LAWS OF YOU SERIES

BECAUSE of YOU

SAMANTHA BRINN

Book Cover Design by Melissa Doughty of Mel D. Designs

Editing and Proofreading by Caroline Palmier

Proofreading by Tina Otero

To all the oldest daughters.
Thank you for your service.

And to Katie and Lou.
Because there is no oldest daughter without the daughters who
come after.
I love you both more than romance novels, Costco pajama sets,
and the fine jewelry counter at a TJ Maxx Runway Store.

Prologue
Ben

Eleven Years Ago

I stand by the front door, impatiently rocking back and forth on the heels of the Jordan 1s my parents got me as a high school graduation gift. My last final was yesterday, graduation is in two days, and we're celebrating tonight at the party my friend Wes' parents are throwing for the whole senior class.

That is, if we ever get there.

I pace at the bottom of the stairs and start yelling up at my twin sister and our shared best friend. "Jules, Hallie, move your asses! We're already late. Your hair looks great! Your makeup is perfect! Now, can we please get the fuck out of here?"

"Benjamin Matthew Parker, you may be eighteen-years-old and an almost high school graduate, but you will not yell *fuck* up the stairs in my house."

My mom walks into the foyer, and I give her a smirk. Rachel Parker has never met a well-placed swear word she didn't like. "Fine, I'll just go up and tell them in person we need to get the fuck out of this house. Then I won't have to yell."

1

"Smartass," she mutters. Then she wraps her arms around me and holds tight, sniffling dramatically. "I can't believe you guys are graduating in two days. It seems like five minutes ago that you and Jules were toddlers and so damn loud I thought this house would never be quiet again. But look at you now."

"Mom, I'm going to college ten minutes from this house. Seven, if all the lights are green. It's not like I'll never see you again. If it makes you feel better, I'll bring home my laundry for you to do on weekends."

She lets go of me then and steps back. "I'll miss you, but not that much. Do your own damn laundry."

"That's what I thought," I mutter. And I start yelling again, because, honestly, how long does it take to put on clothes? I might have a twin sister, and my best friend might be a girl, but whatever they do up there before parties is a mystery to me. "Jules, Hal, if you're not down here in thirty seconds I'm leaving without you."

"Get a grip, Ben. We're coming." Julie and Hallie start making their way down the stairs.

"Fucking finally," I say under my breath. "It took you guys long enou..." I trail off as they come into view, their heads close together, giggling over who even knows what.

Julie is shooting me dirty looks, but I barely notice. All I can see is Hallie. She is wearing tight jeans and a black shirt that shows off a couple inches of flat midriff. Her golden-brown hair is long and loose down her back, and a trio of gold chains circle her neck. We've been to a hundred parties together, and I've seen her dressed up like this more times than I can count. So why aren't my lungs working?

She's standing in front of me now, and her mouth is moving but I can't focus on her words. All I can see is the grin lighting up her face, and her sparkling green eyes that are bolder than normal with whatever eye makeup magic she conjured upstairs in Jules' bathroom. I'm frozen in place. My heart races, and electric tingles shoot through my limbs.

What the actual fuck is happening right now?

"Ben!"

Julie's harsh tone snaps me out of whatever weirdness is going on in my head. She gives me a look, and I know this isn't the first time she has called my name.

"What?"

"I said, are you ready to go? What is wrong with you? Hallie, come on. We can wait in the car until Ben comes back to earth."

They both laugh and turn to leave.

I stand, still frozen, and watch Hallie saunter away and straight out the front door. My eyes are fixed on her ass swaying with every step, and why am I even thinking about Hallie's ass? Never in our entire lifelong friendship have I ever looked at Hallie as anything more than a friend. But it seems like my brain wants to take that detour tonight, and what the fuck am I supposed to do with that?

"You should probably get out there."

I jolt back to reality and turn to my mom. She smirks and gives me that *I know everything there is to know about you* look she's so good at.

"Right. Yeah. Out there. Into the car. With Hallie. And Jules. I'm going. Okay, bye!" *Smooth Ben. Very smooth.*

I leave the house and slide into the car, hoping that whatever just happened was a weird fluke. But as I start the engine, I glance into the rearview mirror and my eyes meet Hallie's. I feel her gaze like a punch to the heart, and in that moment, I know two things.

This isn't a fluke, and nothing is ever going to be the same again.

Chapter One
Hallie

I hammer the final nail into the wall hook, the banging echoing in the large office, empty except for a black spinning chair and a glass desk covered by a vast assortment of beverages. I hang my diploma on the hook and step back to admire my handiwork like the professional I absolutely am. Then I collapse into the chair and spin in a circle like the chaotic human I spend a great deal of my life pretending I absolutely am not. I shove that thought away as quickly as it comes. I don't need an extra existential crisis this morning.

Today is the day we move into our office. The most perfect office on a shady Pittsburgh street with enormous windows and crown moldings and slightly creaky steps and gorgeous built-in bookshelves. The office that will house the all-female private client law firm that my friends Julie, Emma, Molly, and I have been dreaming about starting since we were first year law students buried under ten-pound textbooks and a paralyzing fear of the Socratic method. The law firm we are finally making a reality after paying our dues for five years at big international law firms housed in downtown high rises. We've been in the serious planning stage for more than a year—from the minute we finished our fourth year as associates. And it is all finally happening.

Today. Our name on the deed and my diploma on the wall is proof.

This is ours.

There is only one tiny problem. I'm not one hundred percent sure I want it to be mine.

That thought has been percolating in the back of my mind for the entire year we have been planning in earnest, leaving me feeling guilty and disloyal for even considering abandoning our four-way dream. I have told exactly no one about my doubts.

I keep hoping that as we get closer, they will disappear. The anticipation being worse than the actual event and all that. But instead, the opposite is happening. The closer we get to realizing our dream, the worse it gets.

And today, the day after we closed on the townhouse that would house our firm, and six months before we officially open for business, I am vibrating with anxiety. I absolutely don't know how to say the words, "I don't know if I want this, but I don't know why," to my friends. Conflict is not something I am comfortable with. I usually just go with the flow if that is what makes people around me happy, even if it doesn't necessarily make me happy. Let no one say I'm not self-aware, even if that awareness isn't exactly doing me any good right now.

"Getting an early start, huh?" comes a voice from the doorway.

I gasp, yanked out of my internal monologue. I spin towards my office door where one of my best friends and newly appointed law partner Julie Parker stands. She is balancing a tote bag the size of Texas, a large pink bakery box, and a tray of to-go coffee cups. She's wearing cutoffs, an old college t-shirt, and flip flops; her long blonde hair is pulled up on top of her head to combat the July heat. How she can still look completely perfect despite the casual clothes, messy hair, and swampy summer morning is a mystery I have been pondering for the entirety of our friendship.

Julie and I have known each other our whole lives. My parents started dating their freshman year of college. When they met Julie's parents, who had also recently started dating, they all hit it off immediately and have been friends ever since. Both couples got married a few years after college and then settled in the same Pittsburgh neighborhood. Julie, her twin brother Ben, and I have been best friends since before we could walk. Our families spend a lot of time together, including a two-week vacation every August at the Parkers' lake house in Western Maryland.

Julie and I went to different colleges, but we came back together for law school, and then we both ended up practicing in the private client groups of big law firms. Both of our practices focused on high-net-worth estate planning, which will be the focus of our law firm.

"You scared the shit out of me, Jules. That box better have donuts in it," I say, while standing and reaching for it. If I'm going to have all the Very Big Feelings, I might as well cover them in sugar. Because I am a mature adult who deals with her feelings in a very mature adult way.

"There's nothing in there for you," she says, holding the box out of reach while setting the coffee tray on my desk. "I have your gross maple donuts in a separate bag in my purse, so they don't infect the real donuts. You know, the ones normal people eat. Like chocolate." She reaches into her tote and hands it to me. I immediately tear into it.

"And I'm not surprised you didn't hear me walking up the

stairs, what with all the banging. What are you even doing here this early? It's barely eight."

"Couldn't sleep, too excited," I mumble, my mouth full of maple cream. In fact, I couldn't sleep because of the anxiety and relentless doubt of it all. But I can't—won't—say that to Julie. She has planned our four-way exit from big law, and the start of our new practice, with a strategic precision that would make even the most decorated military general proud. She tends to micromanage people under the best of circumstances and is steadfast in her decision making. I swear she has never had a single regret in all her life. Any expression of doubt would have her reciting a litany of reasons as to why this is the right move for me. And how we have been planning for years, so of course I want this.

That's the last thing I need.

"I'd say take your coffee," she says, pointing at the take-out tray. "But I see your drink lineup is already in full swing this morning." She gestures to the assortment of cups on my desk.

My emotional support beverages have been a running joke for as long as I can remember. I have a massive tumbler of water, a cup of coffee, and a can of seltzer within reach at all times. This is a source of great amusement for the people in my life. But joke's on them, really, because I am always hydrated and appropriately caffeinated.

"Always room for one more." I lift the cup marked with an H and take a sip. I close my eyes as the latte hits my taste buds. *Good choice, Jules.* My night of broken sleep and extra early wakeup are starting to catch up with me, but I shove it down. There is too much to do and too many feelings to avoid. As I savor the extra hit of caffeine, Julie sits down on the floor and immediately pulls a laptop out of her bag. She opens it to display a complex, color-coded spreadsheet on the screen that I know contains the entire universe of things we need to do, buy, and prepare before we officially open for business in January.

"Jesus, Jules, isn't it a little early for that?" I slide down to the floor next to her as I watch her assume the *very serious person doing very serious work* face I have become intimately familiar with over our lifelong friendship. "We don't even have pens. Or phones. Or, like, toilet paper."

"Yes, we do!" calls a voice from the bottom of the stairs. Thirty seconds later, the other half of our foursome appears in the doorway. Emma walks in with a shopping bag in hand full of what looks like pens, notebooks, and the aforementioned toilet paper. She is wearing black shorts and a plain white t-shirt. Her red hair is pulled up in a high ponytail, and her sunglasses slide down her nose. Molly swings in, all bouncing brown curls, cloud of perfume, and sundress in a riot of color. She has stacks of bracelets on both wrists, sundry bags hanging off her arms, and a bottle of Dom in her hand.

"Happy first day, partners," Molly crows, swinging the bottle overhead. She puts the champagne on the floor and digs through one of her bags, emerging with a handful of neon plastic champagne flutes. Molly rarely does anything that isn't at top volume and in full color. She lives life way, way out loud in a way that is equal parts fascinating and mystifying, especially considering her career path. She specializes in the most complex, high-net-worth estate planning that attorneys can do. She is brilliant, detailed, methodical, and has an encyclopedic knowledge of the intricacies of federal transfer tax law that is enviable and absolutely incongruous with her outgoing personality and artist's soul. In short, she is my most fascinating friend. She immediately starts handing the flutes around as she flops down next to Julie and grabs the chocolatiest donut she can find in the box.

"Jules, it is way too fucking early for a spreadsheet that big.

Em, put down your doomsday-prepper supply bag and get down here."

Emma does what she is told, sliding her sunglasses on top of her head, rolling her eyes, and poking through the donut box. When Molly issues an order, people tend to comply. Molly opens the champagne bottle with a loud pop and pours the wine into all our flutes.

"To us," she says, with a brilliant smile on her face. "Best friends and badass women. Who would have guessed back in our first year of law school when we talked about one day opening our own firm while we were bored to tears in that contracts class it would actually happen?"

"Duh, I knew," Julie snarks.

"Yeah, yeah, manifest your shit, blah, blah, blah," I mutter.

What Julie wants, she tends to find a way to get. In all the years I have known her, she has never made a plan—for herself or for anyone else—that she has not followed through to perfect completion. If I didn't love her so much, I would probably have killed her years ago.

"I mean, I kind of knew?" says Emma, her voice rising slightly at the end as if asking a question. "There's no way I was going to survive in a big firm for the long term. All the talking and networking and politicking and up or out? No freaking way." Emma, the youngest of our group, is an actual genius who went to college at sixteen. It was socially traumatic for a girl who already hadn't had the easiest life up to that point. She is an introvert in the extreme, avoids social situations like the plague, and when around anyone except for the three of us or one of her clients, rarely speaks unless absolutely necessary. She is our calm, our voice of reason, and the referee when Julie and Molly get into it, which is often.

"Okay, *anyway*." Molly raises her voice the way she does when our conversation starts veering off the rails, which it does more often than not when the four of us are in one space. "Cheers, bitches. We did the damn thing."

We all clink glasses and take a sip. The champagne tastes like happiness and the kind of joy I only get from sitting in a circle with these women who I love so much that my insides ache with it. I don't know how I ever got this lucky. I look at all four of them—Julie back to perusing her spreadsheet, Molly grinning down into her champagne flute, and Emma taking in the whole room in that quiet and all-seeing way she has. I smile even as my anxiety flares and my throat tightens with an emotion I can't quite name.

I can do this. I will do this. With them. For them. Maybe. What if I can't? How can I ever tell them that I might not want the thing that we have been talking about wanting since we were in school? Especially if I'm still not sure exactly why I don't want it or what I want instead.

I don't get the time to spiral much more. The silence is suddenly broken by the front door opening and closing and then a familiar voice calling out, "Man in the house!"

I smile and yell, "Up here, Benji," to Julie's twin brother, the third in our lifelong trio. His heavy footsteps make their way up the stairs and then his tall frame is crowding my doorway, four wrapped bouquets of flowers in his arms.

He grins at us, all golden hair and ocean blue eyes and woodsy scent and a face that is almost more familiar to me than my own.

"Anyone around here start a law firm today?"

Chapter Two
Ben

Y ou might think with the amount of time we spend together, that eventually I would get used to the heart punch that comes every time I lay eyes on Hallie Kate Evans. You would be wrong. I felt it the first time when we were eighteen and on our way to a high school graduation party. And I feel it right now, at twenty-nine, seeing her sitting cross-legged on the floor of her office, golden brown hair bundled on top of her head, green eyes sparkling, with curves for days.

"I'm surprised you're awake and among the living," my sister pipes up without looking away from her laptop screen. "You know it's still morning, right?"

"Funny, Jules." I walk over and ruffle her hair, making her squawk and shove my hand away. She's not wrong—I am absolutely not a morning person. As the owner of a popular bar on the South Side of Pittsburgh, my nights often stretch out into the early morning, and I am rarely out of bed before ten. But I got my best friend and business partner, Jeremy, to cover for me last night so I could be here before the girls got their day started. I wanted to see the house and help them move in if I could. And I wanted to see Hallie.

"Flowers for the partners," I declare, handing out the bouquets to the girls, who are sprawled on the floor of the office I assume is Hallie's, from the collection of beverages, the e-reader on the glass desk, and the cherry vanilla scent from the shampoo she has been using as long as I can remember. I save Hallie's flowers for last, my fingers grazing hers as I hand them over in a way that I hope seems accidental and not a way to get a part of my body to touch a part of her body. Which it is.

I should probably just say my goodbyes and leave them to their day of whatever it is a bunch of lawyers do when they decide to start a new firm. Instead, I make myself comfortable, dropping down on the floor beside Hallie and stretching my legs out in front of me. I take Hallie's hand and drop two mini-Reese's cups into her palm.

Mini-Reese's cups are Hallie's favorite—just the mini ones, better chocolate to peanut butter ratio, she says. The tradition started the day we graduated high school. She was too anxious to eat breakfast, so by the time we got to the ceremony she was starving. I happened to have had a couple in my pocket that I grabbed on my way out of my bedroom that morning, and I gave them to her while we waited to be called up onto stage. The tradition stuck, and now I always give her mini-Reese's cups on important days in her life.

"You're the best; thanks, Benji." Hallie leans over and kisses my cheek before opening one of the candies and popping it into her mouth. She is the only one who can get away with calling me Benji. I hate that nickname unless it comes from her. She seems different today, though. Quieter. I notice the difference in her immediately. That's the way it is when Hallie is around. My eyes are just drawn to her. She is my true north.

"What kind of coffee today?" I ask, pointing to the to-go

cup in front of her. She is the only person I know who rarely makes her coffee the same way two days in a row. She has a bunch of drinks that she likes and never decides what she will have on any given day until she wakes up. It makes getting her coffee without her input a Choose Your Own Adventure type of situation.

"Jules got me a latte on her way in, but I have my regular with vanilla creamer over there." She gestures idly towards the collection of beverage containers on her desk. Another core Hallie fact—the sheer number of drinks she always has at arm's length. Why she always needs so many drinks is a mystery, but there they are.

"So anyway, any chance you can help us haul stuff today? The moving trucks come at ten with the boxes from our storage unit that all need to be carried upstairs, and we have furniture being delivered around the same time. There's a lot of it, so it's going to take longer than forever. We could use an extra set of hands. How long can we keep you for?"

Keep me forever.

Fucking hell. Shut it down, Benjamin.

"I don't have to be at the bar until six, so I'm yours until then."

"Thanks, we owe you one, Benji." She smiles at me, but it doesn't reach her eyes. Her eyes that are usually the color of freshly cut grass in the springtime today seem muted. What is going on with her?

"You owe me nothing, Hal. I want to help."

I can still feel the ghost of her kiss on my cheek. You would think that we had just stripped naked and fucked on the floor with the way my body buzzes with the energy from it—and with how hard I have to focus to keep from getting a hard-on right here on the floor of her office. It's always like this. Every touch, intentional or not and no matter how friendly, affects me this way. It just lights me right up. I always figured it was because I keep my feelings for Hallie locked up tight. So tight that no one knows. No. One. Not my mom. Not my dad. And definitely not my sister. They know everything about me, except for this. Never this. My family and Hallie's are so close we are basically one giant family at this point. It would take an amount of bravery that I do not currently possess to risk messing with that dynamic.

"So, what do you think, Ben?" Molly's question brings me back to the present. I glance around the circle to find all four girls looking at me. I panic for a minute, wondering if maybe I accidentally spoke my thoughts out loud.

"Huh, what?" I practically yell at her, startled by the disruption of my mental chaos.

"The logo?" she says slowly. The edge of sarcasm in her tone indicates just how little patience she has for repeating herself to people who are so obviously not listening.

Jesus Christ, I need to get a grip. I probably should have waited to deliver my flowers until later in the afternoon. I am not at my best in the morning.

Molly points to the computer she flipped around. The screen shows a proof of the artwork for their logo. "Evans, Parker, Langley, and Jenkins, PC" stands out in black letters against a cream-colored background. It is bold and professional, just like the four women in the circle around me.

"Looks great, Mol," I tell her with a smile. "This whole place looks great too. I can't believe that it's finally yours." They just closed on the property yesterday. They were adamant that they build their firm outside of the downtown Pittsburgh business district. They wanted an office that would be the opposite of the slick, cold spaces where they all spent the first years of their careers. Looking out the window at the quiet, tree lined street, and around at what will soon be Hallie's office, with its original crown moldings, soft yellow walls, and massive fireplace with a walnut mantle and surround, I know they succeeded.

"Thanks, Ben," Emma pipes up with a quiet smile, uttering her first words since I handed her the flowers when I first walked in. She is the quietest of the four but is the protector of the group.

"It may be ours now, but we have a shit ton of work to do before we're in business," Julie declares, glancing down at her ever-present spreadsheet with a satisfied nod. My sister is never happier than when she is telling everyone else what to do, usually with something color-coded in hand.

"God, Jules, enjoy this moment for, like, ten more seconds." Molly pours the last of the champagne into her cup.

"Molly Rae Jenkins, I will kill you if you are too tipsy to help us set up the office when the trucks get here," Jules says while fixing Molly with a death glare.

They continue to bicker while out of the corner of my eye I see Emma slide Molly's neon green champagne flute out of eyesight. I grab it and down what's left, winking at Emma and tossing the flute out into the hallway where it clatters onto the hardwood floor.

Emma grins at me and then I turn to Hallie, who watched the whole thing go down and is turning red while trying not to laugh. She finally can't hold it in anymore and lets it fly, leaning into me while she cackles. *There she is.* Her losing it sets me off and I snort out a laugh, which startles Jules and Molly out of their squabble.

"Hey, where's my champagne?" Molly's question makes Emma start laughing, which sets Hallie and me off all over again, and Jules just looks at us like we're all insane.

I look down at Hallie. She is shaking with laughter, and her body is still pressed right up against me. I put an arm around her shoulders and tuck her into me. Half a foot shorter than my six-two frame, she fits perfectly under my arm, and the warmth at her proximity fills me right up.

And it hits me for the millionth time how much I wish that she were mine.

Chapter Three
Hallie

"Don't you dare, Hal."

I whip around from my desk where I'm reaching for my ever-present e-reader. Ben is standing in my office doorway holding a giant box. He is scowling at me and looks as sweaty and disheveled as I feel after spending the better part of the last five hours lugging boxes from the foyer to the upstairs offices and directing the movers who were unloading furniture.

"There are at least five more boxes with your name on them downstairs, and I need to run home to shower and change before I go to the bar. If you don't want to carry five hundred pounds of legal books on your own, save the smut for later."

He jokes, but Ben is one of the only people who seems to understand and appreciate my love of reading romance.

"Just one chapter. Ten minutes. Twenty tops. I need a break. Too much heavy lifting. Too much peopling," I groan. "Besides, I fell asleep reading at ninety-four percent last night and you know how much I hate that." Actually, I fell asleep reading not last night, but at 4:36 this morning after spending the entire night caught between ruminating and broken sleep laced with sweaty anxiety dreams. I stayed asleep for approximately forty-five minutes before I jerked awake again and started my day, too wound up to go back to sleep.

Ben gives me an amused smile. "And let me guess—you've thought about that last six percent every five minutes since you woke up this morning?"

"Obviously. Now get out of here. Go get another box. Go make sure Molly isn't nagging the furniture delivery people or that Julie hasn't passed out on top of her spreadsheets. I need twenty minutes of quiet time." The truth is I need some time to get my shit together. My stomach has been a fist of anxiety all day long. I thought it would go away as we put the house together. Instead, with every box I lift and every piece of furniture someone puts in my office, it gets worse. I am like twenty minutes away from losing it and breaking down completely unless I have some quiet time. I can break down later at home and consider the "what the fuck do I do" of it all. But in this office, full of all the people I love most in the world who I do not want to let down, I need to hold my scattered pieces together with a death grip.

"Give her the twenty minutes, Ben," I hear Emma yell from down the hall. "You know how crabby she gets when she leaves a book unfinished." *God bless Emma.* She always knows when I need to introvert out for a minute.

"You're lucky I like you," he grumbles, turning to leave.

"You more than like me, Benji. You looooooooove me," I call as he walks out the door.

He turns back around and looks at me, something intense passing over his face so quickly that I think maybe I imagined it. Then he shoots back, "You know it, Hallie girl," and heads downstairs. I smile when I hear him call out, "Mol, quit making the poor guy rearrange the furniture in reception for the fourth time. It looks fine how it is."

I settle back in my desk chair and flip open my e-reader. Before I even finish the first page I hear, "just drink the water, Jules." It comes from down the hall where Julie has been holed up in her office all day, no doubt mainlining caffeine and adding to her spreadsheets. Julie is one of the very best people I know, but she is an insane workaholic who generally forgets basic things like eating and drinking when she really gets into it. Emma is the only one of us brave enough to confront her when she is in this kind of mood.

"Well, if the printer had gotten back to me with the proof for our letterhead and our accountant would actually call me back, maybe I would have had a second to hydrate," Julie gripes back.

I kick back in my chair with my feet up on my desk and my e-reader in my lap. After all the literal and figurative heavy lifting of the day, and the anxiety and doubt that swirl in my stomach, having everyone be so completely themselves—Molly being indecisive and creative, Julie stressing over the details, Emma taking care of us all, and Ben pitching in where he can— is a weird sort of comfort. I lean back and close my eyes and let my friends' voices wash over me. I can't help but wonder whether I am being completely myself, and what the hell I am going to do about it if I'm not.

Chapter Four
Ben

I spend more time than I mean to at the girls' office. I should have anticipated it. Whenever I'm around Hallie, I have a hard time pulling myself away. Being near her makes me feel like we're magnets being drawn to each other. The obvious problem being she doesn't know she's a magnet, and I am far too aware that I am. She spent all day with "best friend Ben," and I spent all day with "desperately wish she was mine Hallie."

I don't know how much longer I can live like this. Being around her without revealing my feelings has gotten harder as we have gotten older. And now, it's nearly unbearable. But the idea of telling her and her not feeling the same is even more unbearable than keeping it to myself. I'm a fucking disaster.

I run home from their office and jump in the shower a mere ten minutes before I'm due to be at Fireside, the bar and restaurant I own and run with Jeremy Wright. Jeremy and I have been best friends since we met our freshman year at the University of Pittsburgh. He is funny, smart, loyal, and dedicated—an amazing business partner and friend. He ended up in the seat next to me in my very first college class, a more untraditional student having played in the NHL for three years before a brutal injury cut his career short. The two of us clicked, and now here we are, years later, as co-owners of Fireside.

When we were looking for space for the bar, we found a gem of a building on the South Side that would become our pride and joy. As we were working on the remodel and pouring our hearts and souls into every inch of the bar, I ended up moving into the loft upstairs. I always assumed it would be short term, but eight years later, I'm still here.

I do a quick rinse and then get out and wrap a towel around my waist. I run a razor over my face and then dig in my drawers for clothes. I am just pulling a shirt over my head when I hear my front door open.

"Hey, Ben, you home?" comes Jeremy's voice from downstairs.

I grab my shoes and jog down the stairs. "Hey, I was just about to come down. What's up?"

"There's a guy in the bar who wants to talk to us. I couldn't get anything out of him, just that he has some business to discuss, and he wants to talk to us together."

"Um, okay. Are we about to get, like, shaken down or something?"

"Nah, didn't get that vibe from him. The guy is corporate all the way down to his wingtips. He was wearing a tie clip, Ben. A tie clip. In the year of our lord 2024."

I chuckle as I bend down to tie my shoes. An athlete to his core, Jeremy abhors anything that comes even remotely close to dressing up. He says it's because of his years of professional hockey where he was forced to wear suits to and from all his games.

"Okay, well, let's go down and see what Mr. Tie Clip needs from a couple of bar owners on the South Side."

The guy is definitely wearing a tie clip, but he also oozes wealth, competence, and sophistication as he sits at a table along the back wall of the bar with a leather portfolio in front of him and a briefcase at his feet. He seems to be in his late forties, in good shape with brown hair styled intentionally to look messy and trendy, dark-rimmed glasses on his face. Seeing us walking in from the back, he stands, reaching out his hand to shake mine.

"Benjamin Parker?"

"Ben," I say, gripping his hand in a firm shake. Something about this guy makes me feel like I need to assert my manhood or something. A thought I haven't had since I was in high school trying to convince the captain of the girls' soccer team that I was a better prom date than the quarterback of the football team. "Can I get you something to drink?" I ask, waving a hand at the bar.

"No, thank you. Please, sit." He gestures to the other chairs at the table, and Jeremy and I sit. *Thank you very much for offering me a seat in my bar. That I own.* I internally roll my eyes.

"I'm Kyle Braverman, CEO of Stonegate Restaurant Group."

Holy. Fuck. That cuts off my metaphorical eye roll as my brain practically stutters, and Jeremy lets out a low whistle next to me. Stonegate Restaurant Group is a wildly successful and well-known company. They started out with one restaurant in Los Angeles and now own restaurants all over the US.

"As you probably know, about five years ago, Stonegate started a new sports division. We are now the concession providers to several hockey arenas, football stadiums, and other sports venues around the country. Fireside, and the two of you, have been on our radar for some time."

"We have?" Jeremy and I say together. Jesus. Way to sound professional in front of the Very Important Person.

"Yes, you have. Jeremy, you may have been out of the league for a while, but you were a Calder Trophy winning forward with more than sixty goals scored in each of your three seasons in the league. You still maintain an active presence in and around the NHL with your charity work, despite being out of play for more than a decade. And Ben, you have been written about both locally and nationally for your business acumen, and your vision and creativity in creating and growing Fireside in this up-and-coming neighborhood, in the city where you were raised, has been highly praised. To put it simply, you have both built something extraordinary here, and Stonegate wants to partner with you."

"Partner? With us?" I will my brain to engage and let me be the intelligent businessperson that this guy seems to think I am.

"What does that mean, exactly?" asks Jeremy.

"As you may know, there has been an increasing demand in the past few years for more high quality, interesting food and beverage options at stadiums and arenas. The days of hot dogs and beers as the main food options at sporting events are long over. This is the biggest reason Stonegate started the sports division. We want to put a Fireside location into each of the stadiums and arenas we service. Stonegate would make the capital investment to get all the locations built and staffed. As owners of Fireside, you would receive a percentage of the sales from each location."

"And this location?" I ask. I'm not sure what I think about

all this, but I definitely know what I want with the bar I am sitting in right now, and it is for it to never be anyone else's but Jeremy's and mine.

"I thought you might ask. This location would remain yours. And with the new locations in the stadiums and arenas around the country making Fireside a nationally recognized brand—at least among sports fans—you could realistically expect a sizable bump in business at this original location. I know you are already a popular bar, but this would make you a destination."

Jeremy and I turn to each other, the deer in headlights look on his face I'm sure mirroring the one on mine. Our bar? National?

"Can we have some time to think about it?" Jeremy asks. "We start getting busy in an hour or so, and Ben and I will need to talk about this."

"Of course." Kyle reaches into the briefcase at his feet and hands us each a black folder with the Stonegate logo stamped in gold on the front. "Take all the time you need. I know this would be a big move for both of you. These folders have the details of everything we discussed, and my business card with my cell number on it is in there. I'll be emailing you first thing tomorrow with digital copies of everything in the folders, as well as additional information on all the financials. Feel free to reach out with any questions that might come up as you discuss this. We would love to have both of you at the Stonegate Los Angeles headquarters to meet the team in the sports division and hear more about what a partnership would entail."

He stands, and Jeremy and I follow.

"It was a pleasure meeting both of you. I hope we speak soon." He shakes both of our hands again, and then leaves the bar.

Jeremy and I stand absolutely still for at least a minute,

before dropping back into the chairs. I feel like I am in another dimension. Did that just actually happen?

"Did that actually just happen?" Jeremy asks, incredulously. I chuckle. Jeremy and I have always had a weird tendency to read each other's thoughts. You would think that I would have the twin telepathy thing with Jules, my actual twin, but nope. I have it with my college best friend instead. "What do you think?"

I shrug. "I don't know what to think. Fireside in stadiums? Nationally? I always figured maybe we would open another location around the city, maybe two. Maybe we'd get wild and open one in Philly or something. But this is definitely more than that."

Jeremy snorts. "I'd say so. Let's give it a little time to settle. Maybe we think about it for a couple of days and talk over the weekend. What do you think about keeping it to ourselves in the meantime? It's a lot to consider. I think getting everyone else's opinions before we settle on ours might make a decision harder."

"Yeah, I can get behind that. Let's get to work."

Chapter Five
Hallie

A couple hours after Ben leaves, all the furniture is where it belongs—at least until Molly changes her mind. Julie finished her to do list for the day and double checked that the rest of us finished ours. All four of us have boxes stacked in our offices ready to be unpacked, and we are exhausted.

I wander downstairs to the kitchen where Emma is unpacking some glassware and putting it away into the glass fronted cabinets. She looks over as I collapse with a groan onto one of the barstools newly arranged around the granite covered island.

"Same, girl, same." She laughs as she places the last glass and tosses the empty box into the corner to deal with later. She sits next to me, putting her arm around me as we both look around the kitchen. At the wide island and the porcelain farmhouse sink and the kelly green cabinets that I lobbied hard for when Molly wanted white everything. And I was right. They look fucking great.

"We're really doing this," Emma says quietly, her voice a little thick. She is the one of us who feels big changes the deep-

27

est. I think it comes from losing her parents when she was eleven and having to build an entire life without them. She was raised by her grandparents, who are amazing, and she is close to my parents as well as Julie's. Even though she doesn't talk about it much, I think she misses her parents the most when she has big shifts in her life. More milestones they aren't here for.

I give her a second of quiet before laying my head on her shoulder. "We are, Em." My stomach twists at my words.

"Well, even if my head doesn't believe it, my muscles do." She laughs. "I need a bath and twelve hours of sleep."

"Well, you're not getting it yet," Julie calls, as she and Molly come into the kitchen and take the two empty stools.

"Jules, no," moans Molly. "We did all the things on your spreadsheets of doom. The furniture is here. The Wi-Fi is set up. We have glasses in the cabinets and cutlery in the drawers. Thanks to Em, we even have toilet paper to hold us over until the office supplies come later in the week. All the boxes are in the right offices thanks to your anal-retentive labeling system. If you are about to suggest we unpack them all before we leave for the day, we'll have to change the name of the firm because you'll be dead, and I'll be in jail for killing you."

"No need to sharpen the knife, Mol; I put the boxes on your lists for tomorrow."

Molly slides Julie a sly look. "Knives are too messy. If I really wanted to kill you, I'd use something clean and quick, like poison."

"Okay, then," interrupts Emma. "If you guys are finished... why is it that I'm putting off my twelve hours of sleep?"

"Oh, yeah, we're going to Fireside," says Julie. "Ben texted and said he's saving us our table, and if I text him when we're on the way over, he'll put in an order for our favorite apps and have drinks waiting."

Opening his own bar was Ben's dream from the time we

were in high school. He works harder than anyone I have ever known—even Julie—and he loves that bar so much. His love is evident in every single corner, from the wooden tables scattered throughout to the exposed ceiling beams and the glossy mahogany bar and bronze light fixtures. It is warm, inviting, a little bit rustic, and one of my favorite places.

"God bless Ben." Molly sighs. "Jules, you were so smart to get yourself a brother who owns a bar."

"Yeah, that's why I'm the smart one," Julie scoffs. "Oh, and Hal, I texted Jo and Hannah too to see if they want to meet us."

"Sounds good." I try to muster up the appropriate amount of enthusiasm in my voice. My sisters Jo and Hannah are younger than us, but now that they are both out of college, they often meet us when we go out. I love them deeply, but they are a lot. More similar and closer to each other than either of them are to me, they are both huge presences in whatever room they inhabit. They are smart and funny and deeply loyal but also loud and a little intense. For our entire lives, I have felt like they sucked the air out of whatever room they were in. They seem to demand everyone's attention and assistance, including our parents' and all the people who inhabit our world. I tend to stay quieter, waiting to see what, if anything, is left for me after they finish expelling whatever thoughts are in their heads at any given time and asking for whatever it is that they need. Whatever I need, I often let take a backseat. It is easier, sometimes, than trying to find a space for myself.

"If you guys are about done with the bickering portion of the night, text Ben to get the margaritas ready, and let's get the hell out of here," I say, standing up. "We're taking an Uber because, drinks. We can all Uber home and then back here in the morning."

"I think Hallie is the smart one," I hear Emma mutter under her breath, too quietly for Jules and Molly to hear.

I shoot her an exaggerated wink and head towards the front door with the three of them following behind me. We lock up and pile into a car headed towards the South Side. As happens a lot when we are all together, I stay quiet, watching them laugh and talk over each other as I exhale the day. I think for the millionth time how lucky I am to have them in my life. But I wonder whether I would still have them if they knew what I was thinking. I'm not sure, and I'm not ready to find out, considering I still have no clue what I would do if not stick with our plan.

So, I stare out the window and watch the city stream by, hoping for the millionth time that maybe I will get lucky and all my doubt will just disappear.

Chapter Six
Ben

"That's the tenth time in the last five minutes that you looked over at the door. Are you waiting for, like, a girl or something?" Jeremy slaps me on the back with a bar towel as he walks past. I whip my head around like a kid caught breaking the rules. Jeremy is way too fucking perceptive.

"Nothing like that. Jules is coming in with the girls and I had the kitchen start their apps. I'm about to do their drinks, but I want them to be cold, so I'm waiting to shake them until they get here." Jeremy gives me a strange look, and I realize that I babbled all that out in a quick, practically incoherent stream. I need to calm the fuck down. "They closed on their office yesterday and spent all day today moving stuff in. They're coming here to celebrate."

"Dude, I know that already. Remember when you asked me to cover last night? I should have been home on my couch with a beer and the baseball game, but instead I was here so that you could get up at stupid o'clock this morning to help your girls and their friends lift heavy shit."

"Shut up, asshole. It was a big day for them." I know Jeremy is kidding—he is as dedicated to the bar as I am and never cares about working late two nights in a row. He and I have been friends for so long that he is almost as close to Hallie and Jules as I am—and Em and Molly by extension.

"I'm just giving you shit. I know what today means to all four of them. They practically set up camp at their table in the corner to plan it out over the last year. I'll go check on their apps." He starts walking back to the kitchen before turning and calling back, "Don't forget that Emma likes sugar on her glass instead of salt." The kitchen door swings shut behind him, and I wonder why he thinks I would forget the drink my sister's best friend has been drinking in my bar for the last seven years. I shrug and glance towards the door again just in time to see the girls walk through.

Julie, Emma, and Molly are laughing as they make their way through the light weeknight crowd. Hallie trails behind them, staring at their backs, and I know something is off. I sensed it all day but seeing her now confirms it.

"Ladies," I drawl as they make their way up to the empty space at the bar. They take the four stools at the end while I stand on the other side, assembling the ingredients for their drinks. "How was the rest of the day in law firm world? Jules, were you able to mark off your scary scary first day spreadsheet?"

Emma and Molly snicker. Jules gives me the murder eye look she perfected when we were kids and uses every time I mention her Type A tendencies and penchant for organization. I'm just as organized as she is, but my intensity is pretty low, while hers is always dialed up to eleven. If we do this partnership with Stonegate and my professional life explodes overnight, maybe I'll be as intense as her. God, I hope not. I have no clue how she has lived this long without an ulcer or a nervous breakdown. I shove it back—not thinking about that now. Bar to run. Drinks to make. No thinking about the massive potential life change dropped on me less than two hours ago.

"Twin," Jules drawls back. "The rest of the day was just fine, thanks, if you think that the Wi-Fi installer being late and the printer forgetting to call back about the firm letterhead is fine. My shoulders are killing me from lifting all the boxes but my brilliant and very fabulous friends crossed off their lists, which means I got to cross off at least most of my list, so I'm taking it as a win."

Out of the corner of my eye, I see Hallie wince at Julie's enthusiasm. She hasn't uttered a word since she walked into the bar. I need to get her alone to find out what the hell is going on with her, and I need to strap my feelings down tight and be best friend Benji while I do it. She is comfortable with that guy. She opens up to that guy, to the extent Hallie opens up to anyone. That's who she needs right now, so that is who I am going to be. I know just how to do it.

I lean casually against the bar. "Jules, it looks like that group of frat guys is stealing your table. Go take Em and Molly and claim it before they can. Hallie can help me carry the drinks over when they're ready."

"Oh no, they fucking aren't." Julie snaps out of her seat, making a beeline for the table with Emma and Molly following in her wake. I smirk, knowing that would do the trick. Julie is territorial over that corner table. All my regulars know not to get near it when Julie is in the house. But this part of Pittsburgh teems with college students from all the local universities and can be transitory during the summer. Julie isn't above kicking someone out of her table if she is feeling extra feisty.

"You really had to put those innocent, puppy dog boys in the line of fire, Benji?" Hallie asks, saying her first words since walking through the door. "You know how she gets, and after a day like today, I don't think she's above throwing a punch if it means getting her table."

"Nah, they'll be fine." I add some ice to the cocktail shaker with their margarita ingredients. "It's been a long day and she's tired, so she'll be all bark. So, what's going on with you, Hal? You're quiet tonight."

She looks up at me while I shake the cocktail, gaze bouncing between my eyes. I can practically see the gears turning in her head as she tries to figure out what to say.

"Nothing," she finally settles on. "Just tired. Like you said, it's been a long day." Her gaze drifts downwards until she's staring at the glossy wood of the bar under her hands.

I should have known she would go with that. Hallie keeps things close to the vest. She rarely opens up to anyone all the way, even the girls and me, and we are the people closest to her, maybe even closer than her parents and her sisters. I pour the margarita into the four glasses I prepped earlier, then fold my arms on top of the bar. I lean a little closer, extending one arm towards her and gently tipping her chin up with one finger so that she looks directly into my eyes. Hers look a little devastated and a lot tired. "Don't lie to me, Hal. I know when you do, and I know that something is up with you. If you tell me, I can help you fix it." I am desperate to help her. I hate seeing her so defeated.

I wait, eyes on hers. Her anxiety hums in the air. My whole body is angled towards her, drawn to her, my mind pleading with her to open up to me, to tell me what is going on. Whatever it is, I want to know. To do what I can to fix it. To take it from her and carry it myself if I can. Partly because I am just a fixer at heart, but mostly because it's Hallie, and Hallie is dug so deeply into my soul that I couldn't extricate her if I wanted to. She never leans on anyone, but I want her to lean on me. To need me like I need her. And I need her like air.

The noise of the bar buzzes around us, but I don't move, my eyes steady on hers. I see the second it starts to happen. Her breath quickens, and her eyes gloss over. Her shoulders fall slightly, as if whatever is going on is weighing her down a little too much. I can practically feel her start to crumble. I stand still, barely breathing, ready to hold whatever pieces of herself she is about to give me.

Her voice comes out in a whisper. "Ben, I..."

"Sisters assemble!" Hallie jerks back from me. She blinks rapidly as her head turns towards the raised voice of her youngest sister, Hannah, who is weaving her way through the crowd. Her middle sister Jo follows closely behind.

"Fuck," I mutter at the interruption. I love Jo and Hannah, but Jesus does their timing suck. When they get closer, the fake grin Hallie pastes on her face and her still-misty eyes are so obvious that I wait for her sisters to comment on it, but they don't seem to notice. How could they not notice? She is all I can see. Hannah and Jo both throw their arms around Hallie and squeeze tight.

"Congratulations, lovey!" says Jo.

"We are so damn proud of you," squeals Hannah.

Hallie closes her eyes and takes a deep breath. When she lets it out and opens her eyes, they are clear again. My need to keep her talking is beating against my chest, so I nudge one of the four glasses on the bar until it tips over, spilling margarita everywhere.

"Crap. Jo and Hannah, can you take these drinks over to Jules, Molly, and Emma?" I ask, waving my hand at the remaining three drinks on the bar. "I'll do another round for you two and Hallie. She can help me bring them over to you in a few."

"No problem." The girls grab the drinks and head over to the corner table.

"Hal," I start.

"Don't worry about it, Ben. Like I said, I'm exhausted. I need a drink, and I need to sleep. I'll be fine tomorrow."

Her eyes are shuttered again, and I know that the moment is over. I'm not getting anything else out of her tonight. Whatever it is will have to wait.

I shake up the next batch of margaritas and fill the glasses. Hallie and I carry them over to the table, where she takes her seat with her friends and her sisters. I go back behind the bar and spend the rest of the night helping Jeremy and my bartenders serve customers and sneaking glances at my friend with her troubled eyes and fake smile, wishing there was something I could do to make it better.

Chapter Seven
Hallie

I sit with my friends and my sisters, their conversations buzzing around me while I stay mostly silent. They are all a little tipsy and don't seem to notice that I have barely said a word in the hour we have been sitting at the table. My feelings are all so close to the surface. If I open my mouth, I'm sure they'll all come tumbling out, like they almost did with Ben.

I can't believe I almost blurted out all of my deepest, darkest, 'I'm in over my head because I don't think I want to do the thing that I have been planning for years to do but I don't know how to tell anyone and get out of it without losing my best friends and if I don't do this, what the hell else would I do' secrets to Ben. And I would have done it if Jo and Hannah hadn't interrupted, even though I have been keeping this secret for more than a year. I've been keeping most of my secrets, if I'm being honest.

I rarely share. I don't go deep with people about my feelings. It's not in my nature. It's not that I don't want to, more that I don't know how. I never have. I have feelings. Big ones. A lot of them. But I've never been able to open my mouth and let them out the way other people can. The way I see my sisters and friends do all the time. It's like everyone else took some class as a kid that taught them how to say, "I'm struggling right now, and I need to talk about it."

It's ridiculous that I'm a twenty-nine-year-old woman and I don't know how to ask for help, or how to let the people who love me support me. I like to please the people in my life, and I don't like to burden anyone with my shit. I mostly shy away from conflict, and I just let things ride when I should confront them head on.

I always keep things inside, and when I struggle, I struggle alone. I'm fascinated and a little jealous of my sisters and their ability to talk about their feelings in a way that lets my parents support them. Or the easy way my friends let loose and lean on the rest of us. Or of people who can confront someone who upsets them. I'm great at supporting other people, but I can never figure out how to get that support for myself. And I think not being able to ask when I need it, or to say what I really think, keeps the people closest to me from really knowing me all the way down. I know all this, and yet, I don't know how to change it.

Which is why my desire to unload on Ben at the bar is so surprising. Sometimes I think that it isn't my parents or sisters or Julie who know me best—it's Ben. When I do try to talk to someone, it is often him before it's Julie. Julie's particular brand of certainty and her tendency to bulldoze through life is enormously intimidating. Ben is the opposite of that. He is quiet and steady. He is a good listener with an uncanny ability to know when I want advice and when I just want someone to listen. And he was right there. His blue eyes calm and understanding and so damn familiar that it made my chest actually ache with the need to tell him everything. I want to lay my head on his shoulder, knowing that he is strong enough to hold me up. And I need someone to hold me up. Because I'm sinking.

"Earth to Hallie!" Julie waves her hand in front of my face. "Where did you go, girl?"

My head snaps up, and I see five pairs of eyes looking at me, all with the same glazed expression that is alcohol mixed with sheer exhaustion. I would look the same if I had taken more than three sips of the margarita in front of me.

"Sorry...I zoned out there for a minute. I'm just tired. I didn't sleep much last night, and all the adrenaline of the day wearing off is getting to me."

Before Julie can say anything else, Jeremy saunters up to the table, all dark hair and brilliant blue eyes and easygoing smile and muscles for days. Ben's best friend might not be a professional hockey player anymore, but he sure still looks like one.

"Another round, ladies?" he asks. And then, for some reason, he arrows his gaze at Emma. "Em, I have the sugar for your margarita glass rim waiting for you behind the bar."

"Oh...um...oh. Okay," stammers Emma. She ducks, her face now bright red, so she is staring at the table. Emma isn't the best at talking to people who aren't either us or her clients, but getting this flustered is unlike her.

"So that's a yes?" Jeremy asks, patiently waiting her out.

"Yes. Wait. No. No more. Drinks. No more drinks. I'm done. We're done. I think. Right? Fuck," she mutters under her breath, glancing desperately around the table with a *save me* expression on her face.

Molly snickers and comes in for the save. Emma rarely swears, so if she's dropping a "fuck," she's desperate.

"Maybe we should call it a night?" asks Molly. "I just thought of a new configuration for the waiting room furniture, and I want to sketch it out before I go to bed."

Julie rolls her eyes but says nothing. Even she knows that Molly is going to move the damn furniture at least ten more times over the next six months. Talking her out of it is a waste of time.

"Jer, we'll settle up with Ben at the bar," Molly says.

"You absolutely will not do that. Our best girls don't pay in our bar on the day they buy an office and start a law firm. Your money is no good here. You, too, Jo and Han. It's on us. Enjoy the rest of your night—proud of you," Jeremy says with a smile. "See you later, Em, and thanks for the thing." He waves and walks back to the bar.

In one motion, all five of our heads turn towards Emma. "Um, what was that all about?" asks Molly.

"What's the thing?" Julie adds.

"Ugh, it's nothing. He just emailed me a couple days ago to review some documents for his foundation." Emma's practice specializes in nonprofit organizations, so it makes sense that Jeremy would go to her. But there is something in the way he was focused on her that has my instincts humming.

"It was no big deal—all we did was email back and forth a little. I don't know why I have so much trouble talking to him."

"Because he's fuck-hot and clearly likes you," Jo declares, blunt as always.

"Definitely," says Hannah. "He practically smoldered. I would kill to have someone look at me the way he just looked at you."

"Seriously? Not possible. And he smolders at everyone. I'm like, a decade younger than him and he's got all that going on." Emma gestures to Jeremy behind the bar, his back to us as he reaches up to grab a liquor bottle on the top shelf. "And I'm just me."

"Seven years, which is absolutely not a decade, but okay." Molly unlocks her phone and opens the Uber app. "I'll refrain from pointing out all the ways what you said is wrong. And I won't tell you how gorgeous and brilliant and successful you are and how I would kill for boobs like yours because we're tired and halfway drunk and tomorrow is another day. Come on, Em; the car is five minutes away." She and Emma stand up and hug Julie and me and then Jo and Hannah.

Molly and Emma live in a house on Walnut Street that had long ago been subdivided into two separate apartments. All four of us lived in one of them together during law school and for the first couple of years after graduation. Two years ago, I bought a townhouse in Shadyside, and then, soon afterwards, Julie did the same. Emma and Molly stayed put. Last year when the landlord wanted to sell both apartments, Emma bought the one we had been living in, and Molly bought the other. It's still kind of weird to be living alone after all the time we spent living together, but there are times when I'm grateful for the privacy. Like, say, when I am in the middle of an existential crisis.

"Bye, favorite ladies!" Molly blows us a dramatic air kiss. Then, with a wave at Ben and Jeremy, and a dramatic nudge to Emma's side when Jeremy waves back, they turn towards the door.

"Be at the office by eight tomorrow morning!" Julie yells after them.

Molly turns around and yells back, "Don't expect me before nine! I can't be both hungover and creative!"

"I told you not to have the third margarita! And you don't have to be creative! No one needs creativity to unpack a box."

"Girl, I always need to be creative."

"Molly, I love you like a sister, and Jules, you are my actual sister and I adore you, but this is not a sorority house. I have actual customers who are not paying to see your particular brand of drama, so very kindly please shut it down in my place of business." Ben has on his serious voice, but I see him snicker when Molly turns back around and sticks her tongue out at Julie before Emma drags her out of the bar.

Jo turns to Julie. "If I didn't know you guys so well, I would think you hate each other."

Julie lets out a snort. "Sometimes I do hate her. But in, like, a sisterly, 'I hate you and you drive me batshit crazy, but I would also die for you and fight anyone who crosses you' kind of way."

"Kind of like I feel about you guys," I say to my sisters with a smirk.

"Hey, I never drive you batshit crazy." Hannah sounds extraordinarily insulted.

"No way," I snark. "Absolutely never. You have never driven me crazy, and I have never had anything but fierce love for you for every single minute you have been alive."

Hannah gives an amused, *yeah right*, look. "Okay, JoJo, time to go." She stands up and comes around to hug me. She holds me a little tighter than usual. And when she says, "I am so proud of you, honey. You guys did good," The tears I have held at bay for hours rise up in my throat again. I will them away with all the force I can muster.

Soon, I can fall apart. Not quite yet.

"Thanks, Han," I whisper. My baby sister might be overwhelming sometimes, but she is kind and happy down to her core. A true sunshine girl. She lets me go and then Jo takes her turn before they leave to catch their own cars home.

"I'm heading out too," says Julie. "I'm going to my parents. I stored some stuff in the pool house I want to bring in tomorrow, so I'll just sleep there and then have my dad drop me off in the morning. Will you be okay to grab a car?"

"For sure. I'm going to run to the bathroom and go home. I'll see you tomorrow, but not until the afternoon. I'm at

Callahan and then in court tomorrow morning to finalize Maya's adoption."

Callahan is a small local Pittsburgh law firm specializing in family law and adoption. I connected with them during a family law clinic I did in my third year of law school, where I assisted one of the attorneys in an adoption proceeding. I loved the clinic and have done some pro bono work with the firm on and off over the years since graduating law school. Maya is a seven-year-old girl who the firm's clients, Eric and Jen Casey, have been fostering for the last four years, and they are formally adopting her tomorrow morning. I have helped them on the long and difficult road to get to this point. There is no way I wouldn't be in that courtroom in the morning to see them officially declared the family they have been since they first laid eyes on Maya.

Eric and Jen are just a year older than I am, and I have become friendly with them in the two years since we first met. I have hung out with them a bunch of times with Julie, Emma, and Molly, and Eric works out at the same gym as the guys whenever they all get the chance. Everyone has met Maya, and they have all seen firsthand what a beautiful family the three of them make. Other than, like, bleeding out on a gurney somewhere, this is probably the only thing that Julie would let me delay box unpacking for.

As predicted, Julie's gaze softens, and she smiles. "I know how much this means to you, Hal. I'm so happy for them, and I'm glad you get to be there to see it. Celebrate with them a little afterward, and I'll see you when you get in." Julie kisses my cheek and I see her stop by the bar for a quick conversation with Ben before she disappears out the door. I head back to the bathroom and as I'm washing my hands my phone dings.

BEN

> Last one standing, huh? Feel like dessert?

I consider this. Part of me wants to go home, crawl under the covers, and wallow. I have been holding myself together all day, and I am so drained of energy I feel like I could just float away. But the memory of Ben's eyes on me earlier has me reconsidering. They were filled with steadiness and understanding, and right now I am so vulnerable that I want to drown in all that comfort. And also eat dessert. Decision made, I text him back.

ME

> I am, in fact, desperate for dessert. Is it ok if I crash in your spare bedroom and Uber home in the morning before work?

I adore Ben's loft. He has big, squishy furniture, fluffy blankets, and an excellent guest room bed. He always stocks our favorite snacks and drinks because we tend to hang out at his apartment after brunch in the area or a particularly late night at the bar. Julie and I each also keep some necessities in the spare room and guest bath, since we both occasionally sleep there when we are too tired to go all the way home.

After getting stuck there one too many times without underwear or a toothbrush, we finally commandeered the dresser as our own. And since Ben is Ben, not only did he not care, but he asked if he should buy a bigger dresser so we could have more room.

BEN

> Always, Hal. Go upstairs and I'll meet you up there when I'm finished here. Shouldn't be long. Jeremy can cover the rest of the night.

Heading back out into the main bar area, I search around for Ben. He is still behind the bar, handing some beers across to a group of women, a couple of whom are openly ogling him. I grew up with Ben and have known him all my life, so I spend a not insignificant amount of time observing women checking him out. He might be one of my best friends, but I'm not blind to how he looks. He is wearing a dark green Henley t-shirt and jeans with a bar rag tucked in the back pocket. His blond hair is a little shorter on the sides and perfectly tousled in a way I know is entirely unintentional. He has a wide smile and sparkling blue eyes, and an air about him that is both smoking hot and incredibly approachable. It is an irresistible combination to most women.

One of the women reaches out and touches his forearm, and I feel a swift tug of something low in my stomach, so foreign and surprising that it knocks me back a step. Territorial maybe? Protective? I can't pinpoint it, so my tired brain stops trying. I need to lay down, stat.

As if Ben can sense me standing there, he looks up and his eyes meet mine. He smiles and gestures towards the door in our usual "head on up" signal. Weird feeling forgotten and awash in relief at the thought of some time with a friend who is not also my soon-to-be partner in a business I may or may not want to actually take part in, I head upstairs to burrow into the couch and wait for Ben.

Chapter Eight
Ben

I can't get out of the bar fast enough.

I make it a habit before leaving the bar to jot down a list of everything I need to remember for the next day. Getting all those little things out of my head and onto paper keeps me from waking up in a panic at three a.m. and sending myself emails with stuff in the middle of the night. I do it every night, without fail. The thought of Hallie sitting on my couch upstairs waiting for me is enough to have me consider skipping it, but the responsible business owner I am at least half of the time has me sitting down at my desk in the back office and making the damn list. The first item is *think about Stonegate offer.* But I know that isn't one I can banish from my subconscious just by writing it down. Then, I head back into the bar to make sure it's stocked for the rest of the night and to check in with Jeremy before I leave.

I'm eyeing the liquor bottles on the wall, my back to the bar, when a voice says, "Hey, what's a guy have to do to get a beer around here?"

I turn around, grinning. Guess I'll be here a little longer

than expected. Sitting on one of the stools is Jordan Wyles, champion shit-stirrer, surgeon, and all-around excellent human. He and I were assigned as random roommates during our freshman year of college. We hit it off instantly, and then I met Jeremy; the three of us have been inseparable ever since.

"Hey, man, you look like shit," I say to him. Jordan is a pediatric surgery attending at the Children's Hospital of Pittsburgh and works insane hours. He looks rough, so he most likely just finished a twenty-four-hour shift—he tries to get into the bar every week or so after one of his shifts since we practically never see him otherwise.

"Thanks, asshole. Two minutes before I was supposed to get off, a five-year-old came in with a broken arm that needed surgery. He wanted to see if he could fly, so he climbed on top of his parents' car and jumped. He was cute as shit and the parents looked so terrified when I saw them in the ER that I stayed and did the surgery myself."

"I did that once," I muse, sliding a beer across the bar to Jordan. "But I just jumped off the kitchen counter. A car, though. Brave kid."

Jordan takes a long sip of his beer. "Yeah, he was pretty proud of himself, and he likes the blue and red cast I gave him. He'll have a good story to tell at school."

"Hey, look what the cat dragged in." Jeremy sidles up to us, takes the seat next to Jordan, and props his leg on the empty stool next to him. His old hockey injury still sometimes bothers him when he's on it for too long. I inwardly wince at the thought of leaving him to close for the third night in a row so I can go up and have dessert with Hallie. "About time that hospital cut you loose. I haven't seen you in a week."

"God, I know," Jordan groans. "It's been a brutal month."

"You're still good for the lake, right?" I ask. Jordan and Jeremy always come to my parents' lake house for our annual two-week vacation in August. Growing up, it was just my family and Hallie's family. But then I met the guys in college, and Jules and Hallie met Emma and Molly in law school, and now they all come too.

"Are you serious? Allie would murder me if she missed the lake. Those two weeks are set in stone for both of us." Allie is Jordan's fiancé. She is smart, funny, and a badass heart surgeon. She is probably on shift tonight since he's here, and she isn't. If their nights off overlap, they usually stay at home wrapped up in each other. They are insanely, disgustingly in love. "So, what's up with you guys?"

Jeremy and I look at each other, and we both nod, silently agreeing to tell Jordan about the Stonegate meeting. He isn't a part of the bar except for all the drinking he does here, so he might be a good, objective voice in the newly formed hurricane of our professional lives.

"What did I tell you guys about doing that weird as fuck telepathy thing around me? It's creepy as hell and I hate it," Jordan mutters.

"Sorry," says Jeremy with a sheepish look on his face. "We kind of do have some news." Jeremy launches into the story of our meeting and everything that the Stonegate guy laid out for us earlier.

"Wow," says Jordan in a low voice. "That is really something. It could be a big opportunity for you guys."

"It could," I muse. "But going national like this is a major deal. When I think about the bar, I think about this." I gesture to the three of us. "Us hanging out here, our regulars, the girls at the table in the corner, people from the neighborhood, the college kids who turn over every year. I know that we're a popular place now, but I worry we would lose the vibe we've built here if there are suddenly Firesides all over the country."

Jeremy nods. "Those are my concerns, too. We decided to

think on it for the rest of the week and see where we are at over the weekend. But keep it to yourself, dude." He points a finger at Jordan. "If you tell Allie, she'll tell Jules and Hallie and the girls, and too many cooks in the kitchen, you know?"

"It's in the vault," promises Jordan. "Speaking of the girls though, where are they? I figured they would be here after their big day. Allie and I felt bad we couldn't be around to help them out today. We're going over on Sunday for a couple of hours to check out the place."

This is what makes Jordan such a good guy. He spent the day putting little kids back together in the OR and dealing with traumatized parents, but still remembers that the girls moved into their office. And I know that Sundays off are sacred for him and Allie, but they're using the day to go over to help the girls out.

"Just missed them," says Jeremy. "They were here until like twenty minutes ago. They all looked wiped and made it an early night. Actually, I didn't see Hallie leave—did she go with Jules?"

"No, she's up at my place waiting for me to finish here. I guess she didn't really feel like going home, so we'll probably watch something stupid, and she'll crash upstairs."

"*Realllllllllly...*" muses Jordan, with a shit-eating grin on his face. I look over and see his expression mirrored on Jeremy's face too.

"Shut up," I mumble. Okay, so when I said that no one knows about my feelings for Hallie, I meant no one except for Jordan and Jeremy. Sort of. A few years ago, in a tequila haze, I might have mentioned something about her being my soulmate and me not being able to breathe without her, or something dramatic like that. I played it off at the time because, tequila. I rarely ever talk about it with them now, but they got the idea, even if they don't really know the details. So, every so often when some of my real, true feelings for Hallie leak through, they catch it, and they pounce.

"She hasn't seemed like herself today, and I think she needs a friend." That's all I'll say about it to the guys, even though I have every intention of going upstairs to try to get her to talk to me.

"It's a big thing they're doing," says Jordan. "It would be weird if she wasn't a little off. If all of them weren't. This is a huge step for them. It's probably just first day jitters."

I shrug and bounce my leg the way I do when I'm anxious to get moving, glancing up at the big antique wooden clock I have hanging on the bar wall. I should be up there already.

"Check you out. Can't even stand still, thinking of her up there," teases Jeremy.

"Whatever, asshole, I just don't want her to be waiting for me. It's late, and she's tired, and I promised her dessert."

"I'm just messing with you, man." He gets up from his seat and comes around to the back of the bar and starts rummaging around. "I love Hallie like a sister. Get up there and keep her company." He shoves a couple of bottles and a jar at me and walks back to his stool.

I look down and see a bottle of ginger ale, a bottle of grenadine, and a small jar of cherries. The ingredients for a Shirley Temple, Hallie's favorite non-alcoholic drink. Jeremy has a photographic memory for people's drink orders, so of course he remembered that Hallie loves Shirley Temples. I give him a grateful look. Luck was really on my side the day I met these guys. Jules is my sister and Hallie is, well, Hallie, but Jordan and Jeremy are my brothers.

"Go," says Jordan. "I have to head out in a few anyway. Allie is off in an hour."

"And don't even think of asking me if I'm sure about closing again tonight, like I know you're about to. It's my bar too, and you've covered for me plenty when I've had to do hockey stuff." Jeremy might be retired, but he still does some charity work that involves the league.

"Wouldn't even think about it. I'm heading out." With a last wave at the guys, I walk out the door and upstairs to my girl.

Chapter Nine
Ben

When I open the door to my loft, Hallie is curled up in the corner of my massive sectional—her favorite seat on the couch. She is wearing one of my hoodies and is wrapped tightly in a blanket. Seeing her here, wearing my clothes, the word *mine* flashes through my brain, and I lose every other thought in my head. The bar, Stonegate, our Very Big Decision. None of it exists when Hallie is in my space like this.

I decided on the way up the stairs not to mention whatever it is she had been about to tell me earlier. She is clearly going through something, and pushing her isn't going to get it out of her. Hallie isn't a sharer. She never has been, even though she comes from a family of girls and a group of friends who probably share more than they should. That isn't her. She keeps her feelings buried deep. Most people, even Jules and the rest of the girls, think Hallie doesn't sweat anything. But I know differently. She opens up her deep depths of feeling to almost no one. I am, occasionally, the exception to that rule, but it's rare. So, the fact that she had been about to tell me something earlier at the bar tells me that whatever it is, is a big deal. I am determined to be her safe space, her soft-landing spot, and I hope she will tell me in her own time.

"Time for dessert, Hal." I toss my keys on the table by the front door and set the box I'm carrying on the kitchen island. I walk behind it to grab a glass out of the cabinet, fill it with ice, and mix the ingredients that Jeremy sent up for her Shirley Temple.

"Please tell me you brought the pie," she says, pausing the TV and looking over at me with a smile. She seems a little lighter, more at ease than she has been all day.

"Hal, it's July. Don't you think I know better than to bring you anything but the pie?"

She aims her gorgeous grin at me. "You're my hero."

The pie is the world's most amazing key lime pie that we get from a bakery in town for our dessert menu every summer from Memorial Day to Labor Day. In the seven years since the bar opened, it sells out every summer night. Eight of my customers are about to be disappointed, but I don't care as long as Hallie keeps smiling.

"And Jeremy and his photographic drink memory sent up stuff for a Shirley Temple. Plates, or forks and the box for the pie?"

"It's almost ten o'clock at night and today was the longest day of my life. Forks and the box."

I grab a couple forks from the kitchen and sit down, leaning my back against the arm of the couch to face Hallie's seat in the corner. Setting her glass on the coffee table and the pie box between us, I hand her a fork, and she wastes no time digging in.

"Jesus, this is good," she mumbles with a full mouth. "What did I do to deserve an entire pie? The public must be rioting downstairs."

"You moved into your new office today. It's a big day, Hal."

When I mention the office, a look flickers across her face. If I wasn't watching her the way I always do, I would have missed it. I put my fork down and lean back against the arm of the couch, legs stretched out in front of me, almost laying in Hallie's lap. I promised myself that I wouldn't push her to tell me what was wrong, but I decide to try some covert digging.

"So, the office looked good. Did you all get everything done you wanted to today?"

"You mean everything that Jules demanded we do?" she says darkly, in a very un-Hallie like tone. Jules may be annoying as shit sometimes with her ordering everyone around and organizing them to within an inch of their lives, but Hallie has never seemed anything but amused by it, even when she's annoyed. This is new.

"Yeah, she was ramped up to a particular level of Jules-ness today. You have all been working towards this for so long—since law school, practically—and now it's finally here. It would be weird if she was calm and all, 'it is what it is' about it. That's not the Jules we know and love," I finish, with a wry smile on my face.

Hallie does not match my energy. "Maybe if she spent a little less time ordering us all around, we would be as excited to do this as she is," she says sharply. Then, seeming to realize what just came out of her mouth, she sucks in a breath and leans forward, covering her face with her hands. I grab her fork and the pie box and toss them both on the coffee table next to her untouched drink. Then I slide closer and pick her up, setting her next to me so that she is tucked against my side, my arm around her shoulders.

This is about the house or the firm. Possibly some kind of fight with Jules, but I doubt that last one. Hallie and Jules rarely fight. I can't even remember the last time I saw them get into it. So, it has to be about the firm. I wrap my free hand around hers, which still cover her face, and gently pull them down to rest on her lap. She sighs, and leans her head against my shoulder, twining her fingers through mine. It feels good, having my hand laced through hers.

"I don't know what's wrong with me, Benji." She says it in a way that makes me think she knows exactly what's wrong with her but doesn't want to speak the words out loud. My heart squeezes at the despair in her tone. She is too far away even though she's sitting right next to me. Shifting so I can lean back against the arm of the couch again, I pull her between my legs. She comes willingly. When I wrap both of my arms around her, she lays her head on my chest, her whole body relaxing in my hold. This is far from the first time I have held her like this, but the feeling hits me in the chest all the same.

I brush a kiss on top of her head, and she sighs. "It's okay to be scared, Hal. Or nervous. Or to feel whatever you need to feel. This is a big thing you're doing, and change is really fucking hard sometimes."

She's silent for a second.

"What if opening this firm is the wrong choice?" Hallie's voice is so low I can barely make out the words.

"The wrong choice for who, Hal?"

She shifts in my lap and sits up, so she is looking at me, eyes tired and sad.

"For me."

I hold her eyes, not saying anything, trying to collect my thoughts. As far as I can remember, Hallie has never expressed any kind of reservations about starting the firm. She, Julie, Emma, and Molly have been talking about this since they were in law school and have been planning in earnest for the past year. None of them, least of all Hallie, have ever seemed anything except excited and dedicated to what they are building. But I know Hallie. If she is saying this now, it means she has been thinking it for way longer. Maybe the whole time.

"Does it feel like the wrong choice?" I ask carefully, wanting her to keep talking to me.

"Sometimes." Then she lays back down, curling her body into mine with her head on my chest, and I know she is done talking for now.

She didn't say much, but even the little she shared is more than I expected she would tell me. I am positive it's more than she has told anyone else. I wrap one arm back around her, using the other hand to stroke her hair the way I know she likes. She sighs and settles back in. After a couple of minutes, her breathing slows.

Just when I think she's asleep, I hear her whisper so quietly it's almost like she hasn't spoken at all.

"Today it did."

Chapter Ten
Hallie

I wake up in the dim, pre-dawn light to the beep of my alarm. I fling a hand out to shut it off and then roll over onto my back in Ben's guest room bed. I guess it's more mine and Julie's bed at this point since everyone Ben knows lives locally and we are the only people to ever sleep in it. As I wait for my body to wake up, images from the night before filter through my brain.

Wrapping myself up in Ben's hoodie and my favorite blanket and collapsing onto his couch like my body couldn't hold me up anymore. Eating pie. My little outburst about Julie. Hinting to Ben that I think opening the firm might be the wrong choice.

I can't believe I let that slip out. I was so comfortable, and Ben was right there with his strong, familiar arms wrapped around me and it just came out. Ben is a vault. I know he won't tell Julie or the other girls what I said, but letting out even that tiny piece feels like I tore myself open and laid my soul bare.

I groan and roll over, burying my face in one of the pillows. It smells like laundry detergent and Ben's woodsy scent, and my body immediately relaxes. Ben and I didn't say much else last night after I let out those tiny truths. I stayed buried in the comforting circle of his arms while we watched TV, and then we both went to bed. As freaked out as I am by what I said last night, I also feel a little bit of relief. For the first morning in months, I'm not waking up with debilitating anxiety about my life choices. Instead, it's more like a low hum in the background. Almost like letting some of it out last night released some of the pressure that has been building up inside of me for the better part of the year. There is a lesson in there somewhere about sharing my feelings, but I am too tired and drained, and it is too damn early for psychoanalysis.

Knowing that I have to get back to the office to pick up my car and get home to change before I have to be at Callahan, I roll out of bed and pad to the bathroom to grab a toothbrush from the stash of new ones that Ben keeps in the bathroom for when Julie or I crash.

After a quick shower, I wrap myself in one of Ben's comically large bath sheets before getting myself as ready as I can and sliding into a pair of old flip-flops Julie must have left here at some point. I open the door quietly so I don't wake Ben, who absolutely would not appreciate being woken up before seven in the morning. I'm already thinking about the coffee I plan on making when I get home. It's going to be a vanilla creamer morning for sure.

I turn towards the kitchen and stop dead in my tracks. Ben is already awake, standing at the stove with a spatula in his hand and a dishtowel over his shoulder.

"Should I be preparing for the rapture?"

Ben whirls around, grinning when he sees me standing there. "Um, what?"

"It's not even seven in the morning. I assumed that the only thing that could get you up and out of bed this early for the second day in a row is if this is, like, our last moment on earth or something."

"I mean, I guess it could be. But also, I'm making breakfast. You and the girls have another big day today and you never leave time for breakfast. I know how you get when you're hungry. So, actually, I'm doing this for Jules, Molly, and Emma, so you don't inflict physical pain because of a disagreement over pens or something when it turns out that you're really just hungry. I heard the shower go on, so I figured I would get a head start."

"That's so nice of you, Ben, but I have to go. I have to Uber to the office to pick up my car then go home to change so I can be at Callahan by nine."

Ben's face lights up. "Oh yeah, it's adoption day. The guys and I hit the gym with Eric earlier this week. I know they've already been a family for four years, but the way he talked about finalizing the adoption makes it feel different. More official, I guess? I'm so happy for them and so proud of you for seeing this through for them. It's a really good thing that you're doing, Hal."

"I love Maya, and I love Eric and Jen. I'm happy to be able to do it. This was a special one for me."

The truth is, they are all special. I love every single case I work on for Callahan, even the heartbreaking ones. And when you are working for and with child services, the foster care system, and parents who have been waiting years to adopt a child, there are a lot of heartbreaking ones. I smile, feeling warm and happy at the thought of standing in that courtroom later today with Eric, Jen, and Maya and watching the judge declare them an official family.

"There you are, Hallie girl."

"What?"

"Your smile. The real one. I haven't seen it in a couple of

days. I missed seeing you happy. Are you doing okay after last night?"

"I'm fine. I was just tired and stressed. Yesterday was such a long day, and I needed some time to recharge. And a decent sleep in your cloud bed didn't hurt either."

He studies me, eyes searching my face like he knows I'm full of shit, and he's looking for the truth. Why did I ever think having Ben as a lifelong best friend was a good idea? He sees too damn much. He looks like he's about to say something and then drops it. I inwardly breathe a sigh of relief. I don't have the time or the mental space to get into it all this morning.

"Okay, well, you're still eating breakfast, so you might as well sit down." He gestures toward the bar stools lined up against his kitchen island.

"I really can't, Benji. I need clothes for court, and I'll be late if I stay much longer."

"Check the closet in the spare room."

"For what?"

"Clothes, Hallie. For court."

"Why would my clothes for court be in your spare room closet?"

"The ghost of Ruth Bader Ginsburg put them there," he deadpans. "She knew one day you would be here, clothes-less and late for court."

"Don't take the queen's name in vain. Are there actually clothes in there?"

"Yes. Jesus, Hallie. There are clothes. You left a suit and shoes once a couple of months ago when you and Jules stayed here. I threw the suit in with my dry cleaning and hung it up in the closet in case you ever needed it. Your shoes are in there too."

"You...huh?" My brain is incapable of forming words. He got my suit dry cleaned? If it were me, I would have just balled it up in a grocery bag or something and given it back dirty. Or, more likely, forgotten to give it back entirely.

"I got your suit dry cleaned. It's in the closet. Okay? Now go, Hallie. Put it on. Come back to the kitchen and sit down where you will eat the omelet I'm making for you so you don't accidentally yell at the judge because you're hangry, and drink the coffee I'm going to give you so you'll be properly caffeinated. I even already filled one of your insane monster tumblers with ice water. You left the purple one here a few weeks ago, by the way. Then, I'll drive you to pick up your car and you can go straight to Callahan. You'll be there well before nine, and you'll spend the morning making Maya, Jen, and Eric officially a family."

I stare at Ben, completely speechless. And then, without warning, my eyes fill with tears. "Shit," I mutter. I frantically try to brush the tears away before Ben sees, but he misses nothing. In three strides he's in front of me, wrapping his arms around me and pulling me into his warm chest, cradling my head in one of his hands, the other arm circling my waist.

"What is it, Hallie girl?"

I shake my head, unable to form words as the tears keep flowing. He doesn't press. He just tightens his arms around me, rubs one hand up and down my back, and says nothing. I bury my head against him and let the tears come. It's the care, I think, that does it.

I'm the original "I'm fine; don't worry about me" girl. The one who takes care of everyone else. I handle the logistics and anticipate what everyone needs and make sure that they have it. I remember all the things for all the people. I remember birthdays and coordinate joint presents and get our friends together when it's been too long since we've seen each other, and I remember when people are sick or hurting, and I check in when they've had a bad day. But it rarely feels like someone does that for me. I think everyone mostly thinks I don't need to be taken care of because I never ask for it. And I guess I don't need it. But god, it feels good when someone just does it without me having to tie myself up in knots worrying about how to ask.

Ben waking up early and making me the breakfast he knew I needed, having a water tumbler for me, and figuring out the logistics of getting me to my car and to Callahan on time and dry cleaning my fucking suit, for god's sake, without me having to ask for any of it? It is a sledgehammer to the already tenuous hold I have on my emotional control.

When the tears finally dry up, I take a deep breath, letting Ben's familiar scent calm me the rest of the way before I step back. Ben reaches up to brush the rest of the tears off my face with his thumbs.

"Feel better?"

"I do." Shockingly, that's the truth.

"Good. Now go get dressed so I can feed you."

I pause, considering. "You're not going to ask me why I was crying?"

He studies me for a second with his calm blue eyes. "I don't have to. You've been holding a lot inside of you, and I don't just mean today or this week. I think you always have a lot going on under the surface you don't let anyone see, and it's not a surprise you need to let it all out. I think you were long overdue for that cry, and I'm glad that you weren't alone when it happened. You're about to start something big and you're worried about it, and I think it's more complicated than just 'change is hard.' You don't want to talk to Jules or the girls about it yet—maybe ever. And it's hard to get a word in with your parents because I know you love Hannah and Jo, but your sisters take up a lot of space and it's hard for you to find room for yourself. You are at my house, so you fell apart with me. If I wasn't here, you would have done it by yourself—or not at all—and then kept moving forward like nothing happened. But I'm glad you're here, and I am too. You're my best friend, and you can always talk to me or fall apart with me and not talk at all. Lean on me. I see you, Hal."

It's the "I see you" that has tears pricking at my eyes again. Ben gives me a look so full of understanding that the relief almost brings me to my knees. Then he leans forward, kissing my forehead before stepping back. "It's going to be okay, Hallie girl. Go get dressed. I'll finish breakfast."

"And coffee. You promised me coffee. I want it with..."

"Vanilla creamer," he supplies.

I look at him, astonished. "How did you know? I just decided when I got out of bed."

"I told you, Hal—I see you. Go. Clothes. Now." Then he winks at me and turns to walk back towards the stove.

Well, okay then. I do what I'm told and go back to the guest room. I open the closet where my favorite black suit I thought I lost months ago is, indeed, hanging with a gray silk shell in a dry cleaner bag on the bar. A pair of my black heels is lined up neatly below it on the floor.

I put it all on, repair the makeup ruined by my impromptu crying jag, and go out to start my day, feeling lighter than I have in weeks.

Chapter Eleven
Ben

"Seriously, Benji, why do we not live together so you can make me breakfast every day?" Hallie asks, as she shoves a fork full of the cheese and mushroom omelet I made her into her mouth. "This is so much better than the granola bar I usually grab on the way out of the house in the morning."

I pin her with a stare. "Jesus, Hal, you're a whole grown-ass woman. Eat breakfast."

"But it takes so much time and effort to make it for myself. I like to cook, but it seems like so much trouble when it's just me."

This woman, honestly. She would make a full meal, plus dessert, for a friend who was sick but can't take out a frying pan to make herself breakfast before work. I have always tried to do things for her, but lately the need to be the person she leans on is overwhelming. I want to be the one who makes her breakfast. Who makes her coffee the way she likes it and is there for her when she needs someone to depend on. Her tears earlier when I told her how the morning was going to go shredded my heart.

I have always seen Hallie in a way that no one else has. She wants someone to take care of her so badly, and she doesn't know how to ask for it. I don't understand why no one else sees it. Why everyone thinks that she is so self-sufficient and happy to run around taking care of everyone else. I mean, god, she practically fell apart when I told her I was making her breakfast and that I dry-cleaned her suit for court.

"Well, you'll just have to start staying here more often so I can get you fed and caffeinated before you go to work." I wink and turn around to grab the coffee pot. I need a second to clear my head of the quick montage of images flickering through my mind of Hallie and me sharing this space for more than just a night of sleepovers between friends in separate bedrooms. The last thing she needs right now is to see how much I want to make that a reality.

"For eggs like this, I would set up camp in your spare room forever." She eats her last bite and pushes her plate away just as my phone dings.

JEREMY

Check your email.

I immediately open my email app and see it. It's an email from Kyle Braverman with the subject "Per Our Discussion." Being with Hallie last night and this morning pushed the meeting from my mind, but now here it is, memorialized in black and white. I open it and see a recap of our discussion. Then I open the attachment and see a proposed term sheet for the deal.

A fucking term sheet. Jesus Christ.

Stonegate would make an investment in Fireside and front all the costs for establishing locations in twenty sports arenas and stadiums over a two-year period, with the option for more as Stonegate contracts with more stadiums for food service. They list the percentage of revenue that we would make from each location, and it details our responsibilities and the control we would have over the look and feel of the bars. It requires that either Jeremy or I travel to each location to approve design choices and various other things I can't focus on right now. The money alone is staggering.

"Guy didn't waste any time," I mumble under my breath.

"What guy?"

I think quickly about the promise Jeremy and I made to each other to keep this to ourselves, even though we told Jordan. But the idea of telling Hallie it's nothing and moving on feels wrong. I want her to open up to me, so I have to do the same.

"Can you keep a secret, Hal?"

"Did you do something illegal? If we have to hide a body or something, I think that the Pennsylvania bar would probably frown on that. But you're my best friend and I love you, so I might not do the actual digging, but I'll drive your getaway car."

I laugh, feeling in this one moment like a one-hundred-pound weight has been lifted from my chest. Having Hallie here in my space, talking to her over breakfast about what's going on in our lives, feels so damn right.

"It makes me feel really special that you would risk your law license to drive my getaway car, but it's nothing like that." Then I tell her everything about Jeremy and I being blindsided by Kyle, about the deal, about the original location becoming a capital L Location since we would be in stadiums all over the country and therefore pretty well known. What I don't tell her is any of my feelings about it because I'm not sure what they are yet.

"And how do you feel about it?" Hallie asks carefully. Fuck. I should have known she would jump straight to the point. Lawyers.

"I have no fucking clue, Hal. I'm a Pittsburgh boy who

went to school to learn how to open a Pittsburgh bar with my best friend with interesting beer and drinks and good food. I wanted it to be a place for people to hang out and relax, a place where Jeremy and I would get to know our customers and let them feel at home. We did that and I love it so damn much. I always figured we would open another location or two, but this? I never considered something like this. I'm not a businessman. I just knew what felt right to me and ran with it. But a stake in bars all over the country? I just don't know."

She studies me for a second, eyes sharp. "It's a big decision."

I let out a sigh of relief that seems kind of silly, but god, yeah, it is a big decision. It feels good to have someone acknowledge that and not just tell me that I should do it because it's a big opportunity.

"It is."

"How much time do you have to decide?"

"Awhile. He wants our final decision by the end of December so that if we go for it, they can start construction on the new locations in the new year. Jeremy and I decided to take a few days to think about it. He and I are going to talk this weekend."

"That makes a lot of sense. Take some time to think about it by yourself, but not too much. You tend to get yourself into trouble when you think too hard on your own. Do you want to talk more about it now, or is just telling me enough?"

It does something to me that she knows me well enough to ask the question. "I think that's enough for now, Hallie girl. It just feels better that someone else knows."

"You can tell me anything. I guess we both have decisions to make now and big secrets to keep." She lets out a little laugh but there's no humor in it. This is the first time she's brought up what she told me last night, and definitely the first time she's mentioned that she has a decision to make. She likely won't tell me if I ask, but I think the decision is whether to stick with the firm or not. I hate that she has been carrying the weight of that choice alone.

"You can always talk to me too, Hal. You don't have to carry any of it on your own."

She looks at me for a second before standing up and carrying her plate around the island into the kitchen. She elbows me out of the way and puts her plate in the dishwasher before taking the last sip of her coffee and putting her mug in the dishwasher too. Then she leans up and kisses my cheek.

"Thanks, Benji. I'm going to grab my bag so you can take me to get my car. I have to get to Callahan and get ready for court."

She turns to walk down the hall but before she gets too far, I reach out and snag her wrist. I turn her back towards me and wrap my arms around her. Everything this morning from her breaking down to sharing breakfast and coffee to telling big secrets in the dim morning light has me thinking about it being like this all the time. What all this *more* with Hallie would be like. I try not to think about it too often or I'll go insane, but right now those thoughts are pinging around my brain like lightning. I need to feel her against me more than I need almost anything else in my life right now.

Hallie relaxes against me, wrapping her arms around my waist and holding on like I'm her only tether. She needs this. She's my anchor, and I'll gladly be hers. But I need more than just to feel her against me. I want to push her up against the kitchen island, kiss her, and drag my mouth down her body until my face is between her legs before carrying her to my bedroom and burying myself inside her until she moans my name. And I need to put a stop to that train of thought immediately before my cock stands up and takes notice that the girl we want to be ours in every way imaginable is wrapped around us. So I give her one last squeeze and let her go.

"Get your stuff, Hallie girl. You have a family to make."

Her brilliant smile before she goes to grab her bag burrows right into my chest where I'm sure it will stay for the rest of the day.

Chapter Twelve
Hallie

"Hallie!" I hear the squeal and look up from where I'm juggling my bag, phone, and coffee cup as I walk down the hall of the courthouse. I grin when I see Maya standing in front of Eric and Jen, one of their hands on each of her shoulders, no doubt keeping her from launching herself down the hall towards me. She is bouncing on her toes, a ball of barely restrained energy.

I reach them and put my coffee and bag on the bench before bending down to her level and giving her a hug. "Hey, kiddo. I'm so happy to see you today."

She squeezes me tight and then lets go and waves a hand down her neon pink and yellow sundress and gold sandals. "Do you like my outfit? Mom said I could pick out whatever I wanted when we went shopping yesterday."

I hear Jen inhale sharply and when I look up, she is clearly barely holding it together. Eric slides an arm around her waist and pulls her close. Maya's case was complicated, and it took a long time for her birth mother to relinquish custody even though she had no intention of caring for Maya and no ability to do it even if she wanted to. It was painful for Eric and Jen, who fell in love with Maya the second they laid eyes on her as foster parents. And it was tough on Maya, who craved the stability a finalized adoption would provide. Even though Eric and Jen tried to shield Maya from as much of the process as possible, she obviously picked up on the vibes because she kept calling them Eric and Jen even after years of living with them. It was only once we scheduled the final hearing that she asked if she could finally start calling them mom and dad. And to all three of them, it meant everything.

My own eyes start watering, but I blink it back so I can focus on Maya. "You look beautiful, Maya. And I have something for you." I dig into my bag and hand her a small jewelry box. She opens it and gasps. Inside the box is a delicate silver chain with three pink stones threaded onto it.

"Hallie, it's so pretty!"

"There are three stones—one for you, one for your mom, and one for your dad. You guys have been a family for a long time, but now you are going to be a legal family, too. You can wear this necklace as a reminder that you have a forever family now."

"Can you put it on me?" Her voice wavers a little.

"Of course, baby. Turn around." I clasp the chain and then turn her back around to face me.

I give her another hug and with her arms around my neck, she whispers, "Thank you for giving me my family."

My emotions have been close to the surface for the past couple of days, and that tiny whisper does me in. My tears spill over as I give her one last squeeze and let her go. "Honey, giving you your family has been the best thing I have ever done in my time as a lawyer."

She smiles and I stand up to face Eric and Jen, who are both a mess. They fold me into a three-way hug and whisper their thanks before we break apart and laugh at the scene we are making—three grown adults crying in a courthouse hallway and a seven-year-old trying to get her arms around all three of us at once.

We have just pulled ourselves together when the court clerk announces that the judge is ready for us. We make our way into the courtroom, but before the clerk closes the door, I hear a familiar voice call, "Wait!" and a parade of footsteps rushing down the hallway. Before I can go out and see what all the commotion is, Ben, Jeremy, Jordan, Jordan's fiancé Allie, Emma, and Molly come barreling through the courtroom doorway.

I grin at them, every part of me lighting up at seeing all my favorite people here. "What are you guys doing here?"

"We would never miss seeing Miss Maya get her family," says Jordan as he and Jeremy hug Eric and then Maya. Allie, Emma, and Molly make a beeline for Jen and throw their arms around her. But Ben comes straight to me.

"Proud of you, Hallie girl," he says quietly, folding me into a hug. I swear this man has hugged me more in the last twenty-four hours than he has in the entirety of our friendship, but I'm not mad about it. He is so warm and solid and familiar. When he puts his arms around me, everything inside me quiets down.

"Where's Jules?" I ask as we break apart, realizing for the first time that everyone is here but her.

An irritated look crosses Ben's face. "She stayed back at the office. Said she wished she could have come, but there's so much to do, and she'll catch up with Eric and Jen later."

I'm disappointed but not surprised. I know she's happy for me that I am getting this done, and she's happy for the Caseys. But I sometimes think her happiness has limits, and those limits are anything that takes her away from work, even if it means supporting me in something important to me and supporting our friends who are fulfilling a lifelong dream. But that's Jules. She has been my friend for my entire life, and I can't expect her to change who she is now.

I just shrug at Ben. "Jules gotta Jules."

"I know you're disappointed she's not here. I can see it in your face. It's okay to tell her that."

"What's the point? This is just how she is."

"The point is telling someone you love who loves you that she did something that disappointed you."

"It won't change anything though, so why poke the bear?"

"Because it's how you feel, Hallie. How you feel matters."

I know Ben is right, and I also know that I will never say anything. Just the latest in a long string of irritations and annoyances that I bury. I hate confrontation. The idea of people being mad at me makes my skin crawl.

How can I expect anyone to change if I never say anything? But I have been living this way for so long. And as uncomfortable as I sometimes am, it's also just easier to live in the status quo. I would rather people be happy, even if it means that sometimes I'm not.

Before I can get too deep in my feelings, the clerk asks everyone to be seated. My friends take the first gallery row, and I sit at one of the tables with Eric, Jen, and Maya.

"All rise," the clerk calls.

We stand, and the judge tells us to be seated. She scans the room and then looks down at Maya and the Caseys with a huge smile.

"It is my absolute honor to be here today," she begins. "Out of all the things I do as a judge in this court, my favorite thing to do is this—to make a family. To make sure that kids like you, Maya, get to find their forever families. And I am thrilled to see so many of Eric and Jen's friends in the courtroom today too. It takes a village, and it is so special that you have so many people who have come here to support you today. You are a very, very lucky family."

I sneak a glance back at my friends, sitting behind us. They are all looking at the judge and beaming, but Ben is looking right at me. He gives me a grin and a wink, and I feel a rush of warmth.

"Now, first, mom and dad, I need your signatures on this document," says the judge. The clerk takes a clipboard from the judge and hands it to Eric and Jen. They sign, and the clerk hands the clipboard back to the judge.

She looks at it and then sets it aside. I have sat through enough of these adoption proceedings to know what's coming next, and my stomach jitters with excitement.

"And that's it," she says with a grin. "Maya, starting now, you are officially Maya Casey. Eric, Jen, Maya, I know that you have been a family in your hearts for a long time. So, it is my absolute honor right now to declare that you are also now a family legally—officially and forever. Congratulations."

At that, Maya bursts into tears and throws herself at Eric and Jen. The three of them hug tightly, rocking back and forth. Tears flow from all of them, from me, and, judging by the sniffles coming from the row behind me, from my friends.

As I watch Eric, Jen, and Maya cling to each other in their first moments as an official family, it is suddenly all so clear to me. This is it. It's so obvious I almost laugh. This is what I want to do. It's not the firm I don't want—it's the kind of work I'm going to be doing at the firm. As I think back on my years in practice so far, I suddenly realize that it has all just been very deeply fine. Nothing particularly satisfying about it at all.

But this? This is what fills my cup. Making families. Helping people navigate the system and giving kids their forever home. This is what I am meant to do. I don't want to do it on the side whenever Callahan has a case that they are too busy to handle. I want this to be my career—what I do for as long as I am still practicing law.

But that rush of clarity and satisfaction also comes with a deep uncertainty because how the hell am I supposed to do that? I have clients waiting to come over to our new firm and Julie counting on me to pull my weight in our shared practice. Emma and Molly have their own niche areas, with their ultra-complex planning and philanthropic practices, but the plan was always for Julie and me to share a practice. We planned our whole firm around it. Telling her that I want to do something else would be a disaster. Could I even do it within the structure of our firm? Would I want to? I shove those thoughts away, happy for now to at least have figured out part of what has been eating at me for the better part of the last year. I can figure out the rest another time.

Before I even have a chance to turn around and look for my friends, I'm attacked by a cloud of bright colors and long brown hair. "I'm such a weepy mess, and I am *never* a weepy mess," Molly declares as she hugs me tightly. "I need brunch and a mimosa, stat. I told Julie, the spoilsport workaholic, not to expect us back at the office."

I chuckle. "Never change, Mol." I give her a grin and turn to see where everyone else is. While Allie is deep in conversation with Jen, Emma is admiring Maya's new necklace, and from what I can overhear from the guys' circle, they are ribbing each other about their workout schedule.

Everyone breaks apart at Jen's declaration that we are going to brunch. Our whole crowd starts moving towards the doorway. Ben falls into step beside me and takes my hand, pressing two mini-Reese's cups into it. I open the candy as we walk down the hall. As I pop them both into my mouth, Ben tosses his arm around me and says, "Bet the brunch eggs won't be as good as my eggs, Hallie girl."

"You know it, Benji. No one makes eggs like you do."

"And don't you ever forget it." He grins at me and drops a kiss on the top of my head. The ghost of his kiss and the weight of his arm warm me to my core as we follow the crowd out of the courthouse.

Chapter Thirteen
Hallie

A few days after Maya's adoption hearing, I am spending some quality Saturday time in my favorite way. I'm at home on my couch under a blanket with my e-reader in hand. I have a Diet Pepsi and a bowl of Cheez-Its, the most perfect snack food ever invented, on the coffee table. My friends have long since unofficially dubbed my frequently required time home alone with my books as Couch Time.

This is the first time I have lived alone in my life, and I love it. I painted my living room dark blue and filled it with big comfortable couches and a deep seated dark green squashy reading chair. It's the kind of chair you can sink into and curl up for an entire day, and it's where Couch Time always takes place. I put sheer curtains around the windows and hung colorful art on the wall. It is a cozy, happy place that is as clean and organized as can be for someone who aspires to be *The Home Edit* but also gets tired putting clean clothes away so usually just piles sweatshirts on top of the dresser.

We have been working our asses off all week to get the office set up, and this is the first moment I have had to breathe since I hung my diploma on my office wall on Monday morning. We had to fight Julie for this time off. She wanted to work straight through the weekend to finalize the office set up and have everything situated before the files we requested from our old firms arrive for clients who were following us. And because in a week, we all leave for our two-week lake vacation and won't be working while we're there. Except, if I know Julie, she will absolutely be working while we're there.

I laugh to myself, thinking of the epic blowout that Julie and Molly had over taking the weekend off. Molly flat out refused to come in. At one point she grabbed Julie's laptop and threatened to delete all of Julie's spreadsheets if she kept insisting. I think the phrases "you don't own me" and "partner bitch from hell" were thrown around. Emma intervened with her typical well-reasoned arguments about burnout and the calmer lifestyle we were all looking for when we left big law like the de facto group therapist she is, and Julie finally relented. Emma is literally the only person who can get Julie to calm down, ever.

And thank god for it, because I don't think I could have lasted in that office one more day without a break. I still haven't recovered from the emotional turmoil of Maya's adoption hearing. The calming effect of my revelation that I don't want to do the thing that I have been doing for my entire career quickly gave way to panic. Because, holy fucking shit, I don't want to do the thing anymore that I have been doing for my entire career.

For some lawyers, a change in their practice isn't that big of a deal. People switch all the time, and it's not like I have been practicing for decades. But for me, it is the equivalent of a bomb detonating in the middle of my life. First of all, because I'm not great with change. Much like I avoid conflict to keep the status quo, I also stay in situations far longer than I should, mainly because I find the unknown really fucking scary. I like my life to be orderly and predictable. I don't like not knowing what is going to happen.

I mean, I dated my college boyfriend for literally years longer than I should have because I was afraid of the chaos of a breakup and what life would look like on the other side. Turns out what was on the other side was freedom and happiness, but who could have known?

Everyone. Literally everyone knew. And they told me. Often.

And more than the change factor, it is the fact that we are a year into planning and a week into executing our new firm. A private client firm where we will be practicing various types of private client law. Sure, we won't actually open for business for a few more months, but the business cards and firm letterheads are being printed. I am a signatory on a bank account and client trust accounts. I have clients from my old firm following me to my new one and counting on me to actually be in practice when I promised them I would be. And I have my three best friends in the world forging on ahead, secure in the belief that I will be right by their side while we do the thing. So, how can I tell them that I don't think I want to do the thing anymore? And how do I build a family law practice almost six years into a career doing something completely different? I could lose my best friends and my career in one fell swoop, and for what? Because I feel emotional when I get to finalize an adoption?

Okay, I know that it's more than that. I know deep in my bones the second I let my mind focus on it that family law is where my heart is. But is that enough to upend my entire life and the lives of my friends?

I groan, burying my face in the blanket I have wrapped around my body. I am so sick of myself. I have been caught up in a cyclone of anxiety and self-pity for too fucking long. I can't sort it all out in my head, and even the very best to-do or pro-con list in the world isn't going to figure this out for me.

Without warning, my mind wanders to the day of Maya's hearing when I broke down at Ben's house, all because he made eggs and handled some of my morning logistics. I cringe thinking back on it. Ben has seen me sick, scared, hungover, and during my extremely unfortunate braces and bad skin phase. But this feels different. What kind of grown ass adult cries because someone makes them eggs and fills a water bottle? But then I remember how he didn't seem put off by it in the least. He didn't even ask me what was wrong; he seemed to already know and understand.

Lean on me. I see you, Hal, he said. And thinking about that almost makes me tear up again. I have never felt as secure and taken care of as I did in that moment.

I consider whether I could talk to him about all of this. I kind of alluded to it with him already, and I know he won't tell Julie or anyone else if I don't want him to. But still. The idea of letting this all out without having an idea of how to fix it myself makes me feel vaguely sick.

Maybe when we're at the lake next week. Even though it scares me shitless, the idea of talking to Ben about my career crisis at the lake house makes it seem less daunting.

The Parkers' lake house is my most sacred place. The place where I am happiest and feel the most like myself. Ben, Julie, and I grew up splashing in the lake, running wild through the backyard and the adjacent woods, and whispering secrets under the stars by the fire pit late at night. At the lake house, it feels like there is nothing and no one else in the world, and summer will last forever. It's where I feel free. If there is anywhere I would feel comfortable giving my deepest secrets to Ben, it's there. I just have to get through the next week first.

My phone beeps, and I jump on it, pathetically grateful for the interruption of my pity spiral.

MOLLY

> It's T-1 week until the gala and there is SHOPPING TO DO.

The gala is the annual fundraising gala for Kids Play—the foundation Jeremy started when he left the league after his injury. It started off as a way to raise money to provide hockey equipment for kids who wanted to play but couldn't afford it. Jeremy was one of those kids when he was younger, and he feels strongly about cost not being a barrier to entry for the sport he loved so much.

Over the years since he left the NHL, the foundation has grown and transformed into a powerhouse that funds equipment for kids in all different sports. The foundation also sponsors scholarships for teams and leagues at all levels of sport, and the foundation board is a veritable who's who of the professional sports world.

The annual gala is held in Pittsburgh every summer. It raises tens of millions of dollars for the foundation, and it is capital F Fancy. It's the one night of the year when we go all out. New dresses are a must, and Molly is the best shopping wing-woman.

JULIE

> Yes, please. Everything in my closet is boring as shit.

ME

> Samesies. I'm thinking I want a color this year.

MOLLY

> GIRL YES.

EMMA

I was thinking of wearing that black dress I wore to my firm's Christmas party last year.

MOLLY

Em, I love you madly, but that dress makes you look like you're going to a fancy funeral. Just, no.

EMMA

But I hate shopping. Just find me something in my own closet. Or one of yours.

MOLLY

Your fabulous boobs that I wish were my own make it hard for you to fit into anything in my closet. But I thought you might say that, so for you, my most favorite women in all the land, I have arranged a treat.

EMMA

Oh no.

JULIE

I love you Mol, but I don't love a surprise.

ME

Bring it sister.

MOLLY

Hallie is my favorite today. The rest of you can suck it up and be at Gallery at 3.

Gallery is a super fancy boutique in Shadyside owned by a friend Molly made in a design class she took one semester for fun a few years ago. I don't know what Molly has planned, but whatever it is, it is going to be fancy, expensive, and fun. Exactly what I need. I get off the couch and go to my bedroom to shower and change before I meet the girls. Just as I'm stripping off my sweatshirt, my phone beeps again.

Because Of You

How's it going Hallie girl? Haven't talked to you since Maya's hearing.

ME

All good. We fought your psychotic sister for the weekend off, so I've been in couch mode all day.

My psychotic sister, otherwise known as your best friend?

When she's insisting we work all weekend, you can claim her.

So is she tied up in a closet or something? How did you convince her to let you take the weekend?

Molly threatened to destroy her spreadsheets and then Emma did her spooky Julie-whisperer thing and convinced her.

I really have no clue how she does that.

I don't know either. She's magic.

So what's your book choice of the day? Are we in a sports mood? Or maybe a good old only one bed situation?

I've been feeling more road-trippy. A+ knowledge of romance tropes by the way.

Seriously, who knew that Ben knew so much about reading romance? Not I, that's for sure.

BEN

I have to, to keep up with your breakneck reading speed. Anyway, there really is something to the happy ever after, you know?

Is Ben reading my books? My brain scrambles and my body flushes hot, thinking of him reading some of the scenes that currently live in my e-reader and rent free inside my head. It's a weird fucking reaction, but I suddenly have an intense desire to know.

ME

I mean, I know, but how do you know? Are you reading my books Benji Boy?

Benji Boy? Where did that come from? That seems uncomfortably close to...flirting? Shit. Is he going to think I'm flirting with him?

BEN

I may have read one or two in my day. Had to see what all the fuss was about.

I knew he was reading my books! I grin at the thought.

BEN

So have you eaten all the Cheez-Its? If you run out, can I convince you to put your book down and do something? Jeremy's at the bar tonight and I have the night off.

ME

I've been on the couch for hours and I have, sadly, eaten all the Cheez-Its. Will have to go shopping before tomorrow's Couch Time. But it's fine because I'm meeting the girls in a couple hours for some super-secret surprise shopping trip. Dresses for the gala.

Super-secret surprise?

Molly.

Say no more. Send dress pictures.

> Huh? You want pictures of the dresses I try on?

I mean, yeah. Maybe you want a guy's opinion.

Or not.

You don't have to.

Kidding.

I was just kidding.

No dress pictures necessary.

Have fun with the girls.

Bye!

I stare at my phone, a laugh bubbling up in my chest. Is Ben high? He rarely ever even sends two texts in a row...but eight? And asking for dress pictures and then backtracking like a psycho? Weird. It makes me feel better about the whole Benji Boy thing. Clearly we are off our game today. Shrugging, I file it away to make fun of him for it the next time I see him and jump in the shower, resolving to find the weirdest dresses in the store to try on and send him pictures of.

An hour later, showered and dressed, I run downstairs to clean up my nest in the living room before I head out. As I'm folding all my blankets, the doorbell rings. When I open the door, there is a box on the stoop from a local grocery store filled with six boxes of Cheez-Its and a case of Diet Pepsi. An Instacart receipt sits on top with a message on it:

Now you won't have to go shopping before tomorrow's couch time.
Have fun with the girls.

Ben

Ben Parker is just too good for this world. With a grin at the thought of him ordering my favorite snacks to save me a trip to the grocery store, I put the box on my kitchen counter and go meet the girls to hunt for the perfect gala dress.

Chapter Fourteen
Ben

S *end dress pictures?*

What the actual fuck was I thinking? Am I an idiot? It's like I blacked out and my fingers just did their own thing for a minute there. I drop my head in my hands and groan. Nothing I can do about it now. I hope the snacks I sent to Hallie before she left distracted her enough not to think too deeply about why I was asking her for dressing room pictures like a pervert. Dressing room pictures.

Jesus fuck, Ben.

At least she has her Couch Time snacks for tomorrow so she doesn't have to go to the grocery store late tonight or get mad at herself tomorrow morning that she forgot. I like being the one to do these little things for her.

I haven't seen Hallie since Maya's adoption hearing. It isn't unusual to go so long without seeing each other, but since that morning at my loft, I have been worried about her. She didn't open up much, but it was more than she had before. The way she broke down when I helped her with the logistics of her morning just killed me. If she would let me, I would take care of all her logistics. I would take care of *her*. She hardly ever lets anyone take care of her. She doesn't seem to know how. But she let me. I am trying not to read anything into it, but I'm obviously failing, and clearly, my brain is melting. See: dressing room pictures. I cringe. I'll be cringing about that for a while.

Since Hallie is busy, I move on to my second choice, although he would kick my ass for referring to him as that. Jeremy is working the bar tonight, but he doesn't have to be there for a few hours. I figure it's time we have the talk about Stonegate that we promised to have this weekend. I still can't bring myself to make a decision about it, but not talking about it is making me antsy, so here we are.

ME

Wings and the baseball game?

JEREMY

Fuck yes. 30 minutes.

We don't have to specify where. Wings and baseball always mean The Dugout, a sports bar we have been going to since college. We grab our usual table along the back wall with the best view of the TV and place our order for beers and wings with the server.

"So, should we talk about it?" The thing about having friends who are as close as Jeremy and I are is that you can hide nothing from them. Jeremy knew what this little get together was about the second I texted him.

"Yeah, I think it's time."

"So, what are you thinking?"

"Honestly, I'm still not sure."

"That's unusual for you. You're usually pretty decisive when it comes to the business. What makes this different?"

He's right. I am decisive about the business. From the location of the bar, to the type of alcohol we stock, to the staff we hire and the color of the stain on the hardwood floor, I make decisions easily and rarely waiver. But something about this one is throwing me, and I can't figure out why.

"I really don't know, Jer. I've been turning it over and over in my head, and I keep going back and forth. It would explode our business, which I guess is good. But it would also turn Fireside into a zoo when all we ever wanted was a neighborhood bar. Being in stadiums and arenas would be cool, but it would also require a lot of travel and time away. I can't settle on an easy yes or no with this, and it's making me feel crazy. You seem so calm about it all."

"It's different for you, I think. I have my work with the foundation, which I love, and I have the bar with you, which I also love. Yes, taking this deal would change the feel of our location here, but that's okay with me. Even though we all forget sometimes, Pittsburgh isn't where I grew up. I love it here, and I never want to leave, but I grew up somewhere else. Pittsburgh is my home, but it's not in my blood the way it is yours."

He is right about that. I am a Pittsburgh boy through and through, raised at the corner of Forbes and Murray and bleeding black and gold. "So, you want to do it?"

"I'm not saying that. I'm saying that I would be fine if we did, but also fine if we didn't. I don't have strong feelings either way, but I get the sense that you have strong feelings all the ways."

"You're right about that," I mutter, irritated with myself that I can't just make a decision and let it go. "We should probably also talk about the money of it all. We would make a lot of it if we did this."

Jeremy scoffs. "I don't need the money, and let's be real, you don't care about the money."

He's right again. I don't care about the money. The bar does well, and we already own the building and my loft upstairs.

And even though I hate thinking or talking about it because it makes me feel uncomfortably elitist, I have a trust fund with more money in it than I will ever need.

I think Jeremy can probably read what's on my face, because the next words out of his mouth are, "I'm not saying we turn it down because we're both swimming in cash. I'm saying that we talk about the legitimate reasons to take or not take the offer and not muddy the waters with the things that don't matter to either of us right now."

"You're right, Jer. I know you're right. And I still have no fucking clue what to do."

"Look, I know that you're struggling with this, and I'm not sure you really know why. I think maybe you need to set it aside for a while. Like, really set it aside and not think about it. We have until the end of the year to decide. We go to the lake in a week, and we'll be there for two. Put it out of your head until after that. We'll all go get some sun, spend time together, and maybe you'll come back with a clearer head. And I know we agreed not to talk to anyone else about it while we decide what we want to do, but maybe talk to your dad? He's a businessman too. He might be able to help."

I consider this. My dad and I are close, but we rarely talk about business. It's my fault. He is a second-generation real estate developer in the city. Parker Inc. developed most of the business district in downtown Pittsburgh and various other neighborhoods around the city, including the South Side where we are currently sitting. Even though he never says anything and has been nothing but supportive, I always feel like maybe he somehow disapproves of me opening a bar instead of going into business with him. Which is why business is never a huge topic of discussion when I'm with him.

"Yeah, maybe."

"Talk to him, Ben. He might be able to help you untangle some of your thoughts about this."

"I'll think about it."

"Good. So, aside from your uncharacteristic indecisiveness, what else is going on?"

My mind immediately turns back to my texts with Hallie, and I cringe all over again.

"What just happened with your face?"

"Huh?"

"You made a really weird face just now."

"No, I didn't." Yeah, I probably did.

"Yes, you did." Dammit.

"Don't worry about it, Jer."

"Oh, I'm not worried. I'm curious as fuck. You have a secret. You never have secrets."

If only he knew.

"I don't."

"You do. Tell me everything."

Embarrassment lowers my defenses enough that I fold like a house of cards. I unlock my phone, which still has my text thread with Hallie on the screen, and hand it to him. Then, I bury my face in my hands so I don't need to see his reaction.

"Wait, dressing room pictures? You asked her for dressing room pictures? Is this, like, an inside joke or something?

"It's not," is all I can manage.

Jeremy bursts out laughing. "Why would you ask her for dressing room pictures, you pervert?"

I groan, and finally lift my head. "I have no clue. My hands just typed it. I take no responsibility. I think I blacked out for a second."

"Why would your subconscious ask Hallie for naked pictures, unless...holy fuck, dude."

"I didn't ask her for naked pictures, and holy fuck, what?"

"You kinda did though. I always thought we were just joking around about the you and Hallie thing."

"We were always just joking around," I say weakly.

Jeremy quirks a brow at me. "Convincing, man."

"There is no me and Hallie thing."

"But you want there to be."

I say nothing, but my silence says everything.

"Whooo boy, this is an interesting development."

"It's not a development," I mumble, regretting the words the second they come out of my mouth.

"What do you mean, it's not a development?"

I think it's feeling like an idiot from texting Hallie earlier and sitting with my best friend in our favorite bar that's to blame for what happens next. I open my mouth and the words come tumbling out. I tell Jeremy everything. About senior year and watching Hallie come down the stairs, and realizing I had feelings for her, and the feelings never going away. About comparing every single woman I have dated for the last decade to her. About feeling like a live wire every time she's around. About how it's getting harder and harder to hide what I feel. And about how terrified I am of telling her and ruining our friendship and messing with our family dynamic.

When I finish, I reach for my beer and drain it, feeling both stripped down and also a little dizzy with relief that, for the first time in over a decade, I'm no longer the only one who knows my biggest secret.

"Jesus, that's a lot to have carried on your own for all these years." Then he eyes me, a smirk crossing his face.

"What?"

"I'm just thinking about college. I was there, remember? Our bedrooms shared a wall for three years. You weren't exactly...saving yourself for the love of your life, if you know what I mean. Don't get me wrong, I'm all for some fun, and from the sounds that came out of your room, I bet you were excellent at that particular brand of fun, but—"

"They weren't her," I cut in sharply, interrupting Jeremy's recap of my string of college one-night stands. Then I take a deep breath and let it out slowly. "They weren't her," I say again, quieter this time. "No one ever could be. I guess I was just trying to..." I trail off, not knowing how to finish that sentence.

"Fuck her out of your system?"

I wince at how that sounds, but also... "Yeah, pretty much."

Jeremy's face softens and he holds my eyes, his filled with a deep understanding.

"Sorry, man, I was just kidding. I understand. Really, I do." He lets out a heavy sigh. "I saw this a lot when I was in the league. Teammates who seemed like playboys when really they were just searching for their person."

Jeremy looks away then. He seems to be collecting himself, but I don't quite understand from what. Before I can ask, his gaze clears, and he starts talking again.

"You could have come to me, you know. I never would have said anything."

"I know, and I trust you with my life, you know that. But it never felt fair to ask you to keep my secret. You're close with Hallie, too."

"I am, but you're my brother." He reaches out and lays his hand over mine.

The matter-of-fact way he says that, coupled with his simple gesture of solidarity, has my throat tightening with emotion.

"So, are you going to tell her?"

"I don't know. It could really mess up both our lives. And Jules' life. And our families. But it's getting harder to keep it in. I'm in love with her. I've been in love with her for eleven years.

I don't know how much longer I can hide it from her. Fuck, Jer, there are times when it's been torture. I've had to watch her for years, dating people who aren't me. Seeing her when she brought her college boyfriend home almost killed me. I wanted to punch that smug asshole. And when she dated that lawyer at her firm last year? Watching them together tore my fucking heart out."

"Look, I know it's not the same thing, but none of us know how long we have with the things we love."

Jeremy's face darkens for a split second and unconsciously, his hand drifts down to his bad knee. I know he's thinking about his hockey career and the way it ended. He never acts anything but okay with the abrupt end to his career, but sometimes I wonder if that's really the truth.

"If you really love her, you should tell her," he says quietly. "Or at least start hinting around and see what happens. Life's too fucking short not to."

I say nothing; he's completely right. It's time.

Not a moment too soon, the server drops two huge baskets of wings and fries on our table. "Can we be done with the emotional wreckage portion of this afternoon now?"

"You know it, pretty friend," Jeremy snarks.

I throw a napkin at him, and we settle in with our wings and our beers to watch some baseball, content to put our big thoughts aside for now.

Chapter Fifteen
Hallie

"Are you fucking kidding me with that, Hal? Take it off." Molly is sprawled on the couch in the big, lavish dressing room of Gallery, champagne in one hand and phone in the other. She convinced her friend to shut down the store for two hours, so the four of us are on a solo shopping excursion. Molly chose her dress ten minutes after we set foot in the store, and she is now doing her very best impression of one of the difficult family members on a *Say Yes to the Dress* episode.

I am wearing a massive pink dress with ten layers of tulle and short, puffy sleeves. It is the most hideous one I could find. I can't figure out why it is in this chic, painfully expensive Shadyside boutique, but the second I saw it, I knew it was perfect for the dressing room picture Ben so weirdly requested.

"Quick, take a picture." I toss my phone to Molly and strike a pose.

"Um, why am I taking a picture of you in a dress that resembles cotton candy?" she asks as she stands up and snaps the picture.

"Ben asked me to send him pictures of the dresses I try on,

so I wanted to find the grossest one I could and send him a picture of that."

She hands my phone back to me. "He asked for what?"

"Dress pictures." I shrug.

"And how did this come up?"

"We were texting. He asked me if I could hang out today, but I told him that we were going dress shopping for the gala. He told me to send him pictures and then got all weird. It was kind of funny, so I figured I would fuck with him a little."

Molly just stares at me.

"Hallie," she says carefully. "Have you ever gotten the feeling that Ben has feelings for you? Like, more than lifetime friendship feelings?"

"What? No way. We've been friends forever. If he liked me like that, I would know."

"Let me see your phone."

"Why?"

"Just hand it over." She holds out her hand and gives me her signature *you will do exactly what I am asking you to do right now or else* face. It works every damn time. I hand her the phone. She holds it up to my face to unlock, and then navigates to my texts with Ben. I know exactly when she sees the dress picture request because she snorts and clicks off the phone. She hands it back to me and collapses onto the couch.

"Well?" I ask.

"Oh, he totally has a thing for you. I think he has for a while now."

"Mol, there's just no way. And keep your voice down." Emma and Julie are still browsing out in the store, and the last thing I need is for them to hear this. I have enough stuff I'm keeping from Julie. I don't need to add this to the list.

"Okay." She just shrugs and leans back on the couch with the look of someone who is satisfied and secure in the knowledge that she planted a seed that she will now sit back and watch grow. This is what Molly does best. She is sly and brilliant and has an uncanny ability to make people see things that no one else knows are there.

But this can't be that, right? Ben doesn't have feelings for me. We're friends. We have always been friends. We have both dated other people—although not lately, I guess. But still. Our families are close. Julie is his sister and my other closest friend in the world. It would never work.

Without warning, I'm assaulted by an image of Ben kissing me and my face heats before I shove it aside. No. Nope. Absolutely not. Molly is wrong. I look over at her and see her smirking at me, as if she knows just where my brain went.

I scowl at her. "Shut the fuck up. You know what you did."

"I sure as shit do," she sings, gleefully, as I flounce back into the dressing room.

As if to prove Molly wrong, I whip out my phone as soon as the curtain closes.

ME

[img attached] I'm pretty sure this is the one.

BEN

You're planning to go to the gala in cotton candy cosplay?

I think it makes a real statement, don't you?

If the statement is, I am a food that little kids eat at a carnival, then definitely.

I laugh and throw my phone in my purse. See, Ben doesn't have feelings for me. Definitely no feelings at all.

I unzip the pink confection and drop it to the floor then rifle through the other dresses I have on the rack in my dressing room. My hand moves to the bright red floor length dress Molly pressed into my hands while we were browsing. It's bolder than I usually go and completely unlike anything I've ever worn before. Without another thought, I pull it from the hanger and put it on. I've been feeling so off kilter for the last year, and particularly for the last couple of weeks, that I'm in the mood for something different.

The silky material of the dress glides up seamlessly. I stick my arms through the spaghetti straps and reach around to zip the back. The front dips just low enough to show a hint of cleavage that, with the right bra, will look amazing, and the dress clings in all the right places before falling straight to the floor. This is the one.

I step out into the outer dressing room where Julie and Emma have just returned, their arms full of dresses. All three of my friends are silent for five full seconds before everyone talks at once.

"Oh my god, Hallie! That has to be the one," says Emma.

"Your boobs in that dress look even better than Emma's boobs," says Julie, grinning. That's the biggest compliment she could ever give me, because it's just common knowledge that of the four of us, Emma has the best boobs by far.

"That dress is so hot I would fuck you in it," Molly chimes in.

There is literally nothing on earth better than girlfriends. "Aw, thanks, pals. I think this is the one."

"No thinking about it," declares Molly. "Go put your clothes back on. You're finished here."

I do what she says, slipping the red dress back onto the hanger and placing it on the rack that the store left us to hold our final choices. I join Molly on the couch where she is scrolling through her phone. She turns to me when I sit next to her.

"Hal, we've barely talked about the Caseys since the hearing. Have you heard anything from them?"

"Jen called me yesterday. They have both sets of grandparents with them this weekend. They couldn't make it for the hearing, so they are having a little weekend family celebration. She says Maya is over the moon and has already written her new name on everything she owns."

"That's the sweetest thing I have ever heard," says Julie, as she walks out of her dressing room in a black halter dress and starts examining herself in the mirror. "I'm so sad I missed the hearing. I would have loved to have been there."

My mind reels with all the things I could say to Julie right now. At first, I say none of them, not wanting to upset our balance or mess up this shopping trip that Molly planned. But then, I hear Ben in my head. *How you feel matters.* And he's right. It does matter.

"You could have been there, you know. I would have liked you to be there. I think Eric, Jen, and Maya would have appreciated it."

Julie turns to me. "I wish I could have, but there was so much to do at the office. The plumber came that morning, and some tech equipment was being delivered, and someone had to be there for all of that. I texted Eric and Jen, and I sent Maya some gifts later that afternoon and promised I would come see them as soon as I could." With that, she turns back to the mirror.

It's nice that she made it right with the Caseys, but what about me? She didn't even apologize or mention she knew how important that hearing was to me. I consider saying more but decide against it. My stomach is churning with nerves, and I know this is just the way Julie is. She gets so tunnel-visioned when she goes into work mode that she forgets about the people around her.

She is impossible to reason with, and trying would just toss a wet blanket over the rest of our day. I stay quiet even though I'm reeling on the inside, words and words and words that I could say to Julie bubbling up before I shove them back down again.

Before long, Emma comes out of her dressing room and all four of us weigh the pros and cons of the dresses that she and Julie picked out.

But in the back of my mind, I keep hearing Ben's soothing and sure voice saying, over and over again, *How you feel matters*.

Chapter Sixteen
Hallie

Our limo glides to a stop in front of the Fairmont in downtown Pittsburgh. Dark green carpet lines the sidewalk in front of the hotel, with press on either side of the entrance behind ropes and crowds of people lining the carpet.

"Our Jeremy doesn't do anything halfway when it comes to his baby," says Molly, snapping closed the compact she was using to check her makeup and sliding it into her gold clutch.

I have been coming to Jeremy's Kids Play annual gala since the very first one back when we were in college. Since Jeremy started the foundation right after he left the league, it was already up and running by the time he met Ben. He played for Pittsburgh's NHL team before his injury and fell so hard for our city that you would think he is a native. After his injury, he never left. He attended the University of Pittsburgh and started the foundation right here. Even with the crowds and the athletes and the razzle dazzle that Jeremy delivers, the gala feels warm and friendly. The food and music are outstanding, and it is one of my favorite nights of the year.

"This is so not my scene," mumbles Emma as the driver

opens the door for us and we exit the car into mayhem. "I don't know why you guys make me come every year when I would be just as happy to stay home and finish packing and let you tell me all about it at brunch tomorrow morning."

Tomorrow we leave for our annual summer vacation at the Parkers' lake house, so the four of us are meeting for brunch in the morning before we drive to the lake.

Julie links her arm through Emma's.

"Because, my dear friend, we all must be equally hung over for our road trip to Maryland." Julie ticks off all the rest of the reasons on her fingers one by one like a teacher giving her class instructions. "Also, you like Jeremy, we can't take our annual 'we're all dressed up and fancy' picture without you, and this year we are networking too. Go forth and find those clients, besties."

"Of course I like Jeremy; we all like Jeremy."

"Not like you do," Julie and I say simultaneously.

"Jesus, Jules, do you ever just turn off work mode?" Molly grumbles.

"You should know her better than that, Mol," I say in a voice that makes me sound cheerier than I feel on the inside. The idea of networking for a firm I'm not even sure I want to be a part of sounds exhausting, and the thong that my clingy dress requires digs into my hips in a way that makes me want to tear it off and go without underwear for the night. "Jules never gives it a rest. There is always an opportunity for networking, and none so much as tonight, in a room full of the wealthiest and most well-known athletes in the country, a lot of whom have probably never even considered the words estate planning, much less tried to do some of their own."

"Fucking right," says Jules, pointing at me. "Now, picture please." The picture is our annual tradition. The first year the four of us came to the gala together during the summer after our first year of law school, we took a picture together on the sidewalk in front of the hotel. It was our first picture all together, and we have taken one together before the gala ever since.

"Excuse me, can you take our picture?" Julie flags down a man who turns out to be Asher Hansley, veteran quarterback of Pittsburgh's NFL team. He is at least six-two and gorgeous in that boy-next-door, purposefully disheveled light brown hair, sparkling blue eyes, bright smile, and blinding white teeth kind of way. That's just the way it is at this event. Athletes everywhere. For a second, he stands frozen, a half-smile on his face as he stares at Julie. But then he seems to snap out of it, and I snicker when he grabs the phone and motions us together. Julie's regular sized iPhone looks like a Barbie accessory in this guy's giant hands. We all put our arms around each other and lean in close. God, I love these women, and this night.

"You ladies look stunning," he says as he snaps a bunch of pictures and then hands the phone back to Julie. "Enjoy the party. Save me a dance, blondie." His gaze locks on Julie, who immediately flushes in a very un-Julie-like way. Then he flashes us a wink and swaggers towards the entrance. I turn to see Julie still staring at what is, admittedly, a superior ass, as Asher makes his way down the carpet, flashing his smile at reporters and fellow carpet-walkers. It's so satisfying that even cool as a cucumber Julie Parker is not immune to the dazzle of the professional athlete.

"Jules, get your eyes off that man's ass." Her head snaps up. Her face is still red, and she is wearing a sheepish smile.

"But it's such a nice ass. Probably looks even nicer in black football pants."

"Yeah, it would," says Molly with a cunning smile that tells me she is also appreciating the exceedingly rare reminder that our very perfect Jules still lives among us common folks.

"That's reason enough to catch a game this season. I bet Jeremy can get us tickets," says Emma.

"I just bet he could. Maybe you should ask him," I say to Emma with a sly smile, refraining from reminding her that Parker, Inc. owns fifteen seats at every game and we can literally always use those tickets if we want to.

She immediately looks away. I will make her admit she has a thing for Jeremy or die trying.

"Anyway, time for mayhem, girls," I say, linking arms with Emma, who needs an extra shot of courage to get through the doors every year. "Let's get in there."

Chapter Seventeen

Ben

"So have you decided yet?" Jordan's fiancée Allie elbows me in the side. I am standing around a high-top table with Allie and Jordan during the cocktail hour of Jeremy's gala. The room teems with athletes, press, and the most wealthy and well-known of the sports world, but Allie only seems interested in nagging me about whether Jeremy and I have decided on the Stonegate offer.

I throw Jordan a glare. "You promised you wouldn't tell her."

"I'm sorry! You should have known better—I can't keep anything from her. She knew I had a secret as soon as I walked in the door the night you told me. I don't know how she does it. It's some witchy shit."

"Fucking right it is," says Allie. "I know everything there is to know about everything and none of you should forget it."

"See? She's spooky man. I don't know what to tell you."

"It's fine." I sigh. "Jeremy doesn't care either way. It's my

105

choice, and I haven't decided yet. We still have some time, and honestly, I'm just not sure."

"What's not to be sure about? It's an amazing opportunity, and it will launch Fireside into the stratosphere."

"I'm not sure I want to be launched into the stratosphere. I always wanted to have a neighborhood bar, somewhere that feels warm and familiar. We figured we would open another couple of locations somewhere, but this is not that. This is a whole other level, and I may not be ready to go there. I like where I am."

"Look, I know it's scary to think about stepping outside of your comfort zone, and you *are* Pittsburgh, so I think it would be even harder for you. But this could be huge for you guys. And we're here to support you—you know that," says Allie, wrapping an arm around my shoulder.

"What she said," says Jordan, kissing Allie on the cheek and grabbing a few glasses of champagne off the tray of a passing server that he hands to us.

"I appreciate the support, Al. I'll let you know when..." I trail off as I see Hallie step into the room. My lungs promptly lose the capacity to breathe air. This is no cotton candy dress. She is wearing a floor-length red dress with tiny straps that dips low in the front and clings to every single curve of her body on the way down. On her feet are gold sandals with tall, thin heels that make her legs look miles long. When she walks, a side slit opens, giving me a glimpse of her toned leg all the way up to mid-thigh. Her hair falls down her back in soft brown waves, and her green eyes are smokey and mysterious looking. She is all woman and hot as fuck, and all the blood in my body rushes south so fast I get dizzy.

"When, what?" asks Allie.

"Huh?" I breathe, still not able to peel my eyes away from Hallie.

"Oh. My. God." says Allie in a low voice.

That breaks my spell. I whip around to find her staring at me and Jordan staring at her.

"Hallie," she declares and points at me. Jordan puts his head in his hands and groans.

"Hallie, what?" I ask her, trying to seem nonchalant even while the back of my neck starts to sweat.

"You. Hallie. You like her. You were looking at her just now like you wanted to devour her. It's the way Jordan looks at me, but it's the way you look at absolutely no one."

I stare accusingly at Jordan.

Jordan throws both of his hands up and takes a step back. "I didn't tell her! I swear!"

"*You knew?*" screeches Allie, staring at Jordan like she might punch him.

"Not really, I swear! Well, kind of. I sort of knew. A little. But no details. Seriously. I never actually knew if it was even true. And I never saw him look at her like *that*."

"I'll deal with you later," she says to Jordan. Then she turns to me. "This is big news, Ben. How long has this been going on? I can't believe Hallie didn't tell me."

"There would have been nothing to tell. Nothing has happened," I say quickly.

Hallie and the girls are still making their way around the room. It's only a matter of time before they spot us, and when they do, they will be over here in a flash.

"But you want it to," declares Allie. Not a question. A statement. It is eerily similar to what Jeremy said at the bar last week when I told him. Fucking hell. Is every emotion I have just written on my face? I look at Allie helplessly. I seem to have completely lost the shield I usually have in place when it comes to Hallie. Telling Jeremy last week and the red dress tonight blew it to pieces.

On the upside, I'm no longer worried about hiding a hard-on in tux pants in a room full of the wealthiest and most important people in the sports world. Having my feelings for Hallie discovered in the middle of this party took care of that pretty quickly.

I shrug, not sure exactly what to say. My biggest secret is out there for the second time in a week, and once again, the thought of someone else knowing is a relief. I'm not so sure how long I can keep up appearances anyway. It's already hard to keep a lid on my feelings where Hallie is concerned, but ever since she opened up to me over her worries about the firm, giving me a piece of her that no one else has, it has been damn near impossible.

"How long have you felt this way?" asks Allie.

"Since senior year," I mumble. "Of high school." If I'm going big tonight, I guess I'm going all the way.

Allie just stares at me, completely still and silent. When I turn to Jordan, I see the same stunned expression mirrored on his face.

"Fuck, Ben. I had no idea it's been that long. I thought you just had, like, a kind of crush on her. I'm sorry, man, I should have realized." Jordan reaches over and squeezes my shoulder in a gesture reminiscent of Jeremy's from earlier in the week. The show of support from the other man I consider a brother has emotion welling up in my throat all over again.

"I kept it from you." I sigh. "I kept it from everyone. Although, Jeremy knows now. He got it out of me last weekend when we met to talk about the business. Hallie and I have been friends our whole lives, and she and Jules might as well be sisters. I've always just been afraid to risk that, you know? If she doesn't feel the same way, or it doesn't work out, it would affect a lot more than just me and her. It always seemed easier to bury it. But lately..." I trail off, not sure what to say next.

Allie says nothing, just puts her arms around my waist and holds tight. I hold her back. "You should tell her," she whispers. "I know it's scary, but life's too damn short not to find your happy, Ben. If she's it, you need to tell her."

Do all my friends share the same brain or something? I close my eyes and rest my cheek on the top of Allie's head. I know she's right, and I also have no clue what to do about it. She gives me one final squeeze and lets go, looking up at me, her face filled with empathy.

"Thanks, Al," I say. "I know it's time. I just have to figure out how. Don't say anything, ok?"

"I would never, Benj. Just know we support you. I love you, and I love Hallie. I think you would be beautiful together." Allie can be prickly and scary sometimes, but she is a good human and a really good friend.

"Look alive," hisses Jordan, before I can say anything else. "We've been spotted."

Chapter Eighteen
Hallie

It takes forever to make it through the ballroom where cocktails are being served. The four of us are stopped a thousand times by friends, family, and people we know from attending Jeremy's foundation events over the years. The Kids Play gala is a major event, which isn't usually my scene, but I look forward to this night every year. Something about all these beautiful and powerful people gathered in one place to raise money to help kids through a foundation started by a man who has become like family to me over the years gives me all the warm and fuzzy feels.

We finally make it through the crowd and approach the high-top table where Ben is standing with Jordan and Allie. Allie rushes forward and, impossibly, catches all four of us in a hug. She squeezes tight, and when she lets us go, she shimmies a little.

"I am so happy to see all of you," she squeals. "I'm excited for the lake tomorrow. Dressing up and the gala is fun and all, but two weeks at the lake where I don't have to cut anyone open or yell at a resident for doing something stupid? Now that is living."

I laugh at her characteristically blunt delivery. I'm excited too. Our two weeks at the lake are a precious slice out of time. I never lose sight of how special it is that we are all able to take the time off every year to make it happen.

"Fuck, yes," says Molly. "It's vacation time. These last few weeks have been exciting as shit, but also fucking exhausting thanks to our resident drill sergeant." She nudges Julie in the side.

Julie must be riding the same happy vibes I am from the gala and from being all together. Because instead of taking Molly's bait, she just smiles and shakes her head. "You'll be thanking me when we open an organized and well-supplied firm in a few months."

Molly opens her mouth, probably to shoot something back about how Julie should thank her for making everything at the office look so amazing and how Julie better not bring all her spreadsheets to the lake and ruin our vacation, but before any words can come out, Emma claps her hand over Molly's mouth.

"Don't even think about it, Mol."

We all laugh, even Molly. "There's something comforting about having friends who know you well enough to know when you're about to lay on the snark. Now, let's find ourselves some drinks."

"Got you covered," Ben calls out from the table behind us. The five of us turn together to see Ben grabbing a bunch of champagne glasses off a server's tray. We crowd around, me standing next to Ben with my shoulder pressed to his, as we all try to fit around the tiny table.

He turns to me and sweeps his eyes down my body and then back up again. "You look beautiful tonight, Hallie," he says, his voice low. His normally ocean-blue eyes are dark and filled with something I have never seen before on him and can't read. Whatever it is, I feel stuck in it, unable to look away, even as a feeling I can't identify swirls low in my stomach. Then Ben breaks the spell, handing me a glass of champagne. He swings his arm around my shoulders and smacks a kiss to my cheek like he always does, as if nothing happened.

What the fuck was that? I look around to see if anyone else caught it. They are all chattering away, oblivious to the moment Ben and I shared. I glance back up at Ben, but he is laughing at something Jordan said and not paying any attention to me. Is it possible I just imagined it? I don't think so. My conversation with Molly in the dressing room last week about Ben having feelings for me flashes through my brain. She got into my head, and now I'm reading into everything Ben does. That has to be it.

Before I can think any more about it, a voice comes over the PA system inviting us all into the main ballroom for dinner and dancing. As I turn to go, I feel a hand on my lower back. I look up to see Ben next to me. He catches my eye and winks at me before guiding me into the ballroom and following our friends toward our table. My entire body flushes with heat, and my breath backs up in my lungs.

No, but seriously, *what the fuck is happening?*

The walk into the ballroom feels like it is ten miles long, with Ben's hand on my back and my breathing shallow. When we get to our table, Ben drops his hand, pulls out a chair for me to sit in, and plops down in the one next to me. I stutter out a breath and mutter something about the bathroom before I turn on my heel and make a quick escape.

I push my way into the women's room and lean against the sink, staring at my flushed face in the mirror and giving myself a little talking to. "*This is Ben. Julie's brother, Ben. Friend Ben. Best friend Ben. We do not get heated for best friend Ben. Get a grip girl."* I'm more off than I think after the last few weeks of worry and little sleep and too much caffeine. I'm not my normal self right now. That's all this is. I wet a paper towel and press it against my neck and take a couple of deep breaths. The cool towel does the trick, and, steadier, I walk back to the ballroom.

The party is in full swing. Dinner is amazing, as always, and the music is rocking the ballroom. Everyone at our table is happy, buzzed, and loud. I'm sitting on one side of the table with Julie, Emma, Molly, and Allie, and we are doing the thing you do when you are in a room full of professional athletes. Discussing their butts. Specifically, which sport provides its players with the best ones.

"It has to be the hockey players," says Allie. "All that skating makes their butts so high and bubbly. It's so fucking hot. Something to grab onto, you know?"

"Hey, now," says Jordan from the other side of Allie. "Don't be grabbing any butt except for mine, baby girl."

"Don't worry, hon," Allie says, dropping a kiss on his lips. "You know yours is the only ass I want to grab." Before she can turn back to us, Jordan grabs her face and kisses her with purpose, one hand cupping her cheek and the other tangling in her hair. He tips her head back to deepen the kiss before breaking it and staring into her eyes for a second, then dropping his hands.

"Fucking right it is," he says, looking satisfied.

Allie turns back around to where we are all laughing. She has a slightly dazed expression on her face, like she isn't quite sure where she is.

"Damn, girl," says Julie.

"I think I had a tiny orgasm just watching that," Molly pipes in.

"How do you find a guy who can kiss like that?" asks Emma.

I stay quiet, replaying the kiss I just witnessed. My eyes have a mind of their own tonight because they drift to Ben. He is looking directly back at me with the same expression I saw earlier. Dark and penetrating and full of something I can't name. What is up with tonight?

"Um, I think I need to get out of here," Allie says. "Like, right now." She stands, pulling Jordan up with her. "Come on, Jord. We're having dessert at home."

Jordan stands and smirks. "We're out of here. Say goodbye to Jer for us. See you at the lake." He wraps an arm around Allie's waist, and they walk away side-by-side, Jordan's hand straying to Allie's ass as they go.

"Should we place bets on whether they have sex in the car before they get home?" asks Molly. "That kiss was capital H Hot."

"I bet they stop in the bathroom before they even leave the hotel," says Julie.

"What Jules said," Ben adds. I snort, and he grins at me. Whatever is going on with Ben tonight is giving me whiplash. From the dark and intense looks I can't read and don't understand, to the fun and playful Ben that I know so well, the whole thing is confusing as fuck. And the weirdest part is that no one seems to notice but me.

"Hey, best pals," a voice calls out. I look over and see Jeremy walking up to us with our quarterback photographer by his side.

"Hey, Jer. Congratulations on a great night," says Ben, standing up to give Jeremy a real hug. Not a one-armed, slap you on the back man hug, but an actual, arms around each other hug. I adore their friendship. I don't know much about Jeremy's backstory, but from the little that Ben has said, I know he didn't have the easiest childhood, and then he got injured and had to leave the NHL. Ben has been with him through a lot. They are friends and business partners, but really, where it counts, they're brothers.

"Thanks, man. Have you guys met Asher Hansley?" he asks. "He's going to be doing some work with the foundation."

"I met these lovely ladies outside earlier." Asher aims that killer smile right at Julie. "They drafted me to be their photographer."

"Great, well, Asher, this is Hallie, Emma, Molly, and Julie." He gestures to each of us, then to Ben. "And Ben, one of my best friends. And wait, where's Jordan?"

"Having sex," Julie and Molly say together.

Asher grins. "I think you all are my people."

We all chat for a few more minutes and then the music, which has been loud and upbeat all night, changes to something softer and slower.

Asher holds his hand out to Julie. "Want to dance, blondie?'

"What the hell," says Julie, taking his hand and letting him pull her up.

"Well, if we're dancing now, I'm going to hunt me down an athlete." Molly grins and stands up.

"Take a walk past table twelve," says Asher, pointing a couple of tables away. "Rookie table." He winks at her and leads Julie to the dance floor.

Molly saunters away, swinging her hips when she gets to table twelve, where wolf-whistles erupt.

"What do you say, Em? Feel like dancing?" asks Jeremy.

Emma looks like she wants the floor to swallow her up, but she manages a quick nod and takes Jeremy's offered hand.

And then it's just Ben and me at the table. "Want to dance,

Hal?" he asks, his voice low. I stare at him for a second, forgetting how to speak because this is Ben, and Ben has never—ever—talked to me in a low, sexy voice before. I am shocked at how much I don't hate it. He holds out his hand to me, and I take it and stand. He leads me to the far corner of the dance floor and I'm weightless, floating over the dance floor as he turns me around, sliding his hand loosely around my waist and bringing our joint hands up between us to rest on his chest. I wrap my other arm around his neck, and we sway together, him turning us slowly as the music floats over the room.

Ben pulls me almost imperceptibly closer, tucking me against him more firmly. He's at least eight inches taller than I am, but my heels give me enough extra height that the top of my head comes up right under his chin. I could rest my head perfectly on his chest if I wanted to. And why do I suddenly want to?

Friend, Hallie. Friend Ben.

Then the hand resting on my waist starts to drift up and down my lower back as we move, and butterflies erupt in my stomach. Ben is giving me butterflies. Ben. My Ben. Friend Ben. We have danced together before, but it sure never felt like this. My entire body buzzes with awareness.

Then Ben dips his head and speaks directly into my ear. A shiver runs down my spine as his lips graze the shell of my ear. "You really do look beautiful tonight, Hal. I saw you in that dress when you walked in, and I lost the power of speech for a full minute."

I freeze and slowly tip my head back to make sure it's still Ben I'm dancing with, because my Ben has never talked to me like this. Never. But there he is. My Ben, who I have known my entire life. Ben, whose face is as familiar to me as my own. Ben, who is suddenly looking at me like he wants to devour me whole.

I would let him. The thought crashes into me without warning. I suck in a breath and tip my head back down, so I'm not looking at him in the eyes anymore. Weird things happen tonight when I look Ben in the eye.

Ben's hand drifts up my back and presses gently so that my head rests on his chest. Then he drifts it back down, his fingers dragging along my spine before his arm loops back around my waist. We finish out the song that way, and when the music changes again to something upbeat, we stand there for a few seconds, not moving a single muscle. I am a tangled riot of feelings from this one dance with Ben, and I have no clue what to do about it. He slowly pulls away from me and searches my eyes before kissing my forehead and leading me back to the table.

The rest of the gala passes in a blur of mingling, dessert, long looks with Ben that I have no idea how to interpret, and conversations with strangers Jules pushes me into to network for the firm. The upside to this weird vibe between Ben and me is that I am too preoccupied to worry that I might be soliciting clients for a practice I don't want, for a firm that I may or may not be a part of when it opens in January. Small blessings, I guess.

And then the night is over. We say our goodbyes to Jeremy and Asher, who has glued himself to Jeremy's side, seemingly pretty serious about getting involved in the foundation.

Molly, Julie, and Emma hug Ben goodbye and turn to go, leaving me standing alone in front of him. This night has been so unexpectedly strange that for the first time in almost thirty years of friendship, I don't know what to say to him. Ben doesn't have the same problem. He pulls me into a hug. His arms band around me, and I can feel his hard chest pressed against me. His lips ghost against my ear again as he whispers, "See you at the lake, Hallie girl."

The butterflies in my stomach flare to life again. We pull apart and I mumble, "See you tomorrow," before running out of the ballroom to catch up with my friends.

I stare out the limo window on the way home, wondering for the millionth time what the fuck happened tonight, why I am so turned on, and what I'm going to do about it.

Chapter Nineteen

Ben

I pace my loft, replaying the entire night in my head. I got back from the gala twenty minutes ago, and all I have done is throw my tux jacket over a chair and untie my tie. After my talk with Jeremy earlier this week and then with Allie and Jordan tonight, it's like something broke free inside me. It is scary as fuck. But for the first time in the eleven years since I started seeing Hallie as more than a friend, I let some of those feelings out.

The looks. The touches. The dance, Jesus Christ.

Nothing has ever felt as good as holding her on that dance floor, and she was not unaffected. I felt the way she melted into me. The way she shivered when I whispered in her ear. The way she looked at me when the dance was over.

There was confusion, sure, but there was also curiosity and a shimmer of heat I have never seen before in those green eyes I have known my entire life. It may be wishful thinking, but somehow, I don't think so. A whole ocean's worth of hope expands in my chest. After eleven years, my head and my heart are in perfect agreement that the possibility of what we could be is worth the risk of whatever might happen if it turns out we aren't that.

I go to the kitchen and grab a beer from the fridge. Then, I sink onto my couch to think. Because this is happening, and I need a plan. A lifetime of knowing Hallie means I know two things for sure. First, she hates change. And second, there is no one more in need of a safe space than her. Come at her with something new and different, something that could shift her equilibrium and change her life and the lives of all the people she loves, and she'll run, all alone, fast and far in the other direction. There is no change bigger than this one. But all I have ever wanted was for her to run to me, not away from me. I have tried to be her safe space for our entire lives, and to make this happen, I have to show her that I can be that for her no matter what our relationship looks like.

Tonight at the gala was as good a start as any, and our lake trip could not be coming at a better time. None of us are ever more ourselves than we are when we are at my family's lake house. For two weeks every summer, we put work and our regular lives away and let loose, just like we did when we were kids. At the lake, everyone is a little bit more. A little happier. A little freer. A little wilder. It is the place where the good things happen.

My phone dings, startling me out of my thoughts. It's the group chat with the guys.

JEREMY

Ben, you ok? Your head was somewhere else at the end of the gala.

JORDAN

What happened at the end of the gala?

JEREMY

Yeah, way to leave early, asshole.

JORDAN

Listen, when your girl tells you that you're leaving for dessert at home, you follow instructions. And dessert was had *winky face emoji*

JEREMY

Gross dude, I don't need to hear about that.

JORDAN

So, details please.

I snort out a laugh. My friends might be grown adults, but they gossip like teenagers. Feeling better with the beginnings of a plan brewing in my mind, I decide to play along.

ME

I'm not sure you deserve any details. Details are for friends who didn't leave early.

JORDAN

Come onnnnnn. Give them to me. You know I hate being left out of shit.

JEREMY

Double your donation from tonight and details will be yours.

JORDAN

Done.

JEREMY

Our Ben had a bit of a moment with Hallie on the dance floor.

ME

Saw that, did you?

JEREMY

Everyone saw that.

JORDAN

I need more please.

JEREMY

> There was no space between them. None at all. It did not look like a friendly dance, and Hallie was definitely picking up what Ben was laying down.

I grin at that, because she sure was. I knew I wasn't imagining it.

ME

> It didn't feel all that friendly either.

JORDAN

> Yeah she was! So what's the plan?

JEREMY

> What makes you think there's a plan?

JORDAN

> Ben, is there a plan?

ME

> There is the beginning of a plan.

JEREMY

> It's the lake, isn't it? That's where you're going to tell her.

ME

> It's the lake. It has to be. I'm going to tell her.

JEREMY

> Fuck. Yes. Proud of you, brother.

JORDAN

> But wait, you can't just blurt it out. You have to wind her up a little first. Take a day or two. Act different. Stand closer. Touch more. Flirt more. Show her. It will confuse the shit out of her. You'll know if she's into it. Then, when the time is right, you tell her.

Fuck, he's right. He is so absolutely right. I'm going to show

Hallie that we are meant to belong to each other. That we are endgame. That no other future makes any sense but the one where we end up by each other's sides. Then, after I show her, I'm going to tell her. Finally.

JEREMY

For what it's worth, I watched her tonight. Her eyes were on you when she didn't think you were looking. She's thinking about you, even if she doesn't understand why.

JORDAN

She's yours Ben. Go get her.

JEREMY

Second that.

ME

Thanks guys. I needed this. See you at the lake.

Decision made, I lift up my beer bottle in a silent toast. Buckle up, Hallie girl. It's so fucking on.

Chapter Twenty
Hallie

I walk into the diner a couple blocks from my house where I'm meeting the girls for brunch before we head to the lake. I'm still off-kilter from the weird energy between Ben and me at the gala. Once I finally got into bed, I tossed and turned for hours. I replayed the way Ben's eyes slid up and down my body when he first saw me in my dress, the way he whispered into my ear, and how his hands ghosted up and down my back while we were dancing. And the looks he gave me on and off all night. Holy hell.

His eyes had a darker edge to them when he looked at me. It almost looked like...need. Or desire. Whatever it was, it was something I have never seen in Ben's eyes before. And it was... well, it was sexy. It was fucking sexy, and that's not something I have ever thought about Ben before.

I replayed those looks in bed last night until my body was so itchy and buzzing with energy that I finally reached into my bedside drawer for my favorite vibrator to relieve some of the tension.

Yep, I got off—twice—to thoughts of Ben's eyes on me. And

if a quick fantasy of him leaning forward and kissing me on the dance floor the way Jordan kissed Allie and then leading me out of the ballroom to go have sex in his car snuck in while my hand was between my legs? Well, let the jury convict me. I'll go quietly because I am guilty as shit.

I am feeling some kind of way this morning and am looking for a distraction, so brunch with the girls is perfect. We're meeting for breakfast at our favorite diner and then heading out. I'm running a little late—because lack of sleep—so Julie, Emma, and Molly are already at a table by the time I push through the door. Julie waves me over and then stands up to hug me before I sit.

"You okay?" she whispers into my ear. "You were quiet last night on the way home. I've been worried about you."

My entire body flushes hot. God bless the August humidity. I'm already sweaty from the walk over, so my getting sweaty for an entirely different reason isn't noticeable. Julie is one of my best friends, but there is no way I can tell her that I was quiet on the ride home because I was hot and bothered and incredibly confused about her twin brother acting positively swoony towards me. So, I do what I do best and deflect.

"Totally fine. I think that last drink was a mistake because I was on the wrong side of tipsy when I got home." She seems to accept that, and I give her an extra squeeze before I blow a kiss to Molly and Emma on the other side of the table and claim the empty chair next to Julie.

"I would have ordered your coffee already, but I wasn't sure which of your drinks you would be in the mood for," says Julie.

"No worries." I flag down a server and order an iced coffee with milk and one Splenda. Without warning, I remember the morning a couple weeks ago where Ben knew what kind of coffee I wanted before I told him. I still can't figure out how he did that. I need to get a grip and stop thinking about Ben.

Once my coffee is delivered and we place our food orders, Molly takes charge of the conversation.

"So, recap," she says, leaning back and crossing her arms. "Em, you're up first. And if you don't include details about your dance with our sexy former hockey player friend, I'll be serenading you alongside Lin Manuel Miranda and the original cast of Hamilton for the entire drive to the lake."

Fuck. The gala recap. All up in my feelings this morning, I forgot about our annual post-gala download of who wore what, who got drunk and did something ridiculous, which athletes were most likely to be dreading the headlines this morning because of the ridiculous something, speculating over who hooked up with who, and a general what's what from the night before. It's always fun and usually hilarious. But this year, I'm not sure I can get through it without turning awkward, stammering, and accidentally sharing my late night...activities with the contents of my bedside drawer.

"I mean, it was a dance," Emma says. "There aren't really a lot of details. It was Jeremy. He's a nice guy. He's my friend, although I still can't speak actual words around him for some reason unless we're talking about work, which will never not be humiliating. I don't know why he even asked me to dance. It was his event, and he probably had a thousand other things to do."

"He asked you to dance because he likes you, Em," Julie pipes in, reaching over to lay her hand over Emma's. "He's liked you for a while, I think. I mean, he keeps sugar behind the bar for your margarita glass, and you know how he's a salt-on-the-rim purist."

"I think he's just trying to be nice. He probably feels sorry for me because I can't manage an entire sentence around him most of the time."

"Bullshit," says Molly. "He has it bad for you. You guys

were so close during that dance I'm shocked either one of you could breathe. I bet he is a fucking god in bed. All that former athlete stamina."

I agree one hundred percent that Jeremy is harboring some serious feelings for Emma. I suspect all her stammering means she likes him right back, but she hasn't figured it all out yet. I stay quiet, though, knowing Emma is uncomfortable talking about her love life under the best of circumstances. It's going to be a wild ride watching the two of them finally get their act together.

"Okay, next," says Emma, eager to turn the spotlight off herself. "Blondie over here and the sexy as sin football player." She uses finger quotes for "blondie," and aims a wicked grin in Julie's direction. "You were dancing, and his hands were basically on your ass. Don't tell me he didn't ask for your number."

"Well, my ass is amazing," Julie says with a smile. "I would have put my hands on it, too. And he absolutely did ask for my number, but I absolutely did not give it to him."

"Why not?" I ask.

"I don't have time to date right now, especially not an athlete."

"Who said anything about dating?" asks Molly. "You could just fuck him, you know. There's no doubt he's amazing in bed too. He has all that *current* athlete stamina."

"What's even the point? His pre-season has already started. I'm sure his schedule is insane, and after the lake, my schedule will be insane too. It seems like a lot of work."

"Sex, Jules. Sex is the point. Hot, dirty sex with a tall, gorgeous athlete who was eye fucking you all night and danced with his hands on your ass."

Our server chooses that moment to arrive at the table with our food. She puts it in front of us and before she turns away, looks at Julie and says, "You should do it, honey. Hot sex is most definitely the point." Then she winks and walks away.

"See, she gets it," says Molly.

"Okay, if I say I will consider the dirty sex with the gorgeous athlete, can we move on to you, Mol? Which football players did you have falling at your feet last night?"

"You know me, babe. They all fall at my feet."

In fact, they do all fall at Molly's feet. She is obviously beautiful, but she is also wholly and unapologetically herself, with a magnetic personality that draws people to her. She dates on and off, always casually. But as soon as a guy starts falling for her, she runs away like her ass is on fire. When we met her during our first year of law school, she told us she was just getting over an explosively bad breakup. She doesn't talk about it much, which is unusual for her because she is an open book about everything else. We know enough to know his name is Gabe, she thought he was the one, and he shattered her heart.

In all the years we have known her, she has never been in a serious relationship. We all think that Gabe is why, even though Molly has never admitted it. Anytime the topic of men or relationships come up, we let Molly act flighty and casual about it. Whenever we press or encourage her to go for more, she gets this haunted look in her eyes that breaks all our hearts. Molly is color and life and happiness. Whatever happened with Gabe was bad enough that it seeps away everything that makes Molly, Molly.

This is an unspoken agreement that Julie, Emma, and I have always had, so it's not surprising when Julie aims a grin at Molly and says, "Because you have fabulous feet for them to fall at. So, what about you, Hal?"

Shit. In my concern for Molly, I forgot that I would have to talk at some point. I opt for casual and hope that the weirdness between Ben and me was invisible to anyone who might have been watching.

"The most action I got last night was watching Jordan and Allie make out at the table and then dancing with a guy who might as well be my brother...so, sadly, nothing to report here. Although, I think I looked amazing, so thanks for making me get the red dress."

Julie points at me. "Hot as fuck for sure. Red is your color, Hal. So, what else?" She looks around the table, and as we eat, we keep talking about who was there, and what everyone was wearing, and Jeremy's speech that made the entire room cry.

I breathe a sigh of relief that, even though my feelings are a mess of confusion and residual arousal, no one else seems to have noticed.

After breakfast, I double check that my e-reader is in my bag and grab my suitcases and the bag of road trip snacks I left by the front door. I fill up my water tumbler and grab a seltzer before heading to Julie's. She is already waiting outside with her bags and our second bag of road trip snacks, chatting with Emma and Molly.

"It's lake time, bitches," Molly yells out when she sees me pull up.

Julie lets out a whoop and throws her suitcases into my trunk. She seems lighter than she has been the last few weeks since we started moving into our office. She hasn't even mentioned work once this morning, although I see her laptop and a stack of files in the tote bag she slides in next to the suitcases. It's probably too much to hope that she would leave work at home entirely. She wouldn't be her if she did. She hands me her bag of snacks.

"I know it's your thing with Ben, but they had the family size bag of mini-Reese's cups at the grocery store, so I got them for you for the drive."

The mention of Ben has my stomach swooping, but Julie's thoughtful gesture has my heart warming. I've felt this underlying irritation with her since Maya's adoption hearing and her cavalier attitude about skipping it. I know that it lingers because I never really talked to her about it, and when I tried, she shut me down. It would have probably been better to press her on it and fight our way to a resolution, but the thought of that makes me vaguely nauseous. I push it aside and hug her.

"Thanks, Jules."

"Anytime. Now let's get this show on the road."

We all slide into the cars. Molly and Emma into Molly's and Julie and I into mine. A little thrill runs through me as I set my GPS to the lake house and then drive away to start my favorite two weeks of the year.

Chapter Twenty-One
Hallie

The Parkers' lake house is a sprawling stone and wood lakefront structure in Deep Creek, Maryland. It has a massive front porch with a row of cushioned chairs and a deck off the living room in the back overlooking the fire pit, the pool, and the lake. It is the most beautiful, interesting house I have ever seen, and it feels more like home than any of my actual homes ever have.

Julie and Ben's parents bought the lake house when we were four years old. At the time, it was a one floor, five-bedroom cabin with a loft that served as a kind of unofficial kid hangout. Over the years, the Parkers have added a second floor to the cabin and wings to flank the original structure on either side to accommodate our growing group.

Rachel and Steven Parker are the most amazing people in the world. As more friends came into our lives, they wanted everyone to feel at home when they came to the lake. For them, that means a bedroom for everyone—no sharing necessary—and two full weeks of friends, family, amazing food, and all our lake house traditions.

It's late afternoon when Julie and I drive up the long gravel driveway and pull up to the front of the house, followed by Molly and Emma. I look up at the house that holds so many of my best memories. Like every time I lay eyes on it after a long time away, my heart lifts and my soul quiets in a way that it doesn't almost anywhere else.

"Mom's really outdone herself on the flowers this year," Julie observes, as we gather up all the detritus of a two-and-a-half-hour road trip from the floor of the car. An interior designer by profession, Rachel gardens as a hobby. Even though Steven has offered to hire a gardener and landscaper many times over the years, she always refuses, insisting that gardening is her happy place. The house is a riot of colors. Flower beds line the front and stretch alongside the driveway, and large planters filled with colorful blooms flank the porch steps and front door. It is happy, gorgeous, organized chaos, and I love every single inch of it.

"She really does get better every year."

"God, don't tell her that. She'll be impossible to live with."

I snort out a laugh because Julie is right. Rachel is amazing at what she does, and she knows it. I pop the trunk and get out to start unloading, as Molly and Emma do the same behind me. I'm just grabbing the handle of my biggest suitcase when the front door opens. I turn towards the sound, as Ben strolls out wearing board shorts, a white t-shirt, and a baseball cap, fully in vacation mode. He looks relaxed and happy and so much like my Ben that I wonder if maybe I built last night up in my head into something that it wasn't. I've been in a weird place lately. It was my mind playing tricks on me, seeing things that weren't really there.

That's definitely it.

Probably.

"Welcome to the lake, ladies." He grins and starts down the

stairs. As he walks directly to me, he takes off his hat, runs his fingers through his blond waves, and resettles the hat on his head, backwards. I have seen him do that a thousand times, but this time it sends a bolt of arousal straight to my core. Okay, so maybe it wasn't my mind playing tricks. He reaches me and pulls me into a hug.

"So happy to see you, Hallie girl," he whispers directly into my ear. I wind my arms around his back to return the hug as my stomach explodes in a riot of butterflies, and that bolt of arousal doubles in size. Okay. Shit. No tricks. None at all. Good thing I packed the good vibrator. He holds onto me for just a second longer than is strictly friendly, and then he releases me. He slides the tote bag off my shoulder and onto his, taking the suitcase out of my hands and grabbing my second one from the trunk.

Stunned a little speechless by my reaction to his greeting, I finally locate my vocal cords. "You don't have to carry all my bags, you know."

"Sure I do, Hal." He tosses me a wink and heads up the porch steps.

"He could have taken my bags," grumbles Julie, as she pulls hers from the trunk and follows Ben up the stairs. Molly trails after her wearing a caftan she must have changed into on the road, massive sunglasses, a big floppy hat, and a tote bag on each arm. Her pile of luggage sits by the car waiting to, no doubt, be carried up to the house by whichever of the men she can charm into doing it. Her dramatic vacation vibe makes me giggle at her retreating form.

She turns around at the top of the porch steps, holds both arms out, yells, "Vacation, baby!" and then sweeps into the house, calling a hello to whoever is in there.

"What was with you and Ben?" I jump at Emma's voice behind me.

"What do you mean?"

"That was a pretty long hug hello, considering you just saw him at the gala last night."

"Oh, was it? I guess maybe. I didn't notice."

She looks at me for a long moment and I get the uncomfortable feeling that, in her Emma way, she is seeing way more than I want her to. But then she just shrugs and says, "Okay. Come on; let's get in there."

Thank all the gods she decides not to press, because I have no idea what I would tell her. Admitting I'm feeling *something* about Ben seems weird and premature since I have no clue what is going on with him. And with me. With him and me? God, no, no him and me. Friend Ben.

Get your shit together, Hallie.

We walk into the house and even though I can hear the chaos of voices back in the kitchen and would kill for an iced latte since my last coffee was two hours ago, I stop for a moment and take everything in. The massive, cheerful great room with the same oversize furniture Julie, Ben, and I tumbled over as kids. The bookshelves overflowing with both classics and well-loved paperbacks I curled up with as a teenager on rainy summer afternoons. I take a deep, cleansing breath as the memories wash over me. Everything about the house is family and love and *home*. I love every gorgeous inch.

Emma and I walk through the great room, back to the kitchen and straight into the arms of Rachel Parker. She hugs Emma and then reaches for me and wraps her arms around me.

"I am so happy to see you, Hallie."

It's not lost on me that her words of greeting are the same ones Ben used outside, but while his led to butterflies, arousal, and confusion, Rachel's greeting leaves me full of warmth. I've always felt closer to Rachel than I do to my mom. There's something about the ways she gets me that is so different from my family. I can let myself be open with her in ways I can't or won't with almost anyone else, except, strangely, Ben. She releases me from the hug but keeps her hands on my shoulders as she studies my face.

"You doing okay, my girl?"

Ben got all his compassion, and the color of his eyes, from his mom. Her expression of concern is so like his that it makes a lump rise in my throat. Terrified I am going either to lose it in this bright, cheery kitchen or spill my guts to her about my existential work crisis and the weirdness with Ben, I just nod, but then I reach out and hug her again.

Over her shoulder, I see Ben around the big farmhouse table with the girls, but he is paying attention only to me. His quiet, steady gaze holds mine, and everything in me relaxes. How this man can give me butterflies one minute and calm my entire being the next is a mystery.

Feeling steadier, I release Rachel. I barely turn around before Ben is handing me a glass with a straw in it.

"Iced latte. Figured it's been a while since your last caffeine hit, and you were probably running on empty. And I put your bags in your room."

He gives me a sexy smirk and then strolls out the back door to the deck. I just stare after him, wondering how he knew what kind of coffee I wanted when I didn't decide until I stepped into the house. And also, why I am suddenly thinking about any facial expression of Ben's as sexy.

God, my head is a mess.

I take my first grateful sip of the latte, and out of the corner of my eye, I see Emma watching me quietly from her place by the glass doors out to the deck. Shit. But I don't have too much time to consider what Emma sees or doesn't see before I am attacked on both sides by my sisters.

"You're finally here!" Jo yells, a little too close to my ear.

"I missed you! And I am so sad I missed the gala! How was it? Tell me *everything*." What Hannah's voice lacks in volume, it makes up for in extreme enthusiasm.

"Oh my god, *yes*," squeals Jo. "Who hooked up? What was everyone wearing? Did you meet any new athletes? I need to see all your pictures!"

The thing about Hannah and Jo is that once they get into it, they can do an entire thing on their own without me ever having to say anything. They keep firing questions at me and bouncing questions off each other without noticing that I still haven't said a word. I take my typical position when the three of us are together and they get on a roll - standing there and waiting for my turn to talk. Just as they are winding down, though, my parents step into the kitchen.

"Hallie!" My dad scoops me up in a bear hug. "Missed you, baby doll." I bury my face in his neck and breathe in his comforting dad scent. I think he's been wearing the same lime-scented deodorant since 1985. It is uniquely him, and to me, it smells like home. Without warning, the same lump that rose in my throat when Rachel studied me makes a reappearance. I let go as quickly as I can, even more unwilling to let loose my emotions that are swimming too close to the surface now that my family has descended.

My dad heads outside and my mom wraps me up next. As she is letting go, she says, "I've barely talked to you in the last couple of weeks, Hallie. How is everything going with the firm?"

Ugh. I should have used the drive up here to strategize in my head about how I was going to answer these questions I knew would be coming from my family. I had, mostly success-fully, avoided phone calls and visits under the guise that we were too busy setting up the office, but my luck has clearly run out. Never great at thinking on my feet, I just mumble, "Things are good."

"Just a few more months until you girls are ready to open. You must be so happy."

"Of course, she's happy," says Jo. "They've been planning this for years, and it's finally happening."

"I would kill to be my own boss and work with my best friends. Work is so annoying lately. Did I tell you about what happened with my boss? You're not going to believe what he did."

Hannah launches into some story, and for once, I'm grateful for my sisters and their need to voice all their feelings about all the things, because it means no one is focused on me and how unhappy I am with my current professional predicament. Hannah is still talking, my mom and Jo's attention on her, as I slip quietly outside onto the deck and into the lake sunshine.

Chapter Twenty-Two
Ben

The grill is going in preparation for our regular first night barbeque. There are tubs full of beer, wine, and sodas on the deck, and all the people I love the most are scattered around the backyard. My dad and Hallie's dad, Max, are at the grill, and my mom and Hallie's mom, Rebecca, have their heads together over something or other. Jordan, Allie, and Jeremy are laying on lounge chairs by the pool. Julie, Molly, and Emma are in the pool with Hallie's sisters, and Hallie is curled up in her favorite rocking chair in the corner of the deck, e-reader in hand and beverage assortment on the table next to her.

Hallie keeps lifting her head and shooting glances at me, and I grin inwardly, thinking of her face when I handed her the iced latte I made for her when I heard their cars pull up earlier. She thinks she's all chaotic and mysterious about her coffee choices, even to herself. But it just takes some attention to figure it out. I don't think anyone has ever paid enough attention to Hallie to really know her completely. But I have. More than anything in the world, I want to be the one to show her what it really means to be known all the way down to her soul.

I can tell from her looks that she's confused right now, and that's just fine by me.

Brace yourself, Hallie girl; you have no idea what you're in for.

I start heading down to talk to the guys when my mom intercepts me.

"Oh my lord, is that my baby boy? The one and only Benjamin Parker? I could have sworn you decided not to come up this year given how little I've seen of you today. Don't you even think about leaving this deck without having a conversation with me."

I grin and open my arms to her. "Put 'er there, pal."

She wraps her arms around me. She smells like the lake, the perfume she's been using for as long as I can remember, and the cookies she was no doubt baking earlier today before we all got here. It all screams *mom,* and it relaxes me almost instantly.

"I know you're all grown up and a man now and blah, blah, blah, but you will always be my baby. We are going to get a beer that I will never believe you are old enough to drink and sit in those chairs over there, and you are going to tell me what's going on in your life."

She points towards the lounge chairs on the opposite side of the deck, and I follow her, grabbing a couple of beers out of the cooler on the way. I may be almost thirty years old, but when Rachel Parker issues an order, you listen. I pop open the beers and hand her one as we sit down.

"Okay, tell me everything," she starts. "What's going on with you, with the bar, with your life? Since we've been at the lake for weeks, I've missed catching up with you."

"Really? I could have sworn someone who sounded like my mom has been calling me at least every other day since you got up here."

"Smartass. It's different in person, and you know it. I need to see your face when we talk. You have a very expressive face."

I snort out a laugh. "Drama much, Ma?"

"I prefer to call it loving mother involved in her children's lives."

"Keep telling yourself that." I take a long sip of my beer and consider whether to tell my mom about the Stonegate deal. I think about Jeremy pushing me to talk to my dad about it, and I decide to test the waters with my mom first.

"There actually is something I wanted to talk to you about."

My mom's face lights up, like I knew it would. There is nothing my mom loves more than when one of her children confides in her. She's both a great mom and an unabashed gossip, so anything that falls into the Venn diagram of those two interests is right in her wheelhouse.

"Please, do go on, Benj."

I give her the broad strokes of the deal. I keep it to just the facts, without letting her know that I'm struggling to decide what to do. She listens, her face giving nothing away. When I finish, she sits for a minute, considering.

"So, what do you think you're going to do?"

"I haven't decided yet. We have a few months before we have to come to a real decision, and I'm not sure what I want. Jeremy would be fine with either choice, so he left it up to me. Jerk."

She laughs. "I think Jeremy knows you well and knows you wouldn't be at peace unless you made this decision for yourself. He's a good friend, Benj."

"The best. But what do you think I should do?"

"You really want to know what I think?"

"Always, Ma."

"I think you should talk to your dad about it."

I make a face, not sure why I didn't consider that talking to my dad would be the first thing she recommended.

"No way. Don't do that. I know you avoid talking to your dad about business, but for the life of me, I don't know why."

"Because he is a wildly successful real estate developer, and I own a bar."

"I'm not even going to explain all the ways that's a dumb reason. And I just decided. I'm also not going to tell you what I think about the deal. Not until you talk to your dad. You talk to him, and then I'll give you my opinion."

"But can't you just tell me now?" My voice is perilously close to whining.

"No dice, baby boy."

"A nicer mom would tell me."

"Well, lucky for you, you got me. Now, what else is happening? How was the gala last night?"

My mind immediately flashes to my arms around Hallie on the dance floor. Hallie chooses that exact moment to get up from her chair across the deck from me, and my eyes follow her as she disappears into the house.

"I'm over here," says my mom.

I snap my head back around to her. "What?"

She's looking at me with a shit-eating grin, and I groan inwardly because it's also her *I have just figured something out about you* grin.

"Looks like you've finally caught up," says my mom with a smirk in my direction.

"Caught up to what?"

"What I've known for your whole life. I saw the way you just looked at her."

"Looked at who?" I don't know why I even bother. No one can play dumb with my mom. She knows everything.

She doesn't even answer my question.

"Are you finally ready to get off your ass and do something about it?"

I open my mouth to respond, and then my brain catches up. "Wait, my whole life? I haven't had feelings for Hallie for my whole life."

She grins triumphantly and I groan, kicking myself for folding that easily.

"You might have only figured it out around high school graduation. But honey, Hallie Evans has been yours since you were six years old, and you handed her your popsicle right over there by the pool when she dropped hers and started to cry. I knew it then and I knew it when you brought Sarah home a couple of years ago and tried to make us all believe you were in love with her. And I saw it every time Hallie brought home that horrible college boyfriend of hers every spring break and you walked around looking like someone told you Pittsburgh was cancelled forever."

Her eyes meet mine, her gaze soft and comforting and so mom-like.

"And honey, I know it now. You and Hallie are meant for each other."

"How did you know I figured out I had feelings for her around graduation?

She just gives me a look. "Benjamin Parker, there is literally nothing that goes on with one of my children that I don't know about. Now the question is, are you finally ready to do something about it?"

I take a deep breath and figure, what the hell. I'm already in deep. "I am. I love her, Ma. I've loved her for years. I know it could be complicated with Jules and our families, but I'm so tired of waiting. I can't do it anymore."

Her face softens and she reaches over and covers her hand with mine.

"Baby boy, this is your life. Jules is going to be fine and so are our families. I know you love her, and for what it's worth, I think she loves you too. She just hasn't quite worked it out yet. She's yours, and while love is complicated, it's worth it." She glances over to where my dad is standing by the grill. As if sensing her, he looks over and throws her a wink. They have always been so in love, so completely in sync with each other.

I want that. With Hallie.

"We had a couple of moments last night at the gala and I think...well, I think maybe she felt it too."

My mom squeezes my hand. "My money's on you, and you have the lake magic on your side. Go get her, pal."

Later that night after dinner and dessert and time spent talking and hanging out around the pool together, the parents go inside. The rest of us strip down to our bathing suits and go to the lake for night swimming. The lake is dark, the water and small beach illuminated only by the moonlight and the landscape lighting along the footpath from the back yard to the beach. Per usual, Hannah and Jo race down the footpath and jump straight in, with Molly and Julie hot on their heels. All four of them swim right out to the floating swim raft we have out towards the middle of the lake. Emma walks in at a regular person pace with Jeremy next to her, and Allie jumps on Jordan's back. I catch up with Hallie on the path and grab her around the waist, taking off at a run.

"Ben, what the fuck?" she screeches. Whatever else she was going to say is cut off as I run straight into the water and submerge us both. We surface, my arms still around her waist, and she turns to face me, a disgruntled look on her face.

"Give a girl some warning next time."

I grin at her. "What would be the fun in that?"

Some of her hair is hanging in her eyes and I bring one of my hands up to push it behind her ear, trailing my finger along her jaw. I hold her chin in place with my thumb and pointer finger so her eyes stay locked on mine. Our faces are inches apart and she sucks in a breath as I lean closer to her. I see her pupils dilate, her eyes darken, and then at the last second, just before our lips meet, I turn my head, kiss her cheek, and pull back.

"Race you out to the swim raft," I say before diving under. When I surface, I turn back and Hallie is still standing where I left her, a stunned look on her face.

A second later, she seems to shake herself out of it, yelling, "Don't think your head start counts, Benji," before diving under and following me out to the raft.

Chapter Twenty-Three
Hallie

B en was just about to kiss me, right? My brain runs it over and over again as we all hang by the floating swim dock. My sisters, Allie, Jordan, and Molly are hanging on to the side while Emma, Jeremy, Julie, Ben and I sit up on top of it. Everyone else is chattering around me, but I hear almost none of it while my brain tries to make sense of what just happened.

My entire body erupts in goosebumps when Ben whispers in my ear. When did he get here? He was just on the other side of the raft.

"You okay, Hal?"

"Totally fine!" I say just a touch too loudly, before standing up and practically throwing myself into the lake. So completely cool, Hal. Super graceful. I groan inwardly. I glance back at the dock and see Ben looking straight at me with a playful grin on his face.

"Jerkface," I mutter under my breath, before swimming over to Molly and my sisters to join whatever conversation they're having. But their argument about which is number one in the definitive ranking of Taylor Swift albums fails to hold my attention—it's *1989*, duh. There is no other answer—when Ben is so *there* with his stupid blond hair and his stupid sky-blue eyes and his low-slung board shorts showing off his perfect fucking six pack and the smirks he keeps tossing at me and I hate him for whatever is it he thinks he's doing right now.

Except I don't hate him at all because what I am is turned all the way on by him and all his perfection, and I hate that I am because I don't know what it all means, and I am absolutely the person who needs to know what it all means.

By the time everyone is ready to swim back to shore, I am fed the fuck up. I want to disappear into my room and curl up in bed with a romance novel where the girl may be harboring weird and confusing feelings for her best friend who is suddenly acting all swoony and strange, but all the confusion is worked out by the end, and everyone lives happily ever after. That's the world I would like to live in tonight, please and thank you.

We all wrap ourselves in towels, grab our clothes, and go inside for the night. Emma, Molly, Julie, and I all have rooms upstairs while Ben and his friends are in one of the wings off the great room. The girls go straight up while I detour into the kitchen to grab my e-reader and my water.

"Looking for this?" Ben is standing in the kitchen leaning up against the big granite island, my e-reader in one hand and my water tumbler in the other.

"I am, actually. I just need to fill up my water and then I'm going to bed. I'm exhausted."

He pushes himself off the island and walks towards where I stand in the kitchen doorway. "I already filled it up for you."

"But I need..."

"Extra ice, I know. I filled the ice all the way to the top, just the way you like it."

How does he know that?

"Okay, well, thanks for doing that for me."

"I like doing things for you." He hands me the cup and my e-reader. "By the way, I checked to see what you're reading, and good choice. Chapter twenty-seven is my favorite." Then he kisses my cheek and saunters away into his wing, calling, "Goodnight, Hal," over his shoulder.

I race up the stairs and drop my towel and water before flipping open my e-reader and navigating to chapter twenty-seven and Fuck. Me. Chapter twenty-seven, it turns out, is a very hot shower sex scene...and how the hell did he know that? And now I'm picturing Ben reading this scene and picturing his face and did he get all hot and bothered over it just like I did and... Nope. No. No way.

I snap my e-reader shut and toss it onto the bed. I take myself to the bathroom to drown myself in my shower which will be, sadly, sexless, and pray that my dreams tonight won't be haunted by my friend Ben and his blue eyes on mine and his hands on my waist and whether he actually did almost kiss me tonight in the lake and how a tiny, traitorous part of me wishes that he had.

I stumble downstairs at eight thirty the next morning towards the smell of coffee and cinnamon. As expected, Rachel is already up and icing the cinnamon buns she must have just taken out of the oven. She has made cinnamon buns at the lake for as long as I can remember, the smell of them our alarm clock, pulling us all out of bed and into the kitchen. I never eat cinnamon buns anywhere except for here. But the smell of them anytime during the year instantly conjures up summer mornings in this house when Rachel and I are the first ones awake, taking a few minutes together in the cozy warmth of the kitchen before everyone else wakes up and chaos descends.

I must make a sound because she turns towards the kitchen doorway and grins at me.

"Morning, honey. I've been waiting for you. Sleep okay?"

Not really, thanks to your son winding me up and then leaving me with a kiss on the cheek and a casual goodnight and I'm really glad I packed my vibrator charger because otherwise I wouldn't have gotten any sleep at all. I can't say that to her, obviously, so I settle on, "I always sleep well here," which is usually true.

I walk over and kiss her on the cheek and then go straight to the coffee pot, reaching into the cabinet above for a glass cup to pour coffee in and stick in the freezer for a while so I can make iced coffee.

"Oh, your coffee is in the fridge, Hallie," Rachel says as she rummages through a drawer for a frying pan.

"What coffee?"

"Ben said to tell you that he made coffee yesterday and put it in the fridge for you so it would be cold by morning. Oh, and there's milk already in it. He said you would want iced coffee but don't like cold brew and wouldn't want to make it with instant. He got Splenda for you on his way up here too. Should be on the top shelf of the cabinet by the fridge."

Seriously?

I open the fridge and right in front of me is a tumbler bearing a sticky note that reads *"Hallie, Caffeinate yourself."* Then I open the cabinet next to the fridge and see the box of Splenda packets. I just stand there, frozen in place. I've been thinking about iced coffee with milk and one Splenda since I opened my eyes this morning, but he made this coffee yester-day. Is he magic?

"Hallie?"

I whip around, coffee in one hand and a Splenda packet in the other, wondering how long I've been standing there considering whether Ben is actually a wizard. I have no clue what my face is doing, but whatever it is, it makes Rachel grin at me before nudging me aside to get the eggs she has obviously been waiting to take out of the fridge.

"Looks like our Ben knows just what you like," she says, cracking eggs into a bowl.

"No shit," I mutter under my breath, more than a little thrown off and not nearly caffeinated enough to make sense of this.

She just laughs and takes the coffee and sugar packet out of my hands, opening the top of the tumbler to add the ice and Splenda herself. She pops in a straw and hands it back to me, kissing me on the head and going back to her breakfast prep.

"So, how are things going at the firm? I know it hasn't been that long since you closed on the house, but you girls must be so excited to be finally hitting the ground running. Jules has been keeping me updated, but I haven't had a chance to talk to you about it."

Oh, hello anxiety, my old friend, it's fucking terrible to see you again.

Between the gala and the weirdness with Ben, I've been able to shove all my angst over the firm and what to do about it to the far recesses of my brain. But with Rachel's question, it all comes roaring back. My stomach tightens, and my shoulders tense up as I consider what to say. I must pause a little too long because Rachel is looking at me with concern.

"Everything okay with the firm, Hallie?"

"Oh, yeah, it's fine. Everything is okay. It's just been a lot these past couple of weeks."

She gives me an unimpressed look.

"That's an evasion if I ever heard one." Turns out Rachel did not earn the title of Best Mom Ever by being stupid.

"It has been a lot. Really. For me especially."

"I'm not going to pry even though I'm dying to, because it's our first morning here and that's always been a special time for you and me. But you know you can talk to me about anything, right? I might not have given birth to you, but you're mine just as much as Julie is."

"Thanks, Rachel," I say, filled with gratitude for her and this quiet morning.

She squeezes my hand. "Okay then. Let's get to it. I'm putting the eggs on now. Will you go wake up Ben? He made me promise not to let him sleep through breakfast this year."

Ever the night owl and extremely not a morning person, Ben sleeps through first morning breakfast more than he makes it. Knowing it pisses him off to miss cinnamon buns, and maybe just a tiny bit eager to see him this morning, I grab my coffee and pad over to his room.

I knock on his door and wait, but there's no answer. I don't hear any movement from inside either. Knowing he's probably still fast asleep, I yell his name, knock one more time, and walk in, expecting to have to haul him out of bed. His bed is empty. The sheets and blankets are rumpled and twisted, and it gives me a rush of satisfaction to think that maybe he spent the night tossing and turning just like I did. That thought is barely through my head when the ensuite bathroom door opens and Ben comes out in a cloud of steam.

I never quite understood the phrase "rooted to the spot," but suddenly, I do. I should turn around and leave, but I can't get a signal from my brain to my feet to get them moving. Ben is rubbing a towel over his wet hair, and he is naked except for a white towel wrapped low around his waist. He's covered in water droplets, and I follow their path with my eyes as they roll from his chest, down his muscled abs, following the light dusting of hair that disappears into his towel. I don't know if it's the towel, or the fact that he's mostly naked and dripping wet. Or because his hair is a wild mess from the towel. Maybe it's that I haven't had enough coffee and this is basically a scene ripped straight out of one of my books, but everything Ben has going on right now is really...doing it for me. God.

"My eyes are up here, Hallie."

I snap my eyes up to meet his. Whatever I'm feeling must be written all over my face because the smirk on Ben's face disappears. His gaze that was playful a second ago changes and turns darker as he takes me in. Our eyes are glued together, and his are intense in a way that makes me itchy and needy and so damn aware of Ben and his body and the woodsy scent of his body wash. Without even realizing what I'm doing, I take a step forward. He holds a hand out to stop me.

"Not yet," he says in a low voice.

That wakes me right up. "Not yet what?"

"Just, not yet." His voice takes on a commending edge, and I don't know what he's talking about, but I stop all the same.

"I'm going to put some clothes on," he says, his voice back to normal. "Tell my mom I'll be out in a second."

I leave his room and close the door behind me, my heart hammering in my ears. I pause and take a deep breath to steady myself before going back to the kitchen. By the time I get there, Julie, Molly, and Emma are sitting around the big kitchen table, coffees in hand. I take a seat with them, and before long, everyone else joins. My mom gives me a hug over the back of my chair and takes a seat next to my sisters, who, per usual, immediately start carrying on about something that is going on at Jo's office and some friend drama Hannah is having. My dad comes in with Steven, already talking about the boards they are replacing on the dock later. Allie and Jordan stumble in with their arms around each other, the beard burn on Allie's neck making it crystal clear what they just got up to. Jeremy squeezes into the seat next to Emma, who turns bright red and pointedly ignores him, which seems to amuse Jeremy. And Molly and Julie are alternating between bickering over god only knows what and giggling over something on Julie's phone.

I'm not in the mood to engage with any of it, the scene with Ben still running through my head like a song on repeat. And then the man himself strolls into the kitchen, kissing his mom on the cheek, pouring his own coffee, and plopping himself next to me. He kisses me on the cheek too.

"Morning, Hal, did you find your coffee?" He is all smiles and easy-going energy, as if we weren't wrapped in a charged stare-off over his naked chest just minutes ago.

I have emotional whiplash. I don't know how to deal with *this* Ben, who can switch so seamlessly from darkened stare to cheerful boy next door.

"Um, I did, thanks. How did you know what I would want?"

"I told you, Hallie girl. I see you."

This time when he says it, I realize that I'm starting to believe he really, truly does.

Chapter Twenty-Four
Hallie

And that's the way it goes all day. We do all the things that we always do on our first day at the lake. We lay by the pool with books and music, jump in the lake, float around on the swim dock, and go into town to our favorite diner for lunch. We make pizza for dinner, play a big game of trivial pursuit, and stay outside until the first fireflies start to blink.

And all day, Ben is just...there. He puts his hand on my back when he passes me and brushes back my hair when we're in the lake. He sits just a little closer on the picnic bench at lunch than is strictly friendly and plops himself down to share my lounge chair by the pool. I have never been aware of another person's presence the way I am of his. By the time we all go up to change for the bonfire, I'm a bundle of nerves and need.

It's fully dark and the guys are just lighting the fire when Molly, Emma, Julie, Allie, and I walk down the path to the lake. We lay out blankets and throw down pillows on the small stretch of sand and gather around the bonfire with bottles of wine, plastic wine glasses, and s'mores supplies. Jordan takes out a guitar because when we are at the lake, we go full-blown summer camp. He absently strums while the rest of us get comfortable. I shiver, silently cursing myself for forgetting to grab a sweatshirt from my room. Before I can get up from my cozy nest and trudge back to the house, a hoodie is dropped over my head. I glance down and see it's one of Ben's University of Pittsburgh sweatshirts. Tugging it down, I look up, and Ben is standing over me.

"You looked cold," is all he says before taking the spot next to me and throwing an arm around my shoulder all friendly-like. His body is so big and cuddly, and the crackling of the fire and the lapping of the water are so soothing. For the first time since Ben and I danced together at the gala, I take a full, easy breath. I settle into Ben's warmth and the heaviness of his arm and I let the lake night wrap itself around me.

Four bottles of wine, two bags of chips, countless s'mores, one game of never-have-I-ever, and at least half of Taylor Swift's discography played on Jordan's guitar later, everyone slowly starts to call it a night.

"I'm going to head up and go over some work stuff before bed," says Julie, standing up and brushing graham cracker crumbs off her leggings.

Molly is next. "I can't believe you lasted all day without doing any work. I'm so proud of you that I'll even go over work stuff with you for an hour or so. I have to finalize the art order for the waiting room anyway."

"Are they ice skating in hell?" asks Jordan. "I don't know the last time I saw the two of you agree on anything."

Molly sticks out her tongue at him.

"We love each other." Then she slides her gaze to Julie with a sly smile. "Most of the time."

Giggling, they head up to the house.

"I'm going up to bed too," says Emma, standing up and grabbing the empty wine bottles.

Jeremy jumps up from his spot on my other side.

"I'll walk with you." He takes the rest of the empty bottles and the garbage bag we brought down for our trash, and they set off.

Jordan packs away his guitar and pulls Allie up. "Come on, my princess; I'm taking you to bed."

"What did I tell you about calling me princess?"

"Um, I don't remember. Maybe you should remind me. In our bedroom." She snickers as he grabs his guitar with one hand and her with the other hand and pulls her up the path.

Then it's just Ben and me. I wait for the tension that has been between us all day to come back, but it doesn't. It's just us and the lake and the fire and the crickets making up the familiar symphony of night at the lake. I take a deep breath and let it out, curling my hands up in Ben's hoodie and wrapping my arms around my legs as I stare into the flames.

Neither of us talk, but it's a comfortable sort of quiet. The kind of quiet that I only really have at the lake. The kind that's filled with magic and possibility and makes me want to give him all my truths. I lean my cheek on my knee with my head facing towards Ben and see that his quiet gaze is already on me.

"I think I'm ready to talk about it now."

"Talk about what?"

"The firm. I mentioned a few weeks ago that I was wondering if maybe it was the wrong choice. I wasn't ready to talk about it then, but I am now."

"Then I'm ready to listen." He swings around and I do the same so we're facing each other, cross-legged, our knees touching. He reaches out and gently pulls my hands from the wrist holes of my sweatshirt, lacing our fingers together but saying nothing. He is giving me the space to say what I need, and I love him for it.

"It started a year ago when we began getting serious with our planning. The girls were all so excited about it and I just... wasn't. Not the way I had been whenever we talked about it before. It was a busy time at work, so I thought maybe that was it, but even when things calmed down, the excitement just never came." I suck in a breath. This is more than I have ever said about the way I've been feeling, and I need a minute.

Ben keeps his steady gaze on mine, and it gives me the courage to keep going. I straighten my shoulders and take a deep breath, steeling my nerves to tell him all of it.

"Julie, Molly, and Emma were forging on ahead, making plans, and slowly starting to put out feelers to their clients to see which ones would follow them, so I did the same. We all kept meeting and planning, and looking for office space. And don't get me wrong, I love being with them and doing something together. I like building something with them, but I could never quite recapture that happiness and excitement I had when we talked about it before."

"Before you started planning?"

"Exactly. It was like every step we took that got us closer to the end, the more anxious I got. But the hell of it was, I could never figure out the why of it all, you know? It was like my instincts were screaming at me that this wasn't the right thing, but I didn't know what the right thing was. I couldn't figure out what was making me so anxious."

"Which made you more anxious."

I smile at him, relieved he gets it. "Yeah. It was an anxiety spiral I couldn't get myself out of, and couldn't figure it out. Part of me thought that maybe it was the change of leaving my firm and striking out on my own because I hate change and it's hard for me. But that wasn't it."

"You keep saying you didn't know what was keeping you from going all in. Does that mean you know now?"

"Jesus, you're good."

"I'm not, really. I just listen when you talk."

I squeeze his hand in gratitude for that and keep going because now that I'm talking, it's like I need to purge it all from my system. "I figured it out the day of Maya's adoption hearing. I was sitting in the courtroom, watching Eric, Jen, and Maya together, seeing their faces when the judge declared them officially a family, and it hit me. I've been practicing trusts & estates law for five years and doing adoption work with Callahan on the side. I guess I went with the flow, assuming that I would continue on that path forever. And that was fine until it wasn't. It's not fine anymore.

"Working on Maya's case made me realize it. I don't want to be an estate planning attorney anymore, Ben. I want to practice family law. And not just a couple hours a month when Callahan has some overflow they don't have time for. I want to do it all the time. Every day. I loved working with the Caseys, and I have loved every single case I've ever worked on with Callahan. Even the hard ones. I want to make families. I want to make sure that kids who wind up in the system are safe and cared for. I want to help parents find the children they are meant to have. There aren't enough lawyers doing this kind of work, and I feel called to do it in a way that I have never felt called to anything. It's what I was meant to do, Benji. I know it for sure."

He looks at me, eyes blazing. "Then you should do it, Hal. You need to do it."

"You know it's not that easy. I'm in the final stages of opening a law firm with my three best friends where we are practicing private client law. I have clients following me to my new firm who are expecting me to be doing the work they have been paying me to do for years. How am I supposed to tell the girls that I'm backing out? Especially Julie. This means so much to her. She'll never forgive me, Ben. But if I don't explore this, I might never forgive myself."

My voice cracks on the last word, and tears spill down my cheeks. All the bravery that pushed my truth out disappears at the thought of either disappointing the three women who mean the most to me or letting go of the dream I didn't even know I had.

Ben drags me between his legs and gathers me up, wrapping me in his warm arms. I cry it out against his chest as he strokes my hair and kisses the top of my head.

He whispers things like, "I'm here," and "I've got you," and "You're safe," and "Let it go, Hallie." The relief of someone else knowing my deepest secret—and that someone else being him— is both heady and draining. When my tears finally dry up, I sit up and face Ben again.

"So that's it. That's all of it. I want to do something else, but I went ahead with plans for the firm and never said anything to any of them. My friends mean everything to me, and I would never want to hurt them, make them angry, or get in the way of our friendship."

Ben takes my hands in his again.

"Hallie, one of the best things about you is that you are so damn loyal. You are such a good friend, and you take care of everyone, all the time. You remember everyone's birthdays, and doctor's appointments, and work milestones. You take people dinner when they're sick and buy their favorite candy when they've had a bad day and check-in when they have a doctor's appointment. And you never ask for anything in return. Most people around you, my sister included, think you don't need or want help or support. But that's not true, is it?"

I shake my head slowly.

"I know it isn't. You have spent so much time worrying about everyone else and holding in all of your thoughts and your truths. You bend over backwards to make sure no one ever worries about you because it's hard for you to open yourself up to other people. And anger isn't an emotion that you are particularly comfortable with, so you would rather go with the flow than change direction if that is what makes the people in your life happy."

I just stare at him, strangely stunned and entirely unsurprised he has me pegged so well.

"But, Hallie, I'm going to say some things now, and I need you to really hear me, okay?"

I nod.

He looks at me with an intensity that turns his clear blue eyes practically navy. "It's okay to lean on the people who love you. You can ask for their support or their help or for whatever damn thing you need. They'll give it to you because they love you and because that's what family does. You can want things and plan for your own future, even if that future looks different than you thought it might. And it's okay to change your mind and take a new path—even if it disappoints the people in your life. Even if one of those people is my sister who you and I both love. Hallie, you are the least selfish person I know, and wanting a new direction for your career isn't wrong. It's life. And yeah, Jules might get mad because it upsets her grand plan. But that's not on you. That's on her, and she'll get over it."

"I know you're right," I whisper. "But this is hard for me."

"I know it is, Hal, but that doesn't mean it's not the right choice."

"So what do I do now?" I ask, like Ben has all the answers. Because honestly, sitting here late at night next to the lake and the dying fire, it feels like he just might.

"I have an idea if you're open to it."

"At this point, I'll take whatever you've got."

"I think you might feel better talking to Julie and the girls if you have a plan. Jules doesn't do well with abstractions, so if you go to her with all your feelings, we both know it won't go well. More likely than not, she'll just bully you into thinking her way."

I snort out a laugh because doesn't Ben just have everyone figured out tonight.

"So, I think in the morning, you should email Charlie Callahan and set up a meeting as soon as you're back in Pittsburgh. He has been practicing family law for his entire career, so he'll have a good perspective on this. Maybe he finally needs another lawyer at his firm, or he knows of another firm looking to hire. Or maybe he has some ideas on how to establish a family law practice under the umbrella of the firm you are already setting up. Whatever it is, he'll be able to give you advice that I can't. Once you schedule the meeting, set it aside for the rest of the time we're here. Take the vacation, read all the books, sit in the sun, let our moms take care of you a little bit. And when we're back in town, you'll have the meeting, and we'll do whatever comes next. But for what it's worth, I think you already do incredible family law work, and if this is the direction you want to take your career, you should do it. I'll be here to support you all the way."

We'll do whatever comes next. I'll be here to support you. My relief at Ben's words, at not being alone in this anymore, at having a plan and someone to shoulder some of my burden after all these months of floundering, is enormous. I wrap myself around Ben, squeezing him tight.

"Thank you," I whisper.

"I've got you, Hal. I'll always be here for you. You don't ever have to go it alone."

Chapter Twenty-Five
Ben

Hallie is pretty wrung out after our talk, so I pour water on the fire, and we gather up the rest of the blankets to carry up to the house. Hallie goes to throw them in the laundry room while I grab her big tumbler, filling it with ice and water. Her look of gratitude last night over me doing something as simple as filling her water cup the way she likes it makes me want to do as many things for her as I can. Hallie Evans has done too much on her own for far too long. She needs someone to take care of her, and I want that someone to be me.

She comes back in, and I hand her the cup. She sets it on the kitchen counter and then throws her arms around me. I wrap mine around her and hold on, resting my cheek on top of her head and breathing in the cherry vanilla smell of her shampoo mixed with a hint of bonfire smoke. She loosens her hold and steps back but doesn't let go of me, and I don't let go of her. We stand frozen, the air around us so charged that I feel my skin prickle with it. I see in her eyes the emotion that my entire body is humming with. *Desire.*

For a split second I think it's going to happen right here in the kitchen of my parents' lake house. That I am going to lean in and kiss her like I have been thinking about doing almost every day for the last eleven years. But, at the last minute, it's me who pulls away, dropping a kiss on Hallie's head and pushing a lock of hair back behind her ear. My fingers graze her ear and then linger on her cheek for a second longer before I drop my hand, eyes never leaving hers.

"Goodnight, Hallie."

"Goodnight, Ben," she whispers.

And then she's gone.

Behind my closed bedroom door, I pace my room. Through the entire shower I just took and now as I wear a path on my bedroom carpet, my only thought is what an idiot I am. The moment was right there, and I hesitated. I know what I saw in her eyes. On her face. I've been waiting eleven years for Hallie to look at me the way she was looking at me in the kitchen.

It's after midnight, but there is no way I'm going to fall asleep tonight after that, knowing that Hallie is just downstairs. The past couple of days have required more restraint than I was aware I possessed. Tonight, down in the kitchen, I reached my limit. It's probably a stupid idea to do this in the middle of the night, and it might end up backfiring spectacularly, but I can't wait anymore. Decision made, I leave my room.

I pause for a second outside my door. This could all go terribly wrong. I could be about to make a mistake that will cost our families decades of easy, uncomplicated friendship. It could screw up my relationship with my sister when I make her feel like she has to choose, at least temporarily, between Hallie and me. But I have come this far, and after our talk by the fire and the moment in the kitchen, I am surer than ever that even if Hallie doesn't feel exactly what I feel, she sure feels something. There's no turning back now.

I take off barefoot down the stairs, avoiding the creaky second step, and walk to Hallie's bedroom door. Praying that I don't completely fuck up my life in the next ten minutes, I lift my hand and knock. A second later, Hallie opens the door, and her eyes go wide when she sees me. It's only then that I realize I'm wearing low-slung sweatpants and an old t-shirt so worn it's practically transparent, and my hair is a disaster from running my hands through it for twenty minutes straight while I paced my bedroom.

Hallie's hair is piled up on top of her head, damp from the shower, and her face is a little pink with that just washed look. Jesus, she's pretty. She is dressed in tiny sleep shorts and an oversized t-shirt. My traitorous eyes drop to her chest, and it's clear that she isn't wearing a bra. Fuck.

"Ben," she stammers, crossing her arms over her chest when she realizes exactly what I'm looking at. "What are you doing here?"

"We need to talk, Hal."

"About what?"

"I think you know what."

That seems to get to her. She stiffens and steps back, letting me into her bedroom and closing the door behind me. She stands there for a second, her hand resting on the now closed door, before she turns back around to face me.

"About what happened in the kitchen..." I start.

"It's okay, Ben, really." And then a flood of words comes out of her mouth. "We don't have to do this now. Or ever. I know things have been weird lately, and it's probably my fault because I've been so off with everything I have going on. You're my best friend, and I can talk to you about things I can't talk to anyone else about, and you really see me, and we're here with all the lake magic, and I just started to feel..." She slams her mouth shut, and her cheeks heat, as if she hadn't meant to say that last thing. But I heard it. I knew I hadn't imagined it. Everything inside me lights right the fuck up.

I take a step towards her. "What did you feel, Hal?"

She takes a step back. "It's nothing. Really. Like I said, it's just being here, at the lake. The whole atmosphere. That's it."

"You sure about that?"

She swallows, visibly. "I don't know what you want me to say, Ben."

"I want you to tell me what you feel." My heart is beating so fast that I wonder if she can hear it and if it's possible I'm going to die of a heart attack before we finish this conversation.

"Why don't you tell me what you feel, and we can compare notes."

"No, Hal. I asked you a question, and I need you to answer it. What. Do. You. Feel?" With each word, I take one step closer to her and I see her take a sharp breath, see the pulse fluttering in her throat. Oh yeah, this is not the look of someone unaffected by what is happening.

"I need words, Hallie."

"I don't know, honestly." She takes two more steps backwards until her back is pressed against her bedroom door and she has nowhere left to go.

"I think I might know," I say, feeling like I'm standing on a ledge one hundred stories in the air, about to jump.

"Well, then could you enlighten me so we can finish this, and I can go to bed?" She says the last part of the sentence in a whisper.

We stand there for a few seconds, staring at each other, both of our chests rising and falling rapidly. We're close enough that each breath she takes flutters over my skin, and I can feel the warmth radiating from her body. It wraps around me and empties my brain of everything except for Hallie and me and this singular moment where everything is about to change.

"I just have to..." I trail off, not sure how to finish that sentence.

"You have to what?"

I know it has to be me. I have to make this move. It's now or never, and it has to be now.

"Fuck it," I say, before grabbing her face in both of my hands and laying my lips on hers. She stands absolutely frozen for a second, and I panic that I misjudged her. But then she winds her arms around my waist and starts kissing me back.

My brain fuzzes, and something loosens in my chest, and my only thought is, "yes, this." I push my hands into her hair, stroking her jaw with my thumbs as I tilt her head back to take the kiss deeper. And she lets me. A groan slips from me when I run my tongue along the seam of her lips and she opens for me, letting my tongue sweep into her sweet mouth and tangle with hers.

Hallie Evans is in my arms, and I am kissing her, and she feels exactly as good as I always thought she would.

In that first touch of my lips to hers, my entire world unspools. We are the friends we always have been, but in this kiss, I can see all the possibilities of what we could be. What I always hoped we would be. It is heady and intense and the closest to a holy moment as I have ever had in my life. I am all feeling and instinct, and we are electric together just like I thought we would be, and all I can think is now that I have her like this, I will never be able to let her go.

Chapter Twenty-Six
Hallie

I'm kissing Ben Parker. I am kissing Ben Parker! And it feels so fucking good I never want it to end. He tastes like mint and the wine we drank by the fire, and he smells like laundry detergent and the woodsy scent that is so absolutely Ben that it should freak me out because *oh my god, I'm kissing Ben. My best friend Ben.* But it doesn't, because Ben is kissing me like he has been thinking about kissing me for his entire life. Sparks dance across my skin, and there is a long, liquid pull low in my belly. I should be shocked by how right this feels, but somehow, I'm not.

Ben drops his hands to my waist and moves them just under the fabric of my t-shirt, his thumbs stroking the bare skin there as his mouth continues to move against mine. It feels like the world is tilting at my feet. I reach up to tangle my hands in his hair, pulling slightly, and he lets out a groan and tears his mouth away to rest his forehead against mine.

"Jesus Christ," he mutters, breathing hard. Then his lips are on mine again, and his tongue is licking back into my mouth in a way that makes my head spin. His fingers leave a trail of fire where they streak up the bare skin along my spine and back down again. I have been kissed before, but I have never, ever been kissed like this.

Ben's mouth leaves mine to drift down my jaw and then to my neck. I let out an honest to god whimper and pull his lips back to mine. He comes willingly, angling his head and kissing me like he'll die without it. He's close enough that I can feel him hard against my leg, and a thrill shoots through me that I did that. He is hard for me. Minutes pass as we stay wrapped up as we kiss and kiss before finally breaking apart and staring at each other, breathing heavily. Ben's eyes are wide and dark, his hair a mess. His lips are wet and puffy, and under the hand that I lay on his chest, his heart is pounding wildly.

"Ben," I whisper, without knowing what I mean to say next.

"I know, Hal." He covers my hand on his chest with one of his. He seems to answer the question I'm not even sure I asked.

We just look at each other for a few seconds longer, the air between us heavy and charged. Our lifelong friendship is cracked wide open, the pieces scattered, waiting to rearrange themselves into whatever new and fragile thing is forming between us right now. I don't know what it is, but I already know it is enormous. That should be terrifying but it's not— because this is Ben, and this is me, and this is Ben and me. Standing here while our eyes search each other's, his filled with heat and longing and what looks strangely like relief, after kissing each other senseless, feels like the most natural thing in the world and the best thing I have ever done.

And then he closes the small distance between us and pulls me against him, one arm looped around my waist and the other hand cradling my head, holding on tight like he's afraid if he lets go, I'll disappear.

But I'm not going anywhere. I am rooted to this spot by the

weight of whatever is happening right now, and I never want to move.

He eases back and looks me in the eyes again. Then he leans down and gives me one more long, slow kiss that has my heart rolling over in my chest before he steps back, his eyes never leaving mine.

We are both silent for a couple of seconds. What do two lifelong friends even say after they kiss the shit out of each other for the first time and like it? It's me who breaks the silence, voicing the only thought in my head.

"How long do you think that's been in there?"

"I don't know," Ben says quietly, in a way that makes me feel like he does know, but I opt not to press it.

The silence descends between us again, and this time it's heavy and filled with something I can't quite name. And then Ben takes another step back and clears his throat.

"So...I guess I'll go back to my room?" He phrases it more like a question than a statement.

The face I know so well is full of uncertainty and hesitation. It's a letdown considering my entire body is still buzzing, and I'm strategizing about how I can kiss him again—and then do a whole lot more than kiss him—as soon as humanly possible.

"Oh, okay, I mean, yeah. I guess it is pretty late," I stammer.

He starts towards the door, but him leaving is the last thing I want right now. So, I pull up my big girl pants.

"Or you could...stay?"

"Yeah?" Ben stops in his tracks, his smile lighting up every inch of him.

"Yeah. Unless you want to go. It's okay if you do, but I want you to stay."

"Hallie, the last thing I want to do right now is walk out that door."

"Really? Okay. Good. Because that kiss was..." I trail off, not knowing what to say. Electric? Mind-blowing? The best kiss of my life?

"Yeah, Hal. It was."

We look at each other, my heart pounding and my need for Ben rising up like a tidal wave. It threatens to swamp me if he doesn't get his hands back on me in the next three seconds. I should probably stop and think about what all this means, but I am so damn sick of thinking all the time. I just want to feel, and this feels absolutely right. It's like all my confusion over the way Ben has been acting over the last couple of days has coalesced into this one single moment. All that is between us right now is want and heat and our chests rising and falling in sync.

As if we decide something at the exact same time, we fly at each other, bodies colliding and mouths crashing together. Our tongues tangle and we are a dizzying frenzy of lips and hands and riotous electricity. I wrap my arms around Ben's neck and stand on my tiptoes, trying to get closer to him, but there is no closer that would be close enough. As if understanding what I'm trying to do, Ben reaches down and wraps a hand around each of my thighs, boosting me up and wrapping my legs around his waist while never pulling his mouth away. He has one hand under my ass and the other gripping the back of my head while his lips assault mine.

I can feel Ben's cock, hot and huge and rock hard, contained only by his thin sweatpants. I grind down on him, trying to ease the ache between my legs. All I'm wearing are underwear and sleep shorts, his cock settled right against my clit, and it feels so fucking good that I could probably come just like this, still fully dressed. The hand on my ass tightens, pulling me even closer to him, and he groans, pulling his mouth from mine and holding me tightly in place so I can't move.

"Nuh-uh, Hallie girl. I've been waiting a long fucking time for this, and the first time you come for me, you're coming on my tongue."

Arousal shoots through me, and I dimly register the "long fucking time." But I'm too buzzed by the proximity of my body to Ben's and the way his mouth grazes the sensitive spot behind my ear and slides down my throat to nip at my collarbone to hold my curiosity for long.

He walks us towards my bed and sets me down on the edge before dropping to his knees. His gaze is fire, the expression on his face hungry as his eyes sweep down my body and back up again, and I'm shocked when I don't burst into flames.

Eyes still on mine, he drifts his hands from my knees up the outsides of my thighs to rest on my hips. He pauses for a second before curling his fingers into the waistband of my shorts.

"Can I?" he asks.

I nod.

"Words, Hallie. I need words."

"Yes. Please."

His smile has a smug edge to it, and fuck if it's not the sexiest thing I have ever seen on his face. I could spend hours pondering the fact that I suddenly find Ben's smile sexy, but then he tugs on my waistband and pulls my shorts down and off in a single move, tossing them onto the floor behind him. Also, so sexy.

He traces a finger down the seam of my underwear and then up the middle over the wet spot I'm sure is there because I have never been this turned on in my life. When his finger grazes my clit, my entire body jolts. Then he leans down and runs his nose up along the center of my underwear, breathing in deeply. He licks along my lower belly, then grasps the sides of my underwear and slides them off and down my legs, throwing them over his shoulder to join my sleep shorts on the floor. With a hand on each knee, he pushes my legs back open, so I am completely bared to him.

"Fuck, Hallie," he breathes. Then, more slowly than I can bear, he traces a single finger up my slit, gathering the moisture that has pooled there and circles my clit. I let out a low moan as a thousand nerve endings spark to life.

Ben looks up at me, gaze molten. "You are so beautiful, Hallie girl." He circles my clit again and my vision blurs, my breath catching in my chest. "Now, lay back."

I fall instantly back on my elbows, eyes never leaving his.

"Good girl."

And bless me Gloria Steinem for I have sinned because every feminist bone in my body turns to dust and floats away at the sound of Ben calling me good girl and looking at me like I am the most desirable being to ever grace this earth. I know without a doubt any sex I have had up until this point was a waste of time because this is already the hottest sexual encounter of my entire life, and Ben hasn't even taken off a single article of clothing.

Ben leans down, flicking my clit lightly with his tongue, and my hands fly down to grab his hair, trying to pull his face closer to me. He lifts his head and gives me one heated look before he cups me, and slides one finger just inside me, and then back out again.

"You are so fucking wet, Hallie. Is this for me?"

"Ben," I breathe.

"Answer me, Hallie girl." He pushes his finger back in, a little deeper this time, and slides his thumb over my clit.

"Yes," I gasp as my hips jerk up.

"Good answer." Ben pushes his finger the rest of the way inside me and rubs his thumb over my clit again and again until my legs start to shake, and my head presses back into the mattress.

"Ben," I breathe. "I need..."

"I know what you need." He wraps a hand around each of my calves, tosses my legs over his shoulders, and covers my entire pussy with his mouth. He curls the finger inside me up, hitting a spot that makes me see stars, as his mouth licks and sucks at my clit until my hips are twisting and I'm crying out at the assault on my senses. Ben on his knees for me. His thick finger stretching me open and his hot, wet mouth working at my clit like he'll die if he has to stop. It's so much and yet not enough at the same time. My grip on his hair tightens as I grind against his mouth, trying to get closer to him.

"Fuck yes, Hallie. Take what you need." He continues to lick and suck and hum against my clit when I roll my hips, and I feel the vibration all the way up my body. Never in my life have I felt like this. My entire body is flushed and vibrating, and I feel like I'm about to combust.

"Ben," I gasp, my chest heaving, not able to suck in enough oxygen to speak a full sentence. "I can't...I..."

"Give it to me, Hallie. Come for me."

Ben slides in a second finger then curls them both up deep inside of me and wraps his lips around my clit, sucking hard. And I detonate. I let out a cry and come so hard my vision blacks out. Waves of pleasure roll through my body, and it's like my world tears apart at the seams. All that's left is Ben and me in this room, on this bed. I tug his hair so hard that I'm afraid I might rip it out, and I keep grinding my hips against him as the waves of what is surely the longest orgasm to ever exist keep pummeling me. My legs are shaking, and my torso is practically lifted straight off the bed. Ben stays with me the whole time, licking and sucking and fucking me with his fingers until finally my hands slide out of his hair and my body drops bonelessly to the comforter.

Ben pulls his fingers out of me and with his eyes on mine, brings them to his mouth and licks them clean. And even though I was sure I had just felt all the pleasure the world had to offer, heat sears straight through me. He looks like a debauched angel, his blue eyes dark and intense, his golden hair a mess from my hands gripping it, and the lower half of his face wet with my release. He stands and crawls over me onto the bed. Supporting his weight on his knees and elbows, he captures my mouth in a kiss that is all tongues and passion and intensity, and I taste myself on his lips. And then we break apart and lock eyes. He lifts a hand and pushes my hair off my forehead, running his hand down my cheek and swiping his thumb along my lower lip.

"Feeling you come on my tongue was the best fucking thing that has ever happened to me. You're mine, Hallie girl."

It shakes me a little how much I deeply, desperately, *want* to be his. I don't make decisions fast, and change makes me itchy, but not right now. Nothing has ever felt as right as Ben and me, together, like this. Something clicks into place inside of me. I am calm, settled, and practically aching with the need to show him how I feel. And then he leans down and kisses me again, watching me the whole time through hooded eyes hazy with lust. Even though two minutes ago his head was literally between my legs, this, right here, is the hottest moment of my life.

Chapter Twenty-Seven
Ben

I have a second of panic that maybe saying, "you're mine" to Hallie only half an hour after we kissed for the first time and two minutes after she came all over my face might freak her out. But I just had the single most transformative sexual experience of my life, and my mouth is moving faster than my brain can think. Hallie just gets a sly smile on her face.

"Yours, huh?'

Fuck it. Might as well just commit. "You know it, Hal. Mine. All fucking mine."

"Well, if I'm yours, that means you're mine, which means this..." She slides down and palms my rock-hard cock and I wheeze out a breath. "Is also mine." She sits up, pushing me back to my feet. Still sitting on the bed, she reaches for the waistband of my sweatpants. Before she can pull them down, I cover her hands with mine.

"Hal, you don't have to." I don't want her ever to think she has to do anything to make me happy. She is always trying so hard to please everyone. I want her to be real with me.

"Fucking duh, Benji. But I felt your cock against my leg

earlier when you kissed me and again just now, and if I don't get to see it soon, I'm going to throw a fit."

"Well then, by all means, have your way with me, Hallie girl, but first…" I lean down and kiss her again, hard and quick, then pull her shirt up over her head. Like I knew they would be, her tits are perfection, exactly a handful, with dusky nipples that are so tempting I can't help but lean down and swipe my tongue over one and then the other. I go to rub my thumbs over them, but she catches my hands and slides off the bed and onto her knees.

"You can play with those later. It's my turn now." In one move, she pulls down my sweatpants and boxer briefs, and I step out of them and kick them away. My cock springs up, long and hard, precum already beading at the tip because the memory of Hallie spread out for me, my tongue inside her, is burned into my brain. And now she's naked in front of me, and naked Hallie is my favorite Hallie.

"Fuck, you're big. Like, really, really big. I guess I shouldn't be surprised that the prettiest person I know has the prettiest cock on the planet."

"The prettiest person you know?"

"Don't act like you don't know what you look like. I've been in your house. You own mirrors."

I grin because playful Hallie is my favorite Hallie, too. I think, in this moment, she is more herself than she has ever been. It shouldn't surprise me that being with her like this is sexy and hot, but also fun and funny. This is the best thing that has ever happened to anyone, ever.

And then I stop grinning because Hallie leans down and swipes her tongue over the head of my cock. I suck in a breath, unprepared for the current that shoots through me. She licks a path along the underside before dipping her tongue in the sensitive spot right below the tip. I grasp the top of her head for balance, so I don't topple over from the sheer pleasure of her on her knees for me and her tongue on my cock. Then she looks up at me with a wicked grin and sucks me into her hot, wet mouth, and Fuck. Me.

I'm dying. This is how I go.

Because Hallie's mouth is on my cock, and nothing has ever felt this good.

Eyes on hers, I rasp, "Fuck, Hallie, you look so good on your knees for me, those pretty lips wrapped around my cock." She must like the praise because she moans and reaches between my legs with one hand and cups my balls, rolling them gently. Her fingers graze the spot just behind my sac as she takes me deeper into her mouth, gliding her tongue along the underside of my cock, and my vision blurs as my balls draw up tight. I would be a little more embarrassed about how fast this is going to be over, but then Hallie takes me so deep I bump the back of her throat. She swallows around me, and embarrassment flees the room as pleasure swamps me.

"Fuck, fuck, fuck," I grit out. I try and pull out, but she grabs my ass with both of her hands and pulls me deeper into her mouth. She slides her mouth up and sucks so hard it's just on the right side of painful.

And I'm gone. My mind blanks, and white-hot pleasure arrows though me as my release barrels up my spine and I explode.

Hallie sticks with me the whole time, swallowing everything I give her. When she has sucked me dry, I haul her up to me and kiss her, pushing my tongue into her mouth as she winds her arms around my neck and tangles her fingers in my hair. The taste of our combined releases has my cock twitching again as need rolls through me, and I wonder idly how soon we can do that again because holy shit.

We finally break apart, chests heaving, and collapse across

the bed, too drained to even move up to the pillows. I roll onto my side and snake my arm around Hallie's waist. I pull her closer to me, marveling at the fact that I can do that now. At least, I think I can. She rolls towards me, our faces inches apart. She reaches up and lays her hand on my cheek, her eyes searching mine. I have never wanted so badly to crawl inside someone's mind and read her thoughts.

"Are you...okay?" I ask. Excellent, Ben. Ask her the world's most generic question after a fucking life-altering experience.

"Are you serious? I'm better than okay. I'm just wondering whether we should, like, talk about it? I don't know. Is that stupid? It's probably stupid. I've never done anything like this before. I mean, I've done this before, obviously. Duh. But never with a friend. I mean, a best friend. Like you. Well, just you. I've never done this with you before. Fuck," she mutters under her breath.

I am so charmed by her uncharacteristic rambling that I haul her into me and squeeze her, raining kisses all over her face until she is giggling and squirming away from me.

"Yes, Hallie girl, we can talk about it." Nerves hit my stomach because I didn't plan for this to happen, and I have no idea what to say to her or how much to divulge.

"So, uh. That...happened," she says, and I see the same nerves I feel reflected in her eyes. For some reason, that makes me feel better. We're both flying without a net here.

"Do you...regret it?"

"God, no. Ben, that was amazing. Like, really amazing, best orgasm of my life. Like I said earlier, I guess I'm wondering, like, how long that's been inside of us. Because that was...wow. But more than just what we did. How it felt. I thought for a second that kissing my best friend would be weird, but it wasn't. It felt kind of...right. Or is it just me?"

"No, Hallie girl, I felt it too."

Hallie looks at me as she considers what I said. And then, "A long fucking time."

"Huh?" I ask, genuinely confused.

"Earlier, before, when you were, um, carrying me to bed, you said you had been waiting for this for a long fucking time. How long?"

Damn her good memory.

"Just...long."

She is quiet for a few seconds, her nose scrunching up as she thinks, then she sits straight up, pulling herself out of our blanket cocoon.

"Wait. You eye fucking me at the gala. The dance. Asking me for dressing room pictures. Jumping into the lake with me. The bonfire. All the other little things I'm probably forgetting right now. Was all of that, like, foreplay?"

I snort out a laugh. This girl. I want to cuddle her and also fuck her into the mattress and isn't that just a fascinating combination.

"Sure, Hal. I guess you could call it that."

"So, you've been thinking of me like...this"—she gestures to the two of us—"all summer?"

I consider what to say to that and decide to let it all out. We are laying here naked and tangled together. Everything that just happened felt so damn good, like all the scattered puzzle pieces of my life are finally fitting together and forming one single image.

"I've felt it for a long time—that you and I would be right together. Longer than the summer. Much longer."

Chapter Twenty-Eight
Hallie

onger than the summer. Much longer. My brain is spinning out a movie reel of all my moments with Ben over the last few years, and I am trying to put my finger on the moment things changed for him. But I honestly can't because until the last few weeks, I thought Ben and I were just...Ben and I. Best friends, family friends, people who care deeply about each other. We have always been close, and he just gets me.

I don't think I ever really considered there might be anything romantic between us. But then I get a flash of a memory. It was a few years ago right here at the lake. Ben brought Sarah, his girlfriend at the time. The second night we were here, I ended up on the deck at two in the morning when I couldn't sleep, and I spotted Ben and Sarah sitting by the lake. They were wrapped in each other, his hands holding her face, kissing like the world was ending. I remember feeling a hot rush of something that at the time I thought was anger at someone else—an outsider—invading our sacred lake vacation. But considering what just happened, I'm looking at that night in a whole new light, and what I felt now seems frighteningly close to...jealousy? And I think about being at the bar a couple weeks ago, and my reaction to seeing those women flirt with him. Holy shit. I was jealous of Sarah and those women and never even realized it.

I've wanted him all this time and I never even knew it.

I think about the looks he gave me during that trip. The glances he tossed my way that I wrote off as nothing. The ones he gave me when he was holding her hand or kissing her head or kissing her in...other ways. I brushed them off at the time, but now...there's no other way to see them. He was with her, but he was looking at me. And holy fucking shit. He really has wanted me all this time.

That's the only reasonable explanation because what just happened was life altering and we didn't even have actual sex. I hope we can fix that soon because bedroom Ben is sexy. Who knew he had such a dirty mouth and that this hot as all fuck in bed was buried inside my lovely, magically knows how I take my coffee, supports me like no one else, and gives me the safe place I've always needed Ben.

I flop down next to him, and he winds his arm around me, rolling me back on my side so we are face to face again.

"How much longer?" I ask. Because for some reason, in this moment, laying naked next to him, knowing how long Ben has been harboring feelings for me is the most important thing in the world.

A blush rises on his cheeks, and he looks away from me for a second before turning back and mumbling, "Since high school."

What the fuck?

"Did you just say since high school?"

Ben blows out a breath. "Yes."

"You've had feelings for me since high school?"

"Yes."

"So, like, more than a decade?"

"Yes," he says, looking away again, clearly embarrassed. Now it's his turn to sit up. He runs his hands through his hair and takes a deep breath.

"It was senior year, the night of Wes Calloway's graduation party. I was standing by my front door, irritated as shit because we were supposed to drive together, and you and Jules were taking forever to get ready. I was about to leave without you when you guys finally came down the stairs. You were wearing the tightest jeans I had ever seen and a black crop top. You curled your hair and did something with your eye makeup that was all dark and sparkly and hot as fuck, and suddenly, you weren't best friend Hallie. You were hot girl Hallie with a body I wanted to run my hands over and an ass I couldn't tear my eyes away from, who made my heart and my stomach feel all weird. We were only eighteen, and I didn't know shit. I thought maybe it would go away, but it never did. It just got stronger. I tried to hide it from you and everyone for all these years, but I couldn't do it anymore." He locks eyes with me. "I can't do it anymore."

I sit up and face him, more than a little stunned. "You remember what I was wearing?" It seems unimportant in the grand scheme of what Ben just revealed, but it's the only detail I can latch onto.

"A guy tends to remember the details about the first and only girl to ever knock him flat on his ass."

"Only girl? But you had other girlfriends. Or, girlfriend, I guess. What about Sarah?"

"What about her? I liked her, but she never knocked me flat on my ass. No one has since I saw you walking down those stairs eleven years ago. And she was the last girlfriend I had because even when I was with her, I could only see you."

"Why didn't you ever say anything?"

"Seriously, Hallie? We have been friends our entire lives. Our families are best friends. You and Jules are as close as sisters. I never wanted to risk messing with that when you had never shown an ounce of interest beyond friendship. But I am only so strong, and eleven years is my limit. I couldn't live anymore without telling you. I don't know what you are thinking about tonight and what just happened, but this isn't a one-time thing for me. You are not a one-time thing for me."

He lifts his hands up to cup both of my cheeks, his eyes dark and intense.

"Hallie girl, you are my best friend and the most important person in my life. And you are also so much more than that. I think *we* can be so much more than that. Maybe this is too much for right now when this is so new, but fuck it. We don't need to label it yet; we can just take it all one day at a time. But I hope you'll give me a chance to show you what I think we can be together. Because, Hallie, I think we can be everything."

I look at him for a few seconds, and it scares me how quickly my feelings shifted. How much I want this. How much I want *him*. For once, though, that trickle of fear pushes me closer instead of away. I lean forward to wrap my arms around his neck.

"I'd like you to show me," I whisper in his ear.

He lets out a little grunt of what sounds like relief and his arms go around my waist, holding tight for a minute before he pulls away and seals his mouth over mine. The kiss is sweet and sexy and a promise of everything that lays ahead of us. Neither of us makes a move to deepen the kiss, but electricity still rolls through me, and I marvel at the fact that this *more* has been inside of me all along, waiting.

We break apart, and Ben moves up towards the pillows, pulling me with him. We crawl under the blankets and lay facing each other again and I ask, "So, what are we going to tell everyone? Should we tell everyone?"

Ben considers this. "I don't really want to keep it a secret, but I also don't want to put any pressure on us before we figure this out."

"I don't want this to be a secret either. I have enough of those. I also don't think we need to make an announcement or anything. Let's just...be ourselves, whatever that means now. They'll figure it out when they figure it out. Hey, it might even be fun to watch everyone react. Except, before we do that, we need to tell Julie that we're more or...whatever we are."

Anxiety shoots through me at the thought of telling Julie and how she'll react. "Actually, I need to tell Julie. I think I should do it alone and first thing in the morning." The thought of a confrontation makes me vaguely nauseous, but the thought of keeping something else from her and letting her find out on her own that her best friend hooked up with her brother and might be *more* is worse.

Ben pushes a piece of hair behind my ear and cups my cheek. "Are you sure? You don't have to tell her alone. I know that's not always easy for you."

"I love that you know that, but I'll be okay. I think."

"You can tell me if you change your mind. I've told you before, Hallie girl. I see you. I'll always see you."

He leans over and kisses me softly, then turns me so that my back is against his front. He wraps an arm around me, and I snuggle back into him, trying to press even closer. Ben drapes a leg over both of mine, tangling us up even more, and tightens his arm around my waist, and I feel calm and safe and so unbelievably cared for.

If this is what it feels like to be *more* with Ben Parker, then sign me right the fuck up.

Chapter Twenty-Nine
Ben

I wake up slowly, stuck for an extra few minutes in that hazy window between asleep and awake. I am still wrapped around Hallie, her arms covering mine, our legs tangled together under the blankets.

Last night comes back to me in flashes. Kissing Hallie at her bedroom door. My head buried between her legs. Hallie on her knees. Laughing. Talking. Deciding to give us a try. Her looking at me the way I always hoped she would. Our talk by the bonfire. Hallie opening up to me in a way I know she doesn't open up to anyone else felt like the world's greatest gift, and I'll do anything to make sure it keeps on happening.

For a second, I'm afraid to move—afraid that the whole of last night might have been a dream. Then I breathe in the cherry vanilla scent that has meant Hallie to me for as long as I can remember, and I crack open my eyes to the morning light filtering through the blinds. She is still fast asleep, her golden-brown hair spread all over the pillow in a tangled mess, so beautiful it makes my chest ache. The fact that I am in her bed, with her in my arms, makes me feel like nothing else matters but this moment, right now. Outside of this room is a houseful of people who are going to have questions. There is my giant career decision and hers. There is wondering whether we can make a real go of this and whether her feelings will catch up to mine. But right now, it's just Hallie and me and this bed—for now, that's more than enough.

Hallie's arms tighten over mine, and she starts to stir. She stretches out her legs and then turns her head to kiss my cheek. "You're still here." She smiles and turns her head back around, tucking herself deeper into me.

"I couldn't miss seeing how you look first thing in the morning."

She reaches a hand up and tries to pat her wild hair into submission. "Going to sleep with mostly wet hair is never my best move."

I grab her hand and pull it down. "Leave it. I like knowing that part of the reason it's a mess is because of my hands in your hair while you were on your knees for me, taking my cock down your throat."

She makes a choking sound. "Jesus, Ben. Has your mouth always been so dirty?"

"Only for you, Hallie girl."

"Well in that case..." She trails off, pushing her hips back, her ass making contact with my already hard cock. I hiss out a breath and push forward, cock sliding between her ass cheeks. I drift my hands up her ribcage and palm her breasts, rubbing my thumbs over her nipples and then plucking at them until she is whimpering and moving her hips, looking for friction.

"Need something, Hal?" I whisper in her ear and then nip at her earlobe, making her suck in a breath.

"Ben," she gasps out. "Touch me, please."

"Touch you where?"

She puts her hand over one of mine on her breasts and slides it down until it's between her legs. "Touch me here."

"Anything for you, Hallie girl." I dip my fingers into her center, where she is already wet and dripping for me. I spread her wetness up and over her clit, drawing lazy circles over the tight bundle of nerves. She's breathing hard, already close. That I can turn her on this much, make her come so fast, has my aching cock hardening even more. I rock my hips against her ass, and she rocks hers back against me and then grinds down on my hand.

"That's it, Hallie girl. Fuck my hand until you come all over it." I thumb her clit and slide two fingers in, curling them up to hit that spot deep inside her that has her moaning so loudly I hope it's too early for everyone on this side of the house to be awake.

"Yes, god, that feels so good," she gasps out, as I press my fingers deeper inside her. "I'm so close." She pushes her hips forward, and I tap her g-spot over and over and press down harder on her clit, strumming it with my thumb faster and faster until she comes, covering my hand in her release and turning her head so her cry is muffled into the pillow.

I stick with her through her orgasm, slowing down the rhythm of my thumb on her clit until her entire body relaxes into the bed. I slide my fingers out of her and roll her onto her back, covering her body with mine, my eyes locking with hers.

She gives me a wicked grin. "I want my hands on you." She slides a hand between our bodies and has barely grazed my cock when there's a knock at the door, Molly's voice then coming through it loud and clear.

"Hallie, why aren't you already at breakfast? Answer the door or I'm coming in."

Hallie drops her head back onto the pillow with a quiet groan.

"She's never going to go away. I think alone time is over, Benji."

I glance over at the clock and see that it's already after nine. "I'm shocked they lasted this long. You're usually in the kitchen with my mom way before now. I guess we're about to go public?" I phrase it like a question, knowing if Hallie changes her mind and wants to hide this, I'll go along with it.

"No time like the present," Hallie sings. "But, tonight? We're doing all of that again, so don't make plans." She grins at me and jumps out of bed, grabbing the clothes scattered all over the floor.

I grin back, already making plans for the next time I have her alone, which fucking better be tonight. I drag myself out of bed and to the bathroom, gathering my own scattered clothes along the way.

Chapter Thirty
Hallie

Waking up in Ben's arms and having an orgasm before breakfast is the best. The second-best is opening the door and finding not just Molly, but also Julie and Emma outside my door and watching their expressions as they take in my appearance. I haven't looked in a mirror yet, but I'm sure that I look exactly like I was doing all the things I was definitely doing last night.

And again this morning.

I plaster a nonchalant expression on my face and play it cool. I wanted to talk to Julie alone, but I guess that's not happening. The new and improved, hooked up with her best friend last night and can't wait to do it again Hallie decides to roll with it.

"What's with the wake-up call?"

"Where have you been?" asks Julie. "We literally never beat you to breakfast."

"And what the fuck happened to your hair?" Molly is nothing if not predictable.

"We just wanted to make sure you were okay," Emma says,

looking at me with concern. "You look okay."

"I am okay. Better than okay, I think."

The bathroom door opens at that moment and Ben walks out looking delightfully disheveled with his hair everywhere and his clothes rumpled from a night in a pile on the floor. And I'm confused now about how I ever saw him as just a friend, because the way he looks right now is doing crazy things to my insides. And other parts of me. He doesn't hesitate. He just crosses the room and comes up behind me, wrapping his arms around my waist and pulling me back into him.

"You think? If you just think you're better than okay and don't know it for sure, I better try harder next time." Then he drops a kiss on my cheek, presses two mini-Reese's cups into my hand—and where the hell did he get those?—and saunters out the door, calling, "See you at breakfast, Hallie girl. I'll have your coffee waiting."

"I want..."

"Iced coffee with milk and one Splenda," he tosses over his shoulder, never even looking back.

Fuck me, he's right again. "How do you know that?" I call at his back.

He finally turns back around. "I've told you a million times, Hallie girl. I see you." Then he throws me a wink and heads toward the kitchen.

I turn back to my friends and snicker, wishing I had a camera. I want to remember their shocked, slack-jawed expressions for the rest of my life. They are all quiet for a second before Molly breaks the silence.

"What. The. Actual. Fuck. You have some explaining to do, Hallie."

"Give her a break, Mol," says Emma. Then she mumbles, "I knew I wasn't imagining things yesterday."

Julie hears exactly what Emma said. "What happened

yesterday?"

"Ben was acting weird, and Hallie was acting all blushy. I don't know if that's a word, but if it's not, it should be, because that's how she was acting."

"Wait. You and Ben were the last to leave the bonfire last night. When Emma came up, I asked her where you were, and she said you were still outside with Ben."

"Wow, nothing gets by you, Mol."

She points a finger at me. "Don't Mol me, Hallie Kate Evans. Benjamin Parker—*our Benjamin Parker*—just walked out of your room in clothes that looked like they spent the night on the floor and you look freshly fucked, girl. Now spill."

Julie has barely said a word yet, and I look at her, a little shimmer of fear slicing through me at her mostly blank expression. I reach over and grab her hand, squeezing it.

"Maybe we should all sit." They come all the way into the room and pile on my bed. I pull Julie down next to me and gather my courage, directing all my attention at her.

"I'm sorry you had to find out like this. I wanted to tell you today before everyone found out, but I didn't expect you all to show up at my door. I understand if you're upset, but I swear I wasn't keeping anything from you. It all just kind of happened after the bonfire last night." I look down at my hands, unsure of what else to say, worried that Julie still hasn't said anything at all.

"Hallie, I'm not upset."

I look up. "You're not?"

"Of course I'm not. I mean, I was pretty fucking surprised to find the two of you all loved up in here first thing in the morning. But it's clear that whatever went on last night made you happy. You are happy, right?"

"Yeah, Jules, I'm really happy," I say, surprised at her reaction.

"That's all that matters to me. So how did this happen? When did this happen?"

"I'm not sure how to answer that question. There's been a weird vibe between us for a few days. Ben has been acting kind of...different, I guess? Like, more than just friendly. I was all confused about it. When we came up from the bonfire last night, we had a moment in the kitchen when I thought he might kiss me, but he didn't. Then he showed up here an hour later and definitely did kiss me. And...other things."

"Yeah, we're going to need details about those other things." Molly flops forward so she is laying on her stomach, her chin in her hands like a kindergartener ready for story time.

"I wish I could disagree with them, but it's been way too long since I've had sex, so if you're having sex, I'm going to need to live vicariously through you for a while," says Emma.

"Guys. No. Just, no. It's too weird." I never have any trouble talking about sex. We talk about sex all the time. But this is Ben, and his twin sister is literally sitting next to me. There is no manual for how to talk about this kind of sex. Julie must sense what my hesitation is all about because she takes my hand.

"It's not weird, Hallie. I mean, don't get me wrong. I don't relish the thought of hearing what my brother gets up to in bed, because, ick. But I love you, and I love Ben. If it's you he's in bed with, it feels different. We talk about this stuff, Hallie. We always have. That shouldn't change now. I don't want it to. And think about it. If you guys get married, then we'll get to be actual sisters." She leans over and bumps her shoulder with mine, and I feel a rush of gratitude for her easy acceptance of what she stumbled in on.

I lean over and hug her. "Thanks, Jules, but no one is getting married. It was just one night."

"But you want it to happen again?"

"I do. I don't know what it is, exactly, but it all felt so...right, I guess? Like, I thought it would be weird because—friend Ben. And shouldn't it feel weird when a guy you've been friends with your whole life kisses the shit out of you? But it didn't feel weird at all. It felt like the easiest thing that has ever happened to me."

"Aww," says Molly. "You are literally blushing. I didn't know you did that. But enough of the sweet stuff. I want to hear the other stuff. Like, is Ben a dirty talker? I bet he is. It's always the sweet ones."

I pause for a second and then decide, what the hell? Last night changed something in me. Being with Ben changed something in me. And it might be a little weird with Julie sitting right here, but these women are *my* women. "His mouth could win an award. For dirty talking and for...other things."

"Fuck. Yes." says Molly. "I don't know why, but I find that so satisfying."

Julie shoves her back into the pillows. "You are so weird, Mol."

"Your brother is hot, Jules, deal with it. And now we know the mouth matches the man. There is nothing better than a man who knows what to do with his mouth. This morning is all kinds of surprising."

I just smile at them all, and as we keep talking, I feel lighter than I have in days. I have my favorite women piled around me. I had the most amazing night with a man who I am starting to suspect I have feelings for that go miles beyond the friendship we have always shared. And it is all happening at my favorite place on earth.

I have big career decisions ahead of me, and everything between Ben and me could implode and take our families down with it, but I'm not thinking of any of that now. Because in this moment, everything feels pretty close to perfect.

Chapter Thirty-One
Hallie

Eventually, we get hungry and wander down in search of breakfast. When I walk into the kitchen, Ben is standing at the island with a frying pan in one hand and a carton of eggs in the other. He tosses me a look so full of heat that I stop short, and my core turns molten.

"Holy god, even I want to jump him after that look," mumbles Molly from behind me.

I snort out a laugh, and Julie elbows her in the ribs.

"Gross, Mol, that's still my brother."

"You were okay when Hallie was talking about him like that!"

"That's different."

"It so isn't."

They keep fighting under their breaths as I make my way around the island to Ben. He hands me the iced coffee he has waiting on the counter and leans down to kiss my cheek, lingering for a second longer than necessary. Butterflies swarm my stomach, and I marvel at my reaction to him. At how much has changed in less than twelve hours.

"How was Jules?" he says in a low voice.

"Surprisingly amazing. I'll tell you later."

"Good. Go sit. I'm making breakfast today."

"Seriously? You never make breakfast when we're here. You usually sleep through it."

"Well, I'm up now." He slides an arm around my waist and pulls me into his side. "It's a really good morning, Hal. I'm making you breakfast." Then he kisses the top of my head and guides me to the table and into a seat right across from Hannah and Jo who are both giving me appraising looks.

"We're going to talk about whatever that was, right?" asks Hannah.

I decide to play dumb. If there's one thing I don't want right now, it's to have this conversation with my sisters at the breakfast table.

"Whatever what was?"

"Um, Ben with his hands all over you and kissing the top of your head. And I've been here for an hour already, and I definitely saw him come into the kitchen earlier from the direction of not his bedroom."

"He what?" screeches Jo.

"Shut. Up." I hiss under my breath. "Can we please talk about this later?"

Jo fixes me with a glare. "We will absolutely talk about this later."

Talking about this with my sisters feels so much more daunting than talking about this with my friends. But it's inevitable, so I better buckle up. My friends all gather around the table, various kinds of coffee in front of them. I let the noise and the chatter and clatter of utensils on dishes settle around me. I try to sneak a look at Ben, but he is already looking at me from his place in front of the stove. I can feel my face flush, and

Because Of You

he grins, then flips off the burner and starts adding food to the plates he laid out on the counter.

He walks over and puts one of those plates in front of me and kisses my head again before taking the chair next to mine. I look down and find the same mushroom and cheese omelet he made for me the morning of Maya's adoption hearing. It was the day I woke up at his house and cried all over him because he took control of the logistics of my day. Thinking back on that morning after last night makes me see it all so differently.

Ben seems to know exactly what I'm thinking about because he slides his hand over my bare thigh and leans in to whisper in my ear.

"I wished that morning I could touch you like this and kiss you after making breakfast. Last night meant a lot to me, Hallie."

"Me too," I whisper, feeling my entire body just beam from the inside out.

He squeezes my leg and then lets go. I go to pick up my fork and see Rachel standing in the doorway of the kitchen, looking at Ben and me with a knowing smile on her face. She catches my eye and gives me a wink, making her way over to the coffee pot. Add Rachel to the list of conversations I'm sure I'll be having today.

The rest of breakfast is uneventful, and we're on lake time, so no one is in a hurry to go anywhere or do anything. I lounge around the table with Ben, my sisters, and the girls for a while, drinking coffee and talking.

We are in the middle of a conversation about whether we want to lounge by the pool or take the boat out later this afternoon when Ben hooks his foot around the bottom of my chair and slides it closer to his. Then he slings his arm around me and tucks me into his side, leaning over and whispering, "You were too far away," into my ear. When he pulls me closer to him and kisses my temple, goosebumps cascade down my arms. He dances his hand along my shoulder and even though it's mid-summer, I give a full body shiver. I can't decide if it's just been so long since someone has touched me like this, or if what happened last night means that I am destined to respond to any part of Ben touching any part of me like this forever. He gives me a sly look that tells me he knows exactly how this is affecting me. And it is in that second that I realize the kitchen has gone deadly silent.

I look up to see the five pairs of eyes around the table focused directly on us and that at some point during our little interlude Jeremy, Jordan, and Allie appeared in the kitchen to join in the staring.

It's Allie who breaks the silence. "Fucking finally." All eyes turn to her.

"What do you mean, finally?" asks Jo.

"It looks like our Ben has finally made his move. He did make his move, right?"

Jordan slides an arm around Allie's waist. "I would tell my blunt and wildly gorgeous fiancée that it's not polite to put people on the spot like that, but I'm nosy, and well, just not that evolved."

Jeremy plops down into the empty chair beside Emma, who promptly scoots her chair a little closer to Molly on her other side.

"Not only is Ben in the kitchen when the clock reads 'before eleven,' but you two are looking awfully cozy at our breakfast table this morning."

Hannah grins at me. "Hallie, I think later is now."

"Definitely now. I love a sexy breakfast story," Jo adds.

"Oh, it's sexy," says Molly.

My buoyant mood from earlier this morning starts to melt away. Telling the girls in my room this morning was one thing—

that was fun—but having everyone's eyes on me like this is making my skin crawl. Like always, Ben seems to know exactly what is going on in my head. He stands suddenly, tugging me with him.

"None of your business, assholes." He directs this to everyone sitting around the table but says it with a smirk. "Now if you don't mind, my girl and I are going to sit by the pool."

Everyone seems stunned silent by the "my girl," so Ben takes the opportunity to grab my hand and pull me out the sliding glass door to the deck.

When we get outside, Ben leads me off the deck and around the corner of the house where we can stand in relative privacy. He leans against the side of the house and pulls me into his arms. My heartbeat immediately slows.

"You okay, Hallie girl?"

"I'm fine." And it turns out that it's actually true. Standing here with Ben like this, I really am fine. Even after that little inquisition.

"You sure?"

"I'm really sure." I lean my head on his chest and the rhythm of his heartbeat soothes every inch of me. It occurs to me that I am never as calm around others as I am around him and that it's been that way my entire life. It feels like the roots for whatever is happening between us now were dug into me the same way they were into him, and I just never noticed. I find I like that thought. That maybe whatever this is has been inside me just as long. It explains why the rapid rearranging of our lifelong friendship feels so right, even among a kitchen full of nosy friends.

"You don't...regret it? Last night? That was a lot back in the kitchen."

Surprised, I pull back so I can look at him. The insecurity I see on his face is so uncharacteristic of Ben that I suddenly want badly to reassure him. I grab both of his hands.

"Last night was amazing, Ben. I don't regret any part of it. I didn't love being the center of attention, but that doesn't have anything to do with last night. I really liked last night. All of it."

"And you're sure you're okay with everyone knowing? I guess it's too late if you're not, but if you're uncomfortable, I want you to tell me. I want you to tell me everything. I know sharing your feelings isn't really your thing, but I hope you'll try with me. You're safe with me, Hal."

God, this man. I have never felt safe enough to tell anyone everything in my entire life, and somehow, he just knows. In this moment, I would walk through fire for him.

"Yeah, Benji, I'm definitely okay with everyone knowing." Reaching up, I circle my arms around his neck, stand on my tiptoes, and lay my lips on his. He reacts instantly, reversing our positions so that my back is pressed against the side of the house. He pulls back for a second, his gaze full of heat and arousal. Then he brings one hand up and tucks my hair behind my ear, trailing his finger down along my jaw.

"There she is," he whispers, before sealing his mouth over mine. His tongue glides over my lower lip, and I open for him, tangling our tongues together. Ben moves one hand to my waist and wraps the other hand around my neck in a gesture of possession that shoots a bolt of need straight through me. This kiss is different from the ones we shared last night. Those were full of shock and heat and frenzy. This kiss is slow and needy and feels like worship. It shakes me to my core and makes me ache with the rightness of it all. As Ben's mouth moves over mine, I have the wild thought that I never want to kiss anyone else, ever again, for as long as I live.

"Well, now what do we have here?"

At the sound of Rachel's voice, Ben and I break apart, startled. I quickly push myself off the house, my first instinct to move my body as far away from Ben's as possible. So extremely cool, Hallie. Very "teenage girl caught kissing a boy" energy.

But Ben doesn't let me go anywhere. He wraps an arm around my waist and pulls me into his side, turning us both to face his mom. Fabulous. Nothing to see here, Rachel. Just me, still in my pajamas, fresh off sharing a soul-shaking kiss with your son while leaning against the side of your house.

"Just a little kissing between friends, Ma. No big deal."

She studies both of us, and I consider for a second what we must look like. Then I immediately stop considering it because I'm sure the answer is...like we were doing exactly what we were just doing. A wide smile breaks out over her face.

"No big deal my ass. Carry on." She turns to walk back to the pool, calling over her shoulder, "Oh and Hallie, come talk to me when you're done doing...whatever it is that you're doing back there."

When Rachel is gone, Ben and I are both quiet for a beat before we burst out laughing. We lean into each other and laugh until there are tears streaming down our faces. Then Ben grabs my face in both of his hands and kisses me hard, and I think maybe this is the best morning of my entire life.

Chapter Thirty-Two
Hallie

After our laughing fit, Ben and I decide that we have given our families and friends enough gossip for the morning. After one last searing kiss and a whispered promise of more later, Ben goes in search of the guys for a morning run, and I go to find Rachel. She is exactly where I assumed she would be—weeding the flower beds in the yard by the pool. I force my feet to move and give myself a little pep talk.

Nothing to be worried about, Hallie. This is Rachel. You love Rachel. She helped raise you. She taught you how to use a tampon when you got your period for the first time and your mom was out of town. You can talk to her about anything. No worries that she caught you practically dry humping her son against the side of her house just now. No worries at all.

Rachel looks up as I approach and kneel down beside her. I have a flash of nostalgia from all the times Rachel and I have talked while pulling weeds in her flower beds after Jules and I fought over some stupid thing as kids, when I came to the lake after my first boyfriend broke my heart when I was sixteen, when my sisters got on my nerves, or when I was frustrated because it felt like no one in my actual family understood me. Just like Ben, Rachel has always understood me. They may be the only two people who do.

"So, having a good morning?" she starts, with a smirk in my direction.

"I'm sorry you caught us like that."

"Oh honey, I'm not. It's well past time you and Ben found your way to each other."

"You knew? How Ben felt about me, I mean."

Rachel pauses for a second. She seems to be choosing her words carefully.

"I'm a mom, honey. I know all there is to know about my children. And that includes you. You have always been as much mine as Julie and Ben. I love you like you're my own blood. The question is, do you know how Ben feels about you?"

I hesitate, but this is Rachel, and we're kneeling in the flower beds in the place where we capital T Talk. Also, if I don't talk to someone, I might explode.

"He told me last night that he's had feelings for me since we were eighteen. That he wants to give being together a try."

"And what do you want?"

I blow out a breath. "I think... I think I want that, too. I'm going to pretend you're not Ben's mom for a second and tell you that he showed up at my door last night after the bonfire and kissed me. Ugh, is it weird to tell you that? It's weird, right?"

"Hallie, I saw what you both were getting up to on the side of the house just now. If you think I don't know that my adult son sometimes kisses girls in bedrooms and other places, you are sorely mistaken. And I know he has wanted to kiss you for a very long time." She stops weeding and sits cross-legged on the ground, motioning for me to do the same. "Did it surprise you?"

"It caught me off guard, I guess, but also, it kind of didn't? It felt like something shifted at the gala. There's been this weird energy between us since then. But then he kissed me, and it just felt...right. I have read one million romance novels, and when the best friends kiss, someone usually panics, but I didn't. I felt everything, but in the good way. It was new and different, but it felt like what we were supposed to be doing. Like maybe I've had feelings for him too but just never recognized it. Kissing him made me happy, Rachel, and I haven't been the happiest version of myself lately." I mentally slap myself for letting that little nugget loose and, obviously, Rachel misses nothing.

"We'll get back to you and the less than happy version of yourself in a minute. For now, I'll say this. When something like this makes you happy, you grab on to it and don't question it too much. If last night made you want to give you and Ben, the romantic version, a try, then you should."

"You don't think it's too fast?"

"I don't. I don't think that your feelings are all that new either. I think maybe you have had the same kinds of feelings for Ben that he has had for you. You just never gave yourself the time and space to consider them."

I think about this, remembering again how I reacted years ago when I saw Ben kissing Sarah. To all the times that Ben was there for me when it felt like no one else was. How I open up to him in ways I don't to almost anyone else. How he feels safe to me, like I can be myself around him. And I think about last night. How being with him like that felt like a missing piece of me clicked right into place. How it didn't feel like a first time at all.

"I think you might be right."

"Honey, I'm always right. I know you don't always trust yourself to feel your feelings and let them out, but I don't mind saying I raised a very good man. You can trust him. He'll be gentle with your feelings just like I know you'll be gentle with his. He will give you the time and care you need to figure this out."

"I know he will." And I do. Ben always makes sure I have exactly what I need.

"Now, what is this about you not being happy?"

For a split second, I consider telling her the way I told Ben last night at the bonfire. Telling her how I want to change my practice entirely, but don't know how to do that without fucking up everything that my friends and I have worked for the past six years and potentially losing them in the process. I love Rachel, but she's also Julie's mom, and I don't feel right opening up to her and asking her to keep it a secret.

"It's nothing, really. Just a big adjustment to leave my job and get the firm ready to open in January."

She eyes me skeptically. She knows I'm not telling her the whole truth, but luckily, she lets it go.

"Okay, but you know that you can talk to me anytime, about anything."

"I do know that."

"Good. Don't ever forget it. Now, these beds won't weed themselves, so get to it, girl."

The last thing I want to do is weed flower beds now that our little heart-to-heart is over, but when Rachel tells you to do something, she doesn't take no for an answer. So, I crouch beside her and start pulling weeds. Lost in the familiar motion of it, I start plotting how to get Ben alone later for a repeat of last night and, hopefully, more.

Chapter Thirty-Three
Ben

"Come on, Jer, move your ass."

"Yeah, man, why so slow? It's almost like you're old or something," Jordan says as he jogs alongside me.

The three of us are out for a run along the lake. This has been an excellent morning, so I have energy to burn, and Jordan can run for hours barely breaking a sweat, but Jeremy is dragging ass today.

"Fuck you both. It's fucking hot."

I poke him in the ribs. "Weren't you, like, a professional athlete or something once upon a time?"

"Yeah, on ice. Where it's cold. And I'm not a professional athlete anymore," he grumbles darkly. It's a rare display of irritation for my normally upbeat best friend, so I am immediately on guard.

"You okay, man?"

"Fine. I just didn't get much sleep last night."

"You want to talk about it?"

"I absolutely do not. Anyway, I think we have more important things to talk about."

"Fucking right, we do," says Jordan, aiming a wide grin right at me. "You and Hallie. Spill it, Benj."

"Yeah, Benj. Spill," Jeremy mocks.

"You guys are worse than old ladies in a hair salon."

"Yeah, but we're your old ladies, so give us the goods, dude."

I know they'll never let up, so I just go with, "I told her."

"You told her what?" asks Jeremy.

"Everything."

They both stop running and turn to me.

"Like, everything, everything?" Jeremy stands with his hands on his knees, trying to catch his breath.

"Everything, everything. I told her I've had feelings for her since we were eighteen. I told her I want to give us a try and see what happens."

Jordan lets out a low whistle. "Jesus, when you go big, you really go big. And what did she say?"

"She said she wants to try."

"Fuck yes she did." Jeremy stands up and swings an arm around my shoulders. "How do you feel?"

"Happy. A bit of disbelief. Scared shitless she'll change her mind, or I'll do something to screw it up. I don't know. How the fuck are you supposed to feel when you kiss the girl of your dreams for the first time?"

"The first time I kissed Allie, I felt like I was about to either pass out or come in my pants like a teenager. So...maybe kind of like that?"

"Yeah, that's about right. I don't know. I kissed her, and it was like realizing a piece of me has been missing all this time, and I didn't even know. I found it last night. Now that I know what we can be like together, I don't think I'll ever be right again without her. But that's way too much fucking pressure to put on us when we've barely started."

Jordan just shrugs. "So don't put that pressure on it. I've known Hallie as long as I've known you, and I've never seen her smile the way she did this morning. So obviously, it felt right to her, too. Just go with it. See what happens. You've been waiting eleven years, and you've finally got your girl. Just enjoy it. Take it one day at a time."

He's right. I know he's right. I have to smother my instinct to go from zero to sixty and dump my feelings all over Hallie before she's ready for them. She needs time to catch up. But now that the lid I've kept on those feelings for all these years has been loosened, it wants to blow all the way off.

I scrub my hands over my sweaty face. "Fuck. Yeah, you're right. One day at a time."

"From the look on Hallie's face this morning, I think you did more than just kiss her. Don't think we're going to let that pitch sail by." Jordan might be the champion shit-stirrer of the group, but when Jeremy is in the right mood, he gives Jordan a run for his money.

"Oh yeah, looked like you brought your A-game straight to Hallie's room last night."

"Do we need to make a stop in town for condoms? I know it's been forever since you got any. Yours are probably all expired."

"I would say you could borrow some of mine, but I fuck my girl bare. We're all committed and shit."

I slap Jordan across the back of his head. "If Allie knew you were talking about her like that, she would string you up by your balls." I'm mostly joking, and I know he is too. I have never seen a guy who loves his girl as much as Jordan loves Allie. He worships every inch of her and the ground she walks on.

"Probably, but it turns me on when she gets angry. Sometimes I make her mad on purpose just to see it."

"You and Allie are so fucking weird. Come on, let's keep

going, or my knee is going to lock up." Jeremy starts walking, and Jordan and I both follow. "And Ben can tell us more about last night."

"It is definitely story time."

"Worse than the old ladies for sure," I mumble under my breath.

There's a knock on my door just as I'm pulling on clothes after my shower. I open it, and Julie is standing there with her "we need to talk" face on. I sigh. Just when I thought maybe I was done with deep conversations for the day.

"Mom said you were up here getting changed. I thought maybe we could talk." Nailed it. We may not have the twin telepathy thing, but I know her faces.

"Yeah, Jules, we should talk." I step back and let her in, closing the door behind her. She sits cross-legged on my bed. I take a seat across from her, our knees touching, just like we used to do when we were kids. We just look at each other for a second, and I'm not sure where to start.

I take a deep breath and start to talk at the exact same time she does.

"Jules, I..."

"Hallie told us..."

We both laugh, and that breaks the tension.

"Let me go first, Jules, okay?"

She nods.

"I wanted to tell you with Hallie this morning, but she wanted to tell you herself. We weren't keeping anything from you, I swear. Last night was the first time anything happened."

"Hallie may not have been keeping anything from me, but you were, weren't you?"

"What do you mean?" I know exactly what she means, but I want to hear it from her. I also haven't gotten all the details from Hallie about their conversation, so I don't know how much Julie knows.

"It may have started for her last night, but I think it started a long time ago for you."

"She told you?"

"She didn't have to. I know you, Benj. From the look of the two of you this morning and from what Hallie told me, last night was more than just a little kissing between friends. And you wouldn't make that kind of move on a whim. You're more careful than that. For last night to have happened the way Hallie told me it did, you have to have been thinking about it for a long, long time."

Why do sisters have to be so damn smart and perceptive?

"I have been."

"How long?"

I know I'm not getting out of here without telling her everything, so I just mumble, "Eleven years."

Julie looks at me, slack jawed. "I'm sorry, did you say eleven years?"

"Yes."

"Jesus fuck, Ben. Hallie left out some key details during morning story time."

"Well, what did she tell you?" Now I'm extra curious, because if she didn't tell them that, then she must have told them about...

"She told us you know exactly what to do with your mouth, which is information I did not need to know about my brother."

The caveman part of my brain lights up at this information,

and I start thinking about what I can do with my mouth again at the earliest opportunity.

Julie slaps my shoulder. "I see where your mind just went, and fucking gross, Ben. Think dirty thoughts about Hallie on your own time. This is my time."

I clear my throat and try to shake out the images flooding my brain—images I have no business having in my head while I'm talking to my sister. Also known as Hallie's other best friend.

"Sorry, Jules. That was weird. This whole thing is a little weird. I'm sorry I didn't tell you. Are you mad?"

"I'm not mad. I'm trying hard not to be offended that you and Hallie both thought I wouldn't be happy for you. I'll tell you what I told her. I love you both so much, and I want you to be happy. If being together like this and exploring whatever this is between you makes you happy, that's good enough for me. I guess I'm just wondering how it's possible that all of this has been inside you this whole time, and I never saw it. And maybe I'm a little sad you didn't feel like you could share it with me. I get it, but still. We tell each other everything."

"I know we do, but this felt like a secret I had to keep. I couldn't let it out because I was afraid it could mess things up for everyone if I did. And Jules, you didn't see it because I didn't want you to. I didn't want anyone to. Even you, and especially Hallie. I never told Jeremy or Jordan either. But the last couple of weeks..." I trail off, wondering what even to say next. One look at Julie's sad face, and I know I owe it to her to give her everything. "My feelings got too big, and they took on a life of their own. I couldn't hold it in anymore. Like I told Hallie, I think eleven years was my limit."

"I understand, Ben. I really do. So, what happens now?"

"Now, we're going to give it a shot—being together, I mean —figuring out what all this means and what it looks like."

Julie studies me. "But you've already figured it out. Haven't you?"

"You're too fucking smart for your own good, Jules. Yeah, I've figured it out. I know what we could be, but I've had more than a decade to work it all through. Hallie has had less than a day, and she deserves the time to work it out on her own, too. I don't want to dump all my feelings on her before she's had time to get her footing."

Julie's eyes gloss over. It's so unusual for her that I reach out and pull her into me. She buries her head in my shoulder, and I hear her sniffle. After a couple of seconds, she pulls away.

"I'm sorry, ignore me."

"What is it, Jules?"

She swipes her fingers under her eyes. "I'm fine. I swear. You are just such a good person, Ben. My favorite person. And Hallie is my best friend. My second favorite person. You are lucky to have each other, whatever this turns out to be."

Jules abhors showing any kind of vulnerability and would rather die than tell me what she's worried about. But I hear what she's saying without her having to say it. I pull her back into me for another hug.

"No matter what happens, you always have me. And Hallie too. You'll never be left behind."

She takes a deep breath and pulls away again.

"Thanks, Benj," she whispers. "I needed to hear that."

"Maybe we do have a little of that twin telepathy after all."

She looks like herself again as she grabs my hand and pulls me up from the bed.

"Come on. Let's go downstairs and make Jeremy bartend an early happy hour. I think we all could use a drink, and he mixes better than you do."

She tosses me a wicked grin, then flies out of the room,

yelling for Jeremy on the way down. I follow behind her, thinking that a drink I don't have to make myself sounds great and plotting a way to get Hallie alone later so that we can pick up right where we left off last night.

Chapter Thirty-Four
Ben

Later that night, after dinner, I slip out of the kitchen and onto the deck. All the parents went to town to meet some other friends from home who are also up at the lake, and everyone else is otherwise occupied. Hallie stands alone by the deck railing, staring out at the sun setting over the lake. She's wearing cutoff shorts, a hoodie, and flip-flops, her golden-brown hair loose around her shoulders. An August night personified. I come up behind her and press up against her back. Resting my hands on the railing on either side of her, I cage her in. She melts back into me and leans her head against my shoulder. We stand there like that for a few minutes in silence. She watches the sun slip lower, and I watch her.

Even in the dimming twilight, her green eyes sparkle at what I know is her favorite view. Her face looks calm and happy. I wrap both my arms around her, and she settles back even deeper against my chest. She fits perfectly against me. Her body curves like we're meant to stand together exactly like this. I lean down and kiss her where her neck meets her shoulder, breathing in her cherry vanilla scent. And I wish, just for a second, that I could stop time and stand here like this forever. The fireflies flash, and the crickets sing, and the lake laps against the shore, and my favorite girl is wrapped in my arms. There has never been a more perfect moment.

The sun drops below the horizon, leaving behind a sky full of brilliant slashes of color. The sunset in this part of Western Maryland never disappoints, and this one is extra brilliant. Like it was sent here just for us, to bless whatever this is that is growing between us. To add a little strength to the still-fragile ties holding it together. Hallie is still staring out at the lake, smiling softly. Her face glows under the painted sky.

"Have you ever seen anything so beautiful?" she breathes.

"I have," I say, my eyes still locked on her. There must be something in my voice because she turns her head to look at me. Our eyes meet, and her breath catches at whatever she sees on my face.

"Ben," she whispers.

I don't know who moves first, but in a heartbeat, our mouths meet. I spin her around and press her back into the deck rail, and she winds her arms around my neck, moaning into me as I take the kiss deeper, sliding my tongue into her mouth. At her taste, need and desire pummel me like a wave crashing onto shore. There is no way she can't tell what this kiss is doing to me, how badly I want her, but neither of us makes any move to leave the deck. Instead, we stand there, bodies locked together, kissing each other senseless under a darkening sky, with the sounds of night all around us. And in this moment, I know that I am going to love Hallie Evans until the day I die.

We stumble into my room, and I kick the door closed before pushing Hallie back against it and sealing my mouth over hers. Once it got too dark to see on the deck, we came inside, skirting past all our friends hanging out in the great room and making a beeline for my room before anyone else noticed. I heard them all talking about going to town to get ice cream, and I hope they do that as soon as possible and leave us the fuck alone. Thinking ahead to our friends' dubious respect for boundaries, I tear my mouth from Hallie's and reach behind her to flip the lock on the door.

"Good thinking," she says, breathlessly before pulling my lips back to hers. I push her back against the door as our mouths move together. Then I drop my hands to her waist, dipping under the hem of her hoodie and skimming my fingers up her ribs to stroke along the sides of her breasts.

Her whole body shivers, and she lets out a sexy little moan I will no doubt be hearing in my dreams. Pulling the cups of her bra down, I rub my thumbs over her peaked nipples, then roll them between my thumb and forefinger. Hallie pulls her mouth from mine, sucking in a sharp breath and arching her back away from the door, pushing herself harder into my hands.

"God, Ben. More. Please."

Her voice sounds breathless and just a little wild. And if she gets that way just from my hands on her nipples, I can't wait to see what she looks and sounds like when I finally get inside her. That thought alone has me hard as steel. I crush my mouth back to hers then grip the hem of her hoodie and pull it over her head. I toss it onto the floor at our feet and reach behind me to pull my own shirt off. Hallie throws her unhooked bra down with it, and then our mouths crash back together. I wrap my hands around her waist and pull her body flush with mine, my hard cock pressing against her stomach. Hallie reaches up and tangles her hands in my hair, and I deepen our kiss, stroking my tongue inside her mouth to taste her. She tastes like summer and the margaritas we drank at dinner and like she is so completely mine.

I kiss and lick down her jaw and skim my lips down her throat and across her collarbone. Then I close my lips around her nipple, sucking it hard while I roll the other one between my fingers. She lets out a throaty moan, and I switch sides, taking the other nipple in my mouth while her hands tug at my hair.

Pushing her back against the door, I move lower, dropping to my knees in front of her. I pop the button on her cutoffs and push them down her legs, taking her underwear with them, before skimming my hands down her legs and lifting one foot, and then the other, freeing them from her shorts. Hallie standing above me completely naked, chest heaving and pulse fluttering rapidly in her throat, has my own heart pounding. I can't wait to get my mouth on her.

My eyes meet hers and she smirks at me. "You look good down there."

"I will get on my knees for you anytime you want me to, Hallie girl. It's my fucking pleasure. Now, I am going to lick you and suck you until you come on my tongue. Then I am going to press you into my bed and slide inside of you and fuck you until you come on my cock so many times that you lose count and can't think of anything but you and me and how good we are together. Does that work for you, Hal?"

"Yes. God. Do that. All of it. Now."

"Good answer. Brace yourself, Hallie girl."

I lift one of her legs over my shoulder, then skim my thumb through her slit, collecting all the moisture already gathered there, and use it to circle my thumb around her clit. Hallie lets out a gasp, and one of her hands flies into my hair, tugging in a way that sends a bolt of lust through me and has me thirty seconds from coming, completely untouched, all over my bedroom floor. I take a deep breath to get my shit together. Then I lean forward and lick along the path my thumb just took, dipping my tongue inside her over and over again. Hallie's taste explodes on my tongue, and Jesus Christ, it's so perfect. I could live down here with my mouth buried in her sweet pussy. I glide my tongue up to circle her clit, and she moans, her head dropping back against the door. I keep circling her clit lightly until she is grinding down, searching for more friction.

"Please, Ben," she begs.

I lift my head and glance up at her. "Tell me what you need."

She meets my gaze and never breaks it as she says, "I need you to suck on me until I come."

Hallie telling me what she needs is a heady thing, and I want nothing more than to give it to her. I dip back down, wrapping my lips around her and sucking her clit into my mouth. She lets out a loud moan, and her leg almost buckles. I reach up and grip her hip, steadying her against the door. With my other hand, I push two fingers inside her. I know I hit the right spot when her muscles contract and she starts to fuck herself on my fingers. I could live a thousand lifetimes and would never get tired of giving Hallie her pleasure.

"Don't stop," she moans. "Right there, please. Don't fucking stop."

Like I would ever. I suck her clit even harder and curl my fingers deep inside her. I feel the second her release starts. Her legs start to shake, and her hands tighten in my hair, pushing my face even tighter against her. Then I graze my teeth over her clit before sealing my mouth back around it, and she comes apart above me with a loud cry. Her release coats my lips and chin, and I stay with her through it, licking up everything she gives me. When her orgasm finally ebbs, she collapses back against the door. I lift her leg off my shoulder and place it on the ground before standing and lifting her up, wrapping her legs around my waist.

"Fuck, Ben, that was... I don't even know what that was."

"That was just the beginning, Hallie girl. You haven't seen anything yet." I carry Hallie over to the bed and drop her down on the comforter. Pushing off my sweatpants and boxer briefs, I crawl on top of her, grinning when I see her gazing down at my cock warily.

"I think I was in such a lust haze last night that I forgot how big you are. Like, you're really, really big"

I snort out a laugh. Jesus, this woman. No woman I have ever been with has made me laugh while I'm so hard that I could hammer a nail into a wall with my dick. "Thanks for the compliment, Hal."

"That wasn't a compliment, Benji. There is no way it's going to fit."

I toss her a wink. "We'll make it fit, Hallie girl."

I lean down to kiss her again, my weight balanced on my forearms. I reach down and push her legs apart, fitting my cock right to where she is hot and wet and ready for me. Never breaking our kiss, I drag myself through her wetness, grazing her clit with my tip over and over again, until we are both gasping into each other's mouths, and I am half-crazy with the need to be inside her. She must feel the same because she slides her hands down my back, gripping my ass and pulling me to her.

"Now, Ben," she says, her hands tightening on my ass.

Fucking hell. "Condom," I manage, starting to roll away to grab one from the box I stuck in my suitcase in a moment of optimism I thank my past self for.

She props herself up on her elbows and looks at me. "Do we...need it?"

"Huh?" I momentarily lose the power of speech at the thought of sinking inside of Hallie bare.

"The condom, Ben. Do we need it? I've been tested. And I have an IUD."

"Me too. I mean, I've been tested, too. And I've always...I mean, I've never...With anyone."

"Me, either."

"Hallie, I want nothing more than to fuck you bare, but are you sure?"

"I'm so sure. I trust you. Now, please, get inside me."

I roll Hallie back under me and fit my mouth over hers in a kiss that is slow and filthy and has her hands back on my ass, urging me towards her. I lift my head, and Hallie stares back at me, lips wet and eyes wide and trusting and filled with lust. My heart bangs against my rib cage with nerves and anticipation, needing Hallie more than I need air in my lungs. I reach down and guide myself towards her entrance. She is so turned on and so wet that I slide inside her in one slow motion and groan at how good she feels. Hot. Wet. Tight. Perfect. I still inside her, giving her time to adjust to me and giving myself a second to gather what's left of my tattered control.

"Look at me, Hallie."

Hallie's gaze is hazy with pleasure. She is so beautiful it reaches out and grabs me by the throat, and I have to swallow down a wave of emotion. She wraps her legs around me and hooks her ankles at my back.

"Fuck me, Ben," she gasps out. "I need you to fuck me now."

I pull out almost to the tip and push back inside her, our moans mingling together as pleasure shoots up my back.

"You are so fucking perfect, Hallie girl. You feel like you were made for me."

I drop my head and kiss her again, my tongue swirling with

hers as I move inside her. I have lived this moment a thousand times in my head over the years, and nothing I imagined comes close to the feeling of being inside Hallie, her legs wrapped around me and her hips rising to meet me thrust for thrust. We are as close as two people can be, and still, it doesn't feel like enough. I reach back and grab one of her legs under her knee, spreading her even wider for me. The change in position has her legs shaking and her inner muscles clenching around me.

"That's it, Hallie girl. Give it to me. Come for me," I growl into her neck, picking up my pace.

"Fuck, Ben," she cries out. "I'm coming." Her orgasm slams into her, her hips jerking up and her pussy choking my cock so tight that I have to grit my teeth to keep from coming myself. But I promised her more than one orgasm, and I'll be damned if I break that promise the first time I fuck her. I slow my pace but keep it steady, until she collapses back against the pillow and looks up at me with a dazed expression on her face.

"Fucking hell, Ben. I have never come that hard."

I smirk at her. "You'll come harder."

I pull out of her then and flip her over onto her stomach. I kiss her neck and then kiss and lick my way down the soft points of her spine as my hands glide down her sides. When I get to her ass, I kiss each round globe and then grip her hips, lifting them until she is on her knees, balancing her weight on her forearms. I reach around and pinch both of her nipples, then roll them between my thumbs and forefingers. She hisses out a breath and lifts her hips higher.

"*Ben*," she whispers urgently. "I need you."

Hearing her say she needs me, even if she just means she needs me to get back inside her, does something to me, and my chest squeezes tight. I grip her hips hard and slide back in, mesmerized by the view of my cock disappearing inside her.

"You look hot as fuck like this, Hallie," I grit out, picking up my pace. She arches her back and moves with me, meeting me thrust for thrust, making the hottest fucking sound every time I slam back inside her.

"Touch me," she gasps out.

Without slowing my pace, I reach around and swirl my thumb around her clit. She cries out so hard I would be worried about the entire house hearing us if I wasn't so lost in the feel of our bodies moving together. Being inside her, moving with her, feels so fucking good, but I suddenly, urgently, need her closer to me. I wrap an arm around her chest and yank her up so that her back is flush with my front. Then I slide my hand up and lightly grip her throat, my other hand strumming her clit. I still don't feel close enough, and she must feel the same because she turns her head back towards me, our mouths meeting in a kiss that is all teeth and tongues and fucking filthy.

"Harder," she rasps, reaching up and wrapping an arm around my neck, anchoring herself to me even tighter.

"Anything, Hallie girl," I whisper in her ear, tightening my hand on her throat. She must like it because her inner walls start to flutter around me. "I'll give you fucking anything."

I pull out and angle my hips so when I slide back into her, I hit her g-spot, and that does it. She clenches around me and comes on a scream. Hallie coming apart around me is every fantasy come to life, and I can't hold it in anymore. The most intense pleasure I have ever felt shoots up my spine, and I explode into her, biting her shoulder as I come. My vision blacks out around the edges, and the orgasm continues to roll through me, my release spilling inside her. My hips slow as my orgasm ebbs, and we both collapse onto the mattress, my arm snaking out around Hallie's waist to pull her against me.

"Holy shit," she gasps, her chest still heaving from her release.

"Yeah," I say, my lips finding the top of her head. I tighten my arm around her and glide my other hand up and down her back.

"That was...wow."

"Yeah, Hallie girl, it was."

"I mean, sex has never felt like that for me. Has it for—"

"No," I say, not even letting her finish her sentence. "Never. It's never been like that for me, either."

I lean down and kiss her again and then untangle myself from her. "Be right back." I go into the bathroom, clean myself up, and then wet a towel with warm water. I take it back to the bed and use it to clean Hallie up and toss it into the hamper in the corner of the room. I lift Hallie up, lay her down on the pillows, and then climb in next to her. I drag the comforter over both of us and then gather her into me so that her head is pillowed on my shoulder, both of my arms around her. I smile as she tosses a leg over me, inching herself even closer.

"You didn't have to do that," Hallie says, her voice thick with exhaustion. "Clean me up like that, I mean. I could have done it myself."

"I did," I say, matter-of-factly. "I will never not take care of you."

"I like being taken care of," she whispers, her voice barely audible. "No one ever thinks I need it, but I do. I just don't know how to ask." Then she nuzzles her face deeper into my neck and drops into sleep.

I lay there for a long time, holding on to Hallie, my heart squeezing at her admission. I know what it cost her to say those words, even half asleep.

Tangled up naked in my bed with the girl of my dreams, I make a silent vow to take care of her for the rest of my life, to give her everything she needs before she ever has to ask.

Chapter Thirty-Five
Hallie

The rest of our two weeks at the lake pass in a blur of bonfires, lake swims, time with my friends, and nights spent with Ben in one of our beds, wrapped up in each other. I thought I'd had good sex before, but it turns out I didn't know what I was talking about. I had no idea sex could be like this, but now that I've had it, I can't get enough.

Which is why, after driving home from the lake in my car with Julie, dropping her off, and then coming home and unpacking, I pick up my phone. I turn it over in my hands while I consider texting Ben. It feels weird. Like, I should be able to spend a night alone, right? I like being alone most of the time.

But then my mind wanders to all our late nights at the lake, our time after everyone else had gone to sleep. Having all the good sex and eating all the snacks and talking for hours about nothing and everything. I think about Ben filling up my water cup every night without me having to ask and knowing how I wanted my coffee every morning in that weirdly clairvoyant way of his. And how he was always touching me in some way—his hand on my back or his arm around my shoulders or stopping to drop a kiss on my head whenever he walked past me.

Ben has been a part of my life in one way or another since I was born, and I thought we knew everything there was to know about each other. But for the past two weeks, it was like I was getting to know him for the first time. It was a time out of time where we didn't have anything to do or anywhere to be. Where I took a break from my angst over potentially upending my entire personal and professional life and my constant worry over where I fit in with my friends and family.

Instead, Ben and I learned every inch of each other's bodies and whispered secrets across our pillows. My feelings for him grew frighteningly fast. I may not always be sure of my place with everyone else in my life, but it's clear to me after these last two weeks that the place I absolutely fit is with him. Being around Ben makes my heart feel like it's too big for my chest. Like I could do anything or be anything as long as he is with me. He makes me want to open myself up and tell him every thought in my head, secure in the belief that he is a soft place for me to lay my secrets.

A knock on the door jolts me out of my reverie. I open it and Ben is there, leaning on my door frame, a take-out bag in his hand, a smile on his face, and his blue eyes sparkling.

"Hey, Hal. I missed your face, so I brought dinner. Figured your refrigerator was as empty as mine."

"How are you even real?" I mutter.

He just smirks at me from his perch against my door frame, wearing athletic shorts, a white T-shirt, and a backwards baseball hat and looking hot as fuck. I suddenly have the wild urge to run my tongue over every inch of his body. I grab the take-out bag from his hand and put it on the floor. Then I pull him inside, shove the door closed, and reach up and wrap my hands around his neck, fastening my mouth to his. He wastes no time gripping my hips and tugging me even closer. I break the kiss and drop my hands to push his shorts and underwear down, so they drop to the floor together. Ben's already hard cock springs up against his stomach and my mouth waters.

"I need to taste you, I just...need to."

He steps out of his clothes and kicks them away, then looks at me. His body is ridiculous. The cut muscles of his abs and the deep V pointing straight down to his cock make me want to run my hands over every inch of him. Whatever Ben sees on my face has his eyes darkening and his cock twitching against his stomach. He reaches behind him and pulls his shirt off, tossing it to the ground along with his hat. Then he gives me a sexy grin.

"Well, then get on your knees, Hallie girl."

Still shocked and aroused by his uncharacteristic dominance, I am instantly damp between my legs. I drop to my knees in front of him and pump his hard length twice before leaning forward and swirling my tongue around him, licking up the drop of precum already beading on his tip. His salty taste explodes in my mouth, and it is like a shot straight to my clit. I wrap one hand around his base and slide down his cock, taking as much of him into my mouth as I can. I drift the other hand up his thigh and around to his ass, gripping as I suck.

"Fuck," Ben mutters, gathering my hair up, guiding me with a firm grip as I bob my head up and down, taking him a little deeper every time. When he bumps the back of my throat and I gag around him, he lets out a throaty groan and then reaches down and pulls me to my feet.

"No. Nope. No. As much as I love having you choke on my cock, and god, Hallie, I fucking do, I want to come inside of you, right where I belong. I haven't been there nearly enough."

My rational brain still tries to square the Ben I have known all my life with the confident, dirty talking man in front of me. But wherever this part of Ben was buried, I am all the way here for it.

"Well, then do it, Benji."

"You got it, Hallie girl." Ben slams his mouth to mine, curling his tongue around mine while he pushes my shorts and underwear down my legs. He pulls back long enough to tear my shirt over my head and then dives right back in, his kiss rough and needy and so damn hot. Ben walks us backward into the living room until the back of my knees hit the couch. Then, he spins us and falls back into it, pulling me down on top of him, his mouth never leaving mine as he runs his hands over my ass. His fingers drift down my crease as he pushes one of his knees between mine, nudging my legs apart and dipping his fingers inside me while he groans.

"You are fucking drenched for me, Hallie."

I lift my head and smirk at him. "Sucking your cock turns me all the way on."

His eyes turn feral, and he brings his mouth back to mine as he plunges two fingers inside of me. He curls them up into my g-spot while his thumb flicks my clit, and I see stars.

I manage to moan out, "Ben, fuck," before he rolls his thumb over my clit again and curls his fingers back up. My back arches, trying to grind down harder on his finger. To get closer. To do fucking anything to ease the ache between my legs while Ben pushes me closer and closer to the brink. He keeps playing with my clit just enough to hold me on the edge but not enough to throw me over, and it's making me wild with need.

"Ben, please," I gasp out.

"Tell me what you need."

"I need to come. Now."

"Then give it to me, Hallie. Come. Now." He curls his

fingers again and increases the pressure on my clit, and I go off like a rocket. My legs shake, and my eyes snap closed as Ben fucks me with his fingers. As my orgasm rolls through me, Ben strokes me through it. When the pleasure finally ebbs, I bring my mouth to his. He locks his arms around me, and it is all teeth and tongues and wild, frenzied need. I feel Ben's hard cock between us, and I push myself up enough to grasp it and give it a long stroke, rubbing my thumb over the head.

Ben grabs my hand and pulls it away from his cock. He lifts it to his mouth and kisses my knuckles. The sweet gesture after the scorching hot moment we just shared has my heart rolling over in my chest.

"As much as I love your hands on me, the only place I'm coming is inside you." He pushes me up so that I'm straddling his hips, before slicking one of his thumbs over my oversensitive clit and sliding his hands up my stomach. Palming my breasts, he rolls my nipples between his fingers in a way that has me gasping and moving my hips, looking for friction, even though I just came all over his hand two minutes ago. I swear, I am insatiable when it comes to this man.

He gives me a wicked grin.

"Ride me, Hallie girl."

My entire body comes alive. I lift up, grasping his cock with one hand and positioning myself over it. Then I sink down slowly, both of us groaning as I take all of him inside of me. I freeze for a second, letting my body adjust to him, eyes closing at the delicious feeling of being so full.

"Eyes on me, Hallie. Always on me." I open my eyes and meet his. They are full of need and desire, and the heat in them spurs me on. I lift up and then sink back down again, rolling my hips so that my clit hits Ben's pelvis. He rolls my nipples again, and I moan at the electricity that pulses through me. Not able to take it slow anymore, I lift all the way up until just his tip is inside me, and I grind hard back down.

"Fuck yes, Hallie," Ben grits out. "Don't fucking stop."

As if I could. I ride him hard, grinding him deep inside me while he moves his hands over every inch of my body.

"God, it's so good, Ben." And it is. My entire body is lit up.

"It's about to get better." Ben brings one of his hands down, circling my clit with his thumb while he fucks up into me. The combination of his thumb on my clit and his cock hitting just the right spot has me climbing higher and higher until I detonate around him.

"Fuck, Hallie. You feel so fucking good. I've never..." Ben doesn't finish his sentence. He just keeps fucking me from below, chasing his own orgasm as mine continues to roll through me. His thrusts lose their rhythm as he gets closer, and then he groans out, "Fuck, I'm coming!"

He spills his release inside me as I collapse on his chest, and we ride out the last of our orgasms. We're both sweaty and breathing hard, our hearts thundering against each other. Ben drifts his hands up and down my back and presses his lips to my hair, my temple, my forehead. It amazes me that even after outstanding, explosive sex, when he is still literally inside me, this sweet moment makes my chest ache. It's the most baffling combination, and I don't hate it.

I lift my head to look at Ben. He smiles and cups my face in both of his hands. He brings his mouth to mine in one more long, slow kiss that makes my head spin, then sits up with me on top of him, leaning in and kissing my nose.

"What do you say to a shower then cold Chinese food right on this couch where you just fucked my brains out?"

I grin at him. "I'd say that is exactly what I need in my life right now."

Wrapping his arms around me, Ben pushes up to standing.

"You can put me down, you know."

"Nah, you just did all the work, Hallie girl. Let me take care of you now."

And take care of me he does. Ben carries me straight to the shower, where he washes my hair and every single inch of my body. He wraps me in one towel and dries my hair with another. Then he sets me on my bed and digs through my drawers for my softest shorts and my favorite hoodie. Every time I protest and tell him I can do it myself, he leans in and kisses the protest right out of my mouth.

After we're both dressed, he deposits me on the couch and covers me with a blanket before disappearing to the kitchen and coming back with a glass of water, a Diet Pepsi, and a can of seltzer, which he puts on the coffee table right in front of me. Then he disappears again to get the food. I had two orgasms and am now clean, warm, properly hydrated, and about to be fed. I should have gotten myself a relationship a long time ago if this is how they go.

But then Ben walks in—clad in only his low-slung athletic shorts, carrying a loaded plate for me—and I think maybe I never had a real relationship before because I was waiting for Ben.

We eat in comfortable silence for a couple of minutes before I blurt out, "I'm meeting with Charlie Callahan tomorrow."

I emailed Charlie while we were at the lake like Ben suggested, the night of the bonfire. He got back to me and told me that he had something he wanted to discuss with me too, so we set up a meeting for my first full day back in the office. And ugh. Just thinking of going back to the office has my stomach knotting up with the anxiety that was largely absent during our two weeks at the lake.

"That's great, Hal, but what's that face?" Damn this man for being able to read me so well.

"I just... I guess I'm nervous about going back into the office tomorrow. I know Jules has a zillion lists of things we need to do, and she wants to jump right back in. But now that I've let myself think a little about what it would be like to practice the kind of law I'm passionate about full time, it's all I want, and I don't even know how I can do it yet. I know that's what the meeting with Charlie is about, but the thought of going to the office and pretending that I still want the same thing as Jules, Molly, and Emma is overwhelming."

Ben takes my now empty plate from my hand and puts it on the coffee table with his, before reaching over and crushing me in a bear hug. He holds on for an extra minute, whispering, "I'm so proud of you, Hal," in my ear before letting go.

"Proud of me for what? For being a hot mess who can't even be honest with her best friends?"

"No, proud of you for telling me what's on your mind. I know that opening up isn't always easy for you, and I want you to know I see that. I'll never take for granted it's me you're opening up to."

Well, hell. My eyes start to water up. I wonder if that's going to happen for the rest of my life whenever Ben says something that makes me realize how well he knows me and how clearly he sees me. And wow, my brain seems to have gotten too far over its skis because the rest of my life? No clue where that came from. But in this moment, I can really see it. I can see us coming home from work every day and having dinner together. Sitting on the couch like this and talking about our days and telling each other what we're thinking and feeling safe enough to do it. And maybe it's too soon, but that picture warms me from the inside out. For one wild second, I want it more than I have ever wanted anything.

Ben glides his thumb over my cheek and catches one rogue tear that managed to spill out, then puts his arm around me and pulls me into his side. I rest my head on his shoulder and let out a deep breath.

"What time is your meeting with Charlie tomorrow?"

"Eight-thirty. I told Jules I'm meeting with him about a case he wants me to take on. Which could be true, actually. He said he's been wanting to talk to me about something, too."

"Good. So go meet with him, call me after and tell me all about it, and then go to work and do whatever jobs Jules assigns you. Then, after work, I hope you'll let me take you on a date."

"A date? Seriously?"

"Seriously. We've been doing this for a couple of weeks now, but since we were at the lake, we haven't had a chance to be together in real life. I want that. Let me pick you up and take you out and hold your hand and be with you out in the world. Please?"

"Yes. Take me on a date and let's be together out in the world. I want that, too."

Ben puts a finger under my chin and tips my head up so he can kiss me. The kiss is long and deep, and it makes my head spin. We break apart and stare at each other before Ben leans in again and lays his lips on my forehead for a long minute before he tucks me back into his side.

Once my brain starts working again, something occurs to me.

"Hey, you know, I'm not the only one with big career decisions on the horizon. Have you thought more about talking to your dad about the Stonegate deal?"

He didn't talk much about the deal at the lake. He just told me that he told his mom, and his mom told him to talk to his dad. But Ben has been hesitant to have that conversation for reasons he still hasn't told me.

Ben shrugs, looking a little uncomfortable. "I know I should."

"So, what's stopping you?"

He lets me go and turns around so we're facing each other. "I feel...inadequate when I talk to my dad about my bar."

I don't say anything, knowing there's more. Ben looks down at his hands and takes a deep breath before continuing.

"You know what my dad does. He's this big real estate developer who does huge deals and makes millions, and I own a bar in my hometown. And it's not that I want his life. I like being a bar owner on the South Side, watching the neighborhood grow and change around me. I love that I have regular customers, and I know them and their families and all their drink orders. I love watching the college kids come flooding back every fall and being the place where they study and eat and date and have fun. And I love running a business with my best friend in the city where I grew up. I am living exactly the life I want. It's not a huge life. My name isn't on buildings, and unless I take this damn deal, my business will never make millions. And whenever I talk to my dad, I feel like it's not enough."

I squeeze his hand, feeling a rush of affection for the Pittsburgh boy I have known my whole life who grew up into this sweet, lovely, amazing man.

"Ben, did you hear yourself? Your bar and your friends and the city where you grew up? You are living the life you want. What we are to each other now might be changing, but don't forget I have known you your entire life. I know how happy your bar makes you. What you're doing is real and special and important. It is what you were born to do. If you don't want to take the Stonegate deal, then don't. What you're doing is more than enough. It's perfect. Talk to your dad. Do it tomorrow before you go to the bar. He loves you. I promise you, he only wants you to be happy. And so do I. You are my favorite person, Ben."

I shift on the couch, so I'm straddling his lap, and wrap my arms around his neck. His arms circle my waist, and he buries his face in my hair. We both hold on tight, breathing each other in.

"You're my favorite person too, Hallie girl."

Chapter Thirty-Six
Hallie

My alarm blares into the early morning. I reach out and shut it off then snuggle back into the warmth of Ben's arms. His hard body is pressed up against my back, both of his arms tight around me and his face buried in my neck. I have never slept as well in my life as I do when he's in bed with me. I start to unwind myself from him, but his arms tighten back around me, and he murmurs something unintelligible into my ear. I roll over in the circle of his arms and talk quietly.

"I have to get ready for my meeting with Charlie. You sleep, Benji. I'll text you after."

Still half asleep, and without opening his eyes, he captures my mouth with his for a long, slow kiss. My entire body lights up. I wonder idly if it will always be this way, and then I banish the thought. It is way too soon to be using words like "always." I lean in and kiss him one more time before reluctantly pulling away. His breathing evens back out almost immediately, and I giggle as I climb out of bed. He is really not a morning person.

I rush through my shower and then pull on the clothes I brought into the bathroom with me so that I wouldn't wake Ben up trying to get dressed in my room. I do some quick makeup, pull my hair back in a ponytail, and call it good enough. But when I open the bathroom door, prepared to slink out of my room, my bed is empty, and I smell coffee.

God, this man.

He is standing at the stove, his back to me, when I walk into the kitchen. I come up behind him and wrap my arms around his waist, laying my lips on the center of his back.

"You didn't have to get up, you know."

He covers my hands with one of his, then turns his head and kisses my temple. "You need to be fed and caffeinated for this meeting."

"I can feed and caffeinate myself, Benji. I've been doing it for years.

He turns all the way around, pressing a kiss to my mouth and then to my forehead.

"Nope, Hallie girl. I take care of what's mine. Go sit down." He hands me a cup of coffee and then turns back around to flip the omelet he has cooking.

What's mine.

It's not the first time he has called me his. But something about him saying it while he makes me breakfast and hands me the exact coffee with vanilla creamer that I had been thinking about while I was in the shower has butterflies swarming in my stomach. They swarm as I eat breakfast with Ben, chatting idly about what's going to happen at my meeting and the conversation he's going to have with his dad. And they swarm when Ben gives me a searing kiss at my front door before I leave. And they swarm when he sends me off with a grin, a second perfectly made coffee in a to go cup, a fresh tumbler of ice water for the road, and two mini-Reese's cups for luck.

Callahan is a small family law firm that has been in business in Pittsburgh for more than forty years. Charlie Callahan started it right after he finished law school, and for all those forty years, it has just been him, his long-time secretary Joan, two associates, and two paralegals. The firm is located in a building on Liberty Avenue in the older section of downtown, and it is vintage Pittsburgh at its finest. The building has a small lobby with mosaic tiled floors, a massive wooden old-school mailbox, and wood-paneled elevators with vintage elevator dials above each car.

While Charlie does a little bit of everything in family law, his practice is mostly centered around kids. He handles foster family situations, adoptions, and does a lot of work with child services. He is brilliant, dedicated, and unwaveringly kind. When I first met him during my family law clinic, I instantly fell in love both with him and with the law he practices. I would have loved to work for him after I graduated, but he didn't have a position open. By the time he did during my second year at my firm, I was so dug into my estate planning practice I didn't even consider leaving, settling instead for handling a pro bono adoption case here and there when I could manage it in between my wealthy and extremely high paying clients. And then when he had another opening during my fourth year, Julie, Emma, Molly, and I had started planning for our firm, so I turned it down again.

After talking it out with Ben and spending some time thinking about it, I see everything so clearly. When Charlie offered me a position the first time, I felt like I should stay at my firm because my clients and the partners I worked with depended on me, even though the work didn't light a fire under me. And when he offered me a position the second time, I felt like I needed to stick with my friends, even though I had already started to suspect that maybe I didn't want the same things they wanted anymore. Both times, I made my decision based on what made other people happy. I make a lot of decisions that way, and I am so tired of it. Being with Ben has made me see that what I want is important too, and I think I'm finally ready to make a change.

The thought of disappointing my friends weighs heavily. I don't know how I will begin to have that conversation, but I want this life. I want to help these kids and these families, and I want to do it every day.

I step off the elevator to Joan's smiling face. "Hallie, honey!" She gets up from her desk and wraps me in a hug. "It's been so long since I've seen you. I heard that the Caseys are doing so well. It's such a good thing that you did."

"It's good to see you, Joan. The Caseys are doing great. Jen emailed me the other day with pictures of Maya from camp, where she is obviously having the time of her life."

"I love that little girl to pieces. Charlie said to go right back to his office when you get here. He's waiting for you. And don't you dare leave here later without telling me every little thing that's going on in your life."

In addition to being Charlie's metaphorical right hand, Joan is a consummate gossip. I grin at her. "Wouldn't dream of it. Thanks, Joan."

When I get to Charlie's office, he is sitting behind his massive desk that is, per usual, covered in stacks of files.

"Nice bowtie, Charlie," I say as I knock on the doorframe.

His face lights up when he sees me. With gray hair, kind eyes, a wide face that is always smiling, and a penchant for wearing wildly patterned bowties, Charlie has serious grandpa energy. It's probably why he is so good at what he does.

"Hallie Evans, just the girl I have been waiting for." Like Joan, he gets up and wraps me in a hug, then motions to the seating area in the corner of his office. Once we're settled in, he asks, "Do you want to start or should I?"

"I'll start." Not sure what he wants to talk to me about, and knowing I'll lose my nerve, I want to get it all out. He nods at me. I take a deep breath and start talking.

"I want to make a change, Charlie. I've felt...unsettled in my practice for a long time now. Like it's just something I do, but I don't have any passion for it. Even while I've been planning for my firm, it hasn't felt right. I've kept moving forward because my friends and I have been making these plans for years and I committed to them, but my heart hasn't been in it. Last month when I was at Maya's adoption hearing, I realized that it's this. This is what I want to do. You know I've always loved working for you on and off over the years, but it's not enough anymore. I want to do it full time. I have no idea how to make it happen and what it will look like, but I figure that if anyone can help me, it's you. So...yeah. That's all of it. That's why I wanted to talk to you."

Charlie has his thinking face on and doesn't say anything for a minute, like he is collecting his thoughts. Then he breaks into a smile.

"Hallie, I wanted to talk to you because I'm retiring at the end of the year."

I don't think anything he could say would shock me more.

"Retiring? But, how? Why?"

God. Way to sound professional, Hallie.

"It's time for me. I have been doing this for a long time, and even though it will probably kill me, I'm ready to say goodbye.

My wife and I want to travel while we can, and I want to spend time with my kids and watch my grandkids grow up."

"But what's going to happen with the practice?"

"One of my associates has already started taking over all my divorces and non-adoption matters, and he will stick with them when I leave. The reason I want to talk to you is to ask if you would take over my adoption practice."

My mind blanks out for a second. "Take over? Like, all of it?"

He chuckles. "Yes, Hallie. All of it. I have never in my entire career seen a young lawyer more dedicated to this kind of work. I know you have stuck with estate planning for all kinds of reasons over the years, and I respect that. But, Hallie, this work is your calling. I knew it the first day I met you when you were a second-year law student, and I know it today. Not everyone can handle the kinds of cases that we see here every day, but you can. It's in your bones, my friend. There is no one I trust to do this more than you. If you take over, I can leave knowing that my clients and the kids are in the best of hands."

I don't know what's wrong with me lately, but having another important person in my life give me that kind of validation makes my eyes fill with tears. It's Charlie, so I let them spill over. He just hands me a tissue, pats my hand, and waits for me to collect myself.

"I'm so sorry. These are happy tears, I promise."

"Hallie, I practice in one of the most tear-soaked areas of the law. I know happy tears when I see them."

I give a watery laugh and try to collect myself.

"Thank you so much, Charlie; you have no idea how much it means to me to hear you say that. I would love nothing more than to take over your cases, but I'm supposed to open an estate planning practice with my friends in January. There's no way I can do both."

"I thought you might say that which is why I've been doing some planning. If you can give me a few more hours today, I have some ideas on how we can make it all work."

At Charlie's words, I feel a shimmer of excitement, and I pull my phone out of my bag.

"One second, let me tell my partners I'm not coming in today."

ME

> Hey ladies. Charlie asked me if I could cover a case for him today. I know we're going over client files and I wouldn't have said yes, but it's an emergency.

My stomach clenches a little at the lie, but it also feels good to be doing something for myself and not worrying, too much, about how I'll explain it to anyone else. Who knew?

JULIE

> On Monday morning after two weeks at the lake? Not ideal, Hallie.

MOLLY

> Don't listen to her Hal. You stay there and help whatever kid needs help. We can go over your files tomorrow.

EMMA

> What Molly said.

JULIE

> Fine. But come in early tomorrow so we can stay on schedule.

MOLLY

> Don't come in early tomorrow. The schedule will be fine.

EMMA

> It really will be. We have plenty of time.

JULIE

Ugh. Fine. But don't come crying to me when we're working on Christmas because you all fucked with my schedule.

MOLLY

[surejan.gif]

I snort out a laugh. Plans changed, I look up at Charlie. "I'm ready, let's talk."

Chapter Thirty-Seven
Ben

My parents' house is quiet when I walk through the front door. It's a big old brick house in the North of Forbes part of Squirrel Hill, one of the residential neighborhoods in Pittsburgh. My parents have lived in this house my entire life. Every inch of it, from the living room with vaulted ceilings and soft old leather furniture, to the big bright kitchen where I spent so much of my childhood, is warm and familiar and will always be home to me.

I considered going back to sleep after Hallie left, but the unsettled business with Stonegate was poking at my brain. Even though we have months to give them our decision, I don't want to wait. I know what I want. But I also know it won't feel final until I have this conversation. My dad is working at home today, so here I am. My mom was right when I talked to her at the lake, and Hallie was right last night. My dad wants what makes me happy. But it still doesn't stop the nagging feeling that my bar isn't enough. That I should do more and be more. Like him.

Frustrated with myself, I walk down the hall and knock on

my dad's closed office door.

"Come in."

I open the door and walk into the office that has changed very little since I was a kid. The big mahogany desk. The shelves covered in books ranging from real estate law tombs to paperback thrillers. The mini-fridge stocked with the lime seltzer he can't get enough of. Walls covered in family pictures. The whole office gives laid back family man. No one would guess that multi-million-dollar deals happen here almost every day.

My dad's face lights up when he sees me in the doorway.

"Hey, Benj," he says, as he gets up to wrap his arms around me in a bear hug. It's the only kind of hug Steven Parker knows when family is concerned. My parents have always been easy with their affection, to each other and to us. Everything I know about being a good partner I've learned from them. I hope I can take care of Hallie even half as well as I have seen my dad take care of my mom over the years.

"What are you doing up and around so early on a weekday?"

I sit down on his office couch, and he joins me. "Hallie had an early meeting. I got up to make her breakfast and got started with my day when she left."

My dad grins at me. "Breakfast for Hallie, huh?"

"Yeah, dad, breakfast. You might be familiar with it. I've seen you make it for mom every day for my entire life."

"Smartass. I like that you're carrying on the Parker tradition of men making breakfast for their girls. And I like even more that your girl is Hallie. So, things are going well? You both seemed happy at the lake."

This, at least, is comfortable territory. I have always talked to my dad about relationships, even though none of mine have ever amounted to much until now.

"Really well. I love her, dad. I want to make breakfast for her every day. She's it for me. I'm just waiting for her to catch up. I know it happened fast, but it feels right, you know?"

My dad smiles, but his eyes get a little misty. "Ben, Hallie has been it for you since you were kids. Your mom and I have been waiting for you both to figure it out. I don't think there is such a thing as too fast when you've known someone your whole life. Enjoy the ride. She'll get to where you are."

"It's not a little weird for you that it's Hallie?"

"Watching one of my children fall in love could never be weird. You are the best man I know, and I have loved Hallie like one of my own for her entire life. I couldn't be happier for you."

Deep down I'm still a little boy looking for his dad's approval. Because at his words, every part of me that has been worrying that Hallie and I are moving too fast quiets. Nothing that feels as right as Hallie and I do could be wrong.

"So, did you just come by to hang out, or is there something on your mind?"

Now or never, I guess.

"There is something, actually." I take a deep breath and dive in. "It's a business thing."

My dad's eyebrows shoot up. I feel a raw edge of guilt at how surprised he is that I'm coming to him to talk about business. It helps me push on.

"Someone from Stonegate Restaurant Group came to talk to Jeremy and me last month. Before the lake. They made us an offer."

My dad nods but says nothing.

"It's a big offer. Huge, actually. They want to put a Fireside location in every stadium they are contracted with for food service. They'll foot the bill to get the locations up and running, and then we get a percentage of the sales from each location. It would make us famous. Well, it would make Fireside famous, and I guess Jeremy and me by extension. Like I said, it's big."

"So, why don't you seem excited about it?"

Here goes nothing, I guess.

"Because I want to turn down the offer." I let out a long, slow breath, feeling my tension ease at having said the words. Because I didn't feel the whole truth of it until now.

"And Jeremy?"

"Jeremy left it up to me. He has his work at the foundation, and he really doesn't care one way or the other if we do this. But I care. I'm not built to be famous, dad. I don't want to have my business known by every sports fan in the country. I'm happy with what I already have. And maybe one day we'll open another location or two, but I want to do it on my terms. Not because a big company wants to come in and explode my career. I want what Jeremy and I have already built. What Hallie and I are building together. That's the life that makes me happy. I know it must seem weird to you..."

"Hang on," my dad cuts in. "I know you weren't just about to insinuate that I might look down on your career because of my business. I'm sure I wasn't about to hear that come out of your mouth, Benjamin."

I look down at my hands, unable to meet his eyes.

"Ben, look at me." I look up, and his eyes bore into mine. "All I have ever wanted is for you and your sister to find what makes you happy. I don't need you to be me. Hell, I don't want you to be me. I love my career, but it's *my* career. Mine. Not yours. Over the past nine years, I have watched you and Jeremy build Fireside from the ground up. I have watched all the love you both pour into it every day, and I see how happy it makes you. If you want to turn down the offer, then you should. If Fireside on the South Side is all you ever want, you never have to justify that to me. You are my son. Your mom and I raised you to be a good man who knows his own mind. If this deal doesn't offer you the life you want, then you absolutely should turn it down."

"Really?" I say, relief pouring through me at my dad's words.

"Yes, really. It's your life, Ben. I couldn't be prouder of how you have chosen to live it."

The door to my dad's office bursts open at that moment, and my mom struts in with a huge smile on her face. She walks straight to me and slaps me across the back of my head.

"Ow, what the fuck, mom?"

"I told you I would give you my opinion after you talked to your dad. That's the first part of it. It was stupid to spend all these years not talking to your dad about your business. Jesus, Ben." Then she leans down and wraps her arms around me. "And obviously, I was listening at the door, and I agree with everything your dad said. We want what you want, Ben. Just be happy, baby boy."

"I am happy, Ma. Really, really happy."

"Good. And your dad's right about Hallie. She'll get to where you are. But if you want to give her a little nudge every now and then, a date night is always a good idea. There was this one time when your dad and I were dating when we..."

"I'm going to stop you right there," I cut in, knowing that my mom's stories of her and my dad's dating days usually end in a way that makes me want to bleach my brain. "I'm taking her out tonight."

My mom grins at me. "That's my boy. Now, tell me everything." She plops down on the couch on my other side and looks at me expectantly.

With the weight of my career crossroads off my shoulders, and my parents on either side of me, I tell them all my plans for sweeping my girl right off her feet.

Chapter Thirty-Eight
Ben

Later that afternoon, in the lull between lunch and dinner, I'm behind the bar taking inventory of our liquor bottles when Jeremy waltzes in, an hour before he's supposed to be here. I was hoping he would be early because telling him and Hallie are the last pieces of my puzzle, and then I can put this whole situation to rest.

"What's up, man?" He comes behind the bar and stands next to me.

"I was hoping you would be here early. I have news."

"So, you finally decided we're turning down the Stonegate deal?"

I just stare at him. "How did you know?"

"Seriously, Ben? You rarely sweat anything. You put your head down and do what needs to be done. In the entire time I've known you, you have agonized over exactly two things. One is Hallie and the other is this deal. Since you and Hallie looked extra cozy at the lake and you smile like an idiot every time you hear her name, I assume it's not her. So, it must be the deal."

"Yeah, but how did you know I was turning it down?"

Jeremy just snorts. "Jesus Christ, Ben. You are the poster child for Pittsburgh Boy. You don't want to go national. You want to be here." He waves his hand around the bar we created. "I knew you would turn it down the second we got the offer. You just had to figure it out for yourself."

Fuck if he isn't exactly right. "Thanks for that, Jer. And thanks for letting me make the choice. I know you said you didn't care, but just...thanks."

"Ben, you're my best friend. We built this business together. You gave me your family when you found out I don't have one of my own. I would do fucking anything for you. But also, the idea of traveling all over the country to look at restaurants? Yeah, no thanks."

"No kidding," I mutter. "So, now I just have to tell Hallie the news. I'm taking her out tonight, so I'll fill her in then."

"Oh, I think you might get to do it sooner than tonight." He nods towards the front of the bar where the door is swinging open.

I turn around just as Hallie flies through it. She storms around the bar and straight to me. She fists my t-shirt in both hands and yanks me down to her, crashing her mouth to mine. My hands go to her hips, holding her against me as our mouths move together. Whatever it is that has gotten into Hallie, I am here for it. She breaks the kiss, panting a little, and grins at me.

"Hi."

"Hey, Hal. What brings you here?"

"I need to talk to you about my meeting. I couldn't wait until tonight." Her green eyes are glowing, and her cheeks are flushed. She looks fucking gorgeous and so elated that I can't help myself. I bring my hands up to cup her face and lay my lips on hers one more time to taste all that happiness. Something important clearly happened at her meeting, and she ran here. To me. To give me the thoughts in her head that she rarely gives to anyone. When we break apart, my heart is drumming out a beat that sounds a whole lot like *mine*.

"Well, hey there, Hal. Whatcha doing here?"

Shit. I forgot all about Jeremy. I turn around, and he is looking at us with a shit eating grin on his face.

"Just need to steal my guy here for a couple minutes. Got some big news."

My guy. My heart speeds right up at the sound of that.

"Seems to be going around. You guys go to the office. I'll take care of things out here."

"Thanks, Jer." Hallie takes my hand and leads me back to the office, shutting the door behind us. She starts talking before the door is even closed. Like the words have been building up in her brain and she can't keep them all from tumbling out.

"Charlie Callahan is retiring at the end of the year, and he wants me to take over his adoption practice."

"Hallie, that's incredible. I am so damn proud of you." I have a million questions, but I stay quiet, hoping she'll keep talking. I fucking love the sound of her voice.

"There's more. He knows about the firm, obviously. And he assumed that I wouldn't want to leave it, so he figured it all out for me. He wants me to move his current clients to our firm and build my adoption practice under our name. He has already spoken to all of them and also to the various family court judges involved in the cases. He got everyone's approval, so all that would be left is to formalize the change of counsel and have the clients sign engagement letters with us once our firm is up and running. He knows this would give Julie a bigger burden since she would eventually have to take over my estate planning clients, so he wants to pay the salary for a year for an extra associate for us to relieve that burden. I still have to contact all my clients to make sure they're okay going with

Julie. But with an additional lawyer, I can focus on my new practice while also helping Julie with my estate planning clients until we get everyone fully transitioned and get the distribution of work right. I still have to talk to Jules and the girls. It's not exactly what we had planned, so they might not want to do it. But Charlie thinks it will work. And, Ben, I really think he's right."

I thought I knew how heavily this decision was weighing on her. I thought I understood how hard it has been for her to live in this limbo, making a choice between two things she wants, thinking she can only have one. But it turns out I didn't have a clue. Her smile is pure sunshine. The kind of smile that comes from deep inside her. She is all lit up, and it hits me right in the chest. It's been so long since I've seen this kind of happy on her. I wrap her in a hug and kiss the top of her head. Then I lead her to the small two-seater couch along the back wall of the office, pulling her down next to me, not letting go of her hand.

"Fucking yes, he's right, Hallie. This may not be exactly what you planned, but sometimes plans change. Jules, Emma, and Molly will be fine, and the four of you will figure out how it's all going to work. They want you to be happy. And so do I. Hallie, I want you to be so happy. Outrageously happy. And this makes you happy. I can see it all over you. You can do this. You were meant to do this."

She takes a deep breath and looks up at me. "You really believe that, don't you?"

I turn and bring one leg up on the couch so that my whole body is facing her, and I take her other hand in mine. "I believe it with every single part of me. I believe in *you*. I always have. I will never not be your biggest fan. I can't wait to watch you help all those kids find their families. You're my fucking hero, Hallie."

Her eyes fill with tears then. One escapes, and I reach up

and catch it with my thumb, wiping it away and holding her face in my hand.

"I didn't think I would figure it out," she whispers. "I really thought I would have to leave the friends I love to do the thing I love. I didn't want to make that choice. But now, I think I can have both."

I pull her to me then. I wrap my arms around her and settle her on my lap. She curls right into me. I guide her head to rest against my chest and stroke a hand down her hair.

"You've been through a lot this past year. I wish I had known how much you were struggling. I would have helped you sooner." It kills me that she went through so much of this on her own, without anyone to lean on.

"You're helping me now. More than you can possibly imagine. Ben, I..." She trails off, and I wait her out, knowing there's more. "This. You and me. It feels...right. Is that weird to say?"

I lean down and kiss her hair. "No, Hal, it's not weird to say. It feels right to me, too. It has since the first night at the lake."

She sits up then and looks at me. "So, are you, like, my boyfriend?"

My heart fucking leaps at her taking this next step first. I have to fight to keep my cool and not maul her on my office couch.

"Hallie, that's all I want. To be yours, and for you to be mine. So, what do you think, Hal? Do you want to be my girlfriend?"

She smiles. "I would really like that."

I do maul her then. I push her back on the couch and fall on top of her, peppering kisses all over her face until she is laughing hysterically and slapping me away. But I can't help it. Until she said the words, I didn't realize how badly I needed to slap a label on what we have. To claim her for the whole world to see. It's caveman thinking, but hell, I guess I'm not really that evolved after all.

My hands press into the couch on either side of her head, and I claim her mouth with mine. The kiss is needy and heated. She moans into my mouth and raises her head up off the couch to take it deeper. I groan as I tear my mouth away from hers. If I let this kiss go on any longer, I'll be fucking her on my office couch, and my staff really doesn't need to hear that. I rest my forehead against hers for a second, trying to get myself together. As my brain re-engages, I realize I never told her about my talk with my dad. No time like the present I guess.

"As much as I would love to keep doing exactly this until the end of time, I have to get back to work. But before we go, I actually have news, too."

"Tell me."

"I, um, talked to my dad today."

Hallie gives me a shove until I'm sitting upright, and she follows me. "Ben! That's really big news. Tell me everything."

"I went over to my parents' house after you left this morning since I knew my dad would be home. I told him everything. How I didn't want to take the Stonegate deal. How I want the life that I have now. This bar. My friends and family. You."

"Me?" She smirks at me.

"You, Hallie girl. You're my girlfriend now. You just said so. That means you are a part of my life." I reach out and twine my fingers with hers. "Hell, Hal, you *are* my life."

A blush spreads over her cheeks, and she looks down at our joined hands, a smile spreading over her face. "God, you can't say stuff like that, or we'll never get out of this room. Tell me the rest." She tries to tug her hand away, but I hold tight.

"My dad was pretty offended that I thought he would feel some kind of way about me turning down the deal because of his big, successful business. He said he wants me to be happy. He said..." I trail off and try and get myself together because even replaying the next part makes the lump rise in my throat. Hallie's hand tightens around mine. She doesn't say anything, just waits for me to continue. "He said I'm a good man who knows my own mind. And that if the deal doesn't give me the life I want, then I should turn it down."

Hallie leans forward and wraps her arms around me. My arms go around her waist. I bury my face in her hair and breathe in her cherry vanilla shampoo. Everything inside me settles. She is my fucking rock. The calm in all my storms.

"I'm so damn proud of you," she whispers into my ear. "I won't even say I told you so."

I let her go, chuckling. "No need to worry about that; my mom already beat you to it."

Hallie laughs, standing up from the couch and reaching out to pull me up after her.

"I mean it though, Ben. I'm so proud of you for making this choice. It can't be easy turning down such a massive deal and so much money."

"That's where you're wrong, Hal. I've got you, which means it wasn't hard at all."

Hallie wraps her arms around my waist and lays her head on my chest. "Your dad is right. You are a good man, Benji. The best man I know."

I drop a kiss on the top of her head, and she lets go, moving past me to open the office door. We walk through the bar, and I lead her outside to the street. I turn to her, propping one shoulder against the side of the bar.

"So, what do you have going on for the rest of the day?"

"I'm going to head home. Everyone thinks I'm at Callahan all day anyway. I need to get my head together to talk to the girls about my plan and hope that they see it the way I do. I need to, like, write a speech or something."

"There's no way they won't. And you can practice that speech for me later tonight. I promised you a date, Hallie girl, and you are getting one."

She grins at me. "Oh, I'm counting on it. Where are we going?"

I grab her face in both of my hands and kiss her nose. "It's a surprise."

"But what if I need to know what to wear?"

"Be casual."

"That could mean all kinds of things. Is it outside? Inside? Are we walking? Are we..."

I cut her off with my mouth on hers. "Outside. There will be some walking. I'll pick you up at five."

"I hate surprises," she grumbles.

I smirk at her. "I know."

"Then why not just tell me?"

"It's more fun this way."

"For you maybe."

She is so damn cute when she gets all irritated that I pull her into me and kiss her one more time, quick and hard.

"Everything with you is fun for me. Now get out of here so I can go back to work."

"You're lucky you're so damn hot, Benji. Because even when you're irritating as shit, I still want to jump you."

I hope it will always be that way. "I'm lucky, Hal, but it's not because of how I look. And feel free to jump me all you want later tonight."

She sweeps her gaze down my body and back up again, meeting my eyes with a look so full of heat that all the blood in my body instantly rushes south.

"Oh, I will. Many, many times. All night long. Later, Benji."

Knowing exactly what she just did, she tosses me a grin and heads down the street to her car. I collapse against the side of the bar. I will my cock to deflate and count the hours until I get to see Hallie again and let her make good on that promise.

Chapter Thirty-Nine
Hallie

ME

ME

> SOS. Ben is taking me on a date tonight and I have no clue what to wear.

MOLLY

FIRST DATE GET IT GIRL.

JULIE

They were together the whole time we were at the lake. Can this really be considered a first date?

MOLLY

I mean, they spent time together and had all the good sex.

JULIE

Seriously Mol. It's still my brother.

MOLLY

You just wish you were having all the good sex Jules.

JULIE

I mean, yeah

MOLLY

Should have given Asher your number when he asked for it at the gala. You could be having hot athlete sex right now.

JULIE

Give my number to a playboy professional athlete? Hard pass.

ME

This is fun but back to me. I need an outfit. I hate everything in my closet. Help. Please.

EMMA

Where are you going?

ME

Ughhh he won't tell me. He says casual. Outside. Some walking. I don't know what to do with that. I hate surprises.

MOLLY

Easy. That patterned maxi dress we bought at the Shadyside sidewalk sale last year. Your flat gold sandals and gold jewelry. The bangles Em got you for your birthday a couple of years ago. Light makeup. Hair down and curl the ends.

ME

You are...so exactly right. How do you do that?

MOLLY

It's a gift. In exchange, we'll need details at the office tomorrow. Especially the sexy ones.

JULIE

MOLLY.

EMMA

Ok have fun, byeeee.

Oh wait, don't forget to wear your good underwear.

MOLLY

I lose friend points for forgetting to remind you about the good underwear.

JULIE

I'm cringing even saying this because, my brother. But wear the red lace that you bought last month when we went to that new store.

ME

It's not like he hasn't seen my underwear.

EMMA

Yeah, but this won't be regular sex. This is after date sex. It's different.

MOLLY

Em speaks the truth. Wear the red lace, Hal. Ben will lose his fucking mind.

ME

Fine, red lace it is.

MOLLY

Debrief. Sexy breakfast story. Tomorrow morning. I'll bring the donuts.

Ben knocks on my door at exactly five that afternoon. I slip into the sandals I had tossed on my bedroom floor while I was getting dressed, grab my bag, and run down the stairs to open the door. My breath catches when I see him. He is wearing a navy blue t-shirt that is the perfect amount of tight to show off his lean, muscled arms. His forearms are tan and strong and so fucking sexy I want to lick them. And there's a thought I have never had about another person's forearms. It's possible that putting a label on our relationship earlier today has made my brain go absolutely haywire. My eyes drift down to the shorts sitting low on his trim hips and then lower.

"My eyes are up here, Hal." I jerk my head up to see Ben smirking at me.

Heat floods my cheeks. "Um, I was just, um..." Yeah, I have nothing.

Ben full out grins and takes two steps towards me, grabbing my waist and pulling me flush against him. My hands find his pecs, and he lowers his head and captures my mouth with his in a kiss so intense it makes my head spin and my skin spark with electricity. He lifts his mouth from mine just far enough to whisper, "Look all you want, Hallie girl. I'm all yours." Then he takes my mouth again in one more kiss before stepping back and doing his own perusal. His eyes are a happy blue as they slide down my body and back up to meet mine. There is a new lightness to him that must have come from finally having his conversation with his dad. It looks so good on him.

"Hallie, you are gorgeous. I could look at you all day." God, I adore every inch of this sweet man.

"Nope, Benji. You promised me a date, so we're doing that. Can I know where we're going now?"

"Not yet. You get to be in suspense for another ten minutes. But I'm sure you'll guess it on the way." He drops two mini-Reese's cups into my hand and then leads me to his SUV. He opens the door for me, and I slide in. I go to reach for my seat-belt, but Ben beats me to it, pulling the belt and leaning over me to click it into place. Then he drops a kiss on my cheek and closes the door. I am so stunned by that small gesture that I don't notice the to-go cup of iced coffee sitting in the cup holder until Ben has already gotten in on his side and started the engine. He slips on a pair of wayfarers, upping his hotness factor at least ten points, and pulls out of his parking spot.

"That's for you." He gestures at the cup. "Iced latte. Thought you might need a caffeine boost."

"Thanks, Benji. How did you know?"

He just shrugs. "You had a big day today. Figured you either forgot or ran out of time to get your own."

He's right, of course. I did forget. I pick up the cup and take a sip. "This is amazing. Coffee Tree?" Ben knows that's my favorite coffee shop in the neighborhood.

"No, I made it."

"You what?"

"I made it for you. Put it in a to-go cup and brought it with me. You don't always like iced lattes from coffee shops. You once told me they don't always get the milk to espresso ratio right, or they put in too much Splenda. You said you like to make it yourself if you can. And I can. My girl gets the coffee she likes."

I turn and just stare at him. "You remember that?"

He reaches over and lays his hand on my thigh, grasping just hard enough to be possessive. Then he shoots me a look filled with something I don't have enough time to name before he turns back to the road.

"Hallie, I have known you my entire life, and there is not a single thing about you that I don't remember."

Ben lets that hang in the air and we lapse into a comfortable silence. His hand is still on my leg, and my entire body is buzzing at the contact. I am so distracted by it that I almost forget to watch where we're going. When we pass a familiar yellow arrow nailed to a tree on South Braddock Avenue, I know for sure.

"We're going to Kennywood?" I squeal.

Bouncing in my seat, I lean over and kiss his cheek, then lay my hand over his on my leg and squeeze, thrilled with him and this night. Kennywood is an old amusement park right outside of Pittsburgh that has been around since the late nineteen hundreds. Every Pittsburgh kid has memories of summer days and nights spent at Kennywood, playing the old amusement park games and riding the rides until our parents dragged us out of the park. Ben and I both love roller coasters, and Kennywood has some of the oldest roller coasters in the world.

When we were finally tall enough to ride them, Roller-coaster Mania was born. The rules were easy: ride every roller coaster in the park twice. We did it every single time we went to Kennywood. Since no one else in either of our families likes rollercoasters the same way we do, it was always just us, running together from ride to ride. Those days are some of my best childhood memories. I haven't been to Kennywood in years, and it feels exactly right that the first time I go back in a long time is with Ben.

Ben flips his hand over, lacing his fingers with mine. "It was worth keeping the secret just to see the grin on your face, Hal. You think we can handle Rollercoaster Mania in our old age?"

"Who are you calling old? We can handle this. Let's fucking go."

We absolutely cannot handle this. Somehow the park isn't all that crowded even though it's a gorgeous late August night. This means there are barely any lines for the rides. The downside to this is we have ridden six rollercoasters basically back-to-back. At first, it was a blast. Holding hands and running from ride to ride. Counting the people in front of us to strategize how to get the front car. Screaming our brains out as we plunged down hundred-foot drops and whipped around double loops. But as we stand in line for the seventh coaster, neither of us are feeling our best, and I am regretting all my life choices.

"So, it's possible I was wrong, and we are, in fact, too old for this."

"No shit, Hal. I think it's safe to say Rollercoaster Mania is best left to the teenage versions of us, with more efficient vestibular systems."

I giggle and lean back against him. "I love that you know the word vestibular. It's so you."

He wraps his arms around my waist and leans down to kiss the side of my neck. It's such a time warp to be here with Ben like this. As kids, Ben, Julie, and I ran wild around this park. Ben and I rode all the roller coasters while Julie waited for us at the exit of each one. Then the three of us would go ride all the rest of the rides together. Looking around, I can practically see the younger versions of us in this exact line, chattering about everything and nothing, waiting for our turn to ride. Just one more in a lifetime of shared memories. Leaning back against his chest, with his strong arms wrapped around me, I make a silent wish for a million more.

"If it wasn't the Racer, I would say let's just cut our losses at six but..." Ben trails off, and I know he wants me to make him get on the ride. Besides me, no one loves a tradition more than Ben Parker.

"No. We can't leave without the Racer. I know we're old, and motion sickness is a thing and whatever, but get your shit together, Benji, because we're doing this. It's tradition. I'm riding red."

Ben grins and kisses me again. "Of course you are. It's not tradition if you don't ride red."

The Racer is an old wooden rollercoaster that has been around since the nineteen twenties. It's famous and has won all kinds of awards from roller-coaster enthusiasts which, it turns out, are a thing. There are two cars—red and blue—that you board on opposite sides of a big wooden platform. The cars run side-by-side on the same track, racing each other at top speed. In all my years, I have never ridden in the blue car. It's red or nothing for me. When it's our turn, we get lucky and each get the front car. The teenage ride attendant straps me in, and I glance over at Ben across the platform. He tosses me a wink as the ride starts to roll, and fuck if that sexy wink doesn't send heat arrowing down to my core.

"Hold on tight, Hallie girl," he calls out to me. And then we fly.

Chapter Forty

Ben

"So, when do you think that you're going to break the news to the girls?"

Hallie and I are sitting side-by-side at a metal table in front of The Potato Patch, our favorite place to eat at the park. Their cheese fries are legendary. We have been eating them here all our lives, and we have a giant pile in front of us right now. I think this is my favorite day. Being here with Hallie as adults, in the place where we ran wild as kids, is more fun than I have had in a long time. I think she feels it too. Her face is flushed, her green eyes bright and happy. She hasn't stopped smiling since we got here, and every time she flashes that wide grin at me, it makes my chest tighten. As we ran from ride to ride, laughing like teenagers, I almost told her I love her at least four times. I swallowed the words down because she's not ready for them yet. I have to keep reminding myself that even though I've had eleven years to come to terms with my feelings, hers are new. She needs more time, and I want to give it to her. I want to do this right. I want a lifetime together, so I remind myself to calm the fuck down and wait a little longer. It will be worth it.

Hallie licks cheese sauce from her fingers and considers my question. "I'll be in the office tomorrow, and you know me. My instinct is to put off any kind of confrontation. But if I don't do it first thing tomorrow, I'm going to spend the day drowning in anxiety. I won't be able to focus on any of the client files Jules wants to get through, and they'll know something is wrong. Also, I'm a shit liar. So...I guess tomorrow?"

"Tomorrow is as good a time as any. And think about how good you'll feel once it's all out in the open."

"I mean, yeah, unless I'm dead because Jules hulked out and killed me when she heard the news. Which might be better than the alternative, which is her doing that scary, freeze-you-out thing that she does so well." Hallie looks down at her hands, hiding what I'm sure is a face lined in concern.

The way she says that makes me think that the freeze-out is what she's most worried about. Hallie's biggest fear is that the people she loves and depends on will abandon her if she speaks her mind and rocks the boat. And changing the entire makeup of their law firm five months before they open for business is a serious rocking of their boat. I shift to straddle the bench and lift her chin with two fingers until she's looking at me. Her eyes meet mine, and the worry written all over her face just about kills me.

"Hallie, things between you and Jules are going to be fine. Will she be mad? Yeah, she probably will be. I know that scares you. It's okay to be scared. But a whole life is a long fucking time, and none of us get through it without pissing off someone at some point. People who love each other can fight and disagree and work through it. I know Jules better than I know myself. Just like there is nothing you could ever say to me that would change even an ounce of the way I feel about you, nothing you say to Jules will make her turn her back on you. You're stuck with both of us. Taking over Charlie's adoption practice is your dream. You and Charlie hammered out a solid plan to make it work for everyone. So do it tomorrow. Go in and tell them. Whatever happens, we will deal with it. Together."

She takes a deep breath and some of the worry on her face disappears. "How do you do that?"

"Do what?"

"Know exactly what I'm thinking even when I'm not sure I do."

"Hal, I've known you my whole life. I've had feelings for you for more than a third of that time. I pay attention to you. How you feel and what you think matters to me more than anything. *You* matter to me more than anything."

"Okay. Tomorrow it is. I'm doing the thing tomorrow. Sunday, I have dinner with my family. If I'm telling Jules tomorrow, I might as well tell my parents at dinner since they'll probably hear about it from your parents. Will you come with me to dinner?"

She looks as excited about telling her family as I look on my way to the dentist. But the fact that she is taking these steps makes me prouder of her than I thought possible. My girl is finding her brave. I take her hand and bring it to my lips, kissing her knuckles. Her sharp intake of breath has me grinning.

"Proud of you, Hal. And definitely yes to dinner. But before we get to all that, there's still more of tonight, and we haven't nearly done these cheese fries justice. Bet I can eat more of them than you."

"Ooh, those are fighting words. You're on, Benji."

And we dive in, my heart practically bursting with love for this woman.

Chapter Forty-One
Hallie

I t's almost ten o'clock by the time I slide back into Ben's car after shoving the biggest stuffed monkey I have ever seen into the backseat.

"You know, you didn't have to pick the biggest prize. A smaller one would have been just fine."

"When we were kids all you wanted was one of the huge stuffed animals from the Shooting Gallery, but we could never win one, no matter how hard we tried. If you think I would pass up an opportunity to win you one now, you're out of your mind."

He leans over me and clicks my seatbelt into place again, kissing my forehead before closing my door and getting in on his side. After eating all the french fries in the entire park, we chased them with ice cream and a funnel cake—because nothing says revisiting childhood memories like eating like ten-year-olds. Uncomfortably full and slightly nauseated, we walked around the old games for a while, playing whatever looked interesting. But when we got to the Shooting Gallery, Ben got all one-track mind and shocked everyone when he actually won, hence the massive pink monkey currently sitting in the back seat. I've been ribbing him about it ever since, even though I secretly love it.

"Thanks for this, Ben. This has been the most fun I've had in a long time."

"Anything for you, Hal. But the night's not over yet. We have one more stop to make."

We drive out of the park and back the way we came, but instead of taking the turn that would take us to my house, he gets on the Parkway headed towards downtown. Weird. He takes the Carson Street exit, and before I know it, we're parking right in front of the entrance to the Duquesne Incline. I turn to him, confused.

"The Incline, seriously?"

He just winks at me. "The Incline. Seriously." He hits the button to unbuckle my seatbelt and comes around to open my door. He takes my hand, and we head into the lower station. I am instantly filled with nostalgia. The Incline is a cable car that goes up and down Mt. Washington. It has been around since the eighteen hundreds and is as much a symbol of Pittsburgh as three rivers, golden bridges, and *Mister Rogers' Neighborhood*. I came to the incline on countless school trips as a kid and even rode a few times as a teenager just for fun. But like Kennywood, it's been years since I sat in one of the red wooden trolley cars. Ben pays our fare, and we enter one of the cars. He sits down first and pulls me into his lap.

"We're the only ones in here, you know. Plenty of seats."

He just wraps his arms around my waist and pulls me back against his chest. "I like you close to me."

Well, okay then. "Benji, you are positively swoony."

"Only for you, Hal." He whispers into my ear, and goose-bumps erupt all over my arms. Something he absolutely does not miss. I can practically feel his smirk against the back of my head.

The incline starts to move, rising up Mt. Washington. The higher we get, the more the view opens up in front of us, and five minutes later, we're at the top. Ben takes my hand, and I follow him out of the trolley and into the upper station.

"So, are you going to tell me what we're doing up here?"

"Come with me." He leads me out of the station and over to the observation deck. No matter how many times I have seen it, the view at night takes my breath away. From up here, downtown Pittsburgh stretches out in front of us, the city lights casting their glow over the three rivers and the fountain at Point State Park, where the rivers meet. We have a perfect view of the golden bridges stretching across the rivers, the illuminated buildings, and the stadiums, empty of people at this late hour.

Ben pulls me in front of him and crowds against my back. His hands rest on the observation deck fence on either side of me, caging me in. I lean my head back against his chest and take in the view.

"This is what we're doing here," he says. "The view. I just... needed to see it." His voice drops at the end until it's practically a whisper. I turn to look at him, curious. But then he keeps talking.

"I haven't let Stonegate know yet that I'm turning down the deal. I don't want that life, but there's a tiny piece of me that wonders what it would be like. So, before I turn it down, I wanted to come up here and look at the view. I have lived in Pittsburgh my whole life. I grew up here and went to college here and started my business here. And I thought that maybe if I came up here, I could quiet that tiny bit of wondering."

I turn in the circle of his arms so I can see his face. "And?"

"Fuck, this view. It reaches in and grabs me by the chest every single time. I can look at this view—at the rivers and the bridges and the shape of the skyline—and understand everything about myself. This is my place. This city. This view. It's a part of me. It's buried deep in my soul. I'm a Pittsburgh boy, Hallie, and I don't want to be anything else. There's no part of me that needs anything different than what I have right here, on the banks of these three rivers. I'm calling Stonegate tomorrow."

Emotion swamping me, I stand on my tiptoes and pull Ben's mouth to mine. His lips are soft and warm. And when he takes my face in both of his hands, his mouth moving softly over mine, I feel it straight down to my toes. The kiss is soft and sweet, and when he pulls away, he leans forward and presses his lips to my forehead, hands still cupping my face. Then he wraps his arms around me and tucks my body into his. I circle my arms around his waist, and he turns us so we can look out over the rivers together. I feel safe in his arms as the warm summer breeze swirls around us, content right down to the tips of my toes.

"Thank you for coming with me. I needed you here with me for this. I just...need you."

My heart squeezes at his words. "You have me."

"You're a part of it too, you know."

"A part of what?"

"A part of this life. My life. The one I see when I look at this view. The only life I want. It might be too soon to say this, but I hope maybe one day it can be our life. That we can live it and build it together."

God, this man. This sweet, kind, big-hearted man. He came to me with his heart in his hands at the exact time I needed him. And it feels like it was supposed to be this way all along. He has always been there when I needed him, and I'm glad I can be that for him, too. His arms tighten around me as he leans down and presses another kiss to the top of my head. My body explodes with warmth, and butterflies swarm in my stomach, and it's all so clear to me. Standing there wrapped around each other, high above the city we both love, staring out at the fountain and the bridges and the city lights, I slide gently into love with my best friend. And it feels so completely right. Ben is it for me. It was always going to be us. Hallie and Ben. We are the most perfect fit.

"It's not too soon," I whisper to him. And then I burrow deeper into his hold, and I let myself dream a little about a shared life with Ben and everything the future holds.

Chapter Forty-Two

Ben

Hallie's porch is dark when we walk up the steps to her front door hand in hand. I'm holding onto my control by a thread. Being with Hallie up on Mt. Washington was more intense than I anticipated. When I looked out onto the city I love while wrapped around the girl I love, I saw more than just the right move for my business. I saw my future with Hallie.

I have always known I wanted a future with her. I have hoped for it for more than a decade of my life. But up on the Incline observation deck with her, I saw it more clearly than I ever have before.

Us living together, going to sleep and waking up together every morning. Hallie sitting at the counter every day with her first cup of coffee, talking to me about whatever case she is working on while I make breakfast. Kissing her goodbye when she leaves for work and her waiting for me in bed when I get home late after closing the bar. Whispering secrets across our pillows and walking around our city through all four seasons. A wedding and a family and a life we build together.

I have never let myself think that far into the future when it comes to me and Hallie. Until tonight. And now that I opened that door in my brain, I can't close it again, and I need her more than I need to take my next breath.

We stop at the door, and Hallie fumbles around in her bag for her keys. She finds them, but before she can fit the key into the lock, I spin her around, press her back against the door, and seal my mouth over hers. The keys drop with a clatter. With my hands on her waist, I press against her so she can feel all of me. So she knows how she affects me. How much I want her. Hallie's arms wrap around my neck and tangle in my hair, tugging just enough to have me groaning into her mouth. Our tongues dance, and I press even more firmly against her, sliding one of my legs in between hers. I lift my leg up just enough to press firmly against her center. She moans and rocks against me, and it almost has me coming in my pants like I'm fifteen again.

My dick is straining against the zipper of my shorts, and I fight to hold on to my control while Hallie grinds onto my leg. Our mouths move together in a kiss that is wet and filthy and so damn hot. I can feel her heat through my shorts, and the noises she's making tell me she's close already. I need to see all of her with a desperation that borders on manic. I tear my mouth away from hers and tighten my grip on her hips. "I fucking love watching you take your pleasure, Hallie girl. But when you come for me tonight, you're going to be spread naked over your bed so I can see every inch of you."

Hallie lets out a whimper that has my cock hardening even more. I lean down and kiss her again, all teeth and tongues until we are both panting for breath. Then I pick up the keys and unlock the door as quickly as possible, kicking it shut behind me. In two strides, I'm in front of Hallie, reaching down for the hem of her dress. I lift it over her head and toss it to the ground behind her. Then I stop dead in my tracks. My breath wheezes out of my lungs as I take her in. She is wearing tiny red lace underwear and a matching bra with lace cups that barely contain her hard nipples. Her eyes are bright, and her face is flushed and glowing. Her lips are wet and red and puffy from kissing me. She is a fucking wet dream. It's a miracle that I don't just pass out right on the spot.

Hallie seems to notice that I'm suddenly unable to form words and she just grins. "You like?"

She does a little spin and I see that the underwear is actually a g-string. Her gorgeous ass on display for me snaps me out of it, and I grab that ass with both hands, lifting her up.

"Do I like it? Fuck, Hallie," I practically growl. I drop my head and bite her nipple through the lace of her bra, then rake my tongue over the tight bud. She groans, throwing her head back and wrapping her legs around my waist. I do the same to the other one, biting and licking until she is squirming against me.

I turn us towards the stairs but I must not move fast enough for her because she leans forward and bites down on my earlobe. *Fuck.* She soothes the spot with her tongue and whispers, "Take me to bed. Now."

I suck in a breath, my cock aching and hard as steel. I carry her across her living room and up the stairs. When I reach her bedroom, I drop her down on the bed and immediately cover her body with mine, bringing our mouths back together. Hallie's legs are still wrapped around me, and I grind into her once before I trail my mouth down her neck, to her lace clad breasts. With my weight on one arm, I tug down the lace cups, freeing her breasts. I pull one hard nipple into my mouth, licking and sucking while I roll the other one between my fingers. Hallie holds me against her, letting out little cries that have me sucking harder and then switching sides so I can worship her other breast with my mouth.

When Hallie is writhing under me, I move lower, kissing my way down her stomach, tasting every inch of her skin. Hallie opens for me the lower I go. The g-string barely covers the thin strip of hair over her pussy, and I groan. It's so hot. There is a wet spot on her underwear, and I drop my head to run my tongue along it, tasting her over the thin fabric. Hallie's hips jerk up, and she lets out a soft cry. I just barely resist the urge to shove the fabric to the side and fuck her with my tongue. There will be time for that later, but tonight I'm worshiping every inch of my girl.

I sit back on my heels, stripping off my t-shirt and dropping it onto the floor by the bed. Hallie's gaze is dark and filled with lust as she trails her eyes over my chest and then lower. "See something you like, Hallie girl?"

She lifts her eyes to mine. "You are so fucking sexy, Ben. I could look at you forever."

Fuck. Me. "We have all night, Hal. Look all you want." I settle between her legs and press a kiss to the inside of her thigh, sliding my lips up and running my tongue along the crease where her leg meets her hip. I lick across her stomach to the opposite hip and back down again, pressing a kiss to the opposite thigh. Hallie writhes under me, tilting her hips up, looking for friction, and I can't resist teasing her a little. I keep running my tongue right along the seam of her underwear, moving closer and closer with each stroke of my tongue, but never quite reaching the place I know she wants me.

Finally, she gasps out, "Ben, please."

"Please what, baby?"

"Please, touch me. Lick me. Something. Anything. You're making me crazy."

"Crazy for me is exactly how I want you, Hallie girl."

I slide my fingers under her underwear and swipe them over her wet slit.

"I can't wait to taste you."

"Do it. Please. Fuck."

I slide her underwear down and push her legs apart. Leaning down right where she is dripping wet, I blow lightly on her clit and her hips jerk up again. I slide my fingers up through her wet heat and trace my forefinger around her clit in light circles. Her hips buck up underneath me and finally, I give her what she wants. Leaning down, I lick her slit from bottom to top and let out a groan as the taste of her explodes on my tongue. I circle her clit with my tongue over and over again. And when her hips start to grind down searching for more friction, I slip two fingers inside her, and she cries out. A dark thrill runs through me at being the person to give this to her. That she is taking her pleasure from me. Hallie's legs tighten around my head as I devour her. Her pussy clamps down on my fingers as I fuck them in and out of her and suck her clit into my mouth.

"Ben," she moans. "It feels so good. Please don't stop."

I lift my head, and my eyes meet hers. Her face is flushed and her chest is heaving. "Never. I could eat you forever. You taste so fucking good. You need to come for me, Hallie girl?"

"I'm so close, please."

I curl my fingers up into her g-spot and suck her clit hard, and she detonates.

"Oh my fuck, Ben. Fuck yes." Hallie's hips jerk up and her legs shake as she comes apart around me, panting and moaning and crying out, her clit throbbing against my tongue. I keep sucking her clit lightly, riding out her orgasm with her, licking up her release. When she melts back into the bed, I kiss my way up her body, stopping to reach around and unhook her bra and toss it away. I kiss and lick her nipples and slide my tongue along her collar bones and her jaw, finally making my way up to take her mouth with mine. The kiss is soft and achingly slow.

My cock is rock hard and begging to be inside her, but then Hallie's arms circle my neck and pull me closer to her as her tongue strokes mine. The kiss changes the energy in the room from frenzied to passion and desire and something deeper. She pushes her tongue into my mouth and tangles it with mine, and I want to keep kissing her for the rest of my life.

"I want you, Ben," Hallie whispers as she looks up at me. Her hair is spread over the bed in a halo around her head, and her eyes are dark and full of an emotion I can't quite name but has my chest tightening. I want to bury myself so deep inside her that I can't tell where I end and she begins.

I stroke my thumb down her cheek, pushing her hair off her face, and press a kiss to her forehead. "Then have me."

Chapter Forty-Three
Hallie

hen have me. There is nothing I want more than to have him. All of him. Forever. But right now, I need him inside me, or I might actually die.

I reach down and push Ben's shorts and boxers down, using my legs to get them all the way off. He kicks them away then hooks his arm around one of my legs, opening me wide. He seals his mouth over mine in a hot, open-mouthed kiss and pushes inside me achingly slowly. I feel every single inch of him, and I gasp into his mouth as he goes still. His eyes close for just a second like he is gathering his control. "You feel so good wrapped around my cock, Hallie. You were fucking made for me."

I wrap my arms around his torso, digging my fingers into his back, and his grip on my thigh tightens as he spreads me even wider. "Move, Ben. I need you to move."

I close my eyes as Ben pulls out so just the tip of him is inside me. He thrusts back in slowly, brushing against my clit and making me slam my eyes shut as a blast of white-hot pleasure shoots through me. I let out a moan, wrapping my legs around Ben's waist, tilting my hips up to take him even deeper.

"Look at me, Hallie girl. Open your eyes and look at me."

I open my eyes and meet his. They are cobalt blue and glazed with pleasure and an emotion that makes my heart thump in my chest.

"Watch me while I fuck you like you're mine. You will never be anything but mine." Ben pulls out again and thrusts back in, our moans tangling together and wrapping us even tighter to each other. He moves in and out of me, slow and steady, eyes locked with mine.

"Hallie," he rasps, as I lift my hips even higher and tighten my inner muscles around him. But it's not enough. I need more. So much more. I buck my hips up to try and flip us over. Ben realizes what I'm doing and wraps both of his arms around me, rolling until I'm settled on top of him. I rock back and forth, grinding down on him, taking him as deep as I can. Ben slides his hands up my torso to rub his thumbs over my nipples, then he rolls them between his fingers. He pinches them, and it's like a lightning bolt to my clit. I let out a groan, bringing my hands up to cover his, while I keep rocking over him.

"You have the most gorgeous tits I have ever seen. I love watching you above me, taking what you want." Ben rocks his hips up into me and I gasp out, my hands flying down to his chest to anchor myself as he does it again and again, his hips rising to meet mine. It feels so good I could come just like this, but I still want more. I need to be closer to him. To feel all of him against me.

"Ben, I need..."

"Tell me, Hallie. Whatever you need. I'll give it to you."

"I need to be closer to you," I moan out as he rolls his hips up into me again.

Ben sits up then, winding his hands around my waist and resettling me so that I am sitting on his thighs, his cock still buried inside me. I wrap my arms around his neck and bring my mouth to his. He glides his tongue along my lips, and I open for him. He licks inside my mouth and slides his tongue around mine as I start to move slowly above him, pleasure ricocheting through me with every rise and fall of my hips. Ben's hands never stop moving. They glide up and down my back, over my ass and down my thighs and back up again. We are joined in every way that two people can be, and it still doesn't feel like enough.

I break the kiss and lock eyes with Ben. His pupils are wide and dark, the same raw, naked emotion on his face that I feel deep in my soul. In this moment, I know there will never be anything for me except me and Ben and these feelings and this life. It hasn't been that long, but two minutes or two years wouldn't make any difference. I know it with more certainty than I have ever known anything. My heart beats with love for his man. He is my past, my present, and my future. I can't bring myself to say the words just yet, so instead, I lean down and kiss him, pouring every ounce of love I feel into it.

Ben must sense the shift in me because he reaches up and cups the side of my face and whispers, "You're gorgeous, Hallie girl." Then he starts fucking into me from below, hard and deep, his eyes never leaving mine. He slips his hand between our bodies, and he rolls his thumb against my clit in a rhythm that has me seeing stars and moaning out his name over and over again. I start to move faster, meeting him thrust for thrust as I climb closer to the edge. Between his cock so deep inside me and his thumb on my clit, I am pummeled with sensation, my movements losing control as pleasure starts to take over.

"Ben, it's so good. I'm so close," I cry out.

"You are so tight around me," he grunts. "I want to feel you come. Feel you squeeze my cock. Come for me, Hallie."

His rhythm never falters, his cock hitting me in the perfect spot every time he rocks up into me. Then he pinches my clit, and I detonate, crying out his name. My orgasm rushes through me, pleasure swamping my body. I'm still flying when Ben rolls us over, grabbing one of my legs behind my knee. Eyes locked on mine, he bucks into me fast and hard, his pelvis hitting my oversensitive clit with every thrust, shooting more pleasure through me as he takes his own.

"Fuck, fuck, fuck. You feel so good, Hallie. So mine. Fuck, I'm coming." His hips jerk, and I feel him spill deep inside as a second release barrels through me. Legs shaking and body slick with sweat, I cry out his name again. Ben's hips slow, riding out both of our releases. He crashes his mouth down on mine in a wet, erotic kiss that has heat pooling in my belly even though I just came twice in a row. Then he rolls us onto our sides and breaks the kiss, both of our chests heaving, and our eyes still locked.

The air is thick and heavy as we stare at each other, both of us a little stunned.

"That was..." I try. "We were..." Nope. Still nothing.

Ben leans forward, kissing my forehead and then my lips.

"I know, Hallie girl. I feel it too." Then he wraps his arms around me and holds me close, our heartbeats returning to normal after that soul-shaking experience.

A minute or an hour later—no way to know for sure—Ben gets up and pads to the bathroom. He comes back with a warm towel that he uses to clean me up so gently that tears unexpectedly burn behind my eyes. No one has ever taken this much care with me. He tosses the towel in the hamper and lifts me up, settling me so my head is on the pillows. Ben slides in next to me, pulling my comforter over both of us. He rolls me into his arms, and I lay my head on his chest. With Ben warm and solid next to me, his hand gliding up and down my back and my ear over his heart, I drop straight into a deep, dreamless sleep.

Chapter Forty-Four
Hallie

After waking up to Ben's head between my legs and an orgasm crashing over me before I even opened my eyes, a round of hot as shit shower sex, and another Ben-made breakfast, my boyfriend—I love saying that— sent me on my way, coffee with vanilla creamer in hand. Ben's psychic coffee abilities have been weirding me out for weeks, but every time I bring it up, he blushes adorably and just says, "I see you, Hal," before changing the subject.

I feel the strangest mixture of light and loose and wired tight with anxiety. Last night with Ben was one of the best of my life. Revisiting one of our favorite places as kids and then going up the Incline to look out over the city is something I will never forget. For the first time in my life, I have someone who gets me, all the way through. Who sees me and all my quirks and chaos and wants to stick around and be a part of it.

Ben sees the real me. I think he always has, and he lets me see him too. The kind, caring, and compassionate man he is. His strength and confidence and his willingness to be vulnerable with me. To tell me how he feels and listen when I tell him. It's a gift we can give to each other. Be each other's safe spaces with wide open hearts. A shelter in all of life's storms.

Which is why I'm walking into my office this morning prepared to do something that is, at best, about to put me on Julie's shit list. And at worst? Well, I'm trying not to think about that.

When I walk in the front door, Emma is in the kitchen, standing in front of the coffee maker. She turns when she hears the door close.

"Hey, Hal. How was last night?"

I may not always share every thought with my friends. But this? This I am dying to talk about. I walk into the kitchen and grab a seat at the island. "God, Em. It was amazing. Every last second of it."

"Hallie Evans, you better not be giving Em a sexy story without me!" Molly comes barreling through the front door in a flowing sundress and wedge sandals. Her usual bags and totes hang over her arms, and she is carrying a donut box.

"As promised, donuts. You can't tell a sexy story without donuts." She drops her bags on the floor and goes over to the stairway yelling, "Jules, I know you're up there! Put the work on hold and get down here! Hallie has a story, and I have donuts!"

Coming into the kitchen, she puts the donuts on the island and gives me a side hug before dropping down onto the stool next to me.

"Hallie, you look positively glowy, girl. I don't have to ask how the sex was last night. I can see it all over your face."

"And twice this morning," I mumble into my coffee, trying to smother the smile that wants to break free.

"Babe, I wish I could say I wasn't jealous, but Jesus Christ. I fucking am. Twice this morning? It's not even nine. That is some impressive stamina."

I look up, and my smile breaks free. "God, you have no idea, Mol. Everything about last night was...I don't even have words. It was perfect. He is perfect. I didn't know it could be like this. I just...I really didn't."

Emma comes over and sits down on the other side of me, covering her hand with mine. Molly just stares at me for a second before suddenly getting up and walking up the stairs to the second floor. Thirty seconds later she comes back, dragging Julie behind her.

"I was almost done, Molly. What is so important it couldn't wait five more minutes?"

Molly points at me. "Hallie is in love with Ben."

My jaw drops. Julie's head swivels around to look at me. Emma puts her face in her hands and mutters, "Molly, locate your tact."

Molly just shrugs. "You are though, right? I mean, your face when you talked about him just now. I have never seen you look like that."

I could deny it, and maybe I should since I haven't said the words to Ben. But I don't have it in me to lie. Not about this.

"I am. I love him. So damn much. And maybe you all think I'm crazy since it's only been a few weeks since we got together like this. But it doesn't feel fast, and it doesn't feel crazy. It just feels... right. It feels like maybe Ben and I have been headed in this direction our whole lives."

"There's no such thing as too fast, Hallie." Emma covers my hand with hers again. "There's no timeline for feelings. They come when they come."

"Em's right." Molly sits back down in her seat and puts her arm around me. "Ben is the best. You've known him your whole life. It's not surprising that once this happened it would be quick."

I look at Julie, who has been studying me quietly. She walks up behind me, putting her arms around me in a tight hug. "No one deserves love more than you do, Hal," she whispers. "I'm happy for you. And Ben. Both of you."

"Okay, but I haven't even told him yet. So maybe we could all keep a lid on it until I do that?"

"Lips are sealed." Molly mimes zipping up her lips and throwing away the key. Even though she would seem like the most likely candidate to spill, Molly is a vault.

"Okay, so now that we're done with the feelings of it all, can we get to the sexy portion of the morning? I need more information about that impressive stamina."

Emma giggles and Julie just rolls her eyes. As much as I want to pretend like discussing my impressive and extremely satisfying sex life is all that's on the agenda today, if I don't get to the thing that I really came here to talk about, the anxiety might just eat me up from the inside out.

"Actually, before we get to that, I have something else to talk to you guys about. Jules, can you sit?"

She tosses me a quizzical look, and I don't blame her. The words "I want to talk" rarely come out of my mouth, but she grabs a stool on the other side of the island and sits.

I take a deep breath and let it out slowly, steeling myself for whatever is about to happen.

"Okay. So. You all know how much I have loved the adoption work I've done with Charlie Callahan since the clinic." Everyone nods, and I see suspicion in Julie's eyes but ignore it and press on. "Well, yesterday, when I was at Callahan, Charlie told me that he is retiring at the end of the year. He has someone to take over his matrimonial practice, but since I have been working with him on and off for so many years, he asked me if I would take over his adoption practice. I would do the work under our firm name, so I would still be here. But my practice would be different."

Julie sucks in a sharp breath. "You told him no, right?"

I shouldn't be surprised that her first instinct is confrontation, but I am.

"I didn't. I told him I had to talk to you." In the past, that's where I would stop, but not this time. "But I want to tell him yes. I love adoption. I know it's a big bomb to drop on you, but this feels like an opportunity I can't pass up. Honestly, I've been thinking about this for a long time. Longer than just since my meeting with Charlie. I'm not happy in estate planning. I don't love it anymore. Maybe I never did. I love adoption. It fulfills me in a way that estate planning never has." I have more to say, but Julie interrupts me.

"A long time?" Julie explodes. "How long? You didn't think about saying something a little sooner? Like maybe before we started planning? Before the client files started coming over? Before we put your name on the fucking letterhead? You can't do this, Hallie. You have clients who are following you here. They are counting on you. I'm counting on you. If you take over Charlie's practice, what am I supposed to do? Em and Molly each have their own thing, but you and I practice together. If you leave, I'll have to take on your clients, and I don't have the capacity for that. You may think I live and breathe work, but I'm not an automaton with no life, Hallie. You can't just pile more work on me and expect me to take it gladly."

"Hang on," says Emma. "There's no need to dismiss it out of hand, Jules. I think we can make it work."

Molly reaches over and squeezes my hand. "If this is important to Hallie, we need to talk about it. This firm is about us enjoying our careers and not paying homage to the big law gods."

As they go back and forth, I start to lose my nerve, and my

instinct to agree and give in takes over. But then I hear Ben's voice in my head telling me that I can do this.

"First of all, I'm not leaving. I will still be right here. I'll just be doing something different. Charlie knows us. He knows this is going to give you a bigger burden since you would have the main responsibility for my clients. So as part of the takeover, he is going to pay an associate salary to us for a year. We can hire someone to relieve the extra burden on you. This way, I can concentrate on my new practice and also help you with my estate planning clients until we figure out the distribution of work. I have done a lot of thinking over which client files I'm going to have coming in from my old firm and the amount of work that they will generate and..."

"No." Julie's voice is low and mean, and it stops me cold. "No fucking way. This is not fucking happening, Hallie. I'm glad for you that you have your little adoption law hobby and that it makes you happy, but that's all it is."

"Fucking hell, Julie." Molly shoots her a dirty look.

"Julie, we need to talk this out." Emma speaks quietly, but her words are no less forceful than Julie's.

"No. She is not going to come in here and change our entire firm less than five months before we open for this. We had plans. We all have plans." She waves her arms around to Molly and Emma. "Those plans do not include upending our whole practice when we still have so much to do to get it established."

The "little hobby" comment hits me straight in the gut.

Julie is a lot of things—focused, intense, and wholly committed to everything she does—but she has never been intentionally cruel. It takes every ounce of courage I have to start talking again. When I do, my words are quiet.

"I want this, Jules. It's the right career move for me. I have turned down two job offers from Charlie over the last four years because it wasn't the right time. But I can't turn this one down. I won't. If I do, I'll regret it forever. This is the right time, and I will do everything in my power to make this work for everyone. You most of all."

Julie just stares at me, gaze cold. "We can't make it work, Hallie. I won't. How selfish can you be? It's enough that you're leaving me for Ben. You are not leaving me at work too. It's. Not. Happening. If you do this, we're done. Fucking done, Hallie." With that, she storms out of the kitchen, leaving me stunned and staring at the counter.

Molly breaks the silence first. "Julie's being a shit, Hallie. She doesn't own this firm, and she certainly doesn't get to tell you what to do with your career. If you want to do this, we'll find a way to make it work. And we all know you're not leaving anyone for Ben. That's just bullshit."

"She's right, Hallie. Life's too damn short for you not to explore this opportunity. Or whatever is happening between you and Ben."

I stay silent and still, the urge to crawl out of my skin coursing through me. I should have just turned Charlie down. Suddenly, I can't sit here anymore. I push up from the stool so quickly that it falls over and clatters onto the floor.

"I'm sorry," I mumble. "I can't be here right now. I just... can't. I'm going to work at home. I'm just... I'll call you later." I leave the kitchen and grab my bag where I left it by the front door before running out and into my car, grateful I brought it today instead of walking.

Holding back the tears threatening to rise in my throat, I drive the half mile home, Julie's harsh words echoing in my mind the whole way. I let myself in my front door, tossing my bag onto the floor and heading straight to the living room. It's not until I'm curled up, wrapped in my favorite blanket, that I let the tears finally come.

Chapter Forty-Five
Ben

I haven't heard from Hallie all day, and it's freaking me the fuck out. I figured she would call me after she talked to the girls. She said she was going to have the conversation as soon as she got to work. When ten o'clock came and went without a word, I wasn't too concerned. I figured she either decided to wait, or she told them, and they got right into planning. When it was past noon, and she hadn't called me or responded to any of my texts, I texted Julie.

Three times. No response.

I had to talk myself down from leaving the bar and going straight to the firm to see what the fuck was going on. My protective instincts were screaming, but I wanted Hallie to know that I believed in her to do this. If I rushed to the rescue before even knowing if anything was wrong, that would send the opposite message.

So instead, I stayed at the bar, trying, and failing, to keep myself busy. When Jeremy waltzed in at six, it was happy hour, and I was trying to restrain myself from snapping at every customer who made the mistake of asking me for a drink. It must be obvious on my face, because Jeremy walks directly behind the bar and starts taking drink orders.

"Everything okay?" he mutters. "You look like you're about to take someone's head off."

I wait to answer until he serves the last customer in line. "I don't know. Hallie was going to talk to Jules, Emma, and Molly about something important today. She said she would call me afterward, but I haven't heard from her all day, and she's not responding to any of my texts. Neither is Julie. I'm worried."

"Did you try asking Molly or Emma?"

"I...No. I didn't. I didn't think of it." And why the fuck didn't I think of it?

Jeremy gives me a look. "Okay, so we're not using our head today. I'm calling Emma." He pulls his phone out of his back pocket and taps a speed dial contact before bringing the phone to his ear.

"Hey Ems. Thanks for getting me that info I asked for. I'm going to go over it and get back to you next week. But right now, I'm with Ben and he needs to talk to you."

He hands the phone to me. I cover up the speaker and ask, "What info?"

Jeremy just shrugs. "She's helping me with something else for the foundation. Talk to her, dude."

I lift the phone to my ear. "Hey Em, is Hallie at the office? I haven't heard from her all day, and I'm getting worried."

"She didn't tell you what happened?"

My stomach drops out of my ass. "No, she didn't. But you're going to. What happened, Emma?"

"She told us this morning about Charlie Callahan's offer, and Julie...she didn't take it well. It was bad, Ben. Really bad."

Jesus Christ, Jules. I'll deal with her later, but right now, I need to find my girl. "Where the fuck is Hallie?" I growl.

"She left right after Jules blew up. She said she was going home. I haven't heard from her since."

"You just let her leave?" I explode.

Jeremy shoots me an angry look and backhands me in the stomach.

"Don't fucking talk to her like that," he hisses.

"Ben, Hallie is an adult, and she was upset. She wanted some space, and we gave it to her."

I run a hand down my face. "Sorry, Em. I didn't mean to yell. I'm worried about her."

"I'm sure she's at home. You should go there. She's been alone long enough."

"I'm on my way."

I hang up and hand Jeremy back his phone. Before I say anything, he jerks his head towards the door. "Go. I'll handle the bar."

"Thanks, Jer, I owe you one."

"You really don't."

I grab my keys and drive to Hallie's, breaking all the speed limits along the way.

When I get to Hallie's, I knock on the door, but there is no answer. My anxiety spikes to intolerable levels. I need to get a grip. I check the handle, and the door is unlocked, so I push right in. The house is dark and quiet, except for the sounds of ragged breathing coming from the living room. I go directly there, and what I see has my heart twisting. Hallie is curled into a ball on the couch, blanket wrapped tightly around her. Her eyes are open but vacant. It scares the shit out of me.

"Hallie girl," I whisper. I sit right down on the couch and

gather her into me. As soon as my arms are around her, her tears spill over. I hold onto her and let her cry it out, murmuring things like "I've got you," "I'm here," and "Let it out, baby." She sobs into my chest, soaking my t-shirt, her shoulders shaking with the force of it. I have never felt more helpless than I do in this moment.

And I have never been more in love with her than I am in this moment.

I would burn down the world for her. But all I can do is be here right now and hold her together while she falls apart. It doesn't feel like nearly enough.

When her cries finally subside, she looks up at me, and my heart shatters. Her face is red and puffy, as if she has been crying since this morning, which I'm now sure she has been. Alone.

The part that absolutely kills me is that the coffee table is completely empty. No coffee cup, no massive water tumbler, and no seltzer can. The image of Hallie crying alone all day without her drinks spurs me to action. I kiss her forehead, murmuring to her that I'll be right back before unwinding myself from her and going straight to the kitchen. I find one of her water tumblers and fill it with ice all the way to the top just how she likes it and then add water. I grab a seltzer can from the fridge and take everything back to the living room. I put both drinks on the coffee table, then pick Hallie up and settle down onto the couch with her on my lap and my arms tightly around her. She buries her face in my neck, and I hold her there for a few more minutes before reaching for the tumbler.

"Drink a little, Hallie girl," I say quietly into her ear. She lifts her head and takes the water, drinking deeply. When she's done, she hands it back to me, and I put it back on the table.

"I know you're sad, Hal," I murmur to her. "Em told me what happened. It's going to be okay. We'll figure it out. I swear we will." I have to practically staple my mouth shut to keep from asking her to relay the conversation she had with Julie word for word. That's not what she needs from me right now.

"It was so bad, Ben," Hallie whispers, her voice scratchy from disuse. "I've never heard Julie talk like that. She was so mean and so mad. I convinced myself she would be okay with it, that she would want this for me. How stupid was that? This was such a big mistake. I never should have said anything. It's never going to be the same."

Fresh tears fall down her face, and I hold her tighter. There is no point in telling her that she's wrong and that Julie will come around. That it wasn't a mistake. Hallie isn't ready to hear that yet. She faced her biggest fear today. She cracked herself open and told Julie—who she loves deeply—exactly what she wants, knowing it might make Julie angry, hoping that it wouldn't. And Julie did exactly what Hallie was afraid of. She got angry and ran, her usual move. But too fucking bad for her. Julie is going to have to deal with this. I'll make sure of it, but now, Hallie is my main concern.

"Have you eaten anything today, Hallie girl?"

"I haven't. But I'm not hungry. I'm so tired, Ben."

"Okay, baby, drink a little more, and then I'm taking you to bed. Do you want the water or the seltzer?"

She points to the tumbler, which I grab after lifting her into my arms. I take her upstairs, straight to the bathroom. I set her down on the counter and flip on the shower before undressing her and shedding my own clothes. When the water warms up, I help her into the shower, closing the glass door behind us. Keeping her back to the spray so that she stays warm, I reach for her shampoo. Pouring some into my hand, I lather up her hair, massaging her scalp with my fingertips. She lets out a sigh and melts against me. I rinse the shampoo out and then do the same with her conditioner. Then I grab her body wash and a loofah and wash her from head to toe. I do a quick rinse of my own, then bundle us both into towels, grabbing a third one to rub over Hallie's hair to dry it off. Every step I take to care for her settles something inside of me. Feeds the deep need I have to be her person. The one by her side for all things. She's here, she's safe, she's mine. As long as those things are true, we can handle everything else that comes.

I've spent enough time in her room to know where everything is. While Hallie sits on her bed, I grab her underwear and a sleep t-shirt and hand them to her. But she shakes her head.

"Not that t-shirt."

"Something wrong with it?"

"No, but I like to sleep in yours." Her face heats at the admission. "You, um, left one here once. I like it. It's in there. Shorts too, if you want those."

I smile at her, trying not to show her the burst of pride I feel at her taking comfort in wearing my clothes, wrapping my scent around her while she sleeps. How it sends my heart thrumming. She's had a rough day. She doesn't need me spilling my feelings all over her right now. I dig through her drawer and find an old University of Pittsburgh t-shirt I have no recollection of leaving here. I hand it to her, and she slips it on while I grab the shorts and tug them up.

"Under the covers, Hallie girl. Let's get you some rest."

Together we climb in and curl ourselves together, my arm slipping around her waist to hold her tightly to my chest. She covers my arm with her own and then scoots back, tucking herself further into me.

"Thank you for being here," she whispers.

"You don't have to thank me, Hal. I never want to be anywhere except for here."

"I'm sorry I didn't call you today after it happened. I just needed to get home. And then, well, you saw where I ended up.

I know I have to tell you everything that happened. I want to tell you. I'm just so tired."

I press a kiss to the back of her head. My heart is cracked wide open and pouring out love for this girl who did her bravest thing today and wants to tell me about it. I will never take any part of this for granted. "Don't worry about it, Hallie. I came looking, and I found you. I'll always find you. Tomorrow is another day. Sleep now."

She laces her fingers with mine and holds on tight. After a few minutes, her breathing evens out. I close my eyes, breathing her in, and before long, I follow her into sleep.

Chapter Forty-Six
Hallie

When I wake up, Ben is wrapped around me, his warm body pressed tightly against my back. My bedroom is dark—it's just after five—but I am wide awake, my brain already cycling through the events of yesterday. My fight with Julie. The horrible things she said. Ben showing up at my house and taking care of me. Even thinking now about how gently he carried me upstairs, washed my hair, and bundled me into bed has tears pricking my eyes. I thought I was all cried out after yesterday. Damn Ben for making me drink all that water. All it did was replenish my tear supply.

Ben is fast asleep, but my body and brain are awash in anxiety, forcing me out of bed. Knowing that Ben has a weird sixth sense for when I'm awake, I untangle myself from him as gently as possible and slide out of bed. Moving as quietly as possible, I sneak to the hall bathroom then to the kitchen. My stomach is still rebelling at the idea of food. Anxiety has a way of killing my appetite, so breakfast is a hard pass, but there's always room for coffee. As if on autopilot, I pour milk into my mug and pop it into the microwave to heat a little. When you're feeling your worst, there is nothing worse than pouring hot coffee over cold milk and instantly ending up with a lukewarm drink. The scent of freshly brewed coffee fills my nose, my brain coming online from the smell alone.

After fishing my phone out of my bag where it has been since I got home from work yesterday morning, I settle onto the couch with my coffee. Unlocking the screen, I wince when I see the missed calls and texts from Ben. He was obviously worried about me, and I feel terrible for not letting him know what happened before I collapsed onto the couch in a ball of misery.

Molly and Emma both sent a bunch of texts too, and I'll have to get back to them at some point today. I love them for sticking up for me, but it makes me feel even worse. This affects their careers too, and I don't want to put them in the middle. I scroll through the rest of my messages before I realize I'm looking for one from Julie that obviously never came. I send her one, hoping she'll answer. I wish I could be mad right now, but I'm too worried I lost my best friend to be angry about what a shit she was.

ME

I'm sorry about yesterday. Can we talk?

I sit, staring at my phone and see the second she reads the message. I watch for the dots to start bouncing, but there's nothing. After five minutes, I give up. She's leaving me on read. Anxiety making me vaguely nauseous, I set my coffee on the table. Then I lean back against the couch cushions and close my eyes, wondering what the fuck I do now.

"You're up early, Hal." My eyes fly open, and Ben is there, leaning against the doorway into the living room. I think morning Ben is my favorite Ben. All sleepy eyes and stubble and disheveled blond hair. Morning Ben just does something to me. Seeing his face cuts right through my anxiety, settling down my tangle of emotions.

"Jesus, Ben. You scared the shit out of me. Why are you up so early? I wanted to let you sleep."

"You weren't there," he says simply. He comes over and lays his lips on mine. It's short and sweet, a good morning kiss between two people who know there is time for deeper, hotter kisses later. It's a kiss that feels like comfort and ease and home.

Ben feels like home.

What a thought to have on the morning after such a fucked-up day. Pulling away, he goes to the kitchen and comes back a couple minutes later with his own mug of coffee. He settles down next to me and takes one of my hands.

"How do you feel this morning, Hallie girl?" His ocean blue eyes are calm, still a little heavy with sleep. I want to burrow into his warm, comforting gaze and stay there forever.

"Honestly, I've been better. Yesterday was so fucked, Ben. I have no clue what to do next."

He squeezes my hand. "I'd like to help you with it, if you want."

"I do want. I'd like to tell you about it."

"I wish you would."

I grab my coffee and take a sip before I dive in. "I was happy yesterday morning. After our date, waking up with you. I was just... happy." He smiles at me and starts stroking his thumb along the sensitive skin on the inside of my wrist. "I felt good going into work. Molly brought donuts, and I was going to give them a sexy breakfast story."

"Sexy breakfast story, huh?" Ben grins at me.

"It's a girl thing. Deal with it, Benji. Anyway, then Julie came down, and I decided to just tell them all before we did anything else." I skip over the part where Julie came down because Molly dragged her down to talk about how in love with

Ben I am. "I told them about Charlie retiring and making me the offer to take over his adoption practice. The first thing Julie said was no. Just, no, this isn't happening. She called it my little adoption law hobby."

"Fucking hell, Jules," Ben mutters.

"Every part of me wanted to shut down. I hate confrontation, and I hate disappointing my friends. But this is so important to me, Ben. I want this, so I made myself tell her that. I mentioned I had been unhappy with estate planning for a while. That I would regret it if I didn't do it. I told her I wanted to see it through, and that I would do whatever I could to make it work. And she said..." I stop, trying to get my shit together. "She said..." I try again and fail, tears burning my eyes again.

Ben puts his coffee on the table and takes my other hand in his, swinging both legs up onto the couch so he is fully facing me.

"It's ok, Hal. You can tell me anything. Whatever it is, it'll be fine. I swear it will."

I take a deep breath and try again. "She called me selfish for asking. She said that it's enough that I'm leaving her to be with you. I can't leave her at work too. She said if I do this, then she and I are done. And then she stormed out." My voice breaks on the last word. My stomach roils, and my hands are cold and clammy, shaking at the thought of losing Julie forever.

Ben grips my hands so tightly that my knuckles are turning white. His jaw is clenched, his eyes stormy with anger. He closes them for a few seconds and takes a couple of deep breaths, like he's trying to get himself under control. When he opens his eyes, he's a little calmer, his grip on my hands looser.

"Hallie, I'm sorry that she said all of that. You are the very best friend Julie could ever ask for. You are so good to her. More than she deserves sometimes. Definitely more than she deserves after her little performance yesterday. I love my sister, but I want to throttle her right now. You don't have a selfish bone in your body. You give and give and give. You do everything for everyone. You aren't wrong to want this. You have to know that."

"I do know that. But is it even worth it? If it's going to cause all this tension and make everyone so angry, maybe it's better to just stay the course."

"I think you may have skipped a part of the story, so let me ask you something. How did Emma and Molly react?"

I shrug. "They were good, actually. They said they thought I should do it. That we would make it work. I had a bunch of messages from them after I left yesterday, but I didn't get them until this morning."

"Hallie, Julie doesn't own you, and she doesn't own your firm. The four of you went into this as equal partners. You went into it to have control over your lives and your careers that you didn't have when you were working at a firm for someone else. Is switching your practice a big change? Sure. But it seems like following your passion is exactly the point of what you're all trying to do."

"It is. But still." I sigh and burrow deeper into the couch. "I tried texting Julie this morning and she left me on read. What if she never talks to me again? I get to have the career I want, but I lose my best friend in the process?"

I huff out a breath and drop my head back. "This is so fucked up."

"It really is, but you don't need to make any decisions right now. I know Charlie doesn't expect that. Take a couple of days. Get a little farther away from the fight. Julie will come around. I promise."

I lean into Ben then. I thought I was done crying, but when he wraps his arm around me and tugs me closer, tears fall all over again. He just holds me, wiping them away, whispering how it's all going to be okay, and how he's not going anywhere. And my chest aches because I love him so damn much, and I just hate this for him.

"I'm sorry that all I'm doing is crying all over you. I'm sure you're regretting all the life choices that led you to this place, where your girlfriend is crying because your sister is a shithead. I hate that you're stuck between us now. That really sucks, and I never wanted to put you in that position. You have given me so much over these past few weeks, and I haven't given you nearly enough. Bet you didn't realize what a chaos agent you were getting yourself involved with."

He sits up then, spinning around to face me.

"Hallie, listen to me. There is nowhere I would rather be than here. I've told you a million times, I see you, Hallie girl, and I know you. I know every damn thing about you, and it all only makes me want you more. There is nothing you could say or do to make me stop wanting you. You're sad right now because you have a soft heart and Julie dented it. It's hard for you to let it out when you're feeling sad. You don't like showing anyone that side of you. But Hallie, I am the luckiest guy on earth because you show it to me. I am so lucky to just be sitting here next to you, holding you when you're sad.

"And Hallie, you have given me plenty. Being with you makes me feel fucking invincible. Because of you, I feel like it's okay to just be me – the Pittsburgh boy who owns a Pittsburgh bar. Who doesn't want to be famous or well known or own bars all around the country or travel the world. Who wants a quiet life in the city he loves with the people he loves."

He pauses then and seems to consider his next words.

"Maybe this isn't the right time, and maybe it's too soon, but fuck it. This is happening. I love *you* Hallie. I'm *in love* with you. I want to go to sleep with you every night and wake up every morning with you in my arms. I want to make your coffee just how you like it every day and make sure you eat breakfast so you don't get hangry and yell at everyone at work. I want to stock the kitchen with Diet Pepsi and Cheez-Its for your Couch Time and fill up your ridiculously huge cups with ice water every night. I want to kiss you and fight with you and fuck you and wipe your tears and be your soft place to land. I want to lean on you and let you lean on me, and I want to hear every single thought you have because your mind is brilliant and fascinating and so damn beautiful. I want to build a whole life with you and make a family with you one day because my love for you is so enormous that it needs more places to go. I have been in love with you since we were eighteen. I was born to love you, and you were made for me to love. I swear that I will love you for the rest of this lifetime and on into whatever comes next. You are mine, Hallie girl, and I have never been, will never be, anything but yours."

I stare at him, trying to suck in a breath, but his words make my lungs shut right down. Those fucking tears fill my eyes again.

"I love you too," I whisper, the tears spilling over.

Has emotional whiplash ever killed anyone? Because I am so sad, but his words filled me with more happiness than I have ever felt in my whole damn life.

"God, Ben, I love you so much. I don't care if it's fast. I'm a mess today, but I want it too. All of it. Everything. I want everything with you."

His breath comes out in a whoosh before his whole face transforms into a grin. He pulls me onto his lap, wrapping his arms around me.

"Eighteen-year-old Ben is fist pumping right now. He finally got his girl," he says into my ear.

I laugh and hold onto him tighter because my personal and professional life are currently a disaster, and I have no clue what to do next, but I have Ben. My soft place to land. My safe place when everything feels like too much.

"Say it again," he whispers into my ear.

"I love you, Benji. So much."

He pulls back, eyes blazing with emotion, and wraps his hand around the back of my head, bringing my mouth to his. He drops his other hand to my waist, gripping tight. His tongue slips against mine in a kiss that is full of passion and fire and all the promises we are making to each other. None of them need words.

Ben tips my head back to take the kiss even deeper, and I feel it all the way to my toes. When we break apart, Ben's mouth hovers over mine.

"You are mine, Hallie girl. Always. Forever."

"And you are mine right back, Benji."

He smiles again and pulls back, tucking my head under his chin. I rest my head on his heart, letting the steady rhythm calm me. I might not know what's going to happen at work, and my best friend might not ever speak to me again. But in this moment, I hold tight to the happiness that is Ben and me and the future we can build together.

It's enough for now.

Chapter Forty-Seven
Ben

"Fucking hell, Ben, are you trying to kill me?"

I snap out of my thoughts in time to catch the barbell I'm supposed to be spotting for Jordan before it lands on his chest. I'm at the gym with him, Jeremy, and Eric Casey trying to get my mind off everything and doing a terrible job of it. It's Sunday—five days since Hallie and Julie's fight, and it's been radio silence from Jules. She won't talk to me, and she won't talk to Hallie. I know she has been to the office because Emma told Jeremy. I don't know what the deal is with all the time they're spending together, but I'm grateful for it now because it's given me at least some information.

Julie has been shutting herself in her office and burying herself in work. She's at the office every day, but she won't say much to Emma or Molly either. Hallie is alternating between weepy and resigned. She can't seem to find her mad. She does better when she's a little bit angry, but she can't quite get there. And even though she opened up to me right after the fight, she's been keeping her thoughts close to the vest the last few days. She's been working at home, and I've been staying at her house at night. I know she's sleeping like shit, but I have no idea what's going through her mind, and it's driving me insane.

"Sorry, man, my head was somewhere else."

"Yeah, no kidding. Maybe we call it a day and talk about whatever's on your mind?"

I clearly need some advice here, so I just nod in agreement.

"Hey guys, wrap it up," Jordan calls to Jeremy and Eric. "We're having breakfast at the diner next door. Ben needs our sage counsel. And I need to avoid having my chest crushed by a barbell."

Ten minutes later we're all seated at a table in the diner, coffee in front of us.

"So, this is about Hallie and Jules, right?" asks Jeremy. "Emma filled me in, and it's not pretty."

"What's the deal with you and Emma? You seem to be spending a fuckton of time together." I wasn't going to ask, but I'm glad Jordan did, because I'm curious as shit.

"It's nothing. She's helping me with some stuff for the foundation. So, Ben, what's the deal?"

I know there's more to it, but I let it slide because I need their help. I fill them in on everything from Hallie's opportunity with Charlie Callahan's adoption practice and the fight, Julie's refusal to talk to either of us, and Hallie's willingness to talk to me about everything except this.

When I'm finally out of words, Jordan lets out a low whistle. "That's some shit, dude. So, what are you going to do?"

I grit my teeth and try to stay calm. "If I knew, would I be here talking to you assholes about it?"

Eric speaks next. "I know I don't know all the girls as well as the rest of you do, but I do know Hallie. She worked with us for years on Maya's case. Without her, Jen and I would never have our family. Hallie was made for this work."

"I know she was. And she wants it badly. If Julie hadn't

reacted the way she did, Hallie would already have accepted Charlie's offer. But she feels like she has to choose between her best friend and her career, and that's a shitty place to be."

"It's not your place to tell Hallie what to do. I know Jen would kick my ass for the mere suggestion of what she should do with her career. But maybe it wouldn't be overstepping to talk to Julie? If she's not returning your calls, just go to her. I don't know Julie that well, but it's possible she doesn't know what to do next either. She's your sister. You can talk to her in a way no one else can."

"He's right, Ben," Jeremy says. "You might be the only person who can get through to Julie right now. You at least have to try. I just texted Emma. Julie's at the office."

I scrub my hands over my face, hating the idea of talking to Julie without mentioning it to Hallie first, but it's probably the best option.

"Okay. You win. I'll talk to her after breakfast."

Jordan elbows me in the ribs. "You are the ultimate fixer, Ben. And I know you love them both. You can help make this right."

Two hours later, I walk through the door of the girls' office and straight up the stairs. Julie's office door is closed, so I knock and wait.

"Emma, I told you I'm not ready to talk," comes Julie's voice from the inside.

"Not Emma."

Silence. "Ben?"

I open the door and stick my head inside. "Yeah, me. Can I come in?"

Julie just shrugs, which I take as a good sign. At least she didn't kick me right out. I sit down in one of the chairs in front of her desk and study her. She looks rough. Dark circles stand out like bruises under her eyes, and her hair is a mess, thrown on top of her head in a knot that's flopping to one side. She's wearing ratty clothes and looks like she hasn't slept in a week. It's a shocking look for my always put together twin sister.

"So, how are you?"

Julie chuckles darkly. "How am I? Well, Ben, my best friend and future law partner kept a huge secret from me and then told me she wants to change our entire plan less than five months before we open for business. How do you think I am?"

"Is that what you think she did?"

"Isn't it?"

"Well, no. She came in here and tried to have a reasonable conversation with you about something that has been on her mind and the direction of her career and some changes you might have to make to your business. This wasn't a whim. She had a plan. She figured it all out. She wanted to tell you, her best friend and partner, about something she wants and is excited about. And you tossed it back in her face, said terrible things, and stormed out."

"She could have talked to me anytime during the last year. She could have told me she was struggling. That she was unsure. But she kept it to herself and dropped a bomb at the last minute."

I blow out a breath. Fucking hell, my sister can be frustrating. "Jules, I love you, but you have never been unsure of anything in your whole damn life. You expect other people to be as certain about everything as you are, or you shove them until they get to where you want them to be. Of course she didn't feel like she could come talk to you about it."

"I wouldn't have done that."

"Are you sure about that? Hallie has spent her entire life as your best friend, walking beside you while you made all the decisions with your ironclad certainty. She has gone along with them because, well, sometimes it's easier that way. And I'm sure that this is hard to hear, but you're not always the easiest person to talk to and to disagree with. And for someone like Hallie, who just wants to please the people who she loves, it's even harder."

"She told you, though. You knew. She opened up to you about it, and she didn't tell me. You didn't tell me."

Okay, so now we're getting to the root of the issue. I start talking, hoping that this all comes out the way I want it to.

"First of all, it wasn't mine to tell. It was Hallie's. But opening up is hard for her. And you getting mad and refusing to talk to her for four days after she told you, her very best friend, her hardest, scariest, deepest secret, just affirms what she believes. That when she lets people really know her, they walk away. You crushed her, Julie. I'm sorry it hurts you that she came to me with this and not you. I'm sorry you felt left out for even a second. I don't want that for you, and I don't want it for the three of us. You're my twin sister. We shared a literal womb. You are one of the most important people in my life. And in Hallie's, too."

"But you have her now, and she has you. There's no room for me anymore. And now she wants to switch practices, so we won't have work. There's nothing left for me."

"I'm so sorry if anything Hallie or I did makes you feel like there isn't a place for you. Because of course there is. But I love her, Jules. I love her so damn much it's almost too much sometimes. She's it for me. My person. My goddamned soulmate. It's always been her for me, and it always will be. What we have is real and true and so fucking right I think my heart is going to explode with it. But I promise, it doesn't make you any less her best friend. The three of us will always be best friends. We will never not be family even if what Hallie and I have makes it look a little different now. And I'm sorry if Hallie opening up to me about what she was thinking in a way that she didn't to you makes you feel like that isn't true.

"Hallie is sorry too, and this is killing her. You have to talk to her, Jules. And you have to listen to her when she tells you what she wants. Really listen and hear her when she tells you what she decides. She is an adult and a whole person who is facing some hard truths about who she is and what she wants, and she doesn't need you bulldozing over her, telling her the way you think it should go. This is her decision, and you need to support her. Support her and help her and be there the way family is. The way we always are. You and I will always have each other no matter what. But I can't live without her, and she can't live without you. It's a tangled web, but it's ours. It's tough love time, Jules. This was a colossal fuck up. You were wrong. You handled this badly. It's on you to fix it."

As I finish, Julie's eyes fill with tears. Julie never cries. Ever. There has always been a layer to Julie that is unknowable, even to me. A part of her that she keeps locked up tight and never lets out for anyone. I see hints of it sometimes, like now. It's a look, or something she says. I wonder a lot what it will take for her to finally set that piece of herself free.

The sight of her tears has me out of my chair and around her desk in less than a second. I pull her up off her chair and wrap my arms around her. She puts her arms around my waist and cries out her tears into my shoulder.

"I'm sorry," she whispers. "I'm so fucking sorry, Ben. I got scared. Everything was so out of control. Like you and Hallie were forming your own unit without me. And then when Hallie told us about the offer, I freaked out." She pulls away from me, wiping her eyes and sinking back down into her chair. I get down on my knees in front of her so we're eye level.

She lets out a shaky breath. "It wasn't really about the practice."

"I know, Jules."

"I feel like my best friend and my brother are slipping away from me. And god, I'm such an idiot. I'm so happy for you both. I swear I am. It just happened fast, and I'm having trouble adjusting. It's a me thing, not a you thing."

"Well, this doesn't exactly fit onto one of your spreadsheets, does it?" I ask in a teasing tone hoping to lighten the mood.

She lets out a short laugh but there's no humor in it. "No, it really doesn't. And if this is what Hallie wants, then I want it for her. Of course we can make it work. What are the chances she'll forgive me?" Jules stares down at her hands clasped tightly in her lap.

"Hallie loves you, Jules. Apologize. Then listen to her, and then apologize again. Then you can move past this and make a plan. She's always going to be yours, Jules. I swear she is."

"I know, and I'm actually ahead of you on the plan. I've been sitting here for four days working out how to integrate Charlie's practice into our firm. I'm almost done. I'll call Hallie tomorrow."

I lean forward and press a kiss to Julie's forehead. She's hardheaded and frustrating a lot of the time, but she has the biggest heart. She just doesn't often show it.

"No one better with a plan than you, Jules."

"Tell me something I don't know." She rolls her eyes, but her smile is real.

I laugh then say goodbye to Julie and walk out of the office. I head for Hallie's, feeling for the first time in a week like things are going to work out just fine.

Chapter Forty-Eight
Hallie

My fingers fly over my laptop keyboard, typing furiously. Sometime between when Ben left for the gym this morning and now, I was consumed by a flood of righteous indignation. Every time I think about Julie, I want to scream. I've stopped myself at least ten times from running out the door straight to her house and telling her exactly how I feel about her and her "no fucking way." Fuck her is how. But I can't go to her like this. I need spreadsheets. Facts and figures. That's Julie's language, and if I'm going to get her on board, I need to speak it. I'll be fucking damned if I'll grovel, but I will go to her with a plan.

I'm almost finished when there's a knock at my door. When I open it, it's Ben with a bright smile and a coffee cup. He leans in to kiss me and then hands me the cup.

"Vanilla latte. Thought you might need one."

"God, this is exactly what I need right now. How did you know?"

"I—"

"Yeah, yeah, you see me and whatever. Are you ever going to tell me how you do the coffee thing?"

"Maybe one day, Hal. Maybe one day. So, you're spicy today."

I lead him back into the living room, which is currently covered in files, papers, and my laptop. "Fucking right I am. After you left this morning, I started thinking. How fucking dare she, you know? I know it's our firm, but this is my career. I want this, Ben. I want it so damn badly. And I'm going to have it."

Ben positively beams. "Damn straight, Hallie girl. Looks like you found your mad. I've been waiting for it."

He has? "You have?"

"Sure. I knew you wouldn't stay sad forever. You do your best work when you're a little bit angry."

He's so right. I do. How is it possible that this man knows me better than I know myself?

"Well, I've done some of my best work today. I contacted all the clients who are coming over with me from my old firm and they are all happy to have their files transferred to Julie. I created a whole bunch of lists and spreadsheets and plans to explain how it's all going to work. If I'm going to talk to Julie, I need to speak her language."

"I'm proud of you, Hal. I know you want this, and you're going to have it. So, here's what's going to happen. You are going to tell me all about these plans you're making. Then, we have dinner with your parents. After dinner, we are going to come back here, and I am going to worship every inch of my gorgeous girl who is going to be a fucking brilliant adoption lawyer. What do you say about that?"

"I say, I've never loved someone more than I love you right now."

Ben scoops me up and tosses me onto the couch, covering

my body with his and raining kisses all over my face until I am breathless and hysterically laughing. He buries his face in my hair and whispers in my ear, "I love you too, Hallie girl. Always."

After spending the afternoon with Ben sprawled around my living room and going over all my plans, we're late getting to my parents' house. My family is already sitting down in the dining room when we walk in the door.

"So, Hallie, what's going on at the firm?" My dad asks, once we all settle around the table.

I hesitate, and Ben squeezes my leg under the table. My righteous anger from earlier today disappears and is replaced by bone deep exhaustion. I'm suddenly so tired. I'm tired of keeping secrets. I'm tired of hiding the thing that has me happier and more excited than anything has since the day I first started the family law clinic in law school. I'm tired of tiptoeing around everyone. I'm doing this, whether Julie likes it or not, so it's time to let it all out. I take a deep breath and start to talk.

"I'll be changing my practice when we open the firm in January." Every head at the table swivels in my direction.

My dad gives me a quizzical look. "What do you mean changing your practice?"

"Charlie Callahan is retiring at the end of the year, and I'll be taking over his adoption practice. I am going to move that part of his practice to our firm, so I'll still be practicing under our firm name. We just won't be exclusively estate planning anymore."

"Honey, that sounds wonderful. I know it's something that

you have always loved, and you are so good at it." I give my mom a grateful smile.

"But what about your clients who are following you from your old firm?" asks my dad.

"I contacted all of them, and they are happy to use Julie, or even Molly for the more complex clients. I will still be there to consult whenever necessary to make sure the transition is as smooth as possible. We were always planning on hiring an associate at some point in the first six months, so I'm hoping that we can speed up the timeline. That will take a lot of the burden off Jules and Molly."

"How does Julie feel about that?" asks Jo.

"Yeah, is she mad? You're changing the whole game. It seems like something she wouldn't be too thrilled about," Hannah chimes in.

"Totally. Julie hates anything that messes up her spread-sheets. And, like, all change."

"Oh, speaking of change, Jo, I hired a guy to come here tomorrow to get the old living room furniture that's in the base-ment. I have the perfect place for it in my new apartment."

"What?" Jo shrieks. "No. No way. They were saving that for me. Mom, tell her she can't."

"You don't have a place for it, Jo, and you still have a year left on your lease. I have a place for it now."

"She's right, Jo," says my mom. "It's silly to just let it sit there. We'll figure out something for you when the time comes."

I'd like to figure out a way back to the conversation we were having about me before my sisters walked all over it. My entire body tenses, another hot bolt of anger washing through me. It feels good though. Not like the constant hum of anxiety I usually have when my sisters take up all the space while I'm left looking for mine.

I open my mouth to start talking, but Ben beats me to it.

In that calm way of his, he says "Jo, Hannah, Becca, Hallie wasn't finished."

They turn to look at him.

"She was in the middle of talking about something important to her, and you all steamrolled right over her."

I feel a rush of love for Ben and his desire to defend me, but for the first time, maybe ever, I'm ready to speak for myself. I put a hand on his arm, lean over and whisper, "Thanks, Benji, but I've got this."

He grins at me, then kisses my forehead and whispers back, "Give 'em hell, Hallie girl."

I look every member of my family in the eye and take a deep breath.

"Ben was right; I wasn't finished. Like I was saying, I'm switching my practice. Charlie Callahan wants me to take over his adoption clients when he retires, and I'm going to accept. I'm moving the whole thing to our new firm. This is what I've always wanted to do. I have the chance now, and I'm taking it. As for Julie, that's between her and me, and we will figure out how to make it work. Even if she doesn't agree, I'm doing it anyway because this is what's best for my career. And ultimately, it's going to be what's best for our firm. I am a whole ass adult, and I can make my own decisions about my own career. And Hannah, Jo, as for that little scene earlier? I love you both, but I'm finished with your shit. I have never stood up for myself in this house. I'm the oldest. I never wanted to upset anyone. I always thought it was better to stand back and let the two of you take up all the space with your melodrama of the day. But no more. Both of you need to learn that the world does not revolve around you. The faster you learn it, the better, because I'm done standing back and waiting for you to figure it out. Mom, you have three daughters. Not two. I'm not the loudest, and I don't always ask for what I need. But that doesn't mean I need nothing. Sometimes I need you to look up from Hannah and Jo and notice me. I'm right here. I've always been right here. Dad, just fucking notice what's going on once in a while. I'm done shoving my heart into a box to make the rest of you happy. I matter too. Pay attention. Now, I'm really sorry that we can't stay for the rest of dinner, but I have something I need to do. Right now."

Breathing hard, I grab Ben's arm and pull him up. I walk him straight through the living room and out the front door. Before I can storm down the front steps to Ben's car, he grabs me and spins me around. He presses me up against the door and attacks my mouth with his. The kiss is wet and hot, and it sends desire straight to my core. He pulls back, his mouth hovering over mine.

"Fucking hell, Hal. Watching you stand up for yourself? I have never been prouder of anyone in my entire life. And it was hot as shit."

"Well, Benji, you might be prouder still because I'm not done. Can you drop me off at Julie's on the way home? I'm done dancing around this. I'm ending it. Tonight."

The most dazzling grin explodes on Ben's face, and he drops his lips to mine in one more punishing kiss.

"Fucking yes, I will. You're a badass, Hal. But she's not home. She's at the office, and I happen to know she's alone. Come on, I'll take you."

I fumble around in my purse on the way to the car. Once we both slide in, I hand my house key to Ben. "Can you wait for me at my house? I want to see you after I talk to Julie."

He takes the key from me and then lifts my hand to his mouth and plants a soft kiss on my knuckles.

"There's nowhere else I'd rather be, Hallie girl."

Chapter Forty-Nine
Hallie

B en drops me off at the office and waits until I unlock the door before pulling away. I assume Julie is working in her office, as usual. So, seeing her sitting at the kitchen island with a glass of wine in front of her stops me in my tracks. She turns when she hears the door close. We stare at each other for a second. And I am utterly astonished when tears fill Julie's eyes and spill over. Julie Parker never cries. Like, never, ever. She broke her leg in two places on a ski slope when we were eleven and didn't shed a single tear.

I have to battle my instinct to smooth everything over. To tell her it's okay, to try and make her feel better. I'm done with that. Instead, I move into the kitchen and take the seat next to her. I get my second shock of the night when she speaks first, and the first thing out of her mouth is an apology.

"I'm sorry, Hallie," she whispers. "I am so fucking sorry."

Seeing Julie in tears, apologizing, is so rare that I barely know where to go from here.

"What, exactly, are you sorry for, Julie?"

She just looks at me for a second, unused to me not accepting her apology without question.

"For everything."

"Yeah, I'm going to need you to be more specific."

She takes a deep breath. "I'm so sorry for dismissing your opportunity to switch to adoption out of hand. I should have let you explain. I should have stayed and talked it through with you and listened to your ideas, how you thought we could make it work. And I'm sorry for saying what I said about you and Ben. I'm happy that you're happy. I swear I am. I love this for both of you. I love you both, and the thought of you happy together is so special. But it's been...harder for me than I expected."

I blow out a breath. Looks like I'm not the only one keeping some feelings close to the vest.

"In what way?"

"I got scared I was going to lose both of you. That you would have each other, and neither of you would need me anymore. You and Ben are my whole world, Hallie. I love Molly and Emma, of course. But it's been you, Ben, and me for as long as I can remember, and the changing dynamic threw me. And maybe I was a little jealous? You guys are building a whole future that I'm not a part of. I should have talked to you about it. I should have explained how I felt. But I didn't know how. The last thing I want is to get in the way of you and Ben figuring out what you are to each other. You haven't done anything wrong. This is a me problem, not a you problem. But the longer I kept it in, the bigger it became, and, well, Tuesday happened. I didn't mean it, Hallie. I didn't mean any of it. I want you and Ben to be happy. And the last thing I want is for you to be unhappy or unfulfilled here in this office. That's the exact opposite of the reason we decided to do this. I have never regretted anything in my life more than I regret what I said to you on Tuesday. I wish I could go back and do it all over again. But since time travel isn't a thing, I hope you'll accept my apology, and know that I hate myself ten times more than you could ever hate me."

I am stunned so speechless it takes me some time to figure out what to say next. Julie offering a heartfelt apology and explanation wasn't on my bingo card for tonight.

"Julie, nothing that happens between Ben and me will ever take me away from you. Ever. You are my sister, just as much as Hannah and Jo are. Ben and I happened so fast, and it caught us all off guard. I love him, Jules. I love him so fucking much that I sometimes feel like I can't breathe. But I love you too. Nothing could ever change that. Ben will never take me away from you, and I will never take him away from you."

Julie sniffles, a couple of tears escaping. "Maybe you guys will get married and then you can be my actual sister. We used to joke about becoming real sisters when we were little. Maybe now it will actually happen."

The thought of marrying Ben makes me feel all warm inside, but...still.

"Let's not jump the gun on that. And I'm sorry too. I should have come to you earlier this year and told you that I was unhappy. But the truth is, it wasn't until Maya's adoption hearing last month that I figured out what I was unhappy about. I don't want to plan estates anymore, Jules. I know you love it, but I don't think I ever did. I love my adoption work. It's what I'm meant to do."

"Then you should do it. Seriously, Hallie. I've spent the last four days coming up with a plan."

I smile. "I have a plan too."

Julie assumes her *very serious person doing very serious work* face. "So, here's what's going to happen right now. We're going to order dessert, then we're going to sit here and go over our plans and figure this out together. And we are going to make sure you have what you need to be the best fucking adoption attorney the city of Pittsburgh has ever seen."

I start laughing and Julie looks at me with a "what?" expression.

"What you just said. 'Here's what's going to happen right now.' It's exactly what Ben said to me earlier today when I told him I had a plan. You Parkers. You really know how to take charge of a moment."

Julie smiles. "What can I say? Twins, you know? I'm ready to take charge of this one, but can I hug you first?"

We stand up at the same time and wrap our arms around each other and hold tight. I cry a little. Julie cries a lot. But they're good tears. Tears of forgiveness and acceptance and deep and abiding friendship. When we break apart, we're both a little bit of a mess, but the good kind of mess. The mid-organization project mess right before everything fits perfectly into place.

"Let's never do that again, okay?" I say to her when we've wiped away our tears.

"Never ever. Thank you for forgiving me even when I don't deserve it. And thank you for coming to me to talk. You didn't have to do that."

"I really did. I want to start trying to face things head on. Speaking of which, I have to tell you about dinner tonight with my parents. It was...unexpected."

"You need to tell me all about that, but first, cake or pie?"

We look at each other for a beat and then say "pie" at exactly the same time and laugh.

Julie places the order, and I go grab her laptop from her office. I don't have mine, but I don't need it. I could give Julie all the details in my sleep.

We chat until the pie comes and then get to work. We sit in

the kitchen of the law firm we built, and we talk and we plan. And with my best friend by my side, my dream starts to come alive.

> Julie and I talked it out and everything is fine. Better than fine.

I'm so happy to hear that. And I'm so proud of you.

> I'm going to be here with Jules for a while, going over our plan. I'll be home late. Like, really late. Don't wait up, ok? Jules said she would drive me home.

Stay as long as you need to. As long as you come home to me at the end of the night, I'm a happy guy.

> I'll be there. I love you.

I love you too, Hallie girl. I'll leave a light on for you.

Chapter Fifty
Hallie

It's almost three in the morning when Julie drops me off at my house. I walk in the front door; it's silent and dark, except for the light on over the kitchen stove. The light was off when I left, which means Ben literally did leave a light on for me. The thought of him walking through my house, turning off the lights for the night, but flipping this one on so I didn't walk into complete darkness when I got home has emotion clogging my throat.

This is what I want, I realize. To leave lights on for each other when we need to work late. To share space with Ben. To share a life with Ben.

My heart full, I go to the kitchen and rummage around in my "all the things I can't find another place for" drawer. When I find what I'm looking for, I put it on the counter, tucked out of view behind the coffee maker. Then I go upstairs to get ready for bed.

In my bedroom, I brush my teeth and wash my face as quietly as I can and slip on a sleep shirt. When I go to get into bed, I see one of my giant tumblers on my nightstand. When I open it, there's ice all the way to the top, just the way I like. And I smile at the man responsible for it.

Ben is fast asleep in the middle of my bed, sprawled out on his back. His face is relaxed in sleep, his long blond eyelashes fanned out across his cheeks. I stand at the side of the bed, just looking at him. He is so beautiful, and he's all mine. His right arm is flung out over my side of the bed, as if he consciously left it there, waiting for me to snuggle into. I do just that. Sliding into bed, I curl up against Ben, my head resting on his chest. His arm comes around me instantly, securing me firmly to his side. He rolls towards me, bringing his other arm around me and pressing a kiss into my hair.

"Missed you, Hallie girl," he mumbles. "Proud of you."

I kiss his chest where my head lays. "Missed you too, Benji. Go back to sleep. I'm here now."

"It never feels right without you next to me."

My heart squeezes. Love for him swamps me.

I go to respond, but his breathing has already evened out. He is asleep again, holding me tightly against him. Laying in the circle of Ben's arms, the future of my career clearly laid, I feel settled and content—maybe more than I ever have been. Exhaustion threatening to overtake me, I let the warmth of Ben's body, his steady breathing, and the beat of his heart lull me into sleep.

The sun is high in the sky when I wake up the next morning. I peer over Ben's shoulder and am shocked to see it's after ten. After working almost all night, Jules and I decided to take the day off. We texted Molly and Emma around midnight, and they enthusiastically agreed. We're all meeting for dinner later, but a whole day of nothing stretches before me, so I settle back down, prepared to doze until Ben wakes up. I don't have to wait long. Ten minutes later, he stirs.

Eyes still closed, he kisses my neck, whispering, "Morning, Hallie girl."

Ben slides his lips up my neck and across my jaw, then takes my mouth in a kiss full of heat and desire. Tongue tangling with mine, the hand wrapped around my hip starts roaming my body. Lips never leaving mine, his fingers creep under my shirt to rub over my nipple, sending lust straight through me. Then he glides his hand down my stomach and below the waistband of my underwear. He drags his fingers through my slit, dipping his index finger inside me where I'm hot and needy.

"Fuck, Hallie, you're so wet for me."

Ben uses my wetness to lightly circle my clit, and I let out a whimper, moving my hips in search of more friction. Crashing his mouth to mine, he sinks two fingers inside me, curling them up while his thumb takes over strumming my clit. It feels so good that I moan into his mouth, right on the edge already. But I want more.

Tearing my mouth away from his, I whisper, "I want you inside me. Please."

"It would be my absolute pleasure." Ben rolls me onto my back, tugs my shirt over my head, and slides my underwear down my legs, where I kick them away. He strips off his briefs and moves back to press his lips to mine while he hooks an arm under one of my knees, pushing my legs apart. In a single motion, he slides inside of me, and our twin moans shatter the quiet morning.

"You feel so good, Hallie girl. There's nowhere I would rather be than inside you."

Ben starts to move, dragging in and out of me lazily, hitting my clit at the perfect angle on every stroke. Dizzy with pleasure, I wrap my arms around his neck and my legs around his waist. He never stops moving, his breath rasping in and out next to my ear, sending shivers up and down my body. I tighten my arms and legs around him trying to get closer, but there is no close that is close enough. I must say that out loud because Ben speaks then, his hips continuing to roll against mine.

"For me either, Hallie. You are my everything. Everything begins and ends with you."

Keeping one forearm on the bed next to my head to support his weight, Ben slides his other arm under me, holding my hips even more firmly against him while he continues to thrust in and out of me. The sensation of him so deep inside me, his hips rolling against my clit, has me climbing higher and higher until my whole body is shaking and begging for release.

"Ben, I can't...I'm so close.

"Come for me, Hallie girl. Show me you're mine."

Ben speeds up his rhythm, holding me impossibly tighter. He angles his hips so he hits the perfect spot inside me, and I shatter, crying out my release against his ear as pleasure rolls through me.

"Fuck, Hallie. You're perfect. So perfect. And mine. You're all mine."

"I'm yours," I whisper. "Always. I love you."

That sends Ben over the edge. He pulls his arm out from under me and anchors it by my head. He seals his mouth over mine and kisses me deeply as his hips lose their rhythm.

"Fuck, fuck, I'm coming." Ben groans into my mouth and I feel his release pour into me.

I'm still clinging to him like a koala when he rolls us onto our sides and brings his forehead to mine. We're both breathing hard, chests rising and falling rapidly as we try to take in oxygen.

"I love you too, Hallie. Sometimes, I can't believe I get to be here with you like this every day."

My chest aches thinking of all the years he watched me, wishing we could be together.

"I wish I had looked more closely. Maybe this would have happened sooner."

He kisses the tip of my nose and leans back to look at me. "I think it happened exactly when it was supposed to happen. We are right where we need to be."

"We are, aren't we?"

"Absolutely. But pretty soon, the kitchen is where we need to be, because I'm fucking starving. What do you think? Shower and then coffee and breakfast?"

"Are you doing the cooking and the coffee making?"

"You know it, Hal."

"Then I say that sounds absolutely perfect."

Half an hour later, I sit at my kitchen counter, an iced coffee with milk and one Splenda in front of me, watching Ben whipping eggs for omelets in a bowl.

"It's kind of becoming our thing, huh? You making me breakfast every morning so I don't starve. And you giving me the exact coffee I want, even though I just decided in my head ten minutes ago and didn't say it out loud, and not telling me how you do it."

"It is our thing. I hope we have lots of things."

"How do you do it, anyway?"

"I told you; I see you, Hallie girl."

I knew he would say that, obviously, and while it used to make me wild with curiosity, it doesn't anymore. Not much, anyway. Because Ben really does see right down to the core of me. And it turns out, it's an extraordinary gift to be seen in this way. A life-changing gift. One I wouldn't trade for anything. All I want in my life is more of this. More of Ben and me. More mornings in the kitchen and quiet nights spent wrapped around each other. As many as I can get. And speaking of which...

"I have something for you."

He looks up from the eggs. "Oh, yeah?"

"Yep." I stand and go to the coffee maker, reaching behind it to pull out the key I hid there last night. I turn and take Ben's hand, pressing the key into it. He stares down at it for a second and then back at me, his blue eyes swimming with emotion.

I reach for his other hand and hold on tight.

"You left a light on for me last night."

"I told you I would."

"I know you did, but when I came in at three in the morning and saw it, it made me realize that I never want to come home late again to a quiet house where no one has left any lights on for me. I never want to come home again without knowing that you're here. I know it hasn't been that long, and maybe this is too much, too soon. But I want to live with you. All the time."

"Yes," Ben says quickly.

"That's it? Just, yes?"

"Hallie, I've been waiting eleven years for you to be mine. It's not too soon. Just, yes. One hundred percent yes."

"Okay, well, I know how much you love your loft, so it doesn't have to be at my house. The key is more of a symbolic thing."

He chuckles. "Hallie, I love my loft, but it was never meant to be permanent for me. I stayed there all these years because it was easy. I want to build a life with you, right here. In this house you bought and made a home. This is your place, and now it will be our place."

"You're sure?"

"Of course I'm sure. I want this with you. I want everything with you. You're my forever, Hallie girl. And I'm yours."

Ben cups my face in his hands and lays his lips to mine. The kiss says things like, "I love you," and "I promise," and "I'm yours," and "forever." It is the best kiss of my life, and when Ben pulls away and wraps his arms around me in a tight hug, I'm home.

Ben is my home.

And I will do my damnedest to make sure that I am his.

"I love you, Hallie girl," he whispers in my ear.

"I love you too, Benji. So, so much. When you move in here, can you bring your couch?"

He laughs then, untangling us from each other. "Anything you want, Hal. Now go sit down. I have breakfast to make. Gotta feed my girl."

I take my seat back at the counter and watch Ben make breakfast. I fill him in on last night with Julie, and he tells me about some plans he has for the bar now that he officially turned down the Stonegate deal. We fill each other in on our plans for the day and little bits and pieces of our lives, and it is extraordinary in its ordinariness.

When breakfast is ready, Ben puts a plate in front of me and kisses me on the forehead before taking the seat next to me with a plate of his own. I sit in my kitchen over breakfast and the perfect cup of coffee with the man I love straight down to the very bottom of my soul. The one who loves me just exactly as I am.

And there is nowhere in the world I would rather be.

Epilogue
Ben

Five Months Later

"Busy, Hal?" I stroll through the doorway of Hallie's office and grin at what I see.

Hallie sits at her desk, surrounded by files, a laptop, and four different drinks. The firm officially opened for business about a month ago, with Hallie working almost exclusively on her adoption cases, and she is wildly happy. She looks up, and her face lights in a smile.

"Hey! What are you doing here? Strangely, I'm not busy at all. All three of my clients on the schedule for today cancelled. Actually, my clients tomorrow and Friday cancelled too. It's a weird week."

"I'm here to kidnap you for a secret mission."

"Oooo, sounds mysterious. Is it a sexy secret mission?"

I laugh. "If you play your cards right."

"I always play my cards right, Benji. And you don't even have to kidnap me. I'll come willingly. Am I coming back here today?"

"You're not, so grab whatever you might need for the night."

Hallie stands up from her desk and comes over for a quick kiss. She starts to pull away, but I spin her back into me, tipping her head back and taking her mouth for a far more satisfying kiss. She hums into my mouth and wraps her arms around my neck, tangling her fingers in my hair. We're both a little breathless when we break apart, exactly the way I like it. Hallie shoves some files into her bag, grabs her phone, and takes my hand to lead me out of the office.

"Do you need to tell Jules or anyone that you're leaving?"

"Actually, none of them are here. I can't even tell you the last time no one was here on a Wednesday morning. Like I said, weird week."

It is not, in fact, a weird week. Unless you count the plans I have for Hallie later today. I know exactly where Julie, Molly, and Emma are, and why all of Hallie's clients mysteriously canceled, but that is embargoed information for now.

"Well let's go, Hallie girl. Secret mission awaits."

We head downstairs and walk out into the frigid January air. I lead her to my car and buckle her seatbelt and kiss her forehead like I always do before I close her door. When Hallie and I first got together, I spent a lot of time thinking about the big moments of a relationship. What I didn't realize was how much I would come to love all the small, everyday moments that make up our life together. I wouldn't trade them for anything.

When I get in the car and start the engine, Hallie's questions start almost immediately.

"Okay, so where are we going?"

"It's a surprise."

"But I hate surprises."

I smirk at her. "I know."

She flops back into her seat, grumbling.

"Check the back seat, Hal. There's a bag back there you might be interested in."

She turns around in her seat and finds the bag I stashed before picking her up. She starts pulling out all her favorite snacks, and I can tell when she gets to the bottom of the bag because she laughs out loud.

Holding up the giant bag of mini-Reese's cups, she says, "That's a lot more than two. This must be one hell of an important day."

"You have no idea," I mumble under my breath.

"What was that?"

"Nothing. There's a cooler back there with drinks, and the tumbler in the cup holder has water in it."

She grins at me, her mouth already full of candy. "You're too good to me, Benji."

I wink at her. "Anything for you, Hallie girl."

The drive goes faster than I thought it would. An hour in, Hallie realizes exactly where we're headed and peppers me with questions the rest of the way. I manage to hold her off, but just barely. As we pull up to our final destination, I breathe a sigh of relief and hope that everything is ready.

Hallie

Ben is acting super fucking weird. He's all one-word answers and nervous energy, and I'm curious as shit. An hour into the drive, I realize we are headed to the lake house. It's not unusual for us to go up in the winter. We all ski, and Deep Creek is a great place for a ski weekend, so I assume that's what we're doing. Lucky all my clients for this week canceled because a long weekend with Ben at the lake house sounds perfect.

When Ben pulls the car up the driveway, my heart lifts just like it does every time the house comes into view. The house is a winter wonderland. Icicles hang from the roof, and the front yard is covered in snow. As much as I like the lake house in August, I've always been a winter girl, and there is something magical about being in the snowy woods in January. Ben parks in front of the house and comes around to open my door. When I get out, I smell the smoke from what I assume is a neighbor's fireplace, and can't wait until we can snuggle into one of the couches inside in front of a fire of our own. Ben grabs my hand and pulls me onto the path that leads to the backyard.

"Where are we going?"

"Just come with me, okay?"

"Um, okay." Weird.

He leads me around the side of the house, and I wonder what we're doing back here. When the lake comes into view, I stop in my tracks and look out in astonishment. The snow has been completely cleared from the small stretch of sand by the mostly frozen over water. There is a bonfire roaring right in the spot where we have all our summer bonfires. And next to the fire are two Adirondack chairs facing each other and covered in blankets.

"Ben, what is all of this?'

"Just come with me."

Ben leads me to the lake and sits me in one of the chairs. He drapes a blanket over my lap and sits across from me. My stomach is a riot of butterflies as he takes both of my hands in his and starts talking, his voice a little shaky. It starts to sink in what is going on, and my eyes preemptively fill with tears.

"I thought about writing a whole speech, but I don't need a lot of words to tell you how I feel about you. Hallie, I fell for you eleven years ago when we were just kids. It took me a while to get my shit together to tell you, but I think everything happened at exactly the right time. Because of you, my whole world makes sense. I love you more than I ever thought possible, and I will love you every day for the rest of my life. My world begins and ends with you."

My breath hitches when Ben reaches into his jacket pocket and pulls out a small velvet box. When he flips it open and I see the diamond ring, I forget how to breathe.

Ben tips my chin up with his fingers so our eyes meet. His beautiful blues are shiny with tears, and that makes my own tears spill over.

"Marry me, Hallie girl. Be mine forever. Let me be yours.

"Ben," I breathe. Ye—"

"Hallie, wait." Ben cuts me off mid-response.

"I'm sorry, what? You asked me to marry you. You can't take it back. It's like, the law. I'd know. Lawyer, remember?"

"Oh, I'm not taking it back. You're stuck with me, Hal."

"So why won't you let me say yes?"

He looks at me, a blush crawling up his face.

"Okay, so before you say yes, there's something you should probably know first. So we don't start off our life together with secrets."

What the actual fuck?

Ben reaches into his pocket for his phone and unlocks it. I see him open his Notes app and scroll through. When he finds what he's looking for, he starts to hand it to me and seems to think twice.

"Okay, so here's the thing. I'm mildly concerned that when you see what I'm about to show you, you're going to want to run screaming. Please don't. I swear I'm not a weirdo stalker. I just wanted to understand you better." He hands the phone to me slowly and sits back.

Confused, I scroll through the note, not quite understanding what I'm looking at. It's line after line of my coffee choices, with notations next to each one, detailing what was going on the day I chose each drink. There must be hundreds of entries going back years. I see everything from "hot with vanilla creamer – first day of big law" to "iced latte – afternoon after the bar exam."

When I don't say anything, he starts talking nervously.

"It started off as a game, trying to guess how you wanted your coffee on any given day. For a long time, I thought it was random. Then I wondered if maybe I could find a pattern, so I could always get you the right coffee on the right day. It took a while, but eventually I figured most of them out. The morning of any important career day, you like hot coffee with vanilla creamer. On lazy mornings, it's iced coffee with milk and one Splenda. On exciting afternoons, it's iced lattes. There are more, but those are the big ones. I know I sound unhinged right now. But it really was a way to understand you better."

I look at him, astonished. I have no words. All this time, I thought my coffee choices were random. A fun little quirk of mine. I never realized there was any pattern to the chaos. It took him years, but Ben watched and learned and figured out about me what I didn't even know about myself.

He shifts uncomfortably in his chair. "Um, can you say something? You're starting to freak me out."

There's only one thing to say. I look him straight in the eyes and grin.

"Yes."

It takes Ben a second, but then his face explodes in the most dazzling smile I have ever seen. He takes my hand and slips the ring onto my finger, bringing my hand up to his mouth, kissing my knuckles, his eyes never leaving mine. He tugs me closer to him and cups my face, kissing me.

When our lips touch, my entire body lights up. The kiss is hard and hungry. It's both familiar and new, sealing this promise we are making to each other at our most sacred place. It's you, and me, and always, and forever, I love you with my whole entire soul. When we finally break apart, both our faces are wet with tears.

"I love you, Hallie girl. Forever."

"I love you too, Benji. So, so much."

Ben leans his forehead against mine and we breathe each other in, reveling in this moment together. But it doesn't last long because suddenly, the quiet is shattered by raucous cheering. I jerk my head around, shocked to see both of our families, Molly, Emma, Jeremy, Jordan, and Allie all assembled on the deck.

Ben looks at me with a sheepish smile.

"So, I needed some help to pull this off. I got Jules to handle your clients—they didn't cancel by the way. I asked my dad to come up to help set up the bonfire so it would be ready when we got here. Word kind of spread from there. I hope that's okay.

I smile at him and lean over to kiss his cheek. "It's more than okay."

"Good. Just so you know, it's a couple of hours with everyone, and then I'm locking the door to our room because tonight, you are mine."

I smirk at him. "Just as long as you're mine, right back."

He winks at me. "You know it, Hallie girl."

Ben pulls me up from my chair and kisses my forehead before dropping two mini-Reese's cups into my hand. Then he wraps his arm around me, and we walk up to the house side-by-side to start celebrating our forever.

Acknowledgments

I am the girl who always flips to the acknowledgements first in every book I read, and I sit here at my computer in utter disbelief that I am writing the acknowledgements for my own book. Writing *Because of You* has been the greatest joy of my life, and I absolutely would not be here without the love and support of all the people I am lucky enough to have in my corner.

Hallie and Ben grew up in Pittsburgh, just like I did. The corner of Forbes and Murray and the banks of the three rivers are my blood, and the city is tattooed on my soul. To the city that raised me and made me, I love every inch of your grit and heart. No matter where I might live on this earth, your bridges and hills will always be my home. I am the proudest Pittsburgh Girl.

Mom, I am everything I am because of you. You have taught me to do the thing and chase the dreams and be resilient and tenacious and stop at nothing. Because of you, I had the confidence to say, "I think I'll write a book today" and then go on to do exactly that. Thank you for being my biggest cheerleader and for never telling me that I can't. I can, because you taught me how.

Dad, there is no better girl dad than you in the world. You taught us football and how to punch and took us to buy bras and pierce our ears. I'm sorry I only ever wanted to look for flowers and fix my braids on the soccer field instead of chasing down the ball, but let's be honest – putting me in any kind of organized sport was just setting all of us up to fail. Thank you for being the voice of reason, the purveyor of chocolate, the maker of drinks, and the best beach buddy, and thank you for knowing that half of my book was more than enough for you to read.

Katie and Lou, see the book dedication. Every girl needs a sister, and I couldn't ask for better ones than you.

David, thank you for being my biggest supporter. I know it wasn't easy when I decided on a random Sunday that I was going to write a book and then usurped all of our TV watching nights so that I could get it done, even when our house was a construction zone and our kids needed to be put to bed and no one had clean pajamas. I love you with my whole heart, and I am so lucky that you are mine.

Will and Bella, I don't think it is possible for a human to be prouder of two people than I am of you. You are funny and smart and curious and the best kids a mom could ask for. Bells, one day I'll write a book that needs an illustrator just like you asked me to, and Will, because I know you're going to ask, my book is 96,254 words. I love you both more than words.

Arielle, Elana, and Karen, they say that it takes a village, and I am so lucky that you are mine. From ice cream nights and pool afternoons and Camp Whatever to Saturday lunches and group texts and all the playdates, I don't know how I would do life without you. Having babies at the same time, raising them together, and "co-parenting" the way we do has been a joy and an absolute pleasure. Thank you times a million for being the emergency contacts on my kids' school and camp forms and for loving my babies like your own. I have never felt lonely in parenting because we do it together. And thank you for being nothing but supportive and enthusiastic when I told you about my harebrained idea to write a book. You are my original hype girls and the best friends I could ever ask for.

Sarah Z., from our early aughts blogger days to raising little boys, to the DJM group and beyond, you have been such a constant, loving presence in my life for more than a decade. Your friendship means everything to me, and sharing this experience with you has been an absolute dream. You are a badass woman and a fabulous friend. ILY.

Ruthie, WHAT EVEN IS LIFE? I don't know what outrageous twist of fate led you to my DMs, but I am so fucking grateful for it. These past months of writing books together, plotting, alpha-reading, late night and early morning voice notes, soapbox moments, and all the rest have been an experience I will never, ever forget. I love that we get to send Hallie and Ben and Luna and Zach – our OG friends to lovers babies – out into the world just a day apart and watch them fly together. Thank you for being the very best confidante and friend in this wild author world. I could never have done this without you.

Brittany, my book doppelganger bestie, from the first moment we bonded over our mutual love of West and Jasper, the very best CU Hockey couple, I knew we were meant to be. Thank you for all the voice notes, the "what are you reading?" chats, and for loving and hyping Ben and Hallie the way that you do. Trading book recs and chatting with you is the highlight of my day, and I am so damn grateful to have met you.

Tina, I always tell everyone that when Tina says to read the book, YOU READ THE BOOK. You are the best book recommender (seriously, *11:11* was one of my favorite journeys), the most fun person to trade opinions on male model covers with (*Irresistibly Risky* = HOT), and my absolute favorite person to talk books with. Thank you for being such a great friend, a fabulous beta reader, and for absolutely saving my book one editing situation. I hope you know you are now stuck with me forever and always.

Sariah, it was the best day ever when I met you. You are absolutely everything – fabulous friend, best hype girl, maker of hilarious content, and winner of best comment award in the beta doc. Thank you for loving Ben and Hallie from day one, shouting about them all over bookstagram, and enthusiastically reading the late-night book two teasers I've been sending you. You are simply the best.

Jessi, LITTLE SIS, I love you and your strawberry bandana and your pink hair and your random messages about your snack and coffee choices of the day in the group chat. Thank you for being such a great hype girl and the most supportive friend.

Grayce, my fellow member of the Late Night in Bed Writer's Club, can you even believe any of this? I sure can't. You were one of the first debut indies I met when I started my author Instagram, and I am so damn grateful for you. Thank you for reading my book so early and for loving Ben and Hallie, and I am so honored to have been able to read Kenna and Griff's story. Writing can sometimes be lonely, but I never feel that way with you just a DM away. I'm so excited to trade alphas for our books 2s, and for everything still to come.

My beta team, Ruth, Sariah, Jessi, Britt, Tina, Candice, Albany, and Kayla, thank you for loving Hallie and Ben from the first page, the hilarious comments, and for taking a chance on an indie author who has no clue what she's doing. Love you all to the moon.

Lemmy, words fail. I simply do not have enough of them to express my gratitude to you for taking a chance on me and for all you have done for me and my book. Working with you these past months has been a joy and a pleasure, and I am still in absolute disbelief that I get to be a part of Luna, alongside you and all the fabulous women you have brought on board. You have worked so hard to make *Because of You* a success, and I appreciate every damn minute of it. I hope you're prepared to keep me forever, because us weird, notebook loving girls have to stick together.

Mel, thank you for designing the book cover of my heart. I am blown away by your talent, and working with you was an absolute dream. Looking forward to many more covers to come.

My fellow indie author girlies, Shann, Tiffany, and Ginsa, what a wild ride. Thank you for being such great friends and confidantes in the author trenches. I am so fucking proud of all of us.

My bookstagram girls, gushing over books with you every day is the highlight of my life. Before I am anything else, I'm a reader, and I am endlessly grateful to have found the most fun, loving, and supportive community I could ask for.

To every reader who picks up this book, I hope you find something to love in these pages. Books have been my joy and my escape since I was a kid, and it was my greatest wish to write a warm hug of a story that someone could lose themselves in for a while. Thank you for taking a chance on an unknown indie author who decided one day to write a book on a whim—having you read my words is the dream of a lifetime. My gratitude is miles wide and oceans deep.

About the Author

Samantha Brinn (Sam to everyone who knows her) is an author of sweet, spicy, and swoony contemporary romance novels. A Pittsburgh girl currently living in the suburbs of NYC, Sam stole her first romance novel off of her mom's bookshelf at age thirteen and has read pretty much nothing but romance ever since. Her Kindle is basically an extension of her hand at this point.

A lawyer by day and author by night, Sam can most often be found in bed with her laptop and writing desk late into the night, having the time of her life writing words and weaving stories and grinning at her characters' hijinks.

Aside from being a reader and a writer, Sam is a lover of French fries, Reese's peanut butter cups, and diet Pepsi, and much like her debut FMC, she rarely makes her coffee the same way twice. A mom of two, Sam cosplays as an organized human, but at her core, she's mostly chaos and prefers it that way, and is loving every second of this wild indie author ride.

Printed by Amazon Italia Logistica S.r.l.
Torrazza Piemonte (TO), Italy

61405691R00199